Spider World
THE TOWER

Fiction by Colin Wilson

Spider World
THE TOWER

Colin Wilson

HAMPTON ROADS
PUBLISHING COMPANY, INC.

Cover design by Grace Pedalino
Cover photography © PhotoDisc, Inc.
For information write:

Hampton Roads Publishing Company, Inc.
1125 Stoney Ridge Road
Charlottesville, VA 22902

Or call: 804-296-2772
Fax: 804-296-5096
e-mail: hrpc@hrpub.com
www.hrpub.com

If you are unable to order this book from your local
bookseller, you may order directly from the publisher.
Call 1-800-766-8009, toll-free.
Library of Congress Catalog Card Number: 00-111234
ISBN 1-57174-239-5
10 9 8 7 6 5 4 3 2 1
Printed on acid-free paper in the United States

For Sally, Damon, and Rowan

Acknowledgements

My chief debt of gratitude is to my friend Donald Seaman, with whom this book was originally planned as a collaboration. The idea was abandoned at a fairly early stage, but I had the benefit of his suggestions and advice throughout. I am also deeply grateful to Professor John Cloudsley-Thompson, England's leading expert on deserts, for his invaluable advice on the first section of this book.

CW

Cornwall, 1986

CONTENTS

PART ONE

The Desert

As the first cold whisper of the dawn wind blew under the flat stone that covered the burrow, Niall placed his ear against the crack and listened with total concentration. Whenever he did that, it was as if a tiny point of light glowed inside his head, and there was a sudden silence in which every noise was amplified. Now, suddenly, he could hear the faint sound of a large insect moving across the sand. The lightness and speed of its movements told him that this was a solifugid, or camel spider. A moment later, it crossed his field of vision—the barrel-like, hairy body glistening in the sunlight, the immense jaws carrying the remains of a lizard. In a moment it was past, and there was no sound but the wind in the branches of the euphorbia cactus. But it had told him what he wanted to know: that there was no scorpion or tiger beetle in the area. The camel spider is the greediest of creatures; it will eat until its stomach is so distended that it can hardly move. This one had looked only half-fed. If there had been any other sign of life in the area, it would have abandoned its half-eaten prey to attack.

Cautiously, he brushed aside the sand with a double movement of his hands like a swimmer; then he slid his underfed body through the gap. The sun was just beginning to show above the horizon; the sand was still cold from the frost of the night. His objective lay fifty yards away, at the edge of the cactus grove: the waru plant whose green flesh, as thick and almost as yielding as an earlobe, formed a cup to capture the dew. For the past hour he had lain awake, his throat burning, and conjured up the joy of dipping his lips into the icy liquid. There was water in the burrow, water gathered by the slave ants fifty feet below the surface of the desert; but it was red in color, and tasted of mineral salts. By comparison, the cold dew of the waru plant was like champagne.

Its cup, formed of two curling leaves, was half full, and there were crystals of ice at the edges. Niall knelt on all fours, lowered his face into the cup and took a long, deep draught. The pleasure made his muscles tingle and relax. For the desert dweller, icy water is one of the greatest of all luxuries. He was tempted to drink every drop; but his training forbade it. The shallow roots of the waru needed this water to live; if he drank it all, the plant would die, and one more source of water would be gone. So Niall stopped drinking while the cup was still half full. But he continued to kneel there, staring into the cold liquid as if drinking its essence, while a chilly wave of delight ran from his shoulders down to his feet. In the depths of his being, strange racial memories stirred: memories of a golden age, when water was plentiful, and men were not forced to live under the floor of the desert like insects.

That mood of deep quiescence saved his life. As he raised his eyes, he saw the balloon against the pale eastern sky. It was about half a mile away, and moving swiftly towards him. Instantly and instinctively, he controlled the reflex of terror. The inner calm of a few moments ago made it easier. At the same moment, he realized that he was kneeling in the shade of the immense organpipe cactus, whose fluted trunk stretched up seventy feet above his head. Against the dark western landscape, with its pools of shadow, his brown body must have been totally invisible. Only the reflex of terror could betray him. And this was difficult to control as the balloon swept towards him, as if the creature inside had marked him for its prey. He thought of the others, lying below in the burrow, and prayed that they were fast asleep. Then the balloon was bearing down on him, and for the first time in his life, he experienced that enormous sense of menace transmitted by hunting spiders. It was as though a hostile willpower was sweeping the desert like a searchlight beam, probing every area of shadow with an almost tangible force, trying to provoke a reflex of terror that would rise towards it like a scream. Niall deliberately averted his eyes to the cup of the waru, and tried to make his mind as still as the clear water. It was then that he experienced the odd sensation of being aware of the soul of the waru, the passive vegetable soul whose only purpose was to drink, absorb sunlight, and stay alive. In that same moment, he was also aware of the prouder soul of the giant cactuses, soaring above him like a challenge to the sky. The ground itself seemed to become transparent so that he could sense the presence of his family, his parents and his brother and two sisters, all lying fast asleep, although his father stirred as the beam of malevolent will swept across him.

A few seconds later, it was gone; the balloon was already a quarter of a mile away across the desert, moving towards the great inland plateau on the horizon. The will-force was sweeping the desert ahead of it, and he could feel its presence as clearly as if it were a beam of light. He sat perfectly still, watching the balloon dwindle into the distance and observing with interest that it swerved aside to avoid a needle-like pinnacle of rock.

When it was gone he hurried back to the burrow, moving swiftly and silently as he had been taught since childhood. His entrance awakened his father, who leapt instantly into a crouching position, his right hand closing on a bone dagger. As he recognized Niall, he also sensed there was something wrong.

"What is it?"

Niall whispered: "A spider balloon."

"Where?"

"It's gone now."

"Did it see you?"

"I don't think so."

Ulf allowed his tension to escape in a long breath. He climbed up to the entrance, listened for a moment, and peered out. The sun was now above the horizon, and the sky was a cloudless blue still tinged with white.

His elder brother, Veig, spoke out of the darkness. "What is it?"

"They're hunting," Ulf said.

There was no need for Veig to ask what he meant. "They," used in that tone of voice, could only mean the death spiders. And when the death spiders were hunting, it was the most serious thing that could happen to this small band of human beings who spent most of their lives underground. For as far back as they could remember, men had been hunted: by scorpions, by tiger beetles, by striped scarabs, and saga insects but most of all, by the death spiders. The beetles and the mosquitoes were natural enemies; sometimes, they could be killed. But the spiders, who were the lords of the earth, were unconquerable. To kill a spider was to invite appalling revenge. When Niall's great-grandfather, Jomar, had been a slave of the spiders, he had seen what happened to a small colony of humans who killed a spider. An army of thousands was mobilized to hunt them. A line of spiders more than ten miles long marched across the desert, with hundreds of balloon spiders overhead. When the human beings were finally captured—about thirty of them, including children—they were brought back to the city of the Death Lord, paraded before the whole populace, and then ritually injected with a nerve poison that brought paralysis. The victims remained fully conscious, yet were unable to move anything but their eyes and eyelids. After that they were slowly eaten, the whole process taking a matter of days; the leader continued to live for almost two weeks, until he was only an armless and legless trunk.

No one knew why the spiders hated men so much: not even Jomar, who had spent his whole life among them until he escaped on a spider balloon. All Jomar knew was that there were thousands of hunting spiders who spent their lives searching for human beings. Perhaps it was because they regarded human flesh as the supreme delicacy. Yet this explanation seemed illogical, since the spiders bred their own human beings for food. Apparently they liked them fat—so fat that they could scarcely walk. So why should a spider prize the flesh of the underfed humans of the desert? There must be some other reason why the spiders regarded humans with such single-minded hatred.

The others were now awake—his mother, Siris, and his two younger sisters, Runa and Mara. Ulf said little within the hearing of the girls; yet they could sense that something was wrong, and their fear was like an unpleasant vibration, or a sweet-sickly smell.

From the entrance stone, Veig beckoned his father. Niall also crept to the mouth of the burrow, and before the two heads blocked the daylight he glimpsed the white balloon, moving fast over the tops of the organ cactus, more than a mile away.

Ulf said softly: "The little ones must be put to sleep."

Veig nodded and disappeared into the depths of the burrow where the ants were stabled. Ten minutes later, he returned with a gourd full of the sweet, porridge-like substance that the ants secreted in their craws. Siris scraped portions of this on wooden platters and the girls ate hungrily, unaccustomed to such generous helpings. When Niall accepted his platter, he smelt the heavy, flowery scent of the ortis plant that came from the forest of the Great Delta. But he had no desire to sleep; he was confident now that he could control his fear reaction. To satisfy his father, he swallowed a mouthful but as soon as no one was looking, pushed the plate under a pile of alfa grass used for bedding. Five minutes later, the little girls were fast asleep again. Niall also felt a pleasant heaviness from the narcotic, a warm glow that soothed the feeling of hunger; but his mind remained alert.

Siris had waited until the girls were asleep before she ate sparingly of the honeydew porridge. Like Niall, she wanted to remain awake. But this was not so that she could help defend the burrow. It was so she could kill the children, then herself, if the death spiders detected their presence.

She was swallowing the first mouthful when the fear-probe invaded the burrow. It was literally an invasion, as if one of the enormous spiders had leapt into the midst of their underground home. For a moment, Niall almost lost control; but his mind instantly grasped that this invisible terror was bodiless and impersonal. Siris was not so lucky. Niall felt as well as saw the fear that poured out of her like a shriek. Ulf and Veig felt it too. The searching will of the death spider seemed to have some quality that amplified their feelings and also released involuntary bursts of fear. Niall alone remained perfectly controlled and calm. He had contracted his mind to a point, so the light seemed to glow inside his head, and he felt strangely detached from his surroundings and from his own personality.

The fear-probe seemed to hesitate, as if it had stopped to listen. But now all the humans had their fear under control, and the inside of the burrow seemed full of a throbbing silence. The two girls breathed peacefully. As the fear-probe faded, like a sound dying away in the distance, Niall experienced a brief glow of satisfaction. If the children had been awake, their terror would have announced their presence in waves of hysteria, betraying them to the spiders as hundreds of other human children had involuntarily betrayed their families. The juice of the ortis plant was a great blessing, even though it had cost the lives of his uncle Thorg and his cousin Hrolf. Both had been overcome by the plant and eaten.

Five times more that day, the fear-probes invaded the burrow; but the minds of the human beings were as still as their bodies; no echo of fear betrayed their presence. Propped against the smooth wall of the burrow, a wall made of sand grains cemented by the saliva of the tiger beetle, Niall felt as if he had been turned to stone.

As the day advanced, the temperature in the burrow rose steadily. Under normal circumstances, they would have sealed the entrance with branches and stones, and the wind would have completed the work by filling the cracks with sand. But Ulf wanted to be able to see the approach of the spider balloons; it was easier to resist the fear-probes when they were expected. So the aperture under the flat stone was left open, and the hot desert wind blew into the burrow, carrying sand that was allowed to form a carpet on the floor. The children perspired as they slept. The adults were indifferent to the temperature; tension kept them at a high level of alertness. Twice during the day Siris brought food—prickly pears and the dried meat of desert rodents—but they ate sparingly, their eyes fixed on the strip of electric blue sky.

At mid-afternoon, Niall was keeping watch when he saw a balloon on the horizon. Minutes later, another appeared to its left, then a third to its right. Soon the sky was full of balloons—he stopped counting when he reached twenty. The sheer number made his heart contract. He hissed to the others, and they joined him, standing back a few feet from the aperture so that all could see.

Ulf said softly: "Why are there so many?"

Niall was puzzled that his father failed to see the answer. The spiders knew they were being scanned by human eyes. It must have been infuriating for the Death Lords to know that down there in the desert, their prey was watching them from some hidden shelter, and that there was no way of driving them into the open. This armada of balloons was designed to cause terror. It might have succeeded in its purpose if it had come from another direction, so as to approach unseen. But in the five minutes or so that it took the balloons to pass overhead, the watchers had time to control their fear. The wind had now risen, so the balloons passed over quickly. The fear stabbed at them for a moment, seeming to illuminate them like a searchlight beam; then it had moved on.

From his vantage point at the side of the aperture, Niall could see that the balloons were spread out in a symmetrical zigzag pattern. He knew instinctively why this was so. A solitary balloon had no chance of getting an exact bearing on its prey. Its powers of observation extended downward in a kind of cone, and unless a spider's attention was focused on the precise point from which it received an echo, it had no way of knowing exactly where that echo had come from. It might be anywhere within a square mile. But if two spiders received the echo simultaneously, each could judge its direction, and their prey could be located at the point at which the two echoes converged. And if more than two balloons received the echo, its source would be even more obvious.

Strangely enough, this insight gave Niall a curious satisfaction. It meant that he was beginning to understand the minds of the spiders, that they no longer represented the terror of the unknown. But an instinct warned him against too much self-satisfaction.

In the late afternoon, the two children stirred. Their faces were flushed from the heat, and their throats were dry—the usual after-effect of the ortis juice. Siris gave them water, and then, as a special treat, the succulent fruit of the opuntia cactus, with its astringent flavor. After that, they were given more of the drugged porridge and fell asleep again. Mara, the youngest, breathed quickly and her long hair was damp with sweat. Her mother sat with her arm extended over her in a protective gesture. Mara was everybody's favorite, and their protectiveness had grown stronger since they had almost lost her. Three months ago, playing among the euphorbia bushes one evening, she had been attacked by a big yellow scorpion. Niall, who had been gathering prickly pear, had heard Runa's screams and arrived in time to see the scorpion disappearing into its lair under a rock, clutching the child's body in its enormous pincers. The sight paralyzed him with shock. He had often watched with morbid fascination as a scorpion paralyzed some creature with that overarching swing of its tail, then shredded and tore the carcass with its chelicerae, the short, powerful claws below the mouth; after that, the wounds would be injected with a digestive enzyme that reduced the tissues to a liquid so the scorpion could drink them. Now his first impulse was to rush in and try to grab his sister; but the sight of that moist stinger, still poised above the creature's back, warned him that this would be suicide. He ran back to the burrow, shouting for his father. Ulf acted with the control of a man whose life has often depended on his coolness. He called to Veig: "Quick, bring fire." It seemed an unbelievably long interval of time before Veig emerged from the burrow with a burning torch of grass. With arms full of the dry, straw-like esparto, they rushed and stumbled through the cactuses to the scorpion's lair. This was underneath a large, flat stone. The creature was waiting for them; they could see its row of eyes gleaming in the darkness, behind the huge pincers. The torch had almost burned out; Ulf blew on it to light the esparto, then rushed unhesitatingly at the entrance to the lair.

The scorpion gave its dry, menacing hiss, and retreated before the flames and the smoke. Ulf kicked the burning fragments into the lair, then gave a leap sideways as the scorpion rushed out, its stinger poised to strike. The giant pincers, like those of an enormous lobster, made it clumsy compared to the man. Veig rushed forward with more burning grass, which he hurled between the pincers, swerving aside to avoid the top-heavy rush. It hissed with agony, tried to turn instinctively towards its lair, and was headed off by Ulf waving a burning torch. Niall knew what he had to do. He plunged into the lair, paused a moment amongst the empty shells of beetles, then snatched up his sister and ran with her into the daylight. The scorpion saw its prey escaping and made a rush at him; Veig jumped forward and hurled his spear between its pincers. Niall handed the cold, still little body to Siris, and turned in time to see their enemy scuttling away across the desert. Veig said later that his spear had destroyed two of its eyes.

It looked as if Mara was dead. The naked, white body was cold and had the peculiar smell of the scorpion's lair. There was no sign of heartbeat. Yet after two days she began to breathe again, and a week later was able to drag herself across the floor of the burrow. It took another month for the effects of the poison to vanish completely. A raised black welt on her shoulder was the only sign of her encounter with the scorpion.

The fourth wave of spider balloons came an hour later. His father touched his shoulder lightly, and he realized he had fallen into a light doze. Still secure in the quiescence of drowsiness, he felt the fear pass over him like a cold wind, and noted that it made the hairs on his arms stand on end. And when the fear had passed, he reflected that it was stupid of the spiders to do it so often. It allowed the human beings to become accustomed to it, and taught them how to resist it. The spiders could not be as intelligent as he had always thought.

The last time was the worst. It happened as dusk was turning the sky a deeper blue. The wind was dropping, and it seemed unlikely that the spiders would mount another reconnaissance. Overhead, through the roof of the burrow, they heard the scrabbling noise of some large insect; it could be a scorpion or a tiger beetle, even a camel spider dragging some heavy prey. The sound was a welcome distraction after hours of silence, and they listened as it moved towards the entrance of the burrow. Suddenly Veig, who was standing on watch, started. Looking past his head, they saw the balloons, now within a dozen feet of the floor of the desert, drifting towards them. At the same moment, sand cascaded through the aperture and the huge lobster claws of the scorpion came into view. This alarmed no one; they assumed it was passing by in its search for food. But the scorpion stopped, and more sand fell into the burrow. The flat stone moved, and Niall realized with incredulity that the creature was trying to force its way in. With the balloons almost overhead, it was the worst thing that could have happened. He could feel the alarm of the others, amplified by fear that their fear would betray them. For a moment, it looked as though the spiders had won.

Niall acted involuntarily, without thinking. Ulf's spear was propped against the wall, its head made of a needle-sharp jackal bone. Neither Ulf nor Veig would have dared to use it, in case the burst of aggressiveness betrayed their presence to the hunters. What Niall did, naturally and spontaneously, was to close his mind, as if drawing a shutter over his thoughts and feelings. Then he took a long step towards the entrance, pushed Veig to one side, and struck with all his force between the claws that were enlarging the entrance. There was a hiss and a blast of a sickening smell. With a lightning reflex, the thing withdrew, and they could see the nearest balloon, only about a hundred yards away, drifting towards them. Niall stood there, freezing into stillness, and continued to shield his mind from the probing beam of will-force. It brushed over him, now so close that he had the illusion he could feel the creature's breath, and its physical presence. A few seconds later, it was gone. They remained there for another ten minutes or so, all experiencing the same fear: that the spiders had detected them and would land in the desert and surround their burrow. As the minutes dragged past, the anxiety receded. Niall thrust his head out of the burrow and saw the balloons far away, outlined against the red and purple sunset behind the mountains. The scorpion had also disappeared. The point of the spear was tinged with blood mixed with a white substance like pus.

Ulf placed one arm round his shoulder and hugged him. "Good boy." The compliment, which Ulf had always used to praise some childish piece of obedience, sounded absurdly inappropriate; but Niall understood the gratitude behind it, and felt a surge of pride.

Ten minutes later, with the suddenness of tropical nightfall, they were immersed in darkness as if in black water. Ulf and Veig blocked the entrance with rocks and stones. Then Veig lit a rush light that burned insect oil and they ate a meal of dried meat and cactus fruit. Niall sat propped in his corner, watching their shadows on the wall and filled with the contentment of fatigue. He knew that his action had saved their lives, and that the others were aware of it too. But he also knew that he was probably responsible for what had happened today. Niall had also killed a death spider.

It had been almost ten years since Niall's family moved into the burrow. Before that, they had lived in a cave at the foot of the great inland plateau, some twenty miles to the south. Even with the cave entrance blocked with stones and rock fragments, the temperature had often reached a hundred during the day. Food was scarce, and the men had spent much time on foraging expeditions. The spider balloon on which Jomar had escaped provided silk for makeshift parasols, which enabled them to survive the midday heat. In a nearby dried-up watercourse there were barrel cacti, whose juice was drinkable. (That of the organ cactus was poisonous.) Yet for the small band of human beings—in those days, Thorg and his wife, Ingeld, and their son Hrolf lived with them—life was a continuous misery of thirst, starvation, and burning heat.

Early one day, farther from home than usual, the hunters had seen a big tiger beetle disappear into its underground burrow. By comparison with their home at the foot of the plateau, this area seemed a paradise. The waru plant gave promise of fresh water, while the distinctly green color of the alfa grass revealed that the night brought moisture in the form of fine mist. Alfa grass meant rope for traps; it could also be woven into baskets and mats. Moreover, the shell of a blister beetle promised a source of oil.

The men were weary, exhausted by the heat and it may have been this that had decided them on the rash enterprise of attacking a tiger beetle. The mandibles of the tiger beetle could sever a man's arm or leg; they were feared for their swiftness and for their incredible voracity—Niall had once seen one capture and eat twelve enormous flies in less than half an hour. But if the beetle could be driven out of its burrow and attacked while it was struggling in the narrow entrance, they stood a chance of killing it before it could make use of its speed.

The first step was to collect a pile of creosote bushes, hacking them out of the ground with their flint knives. With its brittle wood and rank, tarry-smelling leaves, the creosote bush would blaze like a torch after a few hours drying in the sun. They also collected piles of alfa grass, and prevented it from blowing away by weighting it down with stones. Then they collected the largest rocks they could find and piled them in heaps near the beetle's lair. Aware of all this activity, the creature watched them from its burrow, but made no attempt to emerge; there were too many of them. When Hrolf went too close, a pair of claw-like mandibles were thrust out menacingly from under the stone over the entrance.

As the sun rose higher, it became impossible to work for more than a few minutes at a time; even in the shade of the organ-pipe cacti their sweat dried and evaporated before they were aware of it. With the sun directly overhead, they crouched in the shade of their parasols and sipped sparingly of the water to prevent dehydration.

They had retreated into the cactus grove to give the beetle a sense of security. Then, in the early afternoon, Jomar decided it was time to attack; no desert creature expected danger at this time of day. He made fire, using chips of dried bark, then ignited a pile of the alfa grass. The sun was so blinding that the flames were invisible; but when the creosote bushes caught fire, the black smoke billowed into the air. This, they knew, was the most dangerous moment; some distant patrol of spiders might see the smoke. Swiftly, they seized the burning bushes by their roots and dragged them across the sand. With a single powerful movement of his spear, Ulf levered aside the stone that covered the entrance; all prepared for the beetle's swift rush. Then, when nothing happened, Jomar thrust his creosote bush into the hole; the rest of them did the same, and staggered away, eyes streaming and their faces damp with bitter sweat.

It was perhaps half a minute before the beetle emerged, bewildered by the flames and the black smoke. The movement of the entrance stone had made the hole higher and narrower, so the beetle had to struggle to extricate itself. Standing above the entrance, his arms raised above his head, Thorg waited until it was almost clear before he dashed down the heavy rock with all the force of his arms. It struck the thorax just behind the prominent eyes. Another stone, hurled by Hrolf, smashed a front leg at the joint. The beetle opened its great striped wings in an attempt to fly, and Jomar darted forward and drove his spear into the segmented abdomen; the creature twisted in agony, and the powerful mandibles gripped Jomar's leg.

Jomar screamed, and tried to pull himself free. Then another big rock crashed down, destroying an eye and smashing the tough integument that covered the head. The mandibles released Jomar, who was bleeding heavily from the thigh. Hrolf drove his own spear deep into the flesh where the wing joined the body. The beetle gave a convulsive jerk that knocked Ulf and Jomar flat, and landed on its back several yards away. It continued to twitch for perhaps five minutes more.

It was Veig, peering into the burrow, who noticed a movement behind the burning creosote bushes. "There's another in there!" Instantly, they were all alert, prepared for another attack. But none came. Jomar limped into the shade of a parasol and took a long drink of water. Hrolf tended the wound, while the others ignited the remaining creosote bushes and threw them into the burrow. Then, suddenly overcome by the heat, they lay there, panting, and watched to see what happened. Half an hour later, when the creosote bushes had burned themselves to ashes, there was a movement in the entrance to the burrow and the long antennae of a beetle emerged. The female beetle, much smaller than her dead mate, dragged herself out of the hole, followed by half a dozen larvae, each about two feet long. Describing it later to his younger brother, Veig said that he suddenly felt sorry for the beetles—although he knew that if he ventured too close, even the larvae would attack him. The men watched them drag themselves over the burning sand, moving towards a gulley half a mile away. They behaved as if some terrible natural disaster had struck; their only instinct was for self-preservation.

When, later in the day, they explored the burrow, they were surprised to find it was so deep. Jomar's theory was that it had once been the lair of a family of wolf spiders. It was virtually an underground cave, the walls cemented with a mixture of sand and the beetles' saliva. Two half dead larvae lay in its deepest recess, overcome by the smoke; the desert wind, blowing directly on the entrance, had driven the smoke and sparks in like a poison gas. They killed the larvae and threw the corpses outside—the flesh of the tiger beetle has an unpleasant flavor that makes it unsuitable for food. Then they sealed the entrance and collapsed into a long sleep in the cool depths of the lair, which still stank unpleasantly of creosote and smoke.

The next day, two hours before dawn, Ulf, Thorg, and Hrolf set out to fetch the women and seven-year-old Niall from the cave at the foot of the inland plateau. Jomar and Veig remained in the burrow, in case the tiger beetles made an attempt to repossess their home—a precaution that proved to be unnecessary. Later, they discovered that the tiger beetle has a deep antipathy to the smell of burning creosote, and would not even cross a strip of land where there was any trace of it.

Niall could still remember the excitement when his father came back. His first intimation was when Ingeld, Thorg's wife, began to shout, then to wail; she had seen only three men and assumed that the other two had been killed. Then, when the men arrived and described their new home, she became hysterical with excitement. She had always been a woman with poor control of her emotions, and wanted to set out immediately; it took a great deal of persuasion to make her understand that none of them would survive if they set out in the midday heat. Even so, she remained fretful and impatient for the rest of the day.

When they finally left, two hours before dawn, Niall was the most excited of all. They chose this hour to travel because most of the desert predators hunted by night; as dawn approached, they made their way back to their lairs. The temperature was around freezing point; even wrapped in a hide made of caterpillar skins, Niall shivered uncontrollably. But inside, there was a glowing happiness as he peered over his mother's shoulders—for part of the time she carried him in a pouch—and an excitement that made him feel as if he might float up into the air. He had only once been more than a few hundred yards from the cave, and that was in the week the rains came. The wind had turned pleasantly cool; black clouds came from the west, and suddenly water was gushing from the sky. He had stood in the warm rain and laughed and jumped up and down. His mother took him for a walk, to a point where a dried up watercourse cracked the edge of the plateau. There he stood and watched with amazement as the ground heaved and split open and a large bullfrog pushed its way out; half an hour later, it was happening in a dozen places at once. The creatures hopped down to the pools that were beginning to form, and soon there was a loud, non-stop chorus of croaks as they called for the females to join them. The sight of coupling frogs struck Niall as unbelievably funny, and he shrieked with laughter as he splashed in the stream that had sprung up around his feet. Plants and flowers also began to push their way up from the sand, which had now turned into oozy mud. There were hundreds of tiny explosions as dried pods sent their seeds into the air like bullets.

Within hours, the surface of the ground had been covered with an amazing carpet of flowers—white, green, yellow, red, blue, and mauve. Niall, who had never seen any color but the yellow-grey of sand and rock and the fierce blue of the sky, felt as if he was in fairyland. When the rain stopped, bees appeared from nowhere and burrowed into the flowers. The brown pools, looking like mushroom soup, were full of tadpoles who writhed and thrashed and devoured one another. In other, clearer pools, tiny newts devoured fragments of green algae. After four years of living in a lifeless wilderness, Niall was suddenly surrounded by seething, blossoming life, and the sensation filled him with a kind of intoxication.

This is why, as he bounced along on his mother's back or trotted by her side, he experienced the same joy. His father had used the word "fertile" about their new home, and he imagined a place full of flowers and trees and tiny animals. There awakened in him a sense of boundless anticipation of marvels to come. If his father, who had spent his whole life in the desert, had been able to read his mind, he would have shaken his head sadly.

At midday, when the sun became too hot, the men dug deep holes in the sand, covered them with parasols, then poured more sand on top. A few inches below the surface, the sand was quite cool. Less than a mile away, there were pillars of wind-eroded sandstone which might have afforded some shelter; but in the searing heat, they would never have reached them. Niall and his mother and father lay in one of the holes, sweating and chewing at a succulent tuber to prevent dehydration. Niall slept a little, and dreamed of flowers and flowing water. Then once more they were on the move.

The wind had changed direction and seemed cooler. Niall pointed in the direction from which it was blowing and asked his father: "What lies over there?"

"The delta," Ulf said. His voice was tired and indifferent, yet something about the word made Niall shiver.

When they arrived, an hour before nightfall, they were all totally exhausted. Niall's first sight of his new home was of acacia trees on the horizon, then of the immense, many-branched organ-pipe cactus. He had never seen a tree before, although his father had described them. As they came closer, he saw, to his disappointment, that there were no flowers; neither was there the running water he had been dreaming about. Instead, there was barren, rocky ground with a thin covering of sand. The ground was covered with grey-looking shrubs, creosote bushes and alfa grass, and with exposed rocks and stones. Only the tree-like euphorbia cactus, with its deep green leaves, provided a touch of color. In the distance there were more of the strange columns of distorted red rock, while on the southern horizon, behind them, he could see the inland plateau towering like a mountain range. Yet in spite of its dreariness, this was undoubtedly an improvement on the endless sand dunes of their former home.

Jomar and Veig came out to meet them; the burrow was not facing the direction from which they were approaching, but Jomar had sensed their arrival with that natural, intuitive awareness that desert dwellers took for granted. Even if they had known the word, they would not have described their vague awareness of one another's presence as telepathy; it was as natural to them as hearing. And it was possessed in a far more terrifying degree by the death spiders.

Jomar was hardly able to walk; the thigh gripped by the mandibles of the tiger beetle had swelled like a grotesque black pumpkin. Veig had dressed the wound with the crushed root of the devil plant, which grew nearby; it had powerful curative properties. But it could not repair the severed muscle, and Jomar would walk with a limp for the rest of his life.

That night they feasted—at least, it seemed a feast to beings who had never lived much above starvation level. Veig had speared a large, squirrel-like mammal and cooked its flesh by exposing it on hot rocks at midday; for Niall, it was a completely new taste. Then there were the cactus fruits, yellow and astringent, and the juice of the barrel cactus. Clearly, in spite of its barren appearance, this place contained far more life than the inland plateau. It was also, they all realized, far more dangerous. There were the sand scorpions and tiger beetles, the striped scarabs with their poisonous stings, the millipedes and the grey sand spiders, which were non-poisonous but very strong and swift, and which could truss up a human being in their sticky silk in less than a minute.

Fortunately, these predators also had their predators. The spiders were a prey to a wasp called the pepsis, or tarantula hawk, a creature not much larger than a man's hand, which would paralyze them with its sting then use them as a living larder to feed its grubs. And most of the desert insects and small mammals were regarded as fair game by the enormous solifugid or camel spider, an ugly, beetle-like creature with immense jaws which could move so fast that it looked like a ball of thistledown blowing over the desert. Strangely enough, the camel spiders made no attempt to attack human beings; as Niall watched them, he often had a feeling that they were vaguely benevolent, as though they regarded human beings as some kind of ally or fellow-creature. It was just as well; their shark-like jaws could have bitten a man in half.

For many weeks after they first moved into the burrow, Niall spent his days peering out of the entrance at the creatures that went past. There were not many of them—during the heat of the day, most desert creatures retreated to their dens—but to a child brought up in a cave with an endless view of sand dunes, it was like a picture show. He learned to distinguish many of the creatures simply by sound, so that he could instantly tell the movement of a scorpion or desert spider from that of a tiger beetle or a millipede. And when he heard the movements of a camel spider, he knew it was perfectly safe to venture out; most sensible creatures kept out of its way.

During those early days, he was left alone a great deal. The women were delighted with the variety of their environment and wanted to explore. To the civilized eye, this area of shrub-steppe land at the edge of the desert would have seemed a desolate wilderness; to human beings who had lived in the true desert, it was like the Garden of Eden. Many bushes contained spiky, thick-skinned fruit that had to be picked with caution, but which proved highly edible when the skin was hacked away. Brown, dead-looking plants often had tuber-like roots that stored water. In some cases, this liquid was too bitter and unpleasant to drink but could be used for cooling the skin. Guarded by the men, Siris and Ingeld wandered far afield, carrying baskets woven from alfa grass, and returned with all kinds of strange delicacies. The men became experts in setting traps, and often caught hares, suricates, and even birds. Ingeld, who had always been greedy, became distinctly plump.

Niall was ordered to stay in the depths of the burrow while the family was away; but the moment they left, he pushed aside the branches and stones that covered the entrance, and stood on the large rock that formed a step, peering out at the strange creatures that went past. If, as occasionally happened, some huge ant or millipede tried to force its way in, he discouraged it by thrusting a spear out of the hole; as soon as they knew it was occupied, they hurried away.

As with most children Niall's sense of danger was at once exaggerated and unrealistic. To begin with, he was terrified of anything that moved; later, when he discovered that most desert creatures fear the unknown and prefer to avoid trouble, he became over-confident. One morning he grew bored with looking out from the entrance and decided to explore. He carefully closed the burrow behind him, then wandered among the organ-pipe cacti. Because it was still early, the cup of the waru plant was still half full of dew, and it was deliciously cool to the throat. He found a prickly pear and tried to detach one of its fruits, but he had forgotten to bring a flint blade, and it was too tough for his small fingers. He stooped over a devil plant and was fascinated by its grotesque, claw-like appearance. He walked over to the euphorbia that stood a few feet from the burrow and, after making sure that no creature was hiding in its branches, climbed into it and found himself a comfortable perch. It was not unlike being in a cage. This vantage point was far better than the mouth of the burrow, for he could see for miles. When a big tiger beetle came and rested in the euphorbia's shade, he almost stopped breathing. Then it struck him that this might be one of the original inhabitants of the burrow come to reclaim its home, and he had to fight against panic. A large fly more than three inches long alighted on a drooping branch and cleaned its forelegs; with breathtaking speed, the tiger beetle had launched itself off the ground and, although the fly caught the movement and started to rise, it was too late; it disappeared into the beetle's jaws. Niall was petrified as he watched the beetle chew the fly, with disgusting crunching noises, then swallow it. He leaned forward to get a better view and his foot slipped. The beetle pushed itself up on to its front legs, and peered into the tree with its prominent, button-like eyes; Niall gripped the branch, convinced he was about to be dragged from his perch and eaten like the fly. The beetle continued to stare up for what seemed an age, its long feelers waving gently. Then it seemed to lose interest and ambled off. Niall had never experienced such deep and enormous relief. Yet as the beetle had stared into his eyes, the sensation he had experienced had not been fear, but a curious suspension of his senses as if all the normal functions of his body had paused in their activity. In that state of mind, it had seemed that everything had grown very silent, and that he was communicating with the beetle exactly as he might have communicated with another human being. Nevertheless, he ran back to the burrow as soon as he was sure the beetle was out of hearing, and stayed there for the rest of the day.

A few days later, chance saved his life. Having recovered from his fright, he decided to go and see if there was water in the waru cup. It was empty—some creature had been there before him—so he wandered on through the cactus grove and stood looking out over the desert. A few hundred yards away there were more cacti, of another variety; these, he could see, had clusters of the astringent fruit of which he was so fond. There was no obvious danger, but he had the whole day before him, so he sat in the shadow of a cactus and stared out over the steppe. Idly, he picked up a flat stone, cradled it in his fingers, then placed his index finger along its edge and threw it so it spun through the air. It landed twenty feet away, with a puff of sand. At that moment, something happened. It was so swift that for a moment he disbelieved his eyes. Some large creature seemed to be there, in front of him; then, in the time it took him to blink, it had disappeared. He stared hard, wrinkling up his nose. There was nothing there, only the flat, sandy ground, littered with blackish rocks. He threw another stone, and his aim was good; but this time, nothing happened. The air was already trembling with the heat; he wondered if the brief apparition had been some kind of mirage. But the area of ground between himself and the fruit-bearing cacti now communicated an air of menace. He sat there, perfectly still, for perhaps an hour, his chin on his knees. Then, from the other side of the cacti, he saw a movement. It was a crablike insect, slightly more than a foot long—later he would recognize it as a species of darkling beetle—with a greenish-yellow skin resembling a toad's. It ambled on slowly, and paused under the cacti to poke its reptilian face into the empty shell of a dung beetle. Then it kept on coming, straight towards him. As it approached the spot where the stone had landed, Niall held his breath. Then it happened again. With incredible speed, some large, dark creature seemed to leap from out of the ground. As it grabbed the darkling beetle, it paused long enough for Niall to see that it was a big, hairy spider whose segmented body must have been more than three feet long. A moment later it was gone, and a circular trapdoor seemed to close behind it. The beetle had gone too, and the sand looked level and undisturbed. If Niall had glanced away, even for as long as it took to turn his head through ninety degrees, he would have seen nothing. The thought of what would have happened if he had walked across that empty space made his skin crawl with icy shivers.

When his mother returned—with a basket half full of some brown, smooth seeds—he told her about the trapdoor spider and begged her not to tell his father. When his father grew angry, his slaps could leave bruises that took weeks to disappear. But Ulf was not angry. He listened with grave attention, then beckoned Niall and made him point out the place where he had seen the spider. With Veig, Thorg, and Hrolf standing by with raised spears, Ulf threw several large stones to try to lure the spider out of its den. But nothing happened; the creature could probably tell from the vibrations in the ground that the enemy was too numerous. After that, the men avoided the stretch of ground between the cactus groves.

It was more than a week before Niall was again left alone in the burrow. Before leaving, his father made him promise to stay inside, and not, on any account, to move the stones and branches that covered the entrance. Niall, who was afraid of his father, promised in all sincerity. What he had not reckoned on was his nervousness at being left alone. Only a few rays of light filtered into the darkness, and as he lay on his bed of grass, he began to imagine that the trapdoor spider was creeping towards the burrow. A slight sound overhead convinced him that he was under observation. He lay perfectly still, trying to breathe silently. Finally, he crept towards the entrance, stood on the stone and peered out. His field of vision was restricted to a few feet, and nothing was visible; in any case, he was convinced that the spider was waiting overhead, on the roof of the burrow. After standing there for half an hour, his legs began to ache, so he crept silently back to his couch and lay holding the spear that always stood at the entrance to the burrow for instant defense.

About an hour later he heard a sound that made his heart beat violently. There was a scraping noise from the wall behind his head. He sat up and stared at it, expecting to see it crumble and the hairy legs of the trapdoor spider to emerge. He reached out and cautiously felt the wall; it was hard and smooth, having been cemented by the saliva of the tiger beetle. But could it survive an attack from the other side? As the noise continued, he went and stood on the stone inside the entrance and prepared to push aside the branches and run outside. But when he tried to enlarge the hole, he realized that his father had wedged a twisted piece of acacia wood so tight under the lintel stone that it was impossible to budge. And while he was pushing at it with gritted teeth, he thought he heard a slight sound from the roof of the burrow. His imagination immediately conjured up a second spider, waiting there to pounce.

The scraping noises from behind the wall had ceased. He tiptoed over to it and placed his ear against the smooth surface. A few minutes later, the noises began again. As far as he could judge, they were several feet away. He tried to recollect everything his grandfather had said about burrowing spiders: for example, that when they encounter a large stone, they are often forced to change the direction of their tunnel. Perhaps this had happened to the creature on the other side of the wall. As far as he could tell, it seemed to be moving parallel to the wall, not towards it.

The noise continued, sometimes stopping for minutes at a time, then starting again. He began to evolve a plan of campaign; as soon as the wall began to crumble, he would thrust in the spear with all his strength, before the creature had time to enlarge the hole. . . .

The tension was giving him a peculiar sensation in his head, a feeling of pressure as if his heart was trying to force more blood into his brain. It was not unlike the sensation produced by the narcotic juice of the ortis plant. His heart was thumping powerfully and steadily against his ribcage. He soon noticed that if he paid attention to this feeling of pressure inside his head, and to the beating of his heart, he seemed to be able to sense the precise location of the creature behind the wall. By now, he had been listening for more than an hour, straining all his senses. The initial feeling of terror had disappeared—since it was clear that there was no immediate crisis—but the non-stop focusing of attention had produced a heightening of the senses, a feeling of being more wide-awake than he had ever been in his life. It was as if a tiny point of light were glowing inside his head. The sensation was so interesting that he forgot his fear of the invisible enemy. Instead of thumping against his ribs, his heart was now beating slowly and quietly. When he concentrated on its beat, he realized that he could control it—make it go faster or slower, louder or quieter, at will. This realization brought a strange feeling of harmony, a kind of inner richness. And underneath all this, like some dim, shapeless cloud of happiness, was a curious sense of optimism about the future. This was perhaps the strangest thing of all. Niall had never consciously thought about the future. Living in the desert, among people who never spoke more than they had to, there was little to stimulate his imagination to daydreams. He took it for granted that he would be trained as a hunter as soon as he was old enough, and would then spend his life looking for food and praying for success in the hunt. The hunter's life is centered on an obsession with luck, and therefore on a sense of being at the mercy of chance. The sensation that Niall was now experiencing was too vague to translate into words, or even thoughts. Yet its essence was the certitude that his life was not totally at the mercy of chance. Somehow, it was more important than that. This sense of power inside his head—which he could intensify by pulling a face and wrinkling up the muscles of his forehead—aroused a glow of optimism, an expectation of exciting events. He *knew* that for him, fate held something special in store.

The scraping started again, and he transferred his attention to it, but this time with curiosity rather than fear. Half an hour before he had listened with a kind of inner shrinking, as if he preferred not to know what it was. Now the fear was still there but he was somehow up above it, as if it were somebody else's fear. As he listened in this frame of mind, he could sense that the scraping was made by some creature whose legs and mandibles constituted a digging instrument. And that clearly indicated a beetle, not a spider. Then, with sudden clarity, as if his mind had reached through the intervening yards of earth, he seemed to see a brown scarab beetle, little more than six inches long, burrowing its way down in search of long-buried vegetation. His "other self"—the lower self—suddenly breathed a sigh of relief, and the point of light went out inside his head. He was no longer two people, only one, the seven-year-old boy called Niall who had been left alone for the day, and who now knew he was safe. That other Niall had been an adult, the equal—perhaps the superior—of his father or Jomar. And the memory of his existence remained clear and objective, nothing in the least like a dream. It was the boy who seemed in some way unreal.

Niall continued to have nightmares about the trapdoor spider until the day he saw it destroyed.

About a month after he had seen it capture the darkling beetle, he was sitting in the shadow of the organ-pipe cactus, watching the spider's nest. The spear lay at his feet. He knew that if the spider decided to attack him, it would be useless to turn and run; his best chance would be to face it with the spear. The thought terrified him;

yet some deep instinct told him that he had to learn to face his own fear. In the past weeks he had seen it capture insects, birds, and even a gecko lizard.

A big pepsis wasp, about six inches long, buzzed lazily around his head and flew away as he waved his hand at it. It was an attractive creature, with a metallic blue body and great yellow wings. Niall had a vague impression that it was a flying dung beetle.

A moment later, he held his breath as the wasp buzzed slowly above the spider's trapdoor, flew around in a circle, then alighted on the ground a few feet away. He strained his eyes, expecting to see the flash of movement as the spider emerged. But nothing happened. The wasp sat there, obviously unaware of its danger, cleaning its forelegs. Niall, staring unblinkingly with total concentration, caught the tiny movement as the spider raised its trapdoor slightly to look at the intruder. Then it closed it again. Perhaps the spider had dined too well to be interested in a wasp.

What happened next made Niall gasp with disbelief. The wasp had evidently noticed the movement of the trapdoor. It went across to it, inspected it, for perhaps a minute, then began trying to lever it open with its jaws and front legs. At any moment, Niall expected to see a blur of movement followed by the wasp's disappearance. What actually happened so astonished him that he moved forward several feet to get a better view.

The wasp managed to prize open the trapdoor a few inches, at which point it became clear that the spider was pulling on the underside to keep it shut. The contest went on for a long time. At one point, the spider won and the trapdoor closed; but the wasp patiently levered it open again.

The spider decided to fight. Quite suddenly, the trap flew open; the wasp jumped backward, and the big, hairy body crawled out of its hole. The wasp stood its ground, only rising up on all its legs as if to make up for its lack of size. The spider also tilted backwards into a defensive attitude, raising its forelegs above its head so that it seemed to be invoking a solemn curse on the wasp. The dangerous-looking chelicerae, or pincers, were now exposed, and, since the spider was facing towards him, Niall could see the extended fangs. It was a terrifying sight, but the wasp was obviously unafraid. Moving with swift, sure steps, it advanced on the spider as if to drive it back into its nest. The spider rose up on all its legs so that it towered about a yard above the wasp, and was obviously beyond its reach. But the wasp darted under the overarching belly and gripped the spider's rear leg between its mandibles; then, lying on its side, it struck upwards with its sting between the third and fourth legs. At the second attempt, the sting penetrated. The spider closed its legs on its enemy and began to roll over on the ground, trying to bite the wasp; the pepsis kept it at bay with its own long legs. Its sting, which had slipped out when the spider began to roll, now began to probe the spider's armor and drove into a soft spot at the base of the first leg. Now, suddenly, the two became still, the spider still trying to get its pincers down to bite the wasp, the pepsis bracing its legs and driving home the sting. Then it became clear that the spider was weakening; its movements became slower. After about a minute, the wasp withdrew its sting and extricated itself; the spider immediately resumed its previous position, belly high in the air. The rear leg, which the wasp had been biting, seemed to be moving of its own accord. But the legs seemed to lose their strength, and collapsed into their normal position, bent at the joints. With complete nonchalance, the wasp walked towards the spider, climbed up on its back and once more inserted its sting between the joints. It held this position without moving for a long time, and the spider seemed to endure it. As the wasp withdrew the sting, it collapsed onto its belly and lay still.

Now the wasp gripped the spider's front leg between its mandibles and began dragging the hairy body back towards the nest. It had to move backwards, bracing its legs; with each pull, the spider moved a few inches. Finally, the wasp positioned the body on the edge of the hole, went around to the other side and wedged itself under it, then pushed with all its strength; the inert spider toppled down into its own nest. The wasp rubbed its front legs together as if dusting its hands, then vanished down the hole.

Niall felt as if he were bursting with impatience; he wanted to run and tell someone about the battle he had just seen, but there was no one to tell. He considered creeping across the sand to look down the hole, but decided that this might be foolhardy; the wasp might mistake him for another spider. So he sat there for more than half an hour until the wasp emerged from the hole, its metallic body gleaming in the sunlight, and flew away. When he was quite sure that it was out of sight, Niall tiptoed over to the nest. What he saw made his skin crawl with a mixture of fear and disgust. The spider was lying on its back a few feet below him, sprawled exactly as it had fallen. In the center of its upturned belly there was a single white egg, still moist and shiny, stuck to the spider's hairs.

The sight was so menacing—even with the spider on its back that Niall glanced around to make sure that no other spider was creeping up on him. Then, as he peered down at the inert monster, his nervousness slowly vanished, to be replaced by a kind of scientific curiosity. He was able to see that the eight legs were attached to the central portion of the spider's body, the cephalothorax, and that the big round belly, the largest part of its body, had virtually no support. At the far end of the abdomen there were a number of finger-like appendages which Niall guessed to be the spinnerets, or web-extruders. But he was most fascinated by the head, with its two long feelers, and the evil-looking pincers, each with a fang at the end. At the moment, these fangs were folded inward, so Niall could see the tiny hole down which the venom could flow. The pincers looked powerful enough to crunch through a man's arm.

The spider's eyes were on top of its head; by changing his position, he could see two of them, lying directly above the fangs. They were black and gleaming, and he had the uncomfortable feeling that they were watching him.

The nest itself was a tube, only just wide enough for the spider's body; just beyond the place where the body lay it turned through an obtuse angle so that he could not see into its depths. Its walls were lined with a coating of spider silk, and he could see that the trapdoor was made of an ingenious mixture of silk and earth, and was hinged with silk.

Now he could examine these things at leisure, they no longer seemed so terrifying. Finally, afraid that the wasp might return, he jumped to his feet. As he did so, he dislodged some earth, which fell down on to the spider's head. The eyes seemed to flinch, and he suddenly knew with total certainty that the creature was still alive. The thought almost made his heart stop. To restore his courage, he picked up a stone and threw it down the hole; it struck one of the infolded fangs and rolled down to the base of the pincers, where it blocked the mouth. Once again, the two eyes seemed to focus him for a moment. As he walked back to the burrow, he experienced a strange, disturbing feeling that was a mixture of revulsion and pity.

The family returned from their foraging expedition about an hour before nightfall; he could tell from their voices as they approached that they had been successful. They had come upon a swarm of desert locusts, and their woven baskets were full of them. The insects looked a little like big ears of corn, still wrapped in its outer leaves, but with long legs and black eyes. Because they were in such high spirits, they lit a small fire in the entrance of the burrow, and thrust the locusts in to roast, having first removed their heads, legs, and wings. When they were half cooked, they were pulled out of the fire, rolled in herbs, then put back again. Niall found their taste unexpectedly pleasant: crunchy and rather greasy, but saved from insipidity by the herbs and the woodsmoke.

It was only when they had finished their meal, and were sitting around in the darkness, staring contentedly at the ashes of the fire, that Jomar caressed Niall's matted hair and asked:

"What have you been doing all day?"

And Niall, who had been struggling with his impatience, told them what he had seen. He had never had such an attentive audience. Although none of them would admit it, the men—with the exception of Jomar—found the trapdoor spider as frightening as Niall did. Jomar was the only one who had had a chance to exorcise that natural human revulsion towards spiders by observing them at close quarters; and even Jomar found the presence of the trapdoor spider disturbing, purely as a natural hazard. So Niall's news was welcomed with rejoicing, and he had to recite his description of the combat several times—not because they failed to take it in the first time, but because they wanted to savor it to the full. Moreover, his father said nothing about his disobedience in venturing out of the burrow alone.

The excitement made Niall drowsy, and he fell asleep with his head in his mother's lap. Later, his grandfather lifted him quietly and carried him to his bed, which was in a corner next to his own.

Niall woke up as he was being covered with the caterpillar skin; although it was dark, he could distinguish his grandfather by his distinctive smell.

"Why did the wasp lay its egg on the spider's belly?" he asked sleepily.

"So the grub will have something to eat."

"But won't the spider be rotten by the time the egg hatches out?"

"Of course not. It's not dead."

Niall's eyes widened in the dark. He had not mentioned his suspicion that the spider was still alive, for fear of ridicule. "How do you know it's not dead?"

"Wasps don't kill spiders. They want them alive, to feed their young. Now go to sleep."

But Niall was now wide awake. He lay there in the dark for a long time, experiencing again that strange mixture of revulsion and pity; but this time pity was predominant.

Early the next morning, they all went to look at the paralyzed tarantula. Niall was surprised to see that the trapdoor was now shut. With the point of his spear, Jomar levered it open—Niall noticed that, in spite of his confident assertion, he did it with extreme caution. Peering over his shoulder—his mother was holding him—Niall was startled to see that the spider was no longer there. Then he saw that it had been dragged into the bend of the tunnel. The wasp had evidently returned and moved it, then closed the trapdoor—a considerable feat for a creature only six inches long. The women shuddered, and Ingeld said she was going to be sick. But Niall observed that his brother Veig became oddly quiet and thoughtful.

Veig had always been fascinated by insects. Once, as a child, he had vanished from the cave one afternoon when his mother was asleep; she had found him a quarter of a mile away, studying a nest of scarab beetles. On another occasion, the men had returned from their hunting with several live cicadas, each more than a foot long; and although they were half-starved, Veig had begged with tears in his eyes to be allowed to keep one as a pet. (He had been overruled, and the cicada had been roasted for supper.)

So Niall was not surprised, two days later, to see his brother slipping off quietly in the direction of the spider's nest. He waited until Veig was out of sight, then followed him. Niall assumed that his brother wanted to take a closer look at the tarantula, and he was right. From the shelter of the cactus he watched Veig lever open the trapdoor, then lie flat on his stomach to peer into the nest. A few seconds later, Veig lowered himself cautiously over the edge. Niall ran quietly across the sand, approaching from an angle from which his shadow would not betray him. Veig was crouched two feet below him, staring with total absorption; when Niall betrayed his presence by a slight movement, he leapt to his feet, already raising his spear. He sighed with relief when he saw it was his brother.

"Idiot! You frightened me!"

"Sorry. What are you doing?"

Veig simply pointed to the spider. By leaning over the edge, Niall could see that the egg had burst open and that a large black grub now wriggled on the spider's upturned stomach, its tiny legs too feeble to allow it to move. But when Veig gently poked it with his finger, its powerful little mandibles instantly gripped the skin of the spider's belly; for if it rolled off, it would die of starvation. When Veig caressed it, the larva twisted and tried to retaliate with its tiny, undeveloped sting. But Veig persisted; and half an hour later, the grub accepted the light caresses as a matter of course. It was more interested in trying to penetrate the thick, hairy skin of the belly. For two hours they watched it, until the heat of the sun drove them back to the burrow. By that time, it had already gnawed a hole in the skin, and Niall felt no inclination to see more. As they left, Veig carefully closed the trapdoor behind him.

"What would you do if the wasp came back while you were in there?" Niall asked.

"It won't."

"How do you know?"

"I just know." Veig never said much, but he seemed to know things by intuition.

For the next few weeks, Veig spent at least an hour every day in the nest of the trapdoor spider. Niall went with him only once; the sight of the red cavity in the tarantula's belly disgusted him, and he no longer took pleasure in the downfall of his enemy. He found it impossible to understand how Veig could patiently cut tiny slivers of flesh from the spider and feed them to the voracious grub. Soon Veig found it necessary to close the trapdoor, leaving it propped open an inch or so with a stone; otherwise black desert flies were quickly attracted by the exposed entrails. These flies were slightly smaller than the common housefly, being only about three inches long, but the blood-sucking proboscis and sharp mandibles made them capable of destroying an exposed carcass within hours.

One day, Veig came back to the burrow with the wasp on his wrist. It was now almost fully grown, and with its metallic blue body, yellow wings, and long, graceful legs, looked at once beautiful and dangerous. Yet it clearly regarded Veig with total trust; it was astonishing to watch Veig turn it on its back and prod it with his forefinger, while the wasp wrapped its long legs round his hand, nibbled at his finger with its sharp mandibles, and occasionally allowed the long, black sting to slide out like a dagger. It also liked to climb up Veig's arm and hide itself in his shoulder-length hair; then, with its feelers it would investigate the lobe of his ear until he laughed hysterically.

The next morning, Niall was allowed to accompany Veig and Ulf as they took the wasp hunting for the first time. They walked to the acacias that Niall had seen on the horizon when they first came to the burrow. There they soon found what they were looking for: the webs of the grey desert spider. These creatures were smaller than the tarantula, their bodies scarcely more than a foot long; but the legs, by comparison, were enormous. Trussed up in the corner of one of these webs was a grasshopper, helpless in its cocoon of silk. Veig moved around underneath the tree until he saw the spider, concealed in a fork where a branch joined the main trunk. He threw a stone; the first one bounced off the trunk; the second struck the spider. In a flash, it had lowered itself to the ground on a thread of silk. Just as quickly, the wasp was humming towards it, like a hawk descending on its prey. The spider had no time to square up to its antagonist; the wasp was underneath it, gripping its back leg and arching its body upward. They all saw the sting penetrate, and watched the metallic body quiver slightly as it injected its nerve poison. The spider struggled and tried to wrap its legs round the wasp; but its instinct provided it with no defense. A few minutes later, it lay on the ground, limp as a discarded toy. And the wasp, now that it had obeyed its instinct, was also uncertain what to do next; it crawled over the fleshy grey body and seemed to be sniffing it. Veig went and knelt gently beside it, reached out very slowly and moved the wasp onto his wrist. Then, from a bag suspended from his waist, he took a fragment of tarantula flesh and fed it to the wasp. After that, they chopped off the spider's legs, to make it easier to carry, and Ulf dropped it into his own basket. It provided the wasp with meals for the next month.

Ingeld, typically, regarded the wasp with dislike and mistrust, and screamed if it came near her. (It proved to be a friendly creature that liked to walk up and down their bare arms.) She also protested that the dead spider had an unpleasant smell. There was some truth in this; spiders had their own distinct and peculiar smell, which increased after death. But they kept the spider meat in the remotest depth of the burrow, covered with a thick layer of grass, so the smell scarcely penetrated to the living quarters; in any case, human beings who live in close proximity, with little opportunity for washing, soon become accustomed to a variety of natural odors. Niall sensed intuitively that Ingeld's objections arose out of a desire to get herself noticed, and he was amused to observe how quickly her attitude changed when Veig returned a few days later with a bird that the wasp had attacked on the wing. It was a member of the bustard family, about the size of a large duck. Veig described how he had seen it perched in the top of a tree and directed the wasp towards it. (The wasp seemed to respond directly to Veig's mental commands.) Alarmed by the hum, the bird began to fly away, then pecked frantically as the wasp fastened onto its leg and drove in its sting. Veig had to walk two miles to locate them; the wasp was sitting quietly on the back of the bird, which lay with outstretched wings as if it had crashed from a height. Veig gave the wasp its reward of spider meat, then killed the bustard with a twist of his muscular hands.

The women were in some doubt about eating a bird that had been paralyzed with wasp poison, and left it untouched for a while. It was also the first bird they had seen at such close quarters, and they were not sure how to deal with its feathers. Finally, hunger overcame their misgivings; and after Veig had roasted and eaten a slice of the breast without ill effect, the rest was devoured until only the feet remained. The nerve poison—quite harmless when taken orally—had tenderized the flesh, and the result was delicious. From then on, roast bustard was included with running water and colored flowers in Niall's idea of paradise.

Ever since Niall had learned to walk, he had been trained to keep watch for spider balloons. Before he ventured out of the cave at the foot of the plateau, he had to wet his finger and decide the direction of the wind. Then he had to scan the horizon for anything that seemed to reflect the sunlight. Until he was convinced that the sky was completely clear, he had to stay in the cave.

If he saw a balloon heading in his direction, his instructions were to bury himself in the sand—if there was time—or otherwise to remain perfectly still. He was not to follow the progress of the balloon with his eyes, but was to look down at the sand and concentrate on whatever he was looking at. The death spiders, Ulf explained, had poor eyesight, so would probably not see him. They hunted by will, not by the sense of sight, and they could smell fear. This puzzled Niall, who could not understand how fear could have a smell. Ulf explained that fear produced a vibration which was exactly like a scream of terror, and the spider's senses were attuned to this vibration. So if the spider balloons passed overhead, it was necessary to make the mind as silent and as still as the body. To give way to fear would be exactly like jumping up and down and shouting to attract the spider's attention.

Being a cheerful and confident child, Niall had no doubt this would be easy. All he had to do was to empty his mind and tell himself there was nothing to be afraid of. But at night this confidence evaporated. If he lay awake listening to the silence, he often became convinced that he could hear something creeping through the sand outside. Soon his imagination had conjured up a giant spider, trying to peer over the rock that blocked the doorway. Then his heart began to beat faster, and he became aware that he was sending off signals of panic. The harder he tried to suppress them, the more persistent they became. He felt he was caught in a vicious circle, his fear increasing his fear. But eventually, because he was young and self-confident, he learned to counteract the fear before it could send the adrenaline flooding into his bloodstream, and to command his heart to beat more slowly.

His mother was the only one in the family who would talk about the spiders. Later, he understood the reason. The menfolk were afraid that Niall's imagination might become obsessed by the creatures and that his fear might betray them all when the balloons came too close. His mother recognized that fear of the unknown might produce precisely the same effect; so when they were alone, she answered his questions freely. But he knew instinctively that she was only telling him half the truth. When he asked her why the spiders wanted to capture human beings, she said it was because they wanted to enslave them. When he asked her if they ate human beings, she denied it, and pointed out that Jomar had escaped unharmed. But when he questioned Jomar about the spiders, the old man always pretended to be sleepy or deaf. The few things Niall learned about them were picked up from fragments of whispered conversation, overheard when he was supposed to be asleep. And these left him in no doubt that the spiders were not only carnivorous but horribly cruel.

Fortunately, the spider balloons seemed to avoid the desert either because the heat was too great, or because they believed that no human beings could survive in such conditions. Before they moved from the cave to the burrow, Niall had seen only a dozen balloons, and these were on the horizon.

It was different on the edge of the desert; here the spiders kept up regular patrols, usually at dawn or dusk. They were obviously routine patrols, but disturbing all the same. It was as if the spiders knew that, sooner or later, the humans would be tempted out of the desert to these less arid regions with their abundance of cactus fruit and small animals and locusts. One day, when a spider balloon had passed almost directly overhead, they had seriously discussed returning to the safety of the desert. Ulf and Siris were willing, even though Siris was pregnant again; but Ingeld flatly declined even to consider the idea. She said that she would rather be dead than go back to the cave and a diet of prickly pears. Niall was secretly relieved at her refusal; he also preferred food and danger to starvation and boredom.

When his sister Runa was born, Niall ceased to be the baby of the family. He was nearly eleven years old and began to accompany the men on their hunting expeditions. At first he found it exhausting, walking sometimes twenty miles in the heat of the day, his eyes constantly alert for spider balloons or for the telltale signs of the lair of a trapdoor spider or yellow desert scorpion. The men soon realized that his sense of danger was keener than their own. One day, approaching a grove of thorny desert trees where they had set bird snares, Niall experienced a feeling of reluctance, as if some force were trying to pull him backwards. He laid his hand on Hrolf's arm, and his sense of danger communicated itself to the others, who stopped and stared intently at the trees. After perhaps ten minutes, Ulf saw a slight movement, and they all glimpsed the long, thin leg of a cricket. Ulf said: "It's only a decta"—a name for the harmless desert cricket. But Niall's sense of danger remained persistent, and he refused to move. The men finally decided to give the trees a wide berth and struck out across the rock-strewn wilderness towards a clump of fruit-bearing cacti.

On their way back, towards dusk, they again passed within a few hundred yards of the trees. They were moving very quietly, and startled a desert cricket, which frightened them all by suddenly bounding into the air and vanishing with twenty-foot leaps towards the trees. Then, suddenly, there was a blurred cloud and the decta was struggling in the grip of a nightmare creature that towered into the air above it. It was like a very large cricket, perhaps eight feet tall, but its grey-green legs were covered with spikes or bristles. The strange-looking head resembled a long, blank face, surmounted by two spherical eyes; at the lower end of this face were long, pointed jaws, not unlike the claws of a scorpion. As they watched, it pressed the cricket tight against its bosom, lifting the cricket's hind legs clear of the ground, so that they kicked in space. Then, with a single slash of the armored jaws, it ripped open the cricket's throat. They were so horrified at the demonic apparition that they stood and stared. The creature paid no attention to them, but chewed its way into the cricket's head, which collapsed at an unnatural angle. The goggle eyes of the demon seemed to stare unconcernedly over the desert as it crunched its way down its victim's body. When it had almost finished eating, the hunters realized that it might still be hungry; it would be expedient to remove themselves from its vicinity. Badly shaken, they hurried back towards the burrow.

Jomar, who had remained behind that day—his leg was becoming increasingly stiff—recognized their description of the creature, although he had never seen one. It was a particularly savage member of the cricket family sometimes called a saga insect. Its armor made it practically invulnerable, and its long legs meant that it could leap on a prey from a distance of a hundred yards. If the hunters had approached any closer to the trees, one of them would undoubtedly have been eaten as voraciously as the desert cricket was.

After that experience, the men came to accept that Niall's intuition of danger was keener than their own; he became a valuable regular member of the hunting party.

Ulf and Thorg were skilled hunters; but for them, hunting was simply a necessity; when the larder was full, they preferred to rest in the cool depths of the cave, lighted by a flickering oil lamp, and talking in low voices. Veig and Hrolf, being younger, regarded hunting as a sport and an adventure. If this rocky wilderness was like a paradise compared to the desert, then perhaps the lands to the north contained an even wider variety of game. Ulf warned them that the north was also the region of the death spiders. But Jomar had told them that a wide sea lay between this land and the country of the spiders. He had also told them about the great delta that lay to the northeast, a vast green area of forest and lush vegetation. Other hunters had told them about the delta, with its flesh-eating plants; but Veig and Hrolf had the confidence of youth, and did not doubt that even a man-eating plant would be less dangerous than a tiger beetle or giant scorpion. One day, in the cool season, they would cross the wilderness to the great delta. Meanwhile, the land to the north offered promise of adventure.

So one morning, immediately after sunrise, Veig, Hrolf, and Niall left the burrow and marched towards the northern horizon. They were armed with flint knives, spears, and slings, and carried their food in the sheets of spider-silk that would later be used as parasols to protect them from the sun. Niall loved to caress the spider silk; it was smooth and cool and seemed to ripple under his fingers like a liquid. He carried the smallest of the three bundles, containing the cactus fruit and a sealed gourd of water.

An hour later, they passed the distorted columns of red sandstone, worn into strange shapes by the sand-laden wind. They sat down to rest in their shade and ate some cactus fruit. From here, they could see that the land dipped into a shallow bowl, strewn with large boulders. It was important to press on quickly; in a few hours, these boulders would be too hot to touch. On the far edge of the bowl, they could see trees. Veig, who had the keenest eyesight, believed he could also see water.

The distance was greater than they had thought. By midday, they were still in the middle of the rocky wilderness, although the boulders had now given way to flints and shards of granite. They cleared a space of a few square yards, drove the spears into the rocky soil to form makeshift tent-poles, and spread the spider silk over them. With the sun directly overhead, the shade was poor, but it was better than nothing. The ground was too hard and irregular to lie down, so they sat there, clasping their knees and staring out over the depressing wilderness towards the trees on the northern horizon, and the green vegetation that was now clearly visible. Niall was again daydreaming of scented flowers and running water.

After three hours' rest, they again set out towards the north. The day was still hot, but they had to move now if they hoped to reach the trees by nightfall. Niall's legs had become leaden weights, and he was suffering from homesickness; but he kept his eyes fixed on the trees, which grew steadily closer; Veig said they were date palms, which at least promised food. Niall was passionately fond of dates, but seldom had a chance to eat them.

The terrain was now changing; the rocks underfoot were smaller, seldom larger than a fist, and inclined to roll underneath them; plodding wearily with his eyes on the trees, Niall suddenly felt his feet sliding from under him and landed on his back, taking the skin off both elbows. He wanted to rest for a few minutes, but Veig insisted that they had to keep moving. Niall dragged himself to his feet and kept his eyes on the ground, partly to avoid another accident, partly to conceal his tears of fatigue. A few moments later, he caught Hrolf and Veig exchanging a troubled glance and realized both were wishing they had left him at home. It had the effect of making him clench his teeth and force himself to make an effort to control his misery. For a brief moment, the misery became more acute, so that he felt like flinging himself on the ground and giving way to tears. Then, as he concentrated, the point of light glowed inside his head. Quite suddenly, the fatigue vanished—or rather, it was still there in his limbs, but *he* felt quite detached from it, as if observing it from above. He was controlling his fatigue instead of being controlled by it. It was such an exhilarating sensation that he gave a chuckle of satisfaction; Veig looked at him in astonishment and was amazed when Niall smiled back cheerfully.

They strode on, over the hot rocks that shimmered in the heat; through the distorted air, the green countryside ahead looked doubly welcoming. Now Niall observed another change in the terrain. The stones beneath their feet were smaller, varying in size from a hen's egg to a mere pebble, and at fairly regular intervals there were funnel-shaped craters, each about twenty feet deep. As they approached a particularly large crater, they stopped to look down into it. If they had been less tired, they might have scrambled down the sides, merely to satisfy their curiosity; but in this heat, it would have been a pointless waste of energy. As it was, Niall kicked a stone down and watched it bounce to the bottom. Then he noticed a green plant, not unlike the waru, growing a few feet down the side; in its center was a spherical, pale green fruit similar to the cactus fruit. Niall sat down, and cautiously slid down towards it. The ball, about the size of an apple, was hard and unyielding to the touch; a firm twist pulled it loose, and he tossed it up to Hrolf. The movement dislodged the stones he was sitting on and he felt himself slipping. He lay flat on his back and tried to dig in his heels; this worked for a moment, but the stones were too loose and cascaded away from under his feet. His momentum made it more difficult to use his hands or feet as brakes. Finally, halfway down, he came to a halt, and cautiously sat up, aware that any sudden movement would cause him to start slipping again.

Then, very slowly, he turned over onto his hands and knees and began trying to scramble up again.

A shout from Veig made him look round, and his heart contracted with terror. The stones in the bottom of the funnel were moving, heaving as if pushed aside by a giant mole. First, long feelers emerged, reflecting the sun as if they were made of blue metal. The top of the head was a blue dome covered with downy hairs, on either side were large, metallic blue hemispheres, not unlike the eyes of the saga insect; yet to Niall it seemed there were a second pair of eyes at the base of the feelers, narrow and predatory, and surrounded by yellow armor. The rest of the face was also yellow, but with bands of blue, with a protruding, sickle-shaped jaw which made it look not unlike a baboon. The head was followed by a mobile neck, then by powerful-looking forelegs. The armored yellow and black body might have been that of a colored armadillo.

It was unmistakably looking at Niall, and he tried frantically to scramble up the slope. He gained a few feet, then began to slide again. He looked round, expecting to see the armor-plated monster advancing on him; but it was only sitting there, its strange, monkey face turned blankly towards him.

Something struck his hand; it was the end of the rope woven from alfa grass that they always carried on hunting expeditions. Thankfully, Niall grabbed it with both hands. Heaving on the other end, Veig and Hrolf began to pull him up the slope.

Suddenly, a blow on the head, and another in the small of the back, drove the breath from his lungs. For a horrified moment he thought the monkey-faced creature had seized him; but when he looked down, he saw it was sitting in the center of the pit, its face turned away from him. Then, as he watched, it seemed to bury its head in the loose stones and jerk it violently backwards. With astonishing accuracy, the shower of stones struck the side of the pit just above him and rolled down on him; one struck his eye, and he felt blood running down his cheek. Another shower of stones struck his body, making him gasp with pain. At that moment, Veig gave a jerk on the rope; his bruised hands released it, and he began to slide, feet-first, down the side of the pit. Now, at last, the creature turned and began to move towards him, with a slowness that suggested it was quite sure of its prey. Again Veig threw the rope, but it was too short and landed several feet above Niall's hands.

Now Veig, recognizing that the creature's jaws were close to his brother's feet, began to scramble down the slope, hurling stones as he went. One of them struck the creature on the head, and it paused to survey its attacker. There was something very frightening in the robot-like impassivity of that brightly colored face. Veig tried to bring himself to a halt, slid on the stones, and threw himself on to his back to slow down his fall. He managed to dig in his heels, and lay with curved back and bent knees, suddenly aware of his folly in venturing into the pit. Niall had used this diversion to climb a few feet up towards the end of the rope. Slowly, Veig turned over on to his belly and tried to claw his way back up the slope. Immediately, a well-aimed shower of stones struck him on the head and shoulders, knocking him flat.

Niall could see Hrolf lying on his stomach, leaning over the edge of the crater, trying to give Niall a few extra inches of rope. He slipped and managed to retrieve himself and scramble back, sending another shower of stones down on Niall. One of them struck the creature's head, and stopped it briefly.

Niall shouted: "Never mind the rope. Throw stones." Hrolf began to bombard the creature with rocks, but most of them bounced off its armored back.

Veig saw what was happening. "Use the sling!" Hrolf was the best sling-shot in the family. For a moment, he vanished from against the skyline; when he reappeared, he was carrying the sling. He whirled it round his head, and Niall felt the stone whizz past him. Hrolf's aim was excellent, but the creature had again buried its head in the stones, so the missile bounced off its back again. A moment later, another shower of stones struck Veig as he tried to climb and made him slip down.

As the creature moved towards Veig, another stone from Hrolf struck the blue hemisphere on the side of its head. There was a crunching sound, and the dome seemed to disintegrate into blood. Both Veig and Niall shouted with joy. The creature stopped, and for the first time showed signs of indecision. A second stone missed and bounced off its armor; the third missed altogether. Hrolf was becoming over-excited.

"Listen, Hrolf," Veig called. His voice was a strained croak. Hrolf loosed another stone, and it bounced off the armor. "Stop! Listen to me." In spite of its tension, Veig's voice was calm and controlled. "Take your time. See if you can get its other eye." He himself hurled a stone at the creature, which had the effect of making it start towards him again. Hrolf took his time, swinging the sling several times before he released the stone. It was a good shot; it landed square at the point where one of the antennae joined the head and knocked it sideways. A second stone struck the center of the face. The creature stopped, its head turning from side to side as if trying to see its attacker, then turned and buried its head in the stones. Niall thought it was going to throw another shower of stones, then realized, with immense relief, that it was burying itself. There was a final twitch of its back legs, and the striped monster had vanished from their sight.

Both Niall and Veig were too bruised and breathless to move for several minutes. They sat there, staring at the spot where the creature had vanished, expecting to see it looking out at them. When it became clear that it had given up the fight, both renewed their efforts to climb the sides of the pit. Now that they could move more slowly and deliberately, they were able to progress a few inches at a time. Niall soon reached the end of the rope, and Hrolf heaved him up to safety. Then Niall and Hrolf did the same for Veig. Then all three sat at the edge of the crater, looking down at the spot where the creature had disappeared. Niall and Veig were bruised from head to foot, and their hands, feet, and knees were raw; but this seemed unimportant compared to safety.

Veig touched Hrolf on the shoulder.

"Thanks."

Hrolf shrugged with embarrassment. "We'd better get moving."

They knew he was right. This wilderness was no place to spend the night. They collected their bundles and their weapons, and limped on over the stones, towards the green landscape that held promise of rest and water.

An hour later the trees were close, and they came upon the first vegetation: creosote bushes, alfa grass, and waru plants. Then, suddenly, there was real grass under their feet: coarse and wiry, but amazingly soft to their bruised flesh. Now they could see that the trees were bigger than any they had ever seen before, stretching up twice as high as the giant cactus. There was sand underfoot, but it was not the fine, powdery sand of the desert; it was coarser, and pleasant to walk on. And from this sand grew plants and bushes in unimaginable abundance: flowering cacti with bright rose-colored flowers, fleshy green plants like warus, but with big yellow flowers, sorb apple, Rose of Jericho, bright green euphorbias, and dozens of others that Niall had never seen or imagined. Lizards darted from under their feet, and enormous bees hummed among the flowers. There was even the sound of birdsong. Niall found it all so overwhelming that he forgot his fatigue and bruises. It suddenly seemed to him that it would have been worth a week's travel in the wilderness to see a place so beautiful and full of living things.

As they approached the trees, Niall could see that they grew along the sides of a shallow stream that meandered along in its rocky bed. They threw down their bundles and weapons and plunged in without hesitation, dropping onto their hands and knees and drinking greedily. For Niall, the sensation was ecstasy. Even in the middle, the stream was scarcely knee deep, so that when Niall sat down, it hardly came up to his waist. As he stared down into it, the continual movement of the water produced an almost hypnotic sensation. His mind relaxed and blended into the rippling flow, and some deep instinct told him that water and green plants were a part of his birthright.

As he sat there, splashing water over his face and chest, his eye caught a movement on the bank. He stared with incredulity at the huge, blood-red creature that scuttled across the sand and vanished into a flowering bush.

"What's that?" he gasped. Instantly, all three were still, suddenly aware of their vulnerability as they sat there without weapons. Then another of the creatures ran out into the open on its spidery legs, and Veig gasped with relief:

"It's only an ant."

"Do they attack human beings?"

"I don't think so." Veig was obviously unsure.

Reluctantly, they left the water and returned to their weapons. On the opposite bank, ants emerged periodically and vanished into the vegetation. Sometimes they halted, for no obvious reason, then went off in another direction. Most were about two feet long. They had the same blank faces as the saga monster and the crater insect, and the claw-like mandibles looked formidable; yet there was something about those triangular heads, with their flat-looking eyes and the bent antennae which resembled an upturned moustache, that made them seem quite unmenacing.

Veig looked at the sky; the sun was near the horizon. "We'd better move." He heaved himself to his feet. The heat had already dried his wet loincloth. "Wait here."

They watched him splash through the stream and out onto the far bank. A red ant paused in its scurrying, headlong motion, surveyed him for a moment, then hurried on. Encouraged by its lack of interest, he advanced a few feet and stood direct in the path of an oncoming ant. It merely changed direction and scuttled around him. When this had happened half a dozen times more, and it was clear that the ants had no interest in human beings, Niall and Hrolf picked up their bundles and crossed the stream. Once again, an ant stopped to survey them, studied them for a moment, then went on its way. After that, the other ants ignored them. It was as if the first had sent some kind of message, classifying them as harmless.

Nevertheless, they advanced cautiously. This vegetation could conceal the lair of a scorpion or tiger beetle—even a saga insect. But although they saw many beetles, aphids, and bugs, and even a seven-foot millipede, there was no sign of carnivorous insects. Half a mile farther on, they came upon a spot that promised shelter for the night. At the foot of a huge rock, there was a hollow in the sand. They prodded into its depths with their spears to make sure it was not already occupied, then settled down to enlarging it with their hands and flint knives. In less than an hour, it had been transformed into a small den, its entrance concealed by bushes hacked and torn out of the sand. Here, at last, they could feel relatively secure.

The sun was on the horizon; the landscape to the east was already dark. Veig had one more task to perform before they retired for the night: to try and establish contact with his family. Back in the burrow, Siris would be wondering if her sons were safe. As the sun sank below the horizon, she would be sitting alone, emptying her mind, hoping for a message. Veig therefore found himself a comfortable spot at the foot of the rock, where he could stare in the direction of their home. Then he also relaxed and emptied his mind. He should have done this half an hour ago, to allow his thoughts and feelings to become quiescent; but they had been preparing their refuge for the night.

Daylight became dusk; dusk turned swiftly into darkness. Quite suddenly, they were surrounded by a blackness that was like the blackness in the depth of the burrow, without even a gleam of light; it was as if they had been blinded. But in this velvet blackness, Veig suddenly became aware that his mother was listening, as if she were sitting a few feet away. Then, from the depths of his own inner silence, he conveyed to her a picture of the place they were in, and of the den in which they intended to spend the night. The pictures had to be conveyed quickly, for communicating like this was exhausting, requiring a concentration that was difficult to maintain. He also showed her a picture of the rocky wilderness they had crossed, and then of the stream and the scurrying red ants. Their communion lasted, in all, perhaps ten seconds; then, before he could say goodbye, it faded. He could have renewed it with a further effort, but it would have been pointless. Now she knew they were safe and could sleep without anxiety. Veig made his way round the rock, feeling its surface with his hands, groped his way past the barrier of spiky twigs, and stumbled into the shelter, pulling the bush by its roots into the narrow gap. There was no need to ask him if he had established contact; his silence told them the answer.

They were hungry, but too tired to eat. Within minutes, all were fast asleep. Outside, the moon rose, and nocturnal creatures came out to seek their prey.

Niall awoke to the sound of birdsong and the chirping of insects. He yawned and stretched, then gasped with pain. His body felt stiff and bruised all over, and when he tried to sit up, a sharp pain in his elbow forced him to lie down again. But the pleasure of being in these new and strange surroundings made the discomfort seem trifling.

Veig proved to be in the same state. The skin of his back was a mass of bruises where the crater insect had bombarded him with rocks, and he had a lump on the back of his head like a small egg. Hrolf had escaped cuts and bruises, but admitted that it was difficult to bend his knees. They decided there would be no point in trying to return home today; in their present state, they might die in the wilderness.

Niall started to push aside the barrier, then shrank back. Drifting across the morning sky, about fifty feet above the ground, was a spider balloon. A trail of gossamer floated in the breeze behind it. He had never seen one so close. Veig and Hrolf were sitting with their backs to him, and had not noticed his sudden movement. He closed his mind and watched the balloon as it drifted out of his line of vision. If he had alerted the other two, they might have experienced a momentary panic which could have betrayed them to the spider. As it was, Niall was somehow aware that this was a routine patrol, and that the spider inside the balloon was sleepy and inattentive.

Five minutes later, he poked his head out of the den and scanned the sky. The balloon was now a speck in the distance, and there were no others in sight. He waited until it was invisible, then told Veig and Hrolf what he had seen. They were shaken, and he knew he had been right not to alert them.

Veig said: "As close as that?" He was afraid the spiders might know of their presence.

"Just above those trees."

Veig's breath exploded in a sigh of relief. "We were lucky. . . ."

But in his mood of relaxed optimism, Niall knew that it was more than luck.

An hour later, when they were convinced there were no more balloons, they made their way back to the stream. Once again, they soaked themselves in the cool water, lying full length and splashing one another. To Niall, it seemed incredible that Nature could be so wasteful of such a precious commodity. In the desert, a few drops of water could mean the difference between life and death; so could a single cactus fruit or a sand rodent. This superabundance was intoxicating, but also somehow alarming.

They followed the stream for more than a mile. It came down from distant hills; on the other side of those hills, according to Jomar, lay the great delta, where there was even more abundance and even more danger. And somewhere on the far side of the delta, on the other side of the sea, lay the city of the death spiders. He wanted to ask Veig and Hrolf about the spiders, but he knew they would be reluctant to talk about them; they were hunters, and believed that to speak of what one feared most was to invite bad luck.

Here, in this multicolored paradise, they all experienced a continuous sensation of delight mixed with fear. Everything that moved alarmed them, for they were too inexperienced to know what might be dangerous. There were giant dragonflies, as large as a man, whose gauzy, net-veined wings formed a roof over the body when they were at rest, and which turned into vast, buzzing apparitions when they suddenly took to the air. (Niall did not even suspect that these glittering creatures were fully-grown versions of the crater insect that had almost killed them.) There were bright green fungus flies that seemed to take a pleasure in buzzing past their ears so that the high-pitched noise made their heads ring. As they passed close to some immense trees, they saw webs of the grey spiders stretching like enormous nets; in one of these, a big living creature about the size of a man, was still struggling, so encased in spider silk that it was impossible to guess its identity. They kept well clear of the trees. Huge butterflies flapped lazily past them, their great wings creating a pleasant draught. Niall found one of these wings lying on the ground and was amazed at its lightness and strength; he discovered he could lie on it on the surface of the stream, and float along as if on a boat.

They were now ravenously hungry; they had left their food behind in the shelter. The problem was that they were unaware which of these various fruits was edible. Niall took a tentative bite at a purple fruit like an oversized grape, and spat it out immediately; it had a strange, bitter flavor, and the taste stayed in his mouth for the next ten minutes. An experiment with a yellow, fleshy fruit was equally unsuccessful; it tasted like rotten meat. A bright red globular fruit had a pungent, oily flavor.

Then, marching across the sand ahead of them, they saw a number of big black ants, about twice the size of the red ants, each carrying a large, light green fruit. Cautiously, in case the ants were aggressive, they followed the trail backwards until they arrived at a grove covered with a tangle of green plants, among which were the green fruits, in various stages of ripeness. Many kinds of insect were already there, feeding on the ripe fruit, and the air was full of a pleasantly sweet smell. Niall found a large fruit concealed by a tangle of leaves and vines, slashed it open with his flint knife, and scooped out a handful of the ripe flesh. It was deliciously cool and sweet, although the yellow seeds were too hard to eat. It was Niall's first taste of a melon, and he went on scraping and eating until only the skin and the seeds remained.

Their hunger appeased, they sat and watched the black ants collecting fruit. The ants would slice through the vine with their big, dangerous-looking mandibles, then pick up the melon in their two forelegs and march away on the remaining four. They seemed to ignore completely any other living creature that crossed their paths. One of them marched up to a large, overripe melon on which a butterfly was already feeding, snipped through the vine, and proceeded to pick up the melon in its forelegs with the butterfly still eating. The butterfly, apparently indifferent to the ant, went on eating until the fruit suddenly vanished, then flew away past their heads, its wings creating currents of air.

They found all this activity endlessly fascinating. They were accustomed to the desert, where there was little to engage the attention, and to sitting passively for hours in the depths of the burrow. This new world of endless variety was like some marvelous picture show; whenever the attention became fatigued, some new wonder excited it again.

Veig and Hrolf engaged in a discussion about whether ants were vegetarians; Hrolf was convinced that they were, while Veig argued that the serrated mandibles looked as if intended for tearing flesh.

SPIDER WORLD: THE TOWER

This argument was settled when Niall caught a movement in the distance and saw a black ant dragging the corpse of a grasshopper more than twice its own size. The ant was forced to walk backwards; yet it unerringly followed the trail of the other ants without once looking 'round to check its direction. Niall solved this problem when he observed tiny sticky blobs on the trail, and noticed one of the ants dropping a similar blob from the end of its body; it was clearly laying a trail which the other ants followed by smell.

Out of curiosity, they followed the ant that was dragging the grasshopper along the trail. At a certain point, two more ants approached and seemed to offer to help. The human beings watched with interest, expecting to see an instructive example of ant efficiency. In fact, the three ants seemed to have no fixed plan. One of the ants tried to push its way under the grasshopper, with the intention of carrying it; another grabbed it by the wing with its mandibles, while the original ant once again proceeded to drag it backwards. This pulled the grasshopper sideways, so it slid off the back of the carrier, while the membrane of the wing was torn by the force of the pull so that the third ant was left holding a flaky fragment. Then all three proceeded to push, heave, and shove without coordinating their efforts, the result being rather less efficient than when a single ant had been pulling alone. The humans found this confusion uproariously funny and shrieked with laughter.

They soon located the ants' nest, a large hole in the ground close to the roots of an acacia tree. Big soldier ants stood on guard there, and gently touched every ant that went in with their antennae, presumably to check its identity. They settled down at a distance, behind a spiky acacia, and watched the endless traffic. They were unaware that the shelter was unnecessary—that the soldier ants were blind, and the workers had poor eyesight. The ants were guided by an acute sense of smell, and were perfectly aware of the warm-blooded animals watching them from behind the spiny bush. But since food was abundant, and the creatures seemed to intend no harm, they had no reason to attack.

Hrolf eventually began to find the spectacle boring, and Niall found that the warmth of the sun made him sleepy, even though they were in the shade of the acacia. But Veig, who had the instincts of a born naturalist, watched everything with total absorption. It was Veig who recognized that the tree above them and the flowering bushes around were all an integral part of the ants' nest. In the branches of the tree and in the roots of the bushes lived large green aphids, looking like fat grapes, which ate leaves and sap. Periodically, an ant would approach an aphid and stroke the bulbous abdomen with its antennae; then a large globule of a clear, sticky substance would emerge from the aphid's anal cavity and be swallowed greedily by the ant, which might then make a second demand by stroking the aphid's stomach. Veig tried it himself, gently stroking the stomach of an aphid that lay in the roots of a bush; at first, there was no response—his touch was maladroit—but eventually he achieved precisely the right quivering motion of the fingertips and the globule of sticky dew was extruded. Veig tasted it cautiously, frowned, then smacked his lips and tasted it again. Niall and Hrolf were finally persuaded to try the experiment and were agreeably surprised; it was sweet, syrupy, and in spite of a curious vegetable flavor, oddly satisfying to the stomach. As desert dwellers, they found nothing repellent in the notion of eating the product of a green fly's digestive system. They had often eaten far less appetizing things.

Hrolf said thoughtfully: "Pity we couldn't take some of these bugs back home."

"We've got them already. I've seen them." There was no living creature within a mile of the burrow with whose habits Veig was not familiar.

Soon after, they witnessed another curious encounter. A big highwayman beetle, with its broad armored back, blundered past them in the direction of the entrance to the nest. They expected to see it promptly attacked or driven away by the soldier ants. In fact, it approached a passing worker ant and advanced its face towards it as if inviting a kiss, at the same time tapping the ant with its short feelers. The ant stood still, and a small, glistening droplet passed from its mouth into the mouth of the beetle. A moment later, the ant seemed to recognize that it had been stopped on false pretenses and furiously attacked the beetle. Two more passing ants came and joined in. The beetle seemed quite unalarmed; it simply turned on its back, raising its feet in the air as if dead. Two ants tried to bite its armored belly with their mandibles, and another did its best to damage the indrawn head.

After five minutes, they gave up and walked on. The beetle immediately struggled onto its legs, approached another worker ant, and repeated the procedure.

They understood what had happened when a worker ant emerging from the burrow approached a returning worker and stroked it with its antennae, at the same time raising its mouth. The workers had apparently been collecting nectar from flowers, which they seemed to store in the upper part of their bodies. If another ant wanted to eat, it approached the gatherer, indicated its need with its antennae and received a drop of regurgitated nectar. Hrolf and Niall had the utmost difficulty dissuading Veig from trying it; if the worker decided to attack, it would be useless for Veig to roll on his back and raise his legs in the air. Veig finally allowed himself to be persuaded, but nothing would draw him away from the ants' nest. Their activities fascinated him, and he wanted to understand precisely how the ant society operated. Finally, Hrolf and Niall went off in disgust to look for food and to cool themselves in the stream. This was Niall's idea of total happiness: to sit in the deepest place he could find, where the water flowed over his shoulders, and just relax and study the light reflected on the rippling surface. It not only soothed his bruised legs and his scratched hands; it also brought a strange sense of inner control.

An hour before dark, two spider balloons drifted past slightly above the level of the treetops. By this time, all three of them were settled in their shelter under the rock, the entrance sealed with a double barrier of thorny bushes. They watched the balloons through small gaps in the branches, and Veig and Hrolf agreed that this must be a routine patrol; the movement of the balloons communicated no brooding sense of watchfulness.

As they lay in the dark, wrapped in their blankets of spider silk, on thick mattresses of pleasantly scented foxtail grass—which, unlike the esparto of the desert, was yielding and springy—Veig tried to argue them into staying there for another week. Hrolf might have been persuaded, but Niall was homesick; he was missing his mother and sister. Besides, his sixth sense told him that his brother was hatching some dangerous plan.

He proved correct. As they bathed in the stream the next morning, Veig revealed what he had in mind, and even Hrolf, who was usually willing to follow Veig's lead, was incredulous.

"They'd eat you alive!"

"Only if I was stupid enough to let them."

Veig's scheme was to try to obtain some of the ant larvae—the unhatched babies—and rear them in the burrow as he had reared the pepsis wasp. To kidnap the larvae, he was willing to risk venturing into the ants' nest. The secret of admittance, he believed, was to change his smell. Watching the ants throughout the previous day, he had at first concluded that they recognized one another by their sense of touch. The soldier ants felt the workers before admitting them into the nest—which also argued that the soldiers were blind. But he had then observed beetles and millipedes approaching the nest entrance, and the soldier ants had driven them off while they were still some distance away. They had also driven off some large brown ants, which obviously came from another nest. Even worker ants had unhesitatingly shown signs of mistrust of these strangers. This suggested that ants distinguished friends from strangers through their sense of smell, and also seemed to explain why certain creatures—like the highwayman beetle—could persuade ants to disgorge food from their crops. They had somehow succeeded in counterfeiting the ant smell.

Niall asked: "And how do you intend to make youself smell like an ant?"

"That stuff they use to mark their trail—it's a kind of oil."

"But if it doesn't work, they'll kill you. You saw how three of them attacked that beetle."

Veig, who was a man of few words, said stubbornly: "I'm going to try, anyway."

Hrolf and Niall waited at a distance, while Veig concealed himself behind a bush at the side of the ant trail. When a passing ant exuded its drop of oily substance, Veig darted forward, snatched it up and rubbed it on his skin. In half an hour, his body was covered with a mixture of oil, sand, and dust; he even rubbed it into his hair. A black ant approached along the trail, and Veig walked unhesitatingly towards it. Niall had to admire his brother's courage; although the ant was smaller than a man, it looked formidable with its long, spidery legs and powerful mandibles. The ant did not even pause; it simply walked round the human being that blocked its path, and continued without change of pace.

That seemed a good sign. Veig now walked back along the trail towards the nest. Niall ran ahead and concealed himself behind a bush. Several ants passed his brother and paid him no attention.

Niall watched breathlessly, trying to control the pounding of his heart. Veig was still several hundred yards away, approaching very slowly. Suddenly, it struck Niall that he would be better employed trying to stop his heart beating so painfully; it was, after all, something he had learned to do as a child. So he forgot about Veig and turned his attention to his fear, ordering it to stop. For a moment it ignored him; then it began to submit to his control. He tried harder; the point of light glowed inside his head. When he looked up again, Veig was only fifty yards away, and his shiny, mud-coated skin made him look absurd; Niall could sense his fear and his determination. Like Niall, Veig was keeping his tension under control. A worker ant came out of the nest and advanced towards him. Niall could sense its confusion as Veig approached; the smell was familiar, yet it was not the right smell. But then, this creature was obviously not hostile, since he also had the smell of an ant. It was not until the ant and Veig had passed each other that Niall realized he had been reading the ant's mind. It was a sensation like actually being the ant, as if he had momentarily taken possession of its body. And while he had been inside the ant's body, he had also become aware of all the other ants in the nest. It was a bewildering feeling, as if his mind had shattered into thousands of fragments, yet each fragment remained a coherent part of the whole.

Then Veig was approaching the soldier ants, and they had no shadow of doubt that the creature ambling towards them was a stranger who had to be challenged. This thought passed between half a dozen of them, as clearly as if they had spoken aloud, but only two of them responded by making an aggressive movement in Veig's direction. Veig recognized it for what it was, and turned and walked away. Niall's concentration faded, and so did his insight into the minds of the ants.

Niall was struck by an interesting thought. If he had wanted to, he could have interfered with the pattern of communication between the ants. For example, while he was inside the ant's body, he could have suggested that it should stand still instead of walking past Veig. If he had done so, the ant would not have realized it was acting upon his suggestion; it would have assumed it was obeying its own impulse. . . . Was this how the spiders controlled their human slaves?

Veig joined him behind the bush.

"It's no good. It must be the wrong stuff."

"Of course it is. That's the stuff they use for laying trails, not for recognizing one another."

Veig looked at him with surprise. "How do you know?"

Niall could not have told him; he just knew.

The sun was now directly overhead, and the ants had retreated to the coolness of their nest. Veig went and washed himself in the stream, and for the next hour or so they enjoyed the luxury of soaking themselves in the running water, then lying in the shade of date palms to dry. Hrolf climbed one of the palms—covering his arms and legs with scratches from the spiny trunk—and tossed down a bunch of dates; they were less than ripe but were still good to eat.

Then Veig went back to studying his ants, and Niall and Hrolf explored the territory near the stream. There was a tense moment when a big stag beetle rushed out at them from its lair under a bush; but when they fled, it quickly gave up the pursuit. Most of the insects here seemed to be fruit-eaters, and food was abundant. There were many varieties of fruit, few of which they recognized. On the whole, it seemed safe to eat any fruit that the insects found edible, although the most tempting, a large purple globe with green and yellow streaks, proved to be oily and bitter. Others, like the round, hard fruit that had lured Niall into the pit of the crater beetle, were sweet and slightly astringent, and seemed to be a favorite of the ants.

One small tree or bush, not unlike a barrel cactus, grew on the edge of the rocky wilderness. It had long, dry leaves that trailed on the ground—their purpose was probably to collect water—and they were as tough as alfa grass. Niall tore off three narrow strips and plaited them together into a rope. Rope-making was a craft he had learned as a child, and he did it so skillfully that his handiwork was indistinguishable from his mother's. This new material was so easy to use that he went on tearing off strips of leaf and lengthening the rope until it was more than eight times his own length.

Hrolf, meanwhile, was sitting at the top of a pit made by a crater beetle and was trying to lure it into the open by throwing stones. The first stone, rolled cautiously down the slope, had made the beetle peer out of its lair; but when another stone bounced off its head, it had buried itself in the ground and refused to emerge again.

Idly, for want of anything better to do, Niall began throwing stones down the crater, trying to hit the slight bulge that indicated the presence of the insect. Then it struck him that they could lure it into the open if he offered himself as bait. With the rope tied round his waist, it should not be too dangerous. First of all, they tested the rope: Hrolf held one end and Niall pulled with all his might; if anything, it was stronger than their grass rope. Niall sat on the edge of the crater and began to edge his way down, making sure that he caused a cascade of stones. Before he was a quarter of the way down, the creature had poked its head out of the stones. Niall slid another two feet—Hrolf was paying out the rope behind him—then sat still again. The insect heaved itself out of its stones and sat there looking at him. There was something horrifying about that menacing, blank face, and Niall began to experience misgivings—suppose it could bound up the slope quicker than he could scramble to safety?

He felt the rope go slack round his waist, and knew that Hrolf was getting ready to use his sling; the other end of the rope was tied round Hrolf's waist. Then the stone whizzed over his head, so close that it stirred his hair. Hrolf's aim was good; it struck the insect square in the center of its face, and it flinched and jumped backwards, landing awkwardly on its short legs. The massive armored body was not made for swift movement, and it rolled sideways. Another stone struck it on the side of the face, causing visible damage. When a third stone struck it between the feelers, the insect made a sudden decision to retreat; within seconds, a bulge in the stones was the only indication of its presence; then this also vanished. Hrolf grasped the rope and pulled Niall back to safety. They hugged one another and laughed noisily.

A few hundred yards away they found another crater. Once again, the insect was lured out by the shower of stones; once again, it waited with menacing impassiveness as Niall slid down towards it. It was this impassivity that added spice to the game. The nightmare creature seemed to be sure that its victim could not escape. They could almost feel its amazement and outrage when it found itself under attack. This one was so infuriated when Hrolf's first stone smashed one of its feelers that it tried to charge up the slope towards Niall. For a moment he was in the grip of animal terror, but it changed to relief as the cumbersome insect lost its foothold and slid on the stones. Four well-aimed slingshots were all that were needed to make it retreat hastily, and it made no attempt to retaliate by hurling stones at Niall. This, apparently, was a reflex caused by the victim's attempt to escape.

When they found a third crater, shallower than the others, Niall was confident enough to remain upright as he advanced towards the beetle; he simply crouched down as Hrolf bombarded it with stones. He hurled a few stones himself, but they bounced harmlessly off the armor; once again, it was Hrolf's slingshots that made it turn tail.

Niall was becoming bored with his role as bait; he wanted to try using Hrolf's sling. Hrolf was perfectly willing, but he was too big and heavy to serve as bait; Niall could never have pulled his weight back up the sides. Then Niall had a fresh idea. Hrolf stood a few feet away from the edge of the pit, his feet braced apart, and Niall stood as far away as the rope would allow. Then he ran towards the edge of the pit at an angle, ran down the depression, and back up again, like a weight on the end of a pendulum, while Hrolf leaned backwards, taking his weight. The shower of stones brought the crater beetle scrambling out of its shelter. As it looked round in bewilderment, wondering what had become of its prey, Niall had time to loose off several slingshots. Compared to Hrolf, his aim was poor, and only one of them struck the creature on its head. But that was enough to make it decide to bury itself in the stones.

Their entertainment had made them hot; they went back to the stream to cool off. The game with the crater insects had served its purpose and exorcised the fear of their first encounter. They were feeling "lucky" again. As they sat in the stream, Niall raised the idea that had been in the back of his mind for the past two days: persuading the family to move from the desert to this land of abundant food and water. Hrolf's eyes brightened with enthusiasm, but it lasted only a moment.

"The strong one (Jomar) would never agree to come. He is afraid of the spiders."

"But the spider patrols come only twice a day."

"But where we live now, they come only twice a month. And in the desert, they never come at all." He added, after a pause: "Where my mother's people come from, they come about once a week."

It had never struck Niall that Ingeld originally came from somewhere else; he had assumed she had always been a member of the family.

"Where was that?"

"In the place of ruins, three days' march to the south."

"What is a ruin?"

"It's a . . ." Hrolf looked puzzled; he had no words to explain what he meant. "It's a place where men used to live in the days before the spiders."

"The days before the spiders?" For Niall, this was an equally startling concept.

"The legend says there was once a time when men ruled the earth, and thousands of them lived together in the ruins."

"Thousands?" That idea struck Niall as absurd; he found it quite impossible to imagine more than a few dozen human beings. "But how could thousands live in burrows or caves?" He was trying to envisage a city made of underground holes. If the ground was honeycombed with holes, surely it would collapse?

"Not burrows or caves. You've seen a termite's nest?" Niall had, indeed, seen a strange, brown cone on one of their hunting expeditions. "Men used to live in places like that, above the ground."

"And were they not afraid of the death spiders?"

"The strong one says there was a time when the spiders were as small as my fist, and they were afraid of men."

This was such a revolutionary concept that it took Niall some moments to absorb it. It filled him with a tingling excitement that was tinged with a touch of fear. Men who challenged the spiders died a horrible death. Niall was too imaginative to be courageous. Yet this amazing thought—that men might once have been masters of the earth—brought a sensation that was as delightful as running water. Suddenly, there were a hundred questions that he wanted to ask.

He was distracted by a movement further downstream, and for a moment his heart skipped with alarm. Then he recognized his brother Veig, standing in the middle of the stream and beckoning to them. They waded ashore, collected their rope and spears, and hurried to join him.

Veig was in a state of suppressed excitement.

"Where have you been? I've looked everywhere." Niall started to tell him about the crater insect, but Veig interrupted him. "They're fighting." He pointed in the direction of the ants' nest.

"Amongst themselves?"

"No, stupid. The red ants are fighting the black ants. Come and see."

It was an amazing sight. Hundreds of dead ants lay on the ground under the great tree, red ones as well as black. And there seemed to be red ants as far as the eye could see; they were pouring out of the undergrowth in a regular column. And although they were considerably smaller than the black ants, they were far more formidable as fighters, swifter and more compact. When a red ant faced a black ant, it hurled itself towards it with concentrated determination, trying to bite the front leg. The legs of the black ant were longer and more spidery than those of the red ant, and if the red ant succeeded in avoiding the mandibles of its adversary, it seized the leg in its grip and then braced its legs and wrestled. The black ant could only attempt to bite its armored back. In many cases, a second red ant— they seemed to greatly outnumber the black—would grab a rear leg too. Within moments, the damaged legs would be hanging uselessly or lying severed on the ground. With two of its six legs destroyed, the ant was helpless. The red ant would attack it from the side and try to turn it on its back, then would attack the "throat"—the point where the head joined the thorax. While the ant was kicking helplessly, the second aggressor would attack the point where the thorax joined the rear section, the petiole and gaster. What impressed Niall was that the whole operation looked so oddly deliberate and planned: the red ants even seemed to bite and tug in unison. Sometimes—but not often—the black ant could outmaneuver them. If it could keep its front legs out of the clutches of the attacker, then the red ant would disappear under its belly, and the black ant could attack its rear legs, or the "waist" between thorax and petiole. Even so, another red ant could then attack the undefended legs.

They watched the battle with intense excitement. The ants completely ignored them, even when they blundered against their legs. This was obviously a grim war to the death; the red ants were determined to force their way into the rival nest.

"But what are they fighting about?" Niall asked. It seemed incredible that two lots of ants who lived scarcely a mile apart, and who had co-existed in peace—Niall had seen both black and red ants foraging side by side for melons—should suddenly engage in mutual slaughter.

At first it appeared that the red ants were bound to be winners. But after half an hour or so, this was by no means so self-evident. It was true that there were far more red ants swarming around the nest; but as fast as the black ants were killed or disabled, more of them poured out of the hole in the ground. Their tactic, it seemed, was not to try to engage large numbers of the enemy but simply to make sure that the red ants were unable to invade their nest. To Niall, it seemed an incredible example of courage and altruism. When a dozen or so black ants poured out of the nest, each one must have known that it would be dead within minutes; yet there was no sign of hesitation or fear. If there were enough black ants underground, it looked as if they would eventually drive off the enemy by sheer courage and persistence.

Then a strange thing happened. From the direction of the nest of the red ants, a column of black ants came marching. Niall assumed that they were workers who had been out foraging and were now returning to defend their nest. He was baffled when these newcomers advanced on the entrance to the nest and suddenly began to attack the guards. The defenders themselves were obviously just as confused. To judge by their smell, the newcomers were their own kind, friends who could be allowed into the nest. Yet the friends were trying to kill them. They fought back unwillingly, as if convinced that it was all a mistake.

This confusion gave the red ants the chance they needed. While the guards were struggling with the newcomers, the red ants pushed past them and into the entrance. A new wave of defenders poured out, to be met by the bewildering spectacle of the guards fighting to the death with their own kind.

Veig suddenly chuckled; this was so unexpected that they both stared at him in surprise. Veig slapped his thigh.

"Now I understand. Jomar knows all about ants. The red ants are slavers. They capture the larvae of the black ants and turn them into slaves. They're trying to get into the nest to steal more larvae."

Now they understood what was happening. The black newcomers were slaves, and had been summoned to attack their own kind, which they did with blind obedience. At some point in the battle, it had dawned on the red ants that they could use their own slaves as shock troops. This revealed a degree of intelligence. Yet they were not intelligent enough to see that all this fighting was unnecessary. The slaves could probably have walked unchallenged into the nest of the black ants and kidnapped all the larvae they wanted. . . .

The black ant defense had now broken, and red ants were pouring into the nest. In the dark corridors inside there would be slaughter and confusion. Niall suddenly felt saddened. He had hoped the black ants would win. He turned away and waded upstream towards the date palms; he was beginning to feel hungry again.

Fifty yards upstream, he stopped and stared. A column of black ants was pouring out of the bushes—apparently retreating from the conflict. When he looked more closely he understood the reason. They were marching three abreast and the ants in the center column were carrying the larvae in their front legs. They were evacuating the nursery area.

He glanced downstream. Only a few strides away, the red ants were overwhelming the black defenders. It seemed astonishing that none of them should notice the column fleeing from the scene of battle.

Gently parting the bushes, he saw that the ants had opened up a rear entrance. The underground burrow must have been enormous— an ant city with a population of hundreds of thousands. One of the black soldier ants scented him and made a menacing motion towards him; Niall hastily retreated into the water. Clearly, the ants were taking no risks where the precious larvae were concerned.

But where were they taking them to? Some other stronghold? Or did they intend to excavate another nest in some remote spot?

By now, the last of the retreating column had left the nest. Niall caught Veig's attention and beckoned to him. Veig and Hrolf had been so absorbed in the battle that they had not noticed the ants in retreat; now they splashed upstream to observe this new development. A mass of soldiers had formed a tight defense formation around the exit from the nest. As they watched, the first of the red invaders appeared at the exit and was instantly attacked. But, just as Niall had expected, red ants who were pouring into the entrance, fifty yards away, suddenly changed direction and surged towards the exit; the signal to change tactics must have been instantaneous. Some of them surrounded the phalanx of black soldier ants and attacked them; others hurried on the trail of the retreating column. Niall ran along the far bank of the stream to see whether the column would sense the pursuit and increase its pace. What happened astonished him. The column of ants turned towards the stream; without hesitation, the leaders waded into the water. Only the ants carrying the larvae held back. Since the ants were less than a foot high, they were soon submerged; the leaders were swept away by the current. But they continued to pour into the stream, struggling over the backs of their drowning comrades. In less than a minute, there was a solid bridge of ant bodies across the stream, wide enough to resist the increased force of the rising water. Then, as if at a signal, the larvae-carrying ants poured across the bridge. The soldiers massed on the bank to resist the onslaught of the pursuers.

Keeping their distance, the three of them walked parallel to the escaping ants. These were moving fast, but not as fast as they were capable of moving. It was an orderly retreat. Few soldiers now guarded the column; most of them had remained behind on the far bank of the stream to hold back the pursuers. The last of the larvae-carriers had crossed the bridge. It looked as if they were now safe; the mass of black soldier ants defending the bridge was dense enough to hold back the attackers for the rest of the day.

But the red ants had other plans. Their pursuing column also swerved towards the water. It was now shallower, since the bodies of the black ants formed a dam a few yards upstream. Another bridge of corpses was created; within minutes, the red ants were closing in on the retreating column. As soon as they approached the rear guard, the black ants who were defending the bridge suddenly hastened in pursuit; again, it was as if someone had blown a bugle to give them new orders. The three human beings now realized with alarm that they were caught between the two armies, with red ants sweeping towards them. But as far as the ants were concerned, they might have been invisible. For a moment, they were in the middle of the sea of red ants, armor-plated bodies blundering against their legs. They lost no time in withdrawing to a safe distance.

Now there was chaos. Larvae-carrying ants were attacked, sometimes by as many as six at a time, and forced to lay down their burden to defend themselves. Instantly, a red ant would seize the larvae and retreat with it back towards the stream. Here they encountered some of the black soldiers, and there was a further struggle, which sometimes ended in the black ants recovering the larvae.

Niall looked at Veig, and knew what he was thinking. Many of the larvae lay abandoned while the ants struggled. They were white grubs, each about three inches long.

Their eyes met. Here, in this moment of crisis, Veig was asking his brother's advice: shall I risk it? And from Niall's face, he knew the answer was yes.

Veig darted forward among the struggling ants; within seconds he had gathered up half a dozen of the larvae. Niall was carrying his woven shoulder bag, which contained dates and a few other fruit. These he emptied out onto the ground as Veig returned with the larvae.

Veig said: "Let's go."

But a few yards away, a black ant was being attacked by several red ants and had abandoned the larvae to defend itself. One of the red ants instantly snatched up the grub and darted towards them. It was too much for Veig, who leaned over and snatched the grub with a single movement.

Then, for the first time, the ant seemed to notice their presence. Without hesitation it rushed at Veig's leg; Veig twisted aside as the powerful mandibles were about to close on his calf. He kicked out, and the ant was lifted into the air and landed six feet away in the midst of the fighting.

"Run!" Veig yelled.

There would have been no point in running back towards the stream; the whole area that lay between was a battleground. For the time being at least, safety lay in the wilderness.

As they ran towards it, Niall looked back. What he saw confirmed his fears. A column of red ants had peeled off from the main body and was moving towards them. He tapped Veig on the arm and pointed. Veig cursed with dismay.

"Shall I get rid of the grubs?" Niall asked.

The stubborn look crossed Veig's face. "No. They can't catch us."

It was true that the ants were not moving fast. But they were unmistakably marching towards the human beings, and there was something frighteningly purposeful in their motion.

They emerged from the bushes at the edge of the wilderness. The ants were for a moment out of sight. Veig pointed to a big rock twenty yards to their left and they ran towards it. A few moments later, the column of ants emerged from the undergrowth. Without hesitation, they turned towards the rock. They were following the smell of the ant larvae.

Hrolf said: "I don't want to run far over those stones. Why don't we try and get back to the stream?"

But even as they began to run back towards the bushes, more red ants appeared; dozens of them were advancing in a line from the undergrowth. Suddenly, Niall began to experience panic.

There were ants in front of them and ants to their right. If they were not careful, they would find themselves surrounded. They turned and ran back towards the wilderness. Soon the hard, round stones were underfoot. With the bag containing the larvae bouncing up and down against his back, the coil of rope round his shoulders and his spear in his right hand, Niall found it difficult to keep his balance on the slippery stones, which moved under his feet; he almost fell on his knees and used the spear to recover his balance. The ants seemed to experience no difficulty negotiating the stones.

Hrolf, who was about ten yards in front of him, suddenly swerved. He had almost run into the pit of a crater insect. They had to run around its edge, and the change of direction cost them precious seconds; the nearest ants were within fifty yards.

Veig noticed Niall's distress and snatched the bag from his shoulders. "I'll take that." He flung it over his own back and ran on.

A few yards farther on, they encountered another crater. Niall and Hrolf swerved to the left; Veig turned right. The foremost ants changed direction and followed Veig. One of them was not fast enough, and ran over the edge of the crater. Niall glanced back, and saw, to his relief, that all the ants were now pursuing Veig. He also noticed that the ant in the crater was having difficulties struggling back to the top.

Suddenly as if someone had whispered in his ear, Niall saw the answer. The insight seemed to give him new strength and he ran after Veig with relaxed, easy strides. It was not difficult to catch up. Veig was deliberately pacing himself, holding the bag against his side to prevent it from bouncing up and down. But he was beginning to look worried.

"Veig, stop a moment!" Niall called.

"Why?" Without breaking his stride, Veig jogged on.

"I know how to get rid of them."

"How?" This time Veig stopped.

"I'll show you," Niall said. "Give me the bag." He uncoiled the rope from his shoulders and tied the end round his waist. He handed the other end to Hrolf. "I'm going to try to lead them into one of the insect craters." The ants were dangerously close; the humans ran on with Veig in the lead.

A hundred yards farther on they saw a crater to their left. Niall swerved towards it. At the top he paused for a moment, then crouched down and slid over the edge. He halted about ten feet down the side. Stones bounced down to the bottom; the ground heaved, and the hideous face of a crater insect emerged.

A moment later, the first ant appeared at the top of the crater. Without pausing, it ran on, down towards Niall. But its feet slipped on the stones; as it tried to slow down, its legs went into an undignified collapse, and it shot past him. Another ant followed it; this one ran straight towards Niall and he had to jump aside to prevent it from cannoning into his legs. Then a dozen ants rushed over the rim of the crater and descended towards him. All of them encountered the same problem; their forward motion made it difficult to brake, and they skidded past him in a shower of stones. Other ants cannoned into them, driving them downhill.

Hrolf and Veig were standing at the top of the crater, at right angles to the direction from which they had approached; both were holding on to the rope, which was now taut. One of the ants bit into Niall's leg as it went past, and drew blood; it made Niall aware that it would be dangerous to stay there any longer. He began to scramble cautiously across the slope, making for the opposite rim of the crater. Many of the ants followed him but, without the advantage of a taut rope, found it impossible to keep their footing. A few moments later, Niall was safe on the edge of the crater, pulled to his feet by Veig and Hrolf. Behind him, the pit was full of struggling ants. More were pouring over the edge of the pit on the opposite side and joining the heaving mass below.

In the bottom of the pit, the crater insect was demonstrating its formidable strength. It towered above the ants with its armored bulk. As soon as an ant came within range, it descended on it with its full weight, pinning it down with its powerful forelegs. A single bite of the ape-like jaws severed the head, or bit through the waist between the thorax and petiole. The creature was obviously undismayed by the sheer mass of struggling bodies that had descended into its trap; it killed with the efficiency of a machine, and soon the bottom of its pit was slippery with blood. The ants tried to defend themselves with their stings, but it was no use; even when a dying ant succeeded in driving its sting into the creature's throat, it merely severed the sting with its jaws.

The last of their pursuers had plunged into the crater; there must have been more than a hundred ants swarming over one another in the pit. Their sheer number made escape practically impossible. Any attempt to scale the sides of the pit was obstructed by the mass of struggling bodies. A few ants succeeded in dragging themselves out of the mass and reached the rim of the crater; the humans pushed them back with their spears, sending them rolling down to the bottom.

Now Niall understood the disadvantage of the ant communication system. The access to one another's minds which had made them such terrifying pursuers now became a handicap, causing each of them to share the general sense of confusion and defeat.

They watched for perhaps half an hour, until the piles of ant corpses made it difficult for the crater insect to move about. The ants themselves were becoming sluggish, as if they no longer had the strength to struggle. Finally, as the sun began to approach the western horizon, the human beings turned their backs on the slaughter pit and made their way back towards the stream. They walked slowly, for the run across the stones had made their limbs stiff. Niall felt a strange heaviness inside his head, as if all his emotions had become exhausted. Even when he saw the spider balloons floating low over the trees ahead of them, he felt no alarm and watched them as if they were passing clouds.

They made a wide detour and encountered the stream at a spot about two miles below the nest of the black ants. What terrified them at this point was the possibility that the red ants might scent their burden of larvae; they knew that none of them would have the strength to flee back into the wilderness.

But they encountered no ants: only a few beetles and millipedes and one big, grey spider, which contemplated them hungrily from its web between two trees but made no attempt to follow them. Finally, as dark was falling, they reached their shelter under the rock. Several large flies had discovered their store of melons, but they drove these out by using branches as fly swatters. Then they pulled the bushes across the entrance, wrapped themselves in their blankets of spider silk, and sank into a sleep of exhaustion.

The following day they set out before dawn. When the sun rose, they were already in the wilderness. And when, an hour before nightfall, they saw in the distance the great columns of twisted red rock, Niall experienced the pleasure of homecoming with an intensity that brought him close to tears. It felt as if they had been away from the burrow for months rather than days.

Within days, the larvae had turned into baby ants, tiny, grey, helpless creatures with endlessly open mouths. Veig spent his days collecting food for them. He searched for miles around for ripe fruit that could be mashed into a sweet pulp, and spent whole mornings milking aphids for their sweet juice, which he collected in a small gourd. Niall found the ants delightful and entertaining; they had never had pets before—the pepsis wasp was too formidable and independent to be regarded as a pet—and he found them as amusing as his sister, and far more lively and mischievous. Veig made them a nest of the softest grass he could find, and there they crawled over one another, nipped one another's legs with their mandibles, and tried to bite Niall's finger when he poked them. Their soft shells soon hardened, and it amused Niall to flick them with his fingernail and make a metallic clinking sound. He loved to relax until he had tuned in to their simple, instinctive minds. Then it was exactly as if he had also become a baby ant; in fact, it was rather like becoming a baby again. He seemed to be part of some enormous, pleasant, furry, buzzing confusion, a glowing warmth and security that seemed to extend to the whole universe. If he went outside after lying there beside the ants, he continued to experience the same sense of total security. It seemed to him that the cacti and the shrubs were aware of his presence—not sharply and consciously, but warmly and dimly, as if from the depths of a pleasant sleep. And when a huge, sharp-nosed fly tried to alight on his arm to try and drink some of his blood, he felt no irritation or disgust, but a tolerant understanding of its need; he flicked it away gently, without resentment.

Within a few weeks, the ants were enormous, and were investigating every corner of the burrow. Veig had to spend an increasing amount of time searching for food; their appetites seemed to be prodigious.

One morning, very early, Niall was aroused from sleep by a curious scratching noise. It was coming from the depths of the burrow where the ants were kept. He groped his way down the sloping tunnel that led to the lower level and felt cautiously over the bed of dry grass that formed their nest; it was empty. Moving around slowly in the dark, he bumped into a pile of earth. The scratching noise seemed to be coming from the darkness beyond it. The mystery could only be solved with the aid of a light and so as not to disturb the others, he took the tinder box down into the tunnel and ignited a pile of wood shavings. Treading cautiously—in case he set fire to the bed of grass—he made his way into the ants' chamber. It was empty. But behind the pile of earth at the far end, there was a hole in the wall. He held the light inside it and saw that it sloped downward. In its depths, he could see the reflection from the hard carapace of an ant. A moment later, one of the ants came back up the tunnel, its forelegs clutching a load of earth. This it deposited neatly on the pile on the floor. A few minutes later, a second ant emerged, also carrying earth.

The mystery was solved many hours later, by which time the pile of sandy earth had almost reached the ceiling. The forelegs of the ants were covered with mud, and the earth was damp. They were digging down to the watershelf underneath the desert. An hour later, they were no longer muddy, and when Thorg held the oil lamp down the ant tunnel, they could see its flame reflected in water about thirty feet below the surface. And when Veig delicately scratched an ant's thorax with his fingers, it placed its mouth against his and obediently regurgitated a mouthful of water. The water was a brown color, and tasted of mineral salts, but it was cool and refreshing. Veig soon trained the ants to regurgitate into a gourd; after that, they had a permanent source of water in the burrow. It seemed an unimaginable luxury.

Quite suddenly, the ants were adults. They began to wander out of the burrow and forage for their own food. Sometimes they returned carrying fruit or sweet berries; sometimes the stickiness around their mouths revealed that they had been milking aphids of their "honeydew." Their instinct for food seemed to be extraordinary. When they left the burrow in the morning, they would set off into the desert with a certain air of purposefulness, as if they knew precisely where they were going. Sometimes, Niall or Veig followed them, but usually gave up after a few miles; the ants moved fast and seemed indefatigable. They were also totally unselfish. Returning hours later, often at nightfall, they would instantly regurgitate food on command. It became clear that the upper part of the body was basically a storage tank in which food was held in reserve. When the ant became hungry, it simply digested a little of its own reserve, allowing it to pass down into its stomach. In the meantime, anyone could gain access to the larder by simply tickling its thorax lightly and presenting the mouth, or a small gourd, to its face. Niall's sister Runa who was about a year old at the time—developed a passionate fondness for the sticky honeydew nectar, and for the light pink flesh of a fruit not unlike the melon. She soon learned to persuade the ants to regurgitate, and within a few weeks was transformed from a tiny, skinny child with arms like twiglets into a chubby little girl whose face was as round as the full moon.

Suddenly, life was more comfortable than they had ever known it. Under natural conditions, the life of most animals is a continuous search for food, and this had always applied to this small band of human creatures. It was nothing for them to walk twenty miles for the sake of a cactus fruit or a few prickly pears. Ever since he was a baby, Niall had become accustomed to a permanent feeling of hunger. Now, with the ants and the pepsis wasp to do their foraging and hunting, they had almost forgotten what hunger was like. From force of habit, they still spent part of each day in the search for food; but it no longer made any difference if they found nothing. In the wall of the burrow, Ulf had excavated a deep hole to serve as a larder and lined it with stones. In its cool depths, fruit could be kept for weeks at a time. And even when it became rotten, it was not wasted. Jomar recalled that if rotten fruit is left to soak in water, it ferments and produces a peculiarly sickly smell, and that after many weeks, the cloudy liquid would turn into a drink that was both sharp and thirst-quenching and would induce a pleasant sensation of light-headedness. When the men drank this liquid as they sat around in the burrow after dark, the tiny flame of the oil lamp casting huge shadows on the walls, they suddenly became talkative and reminisced about their hunting expeditions. In the past, such talk had been rare, for they came home exhausted and were usually too hungry to waste energy in conversation. Now they were neither tired nor hungry, and often talked until the oil lamp had burned itself dry. The ants, who seemed to respond to the mood of their masters, would come and lie at their feet, occupying most of the floor space, while the pepsis wasp dozed in its own fur-lined nest high on the wall.

And now, for the first time, Niall heard stories about earlier generations: about Ivar the Strong, who had fortified the ancient city of Korsh and resisted all the attempts of the spiders to drive him into the desert; about Skapta the Cunning, who had carried the war into the land of the spiders and had burnt their capital city; about Vaken the Wise, who had lived twice as long as other men, and trained grey desert spiders to act as spies in the land of the death spiders. Little by little, Niall began to understand why the spiders hated and feared human beings, and why they went to such lengths to destroy and enslave them. It had been a long and brutal war between the spiders and humankind, and the spiders had only won it because they had learned to understand the thoughts of human beings. This had come about, according to the legend recounted by Jomar, because a prince named Hallat had fallen in love with a beautiful girl called Turool; but Turool had preferred to marry a poor chieftain named Basat. Hallat became almost insane with jealousy; he dreamed of Turool day and night and made plans to kidnap her from the camp of Basat. Turool's faithful dog Oykel was hunting rats outside the camp and recognized Hallat by his pungent smell; he roused the camp and Hallat was driven away. Hallat was so enraged that he swore revenge and made his way to the city of the spiders. There he allowed himself to be captured by the guards and demanded to see the Lord of the Spiders, a hundred-eyed monster tarantula called Cheb. Taken into the presence of the great tarantula, Hallat offered to betray his ally King Rogor as a sign of his good faith, and King Rogor's city was betrayed to the spiders, who ate two thousand human beings at a great feast. After that, Hallat promised Cheb that he would teach him how to read the thoughts of human beings if he would destroy Basat and capture Turool. Cheb agreed, but he demanded payment in advance, and Hallat spent a year teaching him all the secrets of the human soul. Until the Great Betrayal—as it became known in human legend—the spiders had been unable to understand the complexities of the human mind, for the souls of men were far more intricate and strange than those of the spiders. But little by little, Cheb came to understand the secrets of the human soul. It is said that he had prisoners brought in front of him and made them stand there for hours while he read their minds, until he knew every detail of their lives. Then he made them tell their life stories until he grasped the meaning of all the things he had failed to understand. After this, Cheb ate them, for he felt that he could only truly understand them when he had absorbed every atom of their bodies into his own.

When he understood the mysteries of the human soul, Cheb kept his promise. Thousands of spiders descended on the camp of Basat by night, and the attack was so sudden that all but a few were captured alive. Basat and Turool were brought in front of Hallat, who made Basat kneel down and struck off his head with his own hand. But his cruelty lost him the prize for which he had sacrificed his own kind; Turool became insane with grief and sacrificed her own life by attacking one of her guards with a knife; the spider injected her with its venom, and she died instantly.

There was still one great enigma that Cheb had been unable to solve: the mystery of the White Tower. This tower had been built by men of a bygone age and stood in the center of the city of the death spiders (for this city had once been inhabited by men). The tower had no doors or windows and was made of a smooth substance that seemed impenetrable. The slaves of the bombardier beetles had once been ordered to blast their way into it with explosives, but the tower had remained not only undamaged but untouched. Now Cheb offered to make Hallat the king of all the men on earth if he would help him to penetrate the mystery of the White Tower. Hallat was tempted, for he longed for power. He had many old and wise men tortured in his attempt to learn the secret of the tower. And at last, an old woman—the wife of a tribal chieftain—offered to tell him the secret if he would spare her husband's life. She told him that, according to an ancient family tradition, the secret of the tower was a "mind lock." The mind of a man must interact with the atomic lattice of the walls, which would then yield as easily as if they were made of smoke. The key to the interaction was a magic rod, with which the man must touch the wall. The old chief possessed such a rod as a symbol of his kingship. Hallat took it from him by force and went to the tower the next day at dawn—for, according to tradition, the first rays of the sun would fall upon a hidden door in the wall of the tower. But when he tried to approach the tower with the magic rod, some force threw him to the ground. He tried a second time, and the same thing happened. The third time, he stretched out both his arms to the tower and shouted: "I command you to open!" But when he tried to touch it with the magic rod, there was a flash like lightning and Hallat was burned into a piece of black charcoal. Cheb, when he heard what had happened, had all the prisoners murdered, including the old chief and his wife. And the mystery of the White Tower remained unsolved.

The story made Niall shudder, and that night he woke from a nightmare in which he heard a noise outside the burrow and went out to confront a vast tarantula, tall as an organ-pipe cactus, with a double row of glittering yellow eyes and mandibles big enough to tear up a tree. Yet as soon as he was fully awake, the fear vanished. Ever since he was a child, Niall had been terrified of the idea of the spiders, rather as he might have been terrified of ghosts if he had ever heard of such things. But the knowledge that the spiders were not invincible, that Ivar the Strong and Skapta the Cunning had won spectacular victories against them, endowed them with a reality that was more complex and therefore less frightening. He was intrigued, for example, by the notion that Hallat had to teach the Spider Lord to understand the minds of human beings. Niall had never had to be taught to understand the minds of Ulf or Jomar, or even of the ants. There were moments when he knew what they were thinking or feeling just as if he were inside their heads. So if the spiders found it difficult to understand human beings, that suggested that their minds were totally different, as if they spoke another mental language. And—this was what filled him with a mixture of excitement and terror—if understanding the minds of men had made the spiders the masters of the human race, then would not the reverse also be possible? If men could understand the minds of spiders, could they not one day conquer the spiders?

The next day he set about trying to find the answer. Half a mile away there was a grove of huge pistacia trees, the home of grey desert spiders. When Niall arrived there not long after sunrise he saw that the lower branches of the trees were festooned with tiny webs; above them hung a white egg-sac, from which the babies had recently emerged. The larger web of the mother spider was scarcely visible among the higher branches.

As Niall took up his position in the shadow of a desert shrub, he was aware that the female spider had noticed his approach and was watching him carefully, hoping that he would walk under the tree and give her a chance to drop on his back. He sat there and tried to calm his mind into a state of relaxation, but it was difficult; the knowledge that he was being observed caused a persistent alarm bell to ring in his subconscious mind.

Then a large bluebottle buzzed past, pursued by a robber fly. The robber fly, a large, yellow creature not unlike a wasp, attacked its prey on the wing, pouncing like a hawk; but its first attack had evidently been a failure. The panic-stricken bluebottle swerved upward to avoid the tiny webs spun by the newly-hatched spiders and blundered straight into the web of the mother; the robber fly, too late to change direction, also flew into the sticky silk. A moment later, the grey mother spider, hardly able to believe her luck at this

3

double catch, scuttled swiftly down the web to truss the prey with threads of silk. Then she became aware that the nearest of the two victims was the dangerous robber fly, with his long, pointed snout that could inject a powerful nerve poison. She paused, clinging to the vibrating web as the two insects struggled to tear themselves free by sheer force. The bluebottle almost succeeded, but as five of its six legs freed themselves from the sticky fibers, it keeled sideways and its wing was caught.

Watching all this with total absorption, Niall experienced the sense of deep relaxation that had escaped him a few minutes earlier. He concentrated; the spark glowed inside his head, and suddenly he was picking up the vibrations of terror from the bluebottle and the anger of the robber fly. The robber fly was a far more courageous creature than the bluebottle, and its reaction to its situation was a determination to make someone pay dearly for this indignity. Aware of the watchful gaze of the mother spider, it was saying, in effect: Come near me and I'll pierce a hole right through you . . . and the mother, accustomed to inspiring panic, was disconcerted by this blast of defiance.

Niall could sense her uncertainty; but when he tried to place his mind behind her eyes, he found it puzzling. It was almost as if there were nothing there. He tried again—this time so persistently that the spider might have sensed his presence if she had not been so totally occupied by her more immediate problem.

Now he became aware that, in the branches of the next pistacia tree, another female spider was watching the conflict with interest. Niall tried to place himself on her wavelength, to see the world through her eyes. Again, there was the same puzzling sense of emptiness. At this point, the furious struggles of the robber fly distracted his attention, and his concentration broke. It was several minutes before he felt able to renew the mental effort. And this time, his clumsy attempt to place himself behind the eyes of the watching spider made her suddenly aware of what was happening. He felt her attention sweep around in a probing beam, trying to detect the intruder. Unable to see Niall—who was concealed by the shrub—her watchfulness gave way to alarm. And then, for the first time, Niall began to understand why he found it so hard to pick up the mental vibration of the spider. Its mind was almost as passive as a vegetable. It seemed to exist in a twilight world of pure watchfulness. By comparison, the bluebottle and the robber fly seemed whirlpools of noisy, aggressive energy. And because her mind was so passive, the spider was also aware of the turbulent life energies of her victims.

Suddenly, he understood. The spider spent its whole life in the corner of a web, waiting for passing insects. For her, the vibrations of the web were almost a form of speech; each one was like a word. She had nothing to do but wait passively, studying the thousands of vibrations that surrounded her—the living vibrations of the tree, the vibrations of insects tunneling in the roots, the impersonal vibration of the wind in the leaves, the strange, throbbing vibration of the sunlight beating down through the atmosphere like a great engine. The spider had been aware of his presence long before he came within sight of the trees, for the vibrations of a human being are as loud as the hum of a bee.

At the same time, Niall understood how the death spiders could control other creatures by the will alone. Merely to look at something is to send out a beam of will. Niall could recall many times when he thought he was alone but had an uncomfortable feeling that he was being watched—and turned round to find that someone was looking at him. This was why the grey spider felt uncomfortable when he tried to probe her mind—his will had reached out to touch her like a hand.

Spider consciousness was almost pure perception. The spider is the only living creature that spends its life lying in wait, hoping that victims will walk into its trap. All other creatures have to go out and seek their food. So spiders have developed the ability to turn perception into a beam of pure will. As a fly buzzed through the air, the watching spider tried to will it into its web. . . .

Then why were these grey desert spiders relatively harmless? His intuition told him the answer. Because they were quite unaware that they used willpower to lure flies into the web. When they willed a fly to change direction and blunder into the trap, they believed it was an accident. The death spiders had become masters of the earth when they learned that the will-force can be used as a weapon.

What happened next was an object lesson in the power of the unconscious will. The spider returned to the corner of its web and moved round to the other side, so that the robber fly was no longer between itself and the bluebottle. As the spider advanced onto the web, the bluebottle hurled itself into a frenzy of activity, so that it almost tore itself free, but in its panic, its other wing became glued to the web. Now, as the spider came closer, its eyes fixed on its prey, the fly suddenly collapsed into momentary exhaustion. Swiftly, the spider threw a strand of silk across its body, then another, binding it to the web. A few minutes later, the fly was little more than a cocoon. And, as it struggled in the web, the robber fly experienced an increasing conviction that it was also doomed—a conviction that was almost entirely due to the gentle but demoralizing pressure of the spider's will. In fact, the robber fly was still dangerous; it had enough freedom of movement to defend itself from almost any angle; one thrust of that poisonous snout would have paralyzed the spider in the center of its own web. Yet when the spider had finished trussing the bluebottle, and moved towards the robber fly with a sinister air of deliberation, the fly merely watched its approach and, after one more desperate attempt to tear itself free, allowed itself to be trussed into a bundle. For a moment, Niall's mind entered the stream of its consciousness, and he was appalled by its exhaustion and defeat. As he withdrew his mind, it was like waking from a nightmare.

He walked home in deep thought, shaken by his experience yet also fascinated by it. This insight into the power of the will was a revelation. Because the world around him seemed full of terror and danger, his mind remained alert for any suggestion of a hostile will. And as he passed within twenty yards of the lair of a yellow scorpion, he became aware of its gaze as it watched him from the darkness. It was tired after hunting all night, and therefore disinclined to make a daylight foray. Niall sensed its indecision and deliberately reinforced it by sending out a suggestion that he was armed and dangerous. The scorpion decided that it was not, after all, worth the effort and the risk to attack him.

When he entered the relative coolness of the burrow, he flung himself down on his grass couch feeling utterly drained. But the tiredness was in his head, not his body. It was his attempt to use an unaccustomed will-muscle that had exhausted him so much.

Niall was fifteen when Siris gave birth to another daughter. The child was premature, and for the first two weeks it was uncertain whether she would live. They called her Mara, meaning "small dark one," because her tiny shrivelled face had a curious brown pigmentation. It was undoubtedly the sweet ant-food that saved her life. And as soon as she was out of danger, she began to cry—a piercing, wavering little cry that irritated everyone but her mother. When she was not hungry, she was suffering from colic or heat rash or a runny nose. For the first six months of her life she cried for several hours every night. Ingeld, who had never been fond of children, became very bad tempered and began urging Thorg and Hrolf to look for another home. In fact, they found a roomy lair about a mile away, not far from the twisted red rocks, and the men soon drove out the dung beetles that lived there. But Ingeld spent only one night in her new home, decided she felt nervous, and—to Niall's disgust—moved back again the following day.

Mara's health began to improve when she was six months old; but it was clear that she had a nervous disposition. Any sudden movement made her jump and burst into tears. Loud noises sent her into paroxysms of sobbing. She screamed with fear every time an ant came near her. One early morning, when Thorg and Ingeld thought they were alone in the burrow, Niall overheard them talking about Mara, what would happen when she was older and knew about spiders? "She'll be the death of all of us!" Ingeld said dramatically. Niall felt a mixture of anger and contempt, yet he knew she was right. Mara's terror could betray them all. Yet what could be done? They could hardly murder the child.

It was Jomar who suggested a solution: the juice of the ortis plant. When he had been a child, a dozen brave hunters had ventured into the great delta and returned with gourds full of the juice. The plant was carnivorous and lured its prey with a marvelously sweet smell, a smell so heavenly that it made men dream. When a flying insect settled on the blossom of the ortis plant, it exuded a single drop of a clear liquid. The insect would drink this greedily and then become drowsy. Like tender fingers, the tendrils of the plant would delicately propel it into the mouth of the great, bell-like flower, like a beautiful girl popping a delicious morsel of food into her mouth, and the petals would close round it and digest it.

And how did the hunters avoid this fate? By deliberately choosing small ortis plants that were too weak to kill a full-grown man. One of the hunters would lightly touch the blossom with his finger, causing the juice to be exuded into a tiny cup. If the smell of the plant overcame him, others would rush forward and drag him clear. The problem, apparently, was that the perfume was so intoxicating that some men made no effort to fight it; they allowed themselves to be overcome and woke up later wearing a strange, dreamy smile. One man had allowed himself to collapse into a small plant, and a dozen of the bell-like suckers had instantly fastened on his face, his arms, and his legs. As the others tried to drag him clear, the tendrils resisted, trying to pull him back; they had to be hacked off with flint knives, and meanwhile, clouds of the sweet perfume had stunned two more of the men. When they pulled the suckers off his face and arms, drops of blood lay on the bright red blotches like dew; the tremendous suction of the plant had drawn it through his skin. The man remained unconscious for two days, and when he woke up, moved like a sleepwalker. He returned with the others, but had become sluggish, lazy, and shifty; after he had been caught on several occasions trying to steal the ortis juice he was executed by order of the elders.

As Jomar spoke, Ulf was looking thoughtfully at Mara, who was feeding at her mother's breast. He turned to Thorg. "Would you come with me?"

"Of course."

"Very well. We set out at the time of the full moon."

Niall said: "Can I come?"

Ulf placed his hand on his head. "No, boy. Someone has to stay and look after the women."

So, ten days later, Ulf and Thorg, Veig and Hrolf, set out for the delta. By that time, they had another reason for wanting the juice of the ortis plant: Ingeld was having bouts of morning sickness that convinced her she was pregnant.

It was a well-equipped expedition. The men wore clothes of mil-lipede skin to protect them from the heat, with hoods to draw over their heads. They had strong sandals, with multiple soles, and also carried lightweight shoulder bags of woven grass which could be sus-pended from a yoke. There was no need for a great deal of food or water, since these would be available along the way; they carried only a quantity of meat dried in the sun and gourds of water. They were armed with spears, slings, and knives and also carried ropes.

They left at dusk on the night of the full moon and traveled north to the stony wilderness. Four armed men ran little risk of attack from scorpions, tiger beetles, or other night predators. Niall wanted to accompany them to the edge of the wilderness, but his father refused; returning home alone, a fifteen year-old boy would be an easy prey.

Siris and Ingeld were nervous. The men had often spent days away from home on hunting expeditions, but the women knew this was different. Hunters were accustomed to the ways of giant insects and had a sixth sense for avoiding them. But the delta was full of unknown perils. Even Jomar had never been there, although he had flown over it in a spider balloon.

The next day, at dusk, Siris sat alone in the depths of the burrow while they all remained silent. Mara had been well fed two hours before, and now she slept quietly. After half an hour or so, they heard Siris breathe very deeply and knew that she had established contact. Niall lit the oil lamp as she rejoined them. "They are safe," she said. "Hrolf has been attacked by a mosquito, but they killed it before it could drink his blood." The men were carrying medicinal roots in case of malaria or other fevers.

Ingeld asked: "Is Thorg well?"

"He twisted his ankle, but it is not serious."

Ingeld could have made contact with Thorg if she had been will-ing to make the effort. But she was impatient and found it difficult to relax and clear her mind. She was also lazy, and preferred to leave it to Siris, who was too conscientious to avoid anything that was expected of her.

On the following day, the women went out looking for fresh cac-tus fruit; Niall accompanied them to guard them, carrying the pepsis wasp. It was now old, and had lost much of its skill.

Somehow, the wasp seemed to know that its master, Veig, was far away, and that it was expected to guard the family from trapdoor spiders and other predators. As Niall relaxed and allowed his mind to blend with the mind of the insect, he experienced a stronger sense of kinship and affection than he had ever known before. When they were returning, exhausted by the heat, Niall saw a distant speck in the sky—not a spider balloon but a large bird. As he stared at it, he realized that it was flying directly towards them; he tried to project his mind into the mind of the bird, urging it not to change direction. The wasp, sensing his excitement, also became alert. Suddenly the bird was only a few hundred yards away, flying at the height of a tall tree, and Niall ordered the wasp to attack. It soared up from his wrist, rising straight into the air with a speed and power they had not witnessed for a long time. Like a missile it flashed past the bustard, straight up for another hundred feet or so; then, changing direction, it dived. The bird was totally unprepared; it obviously felt it had nothing to fear from wasps. It fluttered with distress at the impact, and Niall experienced its agony as the sting drove home. A few seconds later, it lay on the ground a few hundred yards away. When Niall arrived, the wasp was sitting quietly on the crooked wing, and the bird's eye was already covered with the film of death. It was enormous, and that night the burrow was full of the smell of roasted bird flesh. Even Ingeld was good tempered and cheerful.

That evening was the end of the time of contentment. The next day, a strong, gritty wind blew from the direction of the delta directly into the entrance of the burrow; when Niall ventured out, it made his eyes run, and the sand grated between his teeth. Mara cried most of the day until even Niall felt like suffocating her. That evening, there was no contact with Ulf or Veig, although Siris sat for over an hour. Jomar told them not to worry; hunters often had other things to do at nightfall. But it was the same again the following day. By this time, Ingeld had become so anxious that she also sat cross-legged on the floor at dusk and tried to empty her mind; but Niall could tell by her breathing that she had no success.

The next day they were all tense and worried. At nightfall, Siris and Ingeld again sat a few feet apart, their heads bowed, while Jomar and Niall lay on their mattresses and tried not to move in case the rustling sound distracted the women. They heard the change in Siris's breathing as she made contact, and Niall sighed with relief. Then, almost immediately, Siris gave a piercing cry and they heard her fall. When Niall reached her, she was lying on her back and her face felt cold. Ingeld was already moaning something about death, and Jomar told her sharply to be silent. Niall propped up his mother, while Jomar forced water between her lips; she gasped and began to cough. When she spoke, her first words were: "They are dead. Thorg and Hrolf are dead." Ingeld began to scream and wail; the children woke up and began to cry. And Siris also sobbed quietly. She could only tell them that the two men had been killed by the ortis plant, and that Ulf and Veig had managed to escape with their lives.

Then Ingeld began to scream with rage. "Why did it have to be mine? Why not yours?"

They let her scream on until she grew tired and began to sob. She cried most of the night. Niall felt ashamed to be so happy that his father and brother were alive.

When Ulf and Veig returned ten days later, both were exhausted. Ulf's right breast and shoulder were covered with circular marks that looked like burns; Veig had become very thin, and there was an expression in his eyes that Niall found deeply disturbing: the look of a man who is haunted by something he cannot forget. Both collapsed on their beds and slept deeply for most of a day and a night.

The juice that had cost Thorg and Hrolf their lives was contained in a small gourd that held little more than a pint; it was sealed tightly with leaves and leather thongs. When, a few hours after Ulf's return, Mara set up her incessant wail, Siris carefully unbound the thongs, levered off the top of the gourd and gave the child a tiny quantity of the clear, syrupy liquid in a wooden spoon. Within less than a minute, Mara was asleep; she was still sleeping sixteen hours later, when Ulf woke up.

At the first opportunity, Niall sniffed the ortis juice. It had a pleasant, sweetish smell not unlike honey, with a touch of a certain mauve flower he had seen in the country of the ants; but after Jomar's story about the plant, he found it disappointing.

For days after their return, Ulf and Veig seemed listless and depressed. Veig later admitted to Niall that during the last thirty-six hours of the return journey, both had been staggering like drunken men, and that neither had expected to reach home alive. In the rocky wilderness, Veig had collapsed three times, and for a while after the last occasion, Ulf had carried him on his shoulders. Fortunately, they had encountered no predators; if any creature had attacked, they would have been helpless. They were too exhausted even to scan the skies for spider balloons.

Ingeld had now recovered from the first shock and had become bitter and surly. They put up with her angry jibes because they felt sorry for her. But one day when she had been drinking the fermented fruit juice, she went too far, and accused Ulf and Veig of being cowards who had allowed her men to die. Ulf gripped her arm so hard that she screamed with pain.

"Never say that again or I will strike you to the ground, even if you are my brother's wife."

She collapsed on the floor and began to sob. "I am too young to be a widow. Am I to live for the rest of my days without a man's embrace?"

Ulf saw the justice in her claim. She was still under forty, and many men would find her beautiful. He said thoughtfully: "There are no men here for you. But you could return to your own people."

She looked up with a gleam of hope. She loved any kind of change. "How could I reach them?"

"We could take you there."

She placed her hands on her stomach. "I shall soon be too big to travel."

Ulf considered this. "All right. We leave on the next night of the full moon."

Siris protested that this was too soon—they were still exhausted after their return from the delta. But Niall caught the hard, stubborn look on Ingeld's face and knew she was determined to have her own way. For her, the thought of any delay was intolerable, although she knew that Siris was right; it would be safer to leave it for another month. It made no difference to her if Ulf and Veig died on the way back; by that time she would be safe with her own family.

As the time of the full moon approached, it became obvious that Veig would not be fit enough to travel; he was still too weak to go outside, and he suffered from a recurrent fever. Jomar's limp made it impossible for him to walk more than a few miles. Siris tried to persuade Ingeld to wait another month; Ingeld, averting her eyes to conceal her true feelings, replied that if she left it that long, she would be unable to walk such a distance. Finally, Siris shrugged her shoulders and gave up the argument; they would all be glad to see the last of Ingeld.

Niall caught his father looking at him speculatively and knew what he was thinking.

"Couldn't I go instead of Veig?"

"Do you think you could walk that far?"

"I can walk as far as Veig."

"But this is a five-day journey, perhaps more." Ulf drew him a map in the sand. Ingeld's people lived near the shores of a salt lake called Thellam, about two days' journey south of the great plateau. The most difficult part of the journey was across the desert that lay at the foot of the plateau, for there were few landmarks. On the far side of the desert there was a country of bare rock and wadis, descending to the salt lake. There was vegetation there, and some water; but there were also poisonous centipedes.

Niall pointed to the plateau. "Could we not avoid the desert by climbing up onto the plateau?"

"There is nothing there but bare rock, and the air is thin."

"But bare rock is better than sand dunes that change every day."

Ulf only said: "Perhaps."

By the time of the full moon, Ulf had recovered his strength. Veig still had hollow cheeks, and his eyes looked tired. Siris was unhappy at the idea of Niall traveling so far, but she knew there was no alternative. It would be dangerous for Ulf to attempt the return journey alone; there were many predators who would attack a lone traveler but would think twice about attacking two men.

At least they were well provisioned. On the day before they set out, Veig went hunting with the pepsis wasp, and caught a large desert rodent. Siris stuffed this with herbs and seeds and roasted it whole. She also baked them thin wafers of bread from a flour made of wild maize. For many days before the journey, the women collected clear water from the waru plant; they had also learned to place gourds under the long, twisted leaves of the welwitschia, to catch the dew the plant intended for its own roots. The brackish water that the ants collected from the depths of the burrow was not suitable for long journeys, for it was full of minerals that left a bitter taste in the mouth and made the throat dry.

They set out an hour before dusk, each carrying two baskets suspended from shoulder-yokes. The day was still hot, although the wind had dropped. When darkness fell, they rested for an hour in the sand, and Niall fell asleep—having been kept awake most of the previous night by excitement. As soon as the moon rose, they went on. The night was cold but the exercise kept them warm. Ingeld—who, having got her own way, now felt slightly ashamed of herself—plodded on silently, making no complaint about the pace. The desert was beautiful in the moonlight, and they could see the plateau clearly ahead of them; but it was a great deal farther than it looked. When the moon set, they were still able to travel by the light of the stars, their eyes having become accustomed to the dark. They reached the foot of the plateau an hour before dawn. As the sun rose, they entered the cave in which Niall had spent the first seven years of his life. They ate a light meal of maize bread and cooked locust, then slept through the heat of the day.

Niall was delighted to see his old home again; but it seemed smaller and somehow different. He had also forgotten how hot and stuffy it could become in the midday heat if the wind was blowing the wrong way. So in spite of his nostalgia, he was not sorry to leave it behind.

They set out while the sun was still hot, because Ulf had decided to take Niall's advice and climb up onto the plateau. Above the cave, it towered up hundreds of feet in the air; to find a point where they could ascend, they had to walk for ten miles or so.

They reached the dried river bed an hour before dusk. Hot and tired, they decided to rest before attempting the steep climb. When the moon rose, they began to ascend the river bed, which became increasingly steep. Then the track became a goat path that zigzagged up the hill; it was too steep to climb except on all fours. Soon it became so precipitous that it made Niall dizzy to look down; where rocks bulged out, forcing them to press tight against them as they edged round, they were aware of the sheer drop below. Ingeld's rather large breasts were here a disadvantage, and in one place she refused to go forward until Ulf had tied a rope round her waist. Before they reached the top of the plateau, sometime after midnight, she was stumbling and staggering, obviously wishing that she had decided to stay at home.

The view here was impressive. Behind them stretched the desert, silvery and peaceful. Before them the plateau sloped to the southeast, rocky and covered with shrubs and mats of thorn. It looked unwelcoming, but the white rock was beautiful in the moonlight. They were tempted to rest, but the ground was so uncomfortable that it was simpler to go on. And after stumbling along for half an hour over the uneven, barren ground, they rejoined the bed of the stream, which was made of white shingle and was pleasant to the feet. Suddenly, Ulf gave a cry of satisfaction and pointed. A hundred yards ahead of them the moon was reflected off something that looked like a silver mirror. It was a small pool of water, little more than a yard wide, in a hollow in the shingle. They dropped down with relief and removed their burdens. The water was white in color, like watered milk, and had a sweet flavor. They had been rationing water since they set out; now it was unimaginably delightful to be able to drink as much as they liked. They ate some cactus fruit and refilled their gourds; then, reluctantly—since their limbs were aching—set out again. The going was unexpectedly smooth, and even when the moon set they were able to march on over the compact pebbles.

At dawn Ingeld wanted to rest, but Ulf refused to allow it. In a few hours, the sun would be directly overhead, and in the meantime they had to look for shelter.

In fact, before the sun was high, they saw a thicket of trees on the southern horizon and cut across towards it. They looked like overgrown bushes, about six feet high, and the lower branches formed a concave arch. They were able to stretch sheets of spider silk over them to form a sunshade, and to use another sheet, pinned to the ground with heavy stones, as a windbreak. It felt almost like being in a cave, and they slept deeply and heavily until the sun was low in the sky. Then, after a light meal, they moved on again.

The track now lay across a lava field covered with large boulders; after a few miles, this became unexpectedly smooth, like hard-packed sand. Ingeld was beginning to complain that her feet were sore; Ulf and Niall glanced at each other, anticipating that her period of good behavior was finished and that the difficulties of the journey would now be augmented by her complaints. Fortunately, they came upon another pool of water, larger and deeper than the first; after they had drunk their fill and refilled their gourds, Ingeld asked them to look the other way, then stripped off her clothes and plunged in. Standing there, up to her waist, she looked so happy that Niall decided to join her. The water was still warm from the heat of the day, and refreshing to the limbs. When they set out again, he felt as if he had just awakened from a pleasant sleep.

By dawn, the ground was sloping upward again, and since the plateau was basin-shaped, they assumed they were nearing its southern edge. An hour later, they were standing on this edge, looking at the reflection of sunlight on distant water—the salt lake called Thellam. Ingeld was excited; she felt that another day's march would bring her to her own people; Ulf pointed out that the height made distance deceptive and that they probably had at least another fifty miles ahead of them.

Since there was no sign of shelter at the top of the plateau, there was nothing for it but to look for a way down, and seek a camping place on the plain below. Niall went to the edge and looked over. The drop made him feel dizzy; it must have been a thousand feet. Moreover, the cliff curved back underneath him; it had been sandblasted into a hollow by the desert winds. If the edge had crumbled, nothing would break his fall straight down to the rocks below.

It was a question of turning either left or right—to the west or east. And since the westward direction would eventually lead them back to the place at which they had ascended, they decided to go east. They also chose to return half a mile inland, since the terrain at the edge of the plateau was rocky and split with rifts; inland the going was smoother. But it was also hotter; the sun reflected back from the white lava underfoot. Glancing at his father out of the corner of his eye, Niall realized with concern that he was very tired. He was not yet recovered from the journey to the delta. He glanced at Ingeld, plodding sullenly along with a martyred expression, and experienced a flash of hatred.

An hour later, he saw a huge shape against the western horizon; it might have been a hill, but it was too irregular.

"That must be the citadel of the warriors," Ulf said. He was so obviously tired that Niall decided against asking for more information, but as they drew nearer he was amazed by the sheer size of the citadel; it must have been five hundred feet high. He had never seen anything so magnificent and majestic. Now he could see that it had been built on top of a natural hill of rock in such a way that it seemed a continuation of the hill. It was made of great stone blocks, each about six feet long and three feet high. Against the skyline were the remains of rectangular towers, some of them half ruined. These were supported below by immense buttresses. The closer they came, the more obvious was the devastation. There were great rectangular

81

columns, more than ten feet wide, which had once supported a roof; now only two of these were their original height; the others were shattered stumps.

At the foot of the hill they paused to rest and to drink some water. But the heat was now so great, in spite of the wind from the south, that they were in danger of sunstroke. Unwillingly, they dragged themselves to their feet and began to look for the easiest way to ascend.

Halfway round the northern face, they found it; a stairway, scarcely a foot wide, cut into the rock. It seemed to go on forever. But since there was obviously no alternative, they began plodding upward, their suspended baskets dragging on the stair. Its steps were irregular, some narrow, some deep, some badly crumbled or eroded. Ulf went first; Niall followed, with Ingeld in the rear (this being from motives of modesty—her spider-silk dress came only halfway down her thighs). Niall clambered on wearily, keeping his eyes fixed on the next step; when he finally paused to look round, he was surprised to see that they were now high above the plain and that the walls of the citadel were only a few feet above them. A few minutes later they staggered in through an arched doorway into the outer courtyard.

Niall found it all so astonishing that he forgot his weariness. If someone had described such a place to him, he would have assumed they were exaggerating. The courtyard was full of rubble and gigantic tumbled blocks from the walls; yet even so it looked vast and empty. Arches all around led into great halls. Part of the main building had been cut out of the rock itself, and the red and yellow rock gave it the appearance of a castle out of a fairy tale. The summit of the citadel still towered more than a hundred feet above them.

The immediate necessity was shade, somewhere to rest. They crossed the courtyard and went in through one of the arched doorways. They found themselves in a hall so immense that the far walls and the ceiling were lost in the shadows. It was startlingly cool, being on the side of the building that was protected from the morning sun. Here they spread out their blankets, flung themselves down and lay panting, listening to the endless thunder of the wind. Within minutes, Niall was fast asleep.

He had a strange dream; the Spider Lord, Cheb, was looking down on him from some immense height and mocking him. As he began to struggle back to consciousness, he realized that he was cold. Outside, the sunlight was blinding on the white courtyard; next to him, his father and Ingeld were both fast asleep. He sat up, pulled some of his blanket out from underneath him and wrapped it round to form a sleeping bag. In one of the baskets, he had another light-weight blanket made of caterpillar skin, but he was too sleepy to get it out. The memory of his dream disturbed him; the Spider Lord had been sitting on the topmost tower of the citadel, looking down at him. But with his father beside him, he felt safe; a few minutes later he was asleep.

He woke with the feeling that someone had touched his shoulder. Somewhere above him, a fly was buzzing. The blanket had slipped off his shoulder, and it was cold; he reached up to cover it and had difficulty raising his arm; it was as if his blanket had become tucked underneath him, restricting his freedom of movement. At the same time, the buzzing took on a note of frenzied alarm, the sound of a fly caught in a web. He raised his head and looked across the hall; something seemed to scurry into the darkness, and he thought he could see a hundred gleaming points. Suddenly, he was fully awake, trying to sit up. Then he saw what was preventing him. Bands of spider web had been stretched over him and somehow fastened to the floor. The web was lying all over him, like a soft blanket. He looked at his father and Ingeld; they were also covered with a loose-meshed web of spider silk that was still damp and sticky with the spider secretion. And now he saw that the gleaming points were the eyes of dozens of spiders, watching from the shadows.

His cry woke up the other two. As soon as they tried to sit up, they found themselves tangled in the sticky blankets that covered them. Before they tried to move, the web had been stretched over like a loosely flung sheet; as soon as they sat up, their bodies came into contact with the sticky silk, which clung to them, and as they tried to pull it free their hands and arms became entangled.

The spiders had now moved forward out of the shadow as if to get a closer view. To his relief, Niall saw that they were fairly small—with bodies about six inches long and a leg-span of about eighteen inches. He could also tell at a glance that they were related to the grey desert spider, and that they were non-poisonous.

It was now that Niall realized how fortunate he had been to wake and cover himself with the blanket. The spider net covered his blanket, and came into contact only with his shoulder, right hand,

and left foot. He was able to reach out with his left hand and pull his yoke, with its attached baskets, towards him. He found his flint knife and sawed away the web at his wrist; then freed his shoulder and left foot. He slipped out of the blanket and stood up, and the spiders retreated into the shadows. He picked up a large fragment of stone and flung it among them; he heard them scuttling away.

"Lie still!" he told Ingeld. She had given way to panic and was making unpleasant gasping noises as she tore at the web; he could see from her eyes that she believed this was the end. He sawed at the ends of the web where it was stuck to the floor, and a few minutes later she was able to stagger to her feet, although she was still covered with the sticky silk.

"Go outside," Niall said. She needed no encouragement; trailing loose ends of web she rushed into the sunlight. Then Niall freed his father. As he did this, the spiders began to advance again, and he threw more stones at them. Once more they retreated. It was now clear that they were in no immediate danger; the spiders would not dare to attack now that their prey was awake.

Outside, the sunlight was blinding; it was mid-afternoon. Niall helped them peel off the web by hanging on to it as they pulled in the opposite direction; it left behind sticky filaments and lines of shiny stickiness on their skin. It took nearly an hour for Ulf and Ingeld to disentangle themselves from the fragments.

Their bags were still inside: when they went in to fetch them, they again found themselves watched from the darkness by hundreds of tiny eyes. The ends of the web still attached to the floor seemed quite solid and immovable, as if the spider-glue had hardened into a kind of resin. The spiders had exuded their light filaments, then thrown them over the sleeping human beings so that they settled as lightly as flakes of snow. It was the touch of one of them that had awakened Niall. If he had not been covered by his blanket, he would have been entangled as tightly as the others. And by now, the three of them would probably have been wrapped from head to foot in cocoons of spider silk.

At least the danger had removed the last vestiges of tiredness; they all felt capable of walking a hundred miles to escape this frightening place. Yet there would be no point in leaving until they were sure of their direction. Leaving their shoulder bags in the shade, they set out to look for a vantage point over the southern plain. They found what they were looking for in an adjoining courtyard—a flight of stone steps that went up the side of the outer wall. This was one of the few places where it was undamaged. More than a hundred regular steps brought them out on top of the wall, which was about six feet wide with a stone sentry box at the junction with the wall of the next courtyard. Niall went into the box and looked out of its window; he felt safer there than standing on top of the wall in the strong wind.

In the distance, he could see the gleam of the waters of the salt lake. Below, there was a sheer drop of fifteen hundred feet to the plains. Here the wall of the cliff was less precipitous, but it was still far too steep to climb down.

Ulf had reached the same conclusion. He said gloomily: "No way down for miles."

Niall stood staring out over the plain. "But what did they do if they wanted to go over there?"

Ingeld said irritably: "Walked."

"But which way? I can't believe they went across to the other side of the plateau."

Ulf was struck by this observation. "You must be right. There must be some other way down."

They began walking along the top of the wall. At twenty-yard intervals, there was another "sentry box," usually perched on an obtuse angle between two courtyards. Walking along the walls made them aware of the size of the place. It was far bigger than it seemed from below.

Niall asked: "Do you think giants built this place?"

Ulf shook his head. "No. Those stairs were made for men the same size as you and me."

Niall found the idea staggering. So men like himself had built this vast citadel. But surely it must have taken many lifetimes? That depended, of course, on how many there were. . . . For the first time, it dawned on Niall that perhaps there *had* been a time when men were lords of the earth. Before this moment, he had entertained it as an idea but never actually grasped it as a real possibility. Now the thought of thousands of men carving stone blocks, building these tremendous walls, brought a strange sense of exhilaration that was as delightful as cold water poured over his head.

It was at the next guard house that Niall saw what they were looking for: steps cut into the side of the cliff. They were only visible from directly above. At this point, the cliff was no longer a sheer rock face. The sand-laden wind had cut into it, carving away softer material so that the rock was a series of irregular columns and hummocks. Trees and bushes grew out of crevices. This was more like the point at which they had climbed up to the plateau. And immediately below them they could see steps leading down, and vanishing from sight around a great hump-backed rock which had been carved into wrinkles until it looked like the skin of a living creature.

They found more steps and descended into the courtyard. But there seemed to be no archway in the outer wall. They walked through into the next courtyard, then the next. There were no doors. And that, Ulf pointed out, made good sense; what was the point of building an immense fortified castle and then putting hundreds of doors in its walls through which enemies could gain entrance?

That still left the problem of how the inhabitants had gained access to the top of the stairway. Niall climbed back to the top of the wall—being the youngest and most active—and looked down directly on the flight of steps. Now he noticed something he had not seen when inspecting them from the side. They apparently started twenty yards down the cliff. But if they stopped there, how could people who had climbed all the way up from the plain reach the citadel?

He went to the other side of the wall and looked down into the courtyard. Immediately below was a dim circular mark on the ground, about six feet in diameter. He called down to Ulf: "What's that?"

"What?"

"There's a circle on the ground right below where I'm standing."

"I can't see it."

"You're standing right on it now."

He hurried back down the stairway. Back in the courtyard, the circle had become invisible; but since he knew his father was standing inside it, he went on all fours, examining the ground closely. With his flint knife, he began to scrape where the dust seemed soft. There was a crack between two stones. Now Ulf, Niall, and Ingeld all used their knives, and in five minutes had uncovered the circle of stone. Further examination revealed a metal ring. Niall had never seen any kind of metal in his life, and thought it must be some rare kind of stone. The ring was about six inches in diameter, wide enough for all three of them to be able to grip it simultaneously. They braced their feet and heaved; nothing happened. They tried again, and this time the great stone trapdoor seemed to move very slightly. They tried for five minutes until they were panting, and had succeeded in raising the lid about two inches.

Now, in spite of their dislike of the inner rooms, they decided to look into the hall across the courtyard. This was smaller than the one in which they had slept, and was full of strange objects made of wood. Never having seen a chair or table, none of them guessed that they were in an officers' mess room. Much of the furniture was worm eaten, and a chair broke when Niall tried to pick it up. Fragments of carpet on the floor were bleached with the sunlight, although in remote corners, where the sun had been unable to reach, there were still colored patterns, badly faded, but oddly rich and exciting.

And protruding from a heap of rubble in a corner there was a wooden beam, ten feet long and four inches wide. Ulf held it by one end, and pressed his foot on it; the wood was unyielding. Niall took the other end and they carried it into the courtyard.

They placed it through the metal ring, and Niall and Ingeld took one end while Ulf took the other. They braced their knees and gave a tremendous heave; the stone lid came out of the ground, and a six-inch gap appeared. The weight was too great, and they had to let it fall. Niall went back into the room, and found another piece of wood. And next time they raised the stone lid, he used his foot to maneuver the wood into the gap. Then, using the other beam as a lever, they forced open the trapdoor and succeeded in pushing it to one side. A blast of wind blew up into their faces. Below, they could see stairs descending into darkness.

Ten minutes later, they were climbing down cautiously. For a space of twenty feet or so, the tunnel became so black that they had to move very slowly, testing each step with their feet. Then there was a glimmer of light, and around the next bend, the entrance admitted a blinding beam of sunlight. Then they were standing in the narrow doorway and experiencing vertigo at the sheer drop below them and the distant horizon.

Looked at from above, the steps seemed to descend almost vertically, like a ladder. Ingeld sat down, pressing tight against the wall of the tunnel.

"I'm sorry. I can't go down there. I can't stand heights."

Ulf looked at her in astonishment. "You climbed up the other side."

"But that was going up. Besides, it was nearly dark."

Ulf grinned sarcastically. "All right. We'll wait until it's dark."

She began to cry. "I'm sorry, but I just can't do it."

Ulf shrugged. "Do you want to spend the night sitting there?"

"But there must be a better way down."

"There's nothing wrong with this."

The sullen stubborn look came into her eyes. "I'm not going down that way."

It was the worst possible thing to say to Ulf; he had often felt infuriated with Thorg for giving way to his wife's determination to have her own way. Now he stared back at Ingeld with a stony, set expression.

"You can do what you like. We're going down to spend the night at the bottom."

Ingeld was not accustomed to being thwarted.

"And what am I supposed to do?"

"You can go and spend the night in the fortress."

"What about the spiders!"

"What are you more afraid of—spiders or heights?" He began descending, his face towards the steps. "Come on, Niall."

Unwillingly—for although he felt as his father did about Ingeld, he still felt sorry for her—Niall began to descend the stairway. It was, in fact, less dangerous than it looked, for although each step was only a few inches deep, hand-holds had been cut in the rock beside them. A hundred yards farther down, where the steps turned at an angle behind the hump-backed rock, the slope suddenly became less steep. Here, out of sight of Ingeld, Ulf beckoned him to sit down. They stayed there for a quarter of an hour, and ate a prickly pear and some maize bread. After that, Ulf left his baggage and went back up the cliff. A few minutes later, he reappeared with Ingeld. Her face was stained with tears and her lips were set in a sullen pout; but the mulish expression had disappeared.

There must have been over three thousand steps. They followed a twisting curve, sometimes descending into clefts, sometimes exposed on the face of the cliff, and at one point passing through a valley with massive and rectangular carved rocks, sculptured with bas reliefs of strange animals. Some of the creatures looked a little like desert rodents; but they were as big as insects. They stood and contemplated these things with a feeling of awe. Niall pointed to a particularly fierce looking creature that seemed to be surrounded by hunters. "What is that?"

"I'm not sure."

Ingeld said contemptuously: "It's a tiger."

"Did such things really live on Earth?"

"Of course."

Ulf said: "The spiders killed off all the larger animals."

"Then why did they allow man to survive?"

"Because man cannot protect himself. He has no claws, no tusks, no sharp teeth."

"But he has weapons."

Ulf said grimly: "But weapons can be taken away. You cannot take away a tiger's claws without killing it first."

They tramped on. For the last few hundred feet the descent became more difficult, for the cliff was broken and eroded. At its base it had been hollowed out by the wind; they had to throw down their baggage and jump the last ten feet, landing in soft sand. Looking back up, they saw that the stairway was now invisible. Its builders had taken care not to make it obvious to enemies.

By traveling over the plateau, they had avoided the worst of the desert. The countryside ahead was not unlike the region around the burrow, but with more vegetation. Compared to the plateau, the atmosphere here was hot and oppressive. In spite of the menace of the spiders, which now lay behind them, Niall felt a sharp pang of regret at leaving the ruined citadel. For him, it represented something he had never before encountered: romance and mystery.

The sun was near the western horizon. The long descent of the stairs had made them all tired. Ulf decided to rest until the moon rose. The hollows worn in the base of the cliff argued that there should also be caves. They walked due west for almost a mile but found nothing deeper than a few feet. However they encountered another group of the low trees or bushes under which they had slept on the plateau. They selected the lowest one, spread blankets over it to form a sunshade, then lay down to rest. Ingeld lay several yards away; she had still not forgiven Ulf for making her climb down the stairway.

When the edge of the sun neared the horizon, Ulf took himself off into the middle of the bushes, and sat cross-legged, his back against the twisted root of a tree. It was time he tried to make contact with Siris. Since they were roughly in the same longitude, they should observe the sunset at the same time. Their agreement was to attempt contact as the sun touched the horizon. This moment seemed to facilitate contact between minds.

Niall moved his position slightly so he could watch his father. Ulf was tired, and instead of relaxing, might easily fall asleep. Therefore he intended to keep Ulf in sight, and to make some small movement to arouse his attention if he seemed to be dozing.

Suddenly, he stiffened with horror. In the twisted root behind his father, something was moving. As he watched, the long, sinuous body of a grey centipede crawled into the open. It was about three feet long, and the many-jointed antennae were vibrating curiously; it had sensed intruders in its territory. But it had not yet noticed Ulf, who was sitting still as a stone. Niall had seen very few centipedes, and the movement of their tiny legs fascinated and repelled him. Unlike the millipede, the centipede is poisonous; this one was of the soil-burrowing type. And when, in the course of its cautious survey of its territory, it became aware of the man, its head reared upward into a position of alertness, revealing poison claws like those of a spider.

While Ulf remained still, he was in no danger. But if he became aware of the centipede, and moved suddenly, he would instantly be bitten.

Niall also realized that Ingeld was lying in a position from which she could see Ulf. Her eyes were closed; but if she opened them and saw the centipede, she would scream.

Niall suppressed the panic surging in his veins and made his mind calm. At that moment, Ulf's deeper breathing indicated that he had made contact. The centipede was still poised, its poison claws within a few inches of Ulf's bare back. But as Ulf remained immobile, this fighting posture gradually relaxed. Very cautiously, Niall looked around for his spear; it was propped against the trunk of the tree a few feet away. Moving very slowly, in case he disturbed Ingeld, he reached out towards it. It was slightly too far for his reach; he had to edge forward. His hand closed round its shaft; silently, he raised it into the throwing position. But Ulf's breathing told him that he was still in contact. Everything was silent. Then Ingeld stirred, and the bone bracelets on her wrists rattled. Instantly, the centipede was again in the striking position. When silence ensued, it again relaxed.

A full minute went by. Suddenly, Ulf sighed deeply and stirred. Without hesitation, Niall hurled the spear. It struck the ground a few inches from the centipede, but its momentum drove it on so that its point ploughed through the ground and under the centipede's belly. Startled, Ulf looked round. The spear had carried the centipede several feet away. A moment later, Niall was standing over it with his father's spear, stabbing the writhing body again and again. Ingeld woke up, saw what was happening, and screamed piercingly. Two minutes earlier, the scream would have cost Ulf his life. Now it only galvanized him into action; he seized the other spear and helped Niall dispatch the thrashing predator, whose erect fangs were now harmless since the head was half-severed from the body.

When the creature lay still, Ulf placed his hand briefly on Niall's head. "Good work, son." He seldom addressed Niall as "son," and Niall blushed with pleasure.

Ingeld was still frantic. "Oh, let's get away from here! It's horrible."

Ulf shrugged. "It should be safe enough now." He prodded with his spear deep into the roots of the tree.

"I can't bear it here!" Her voice was tense with hysteria.

Ulf sighed. "There's no point in moving until the moon rises. We can't see where we're going."

"Then I'm going over there!" And she moved out into the open, fifty yards away, and sat there defiantly. Niall wanted to tell her that she was in more danger from scorpions and centipedes in the open than under the bushes, but decided it was not worth the effort. The thought that they would soon be seeing the last of her filled him with relief.

An hour later, the moon rose and they began the march south. A few miles on, they came upon a well-worn road that seemed to run from the plateau in the direction of the salt lake. They followed this for the remainder of the night. Often they were alarmed by movements from the desert on either side of them—scrabbling noises, scuttling sounds, and on one occasion a menacing hiss but they saw nothing; few desert creatures would risk attacking a group of three.

When the moon set, they rested for an hour. Ingeld flung herself down on the ground and gave a deep sigh. Ulf lay on his back, using a flat stone as a pillow. Niall preferred to sit with his back against a boulder; the sounds from the desert had made him nervous. He began to doze, but a rustling sound woke him; he listened intently, but there was no further noise. He allowed himself to relax, while concentrating at the same time. Because of his fatigue, it worked more easily than usual, and he suddenly experienced that deep inner quiet as if he had walked into some vast empty hall. Ingeld stirred, and as his attention switched to her, he became aware of her thoughts: of her feeling of weariness and her resentment at the efforts she was being forced to make. He saw that she felt no gratitude towards himself or his father for bringing her this far: only a feeling of angry contempt. She was, he now realized, deeply resentful about the deaths of Thorg and Hrolf, and blamed them on Ulf and Veig. Still nursing her sense of injury, she fell asleep. Ulf was already asleep; when Niall turned his attention to his father, he was aware of a sensation like a grey, pulsating mass, full of images and dreams.

When he used this new sense of inwardness to scan the desert, he immediately became aware of hundreds of living creatures: beetles, spiders, ants, solifugids, centipedes, rodents, all thinking about food. It was a strange sensation, like becoming the desert. Some of the creatures, the grey spiders, for example, were aware that his mind was scanning them; others were completely oblivious.

Something was disturbing him, like a nagging worry at the back of his mind. His mind came back to the here-and-now and he realized it was already daylight. Then he started as something brushed his leg. He was sitting in the midst of small, moving bodies, dark, hairy creatures like caterpillars that had emerged from the underbrush a few feet from the road. His first thought was that they were poisonous centipedes; a closer look revealed that they had the typical hump-backed locomotion of a caterpillar. Their length varied between six inches and a foot. Ingeld was lying on her back, her mouth open, her arm flung above her head, and one of the caterpillars was crawling over her dress. Niall bestirred himself to shake her awake. At that moment, the caterpillar rose up on her chest, like a striking snake, and made a plunge forward. Ingeld woke up and began to choke. To his horror, Niall realized that the creature was in her mouth, about six inches of its length hanging over her chin; as he watched, the six inches diminished to three. Ingeld was thrashing and struggling helplessly. Niall rushed forward, grabbed at the creature's furry body and pulled violently. It came out, struggling and writhing, and he felt its sharp mandibles bite his wrist. Ingeld began to be sick. As he hurled the creature to the ground, Niall became aware of others crawling up his legs and saw that his father's body was also covered. As Niall yelled, Ulf woke with a start and jumped to his feet. One of the hairy creatures tried to enter his mouth; he clenched his teeth, biting its head off, and hurled the rest to the ground.

Ignoring their baggage, they ran, beating off caterpillars that tried to climb their legs. Fifty yards away, they halted; the caterpillars had made no attempt to follow. Ingeld was gasping convulsively, and Ulf, his face distorted by disgust, spat repeatedly to clear his mouth. The air was filled with a sickening smell like rotting vegetation.

Niall said: "What are they?"

"Bore worms. One of the vilest creatures in the desert. Ugh!" He spat again.

Ingeld, sobbing like a frightened child, said: "It tried to get into my mouth."

Ulf nodded. "And if it had succeeded, you'd be dead by now. They feed off intestines."

This was too much for her; she collapsed on the ground, sobbing hysterically. Ulf made no attempt to comfort her; he knew that crying was the quickest way of exorcizing her disgust.

A few minutes later, the bore worms had gone, vanishing into the bushes on the other side of the road. They went back to collect their weapons and baggage but all the food was ruined. It had not been eaten, but the maize bread, meat, and cactus fruit were covered with a slimy excretion that had a bitter, sickening smell. Reluctantly, they emptied their baskets onto the road. At least it lightened their burden. Then, their baskets now containing only the water gourds, they tramped on. But as the sun rose, the slimy substance that covered the baskets like the trail of a slug began to decay, producing a pungent, rotting stench. Finally, they decided to abandon the baskets. The smell was now so nauseating that they did this without regret.

Half an hour later, Niall heard a sound that made his heart lift with joy: the gurgle of running water. They parted the bushes at the side of the road and found a small stream. The clear water flowed over smooth white pebbles. They plunged in, dropping on all fours to drink. Then Niall sat down in the water and washed himself all over. When they left the stream half an hour later, they no longer smelt of decay.

A few miles farther on, their route took them through boulder-strewn slopes of white scree; the road had been carved out of the limestone. Now they could see clearly the shimmering expanse of the salt lake. The sight of the water produced in Niall an almost choking feeling of breathless excitement. The road descended into a valley between walls of rock. High up on one of these were a number of immense carvings: men wearing strange head-dresses, with rectangular beards and long garments.

"Who are they?" Niall asked.

Ulf said: "No one knows."

Ingeld said: "I know. They are my ancestors." She glanced at them contemptuously.

At that moment, there came a sound that made Niall's heart stand still with astonishment. It was a human shout. At the next bend of the road, half a mile ahead, men were coming towards them and waving.

"You see—my people are coming to meet me," Ingeld said proudly.

Niall said incredulously: "How did they know you were coming?"

She smiled disdainfully. "They know many things that are beyond your understanding."

Ulf glanced at her mockingly, but said nothing.

A few minutes later, they could see the men clearly. There were about a dozen and the one who walked in front was tall and wore some kind of white garment. He raised his hand in salute and, when they were within hailing distance, called: "Welcome to the land of Dira."

His voice echoed between the cliffs. This in itself astonished Niall. Since childhood, he had been taught never to shout, except in cases of absolute necessity: survival depended upon being unheard and unseen. But this tall man behaved as if he didn't care if he alerted all the predators for miles around.

A moment later, he and Ulf had locked forearms in a clasp of friendship.

"My name is Hamna," the young man said, "the son of Kazak. These are my kinsmen. We have been sent to greet you and bid you welcome."

Niall asked: "How did you know we were coming?"

"My mother Sefna received a message from her sister to say that you had arrived in our land."

Ulf smiled at Ingeld with a trace of satire. "So it's not beyond our understanding after all. Siris said she was going to try to contact her sister."

Ingeld ignored him as she stepped forward and embraced Hamna. "I am your cousin Ingeld." With a glance at Ulf she added: "I am glad to be back among my own people."

Hamna said formally: "You are welcome."

Ulf said dryly: "We are also glad she is back among her own people."

Fortunately, the ambiguity of this comment seemed to be lost on the newcomers.

Introductions followed; Niall was fascinated and impressed by everyone he met. They all seemed so much bigger and stronger than the males of his own family; it was obvious they were better fed. Instead of garments of caterpillar skin or spider silk, they wore a woven cloth; but what astonished Niall was that their clothes were of different colors; he had never heard of dye. The stout sandals on their feet were all of the same design.

Hamna and his companions had set out at dawn, so there was still a long way to go. But now he was among other men, Niall's fatigue had vanished in eager expectancy and he was indifferent to the heat.

The youngest of Hamna's companions was a youth named Massig, who was apparently about Niall's age; but he was at least six inches taller and had a broad, powerful chest. His hair fascinated Niall, for it seemed strangely tidy, all its strands running parallel; it was held around the forehead by a white band of cloth. Massig seemed an amiable, good natured youth, and he asked Niall all kinds of questions about the journey. It was some time before Niall realized, to his astonishment, that Massig envied him for having traveled so far from home. Niall also observed that Massig cast admiring glances towards Ingeld; it had never struck Niall that anyone might regard her as attractive. Ingeld herself was so intoxicated at being surrounded by strong males that her eyes sparkled and her cheeks glowed; Niall had never seen her look so happy. The only thing that troubled him was that his father was limping badly, and was obviously tired; this journey had drained his resources.

Niall asked Massig about the great carvings on the cliff-walls, but Massig knew little about them. "They were made by men of a remote age—so long ago that no one knows when it was. In the face of the cliff, there are also tombs where ancient men are buried."

"Have you been there?"

"No. They say they are haunted."

"Haunted?" Massig explained about the spirits of the dead, and Niall shuddered; no one in his family had ever mentioned ghosts.

The welcoming party were carrying food and drink, and they ate as they walked in the midday heat. The drink was water flavored with a fruit Niall had never tasted; it was, in fact, lemon. The sharp flavor made it marvelously refreshing. The dried meat was of the same kind they had been forced to throw away, but more abundant and of a better flavor. There were also cactus fruit, persimmons, and oranges—the latter again a new sensation for Niall.

The scenery became less barren; palm trees and flowering bushes reminded Niall of the country of the ants. The lake shimmered ahead and a stream ran parallel to the road. Niall suddenly experienced keen regret that his mother and sisters were not here to see all this: it would have made it somehow more real if they had shared his sense of wonder.

Then, to Niall's surprise, they turned away from the lake and took a path that led into the desert again. The road began to ascend; the landscape became barren. He asked Massig: "Why do you not live near the water?"

"Because of the spiders. They expect men to live near water, so we live in the desert. There was a time when our people lived close to the water, but the spiders found us and took away many captives."

It saddened Niall to think that even here, in this land of plenty, no one could afford to forget the spiders.

His eyes scanned the distance; he was looking for any sign of the habitations that Veig had described. But there was nothing; only the rocks and the sand stretching towards the distant plateau. He began to wonder how much further he had to walk.

The question was answered immediately. Hamna came to a halt in the midst of a patch of rock-covered sand that looked indistinguishable from the rest of the landscape. He picked up a heavy stone and, dropping to one knee, gave several hard bangs on the ground. There was a hollow sound. A few moments later, an irregular patch of desert rose upward and a man's head emerged. Hamna turned and beckoned the guests to follow him. Niall found himself looking down at a flight of narrow steps only a few feet wide. He also noticed with interest that the sand and rocks on the upper surface of the trapdoor were stuck fast, and did not slide off even when it was turned upside down.

Hamna went first. The steps led into darkness, so they had to feel their way with their hands. A narrow corridor, not unlike that which led to the lower depths of their own burrow, sloped downward at such a steep angle that it was necessary to press both hands against the walls. These seemed to be made of stone. In the air, Niall noticed the distinctive smell of burning beetle oil, although he could see nothing in the pitch darkness.

They came to a halt, and three loud raps sounded. After a silence, there was the sound of something heavy being moved. Then the first gleam of light came from ahead, revealing that they were in a low-ceilinged chamber, about ten feet square. The light was admitted past great slabs of stone, which were being moved aside, and a cooler air blew in their faces. Two large stone slabs were being carried bodily apart, each by four men; beyond them, dozens of lighted lamps illuminated a broad chamber. Niall gasped. It was an enormous room, at least fifty feet long, and the lights, set in alcoves in the walls, made it almost as bright as daylight. But this, apparently, was only a kind of corridor. Hamna led them forward, and more slabs of stone were moved aside. There was yet another lighted room, whose ceiling was higher than the previous one and whose walls were supported by stone buttresses. And this was also apparently a corridor, for beyond it he could see a large chamber whose stone doors had already been moved aside. As they approached, he saw that it was filled with a crowd of people, including women and children. They parted to make way for Hamna, and down the aisle between them, Niall could see a big stone chair, approached by several steps. In it sat a tall heavily built man, his grey hair held in place by a gold-colored band; the white garment he wore came within a few inches of his feet. The old man stood up, smiling, and held out his hand to Ulf; they clasped forearms.

"Welcome to Dira. My name is Kazak." He had a strong, broad face, somewhat too flabby, and the look of a man who expects unquestioning obedience.

Niall was less interested in the old man than in the tall, graceful girl who stood by his chair. Her face bore a family resemblance to Ingeld, but the features were more clean cut. Her red-gold hair was held in place by a circlet of shiny metal. When he noticed that she was also looking at him with curiosity, he quickly looked away.

Ulf introduced himself, then Niall and Ingeld. The old king, Niall observed, looked at Ingeld with keen interest, taking in the short, spider-silk garment that revealed the curves of her body. Ingeld's dress was far shorter than the tunics worn by the other women, including the beautiful girl beside the throne.

Kazak was saying: "This is my daughter Merlew, who runs my household." When Niall clasped forearms with Merlew, he was thrilled by the softness of her skin, and by the delicious scent that came from her, quite unlike his own rank smell of sweat. When she smiled at him, showing even white teeth, his heart seemed to collapse with an emotion that was like fear, but far more agreeable. But with the self-control that came naturally to him, he gave no sign of his feelings.

Niall found himself being kissed and hugged by a large-breasted woman with very white shoulders and a firm chin. This, he gathered, was Sefna, his mother's sister. She was ruffling his hair.

"Poor boy, you must be tired. Come and eat, then you can rest."

She made a perfunctory obeisance to Kazak, bringing her right knee close to the floor, then, taking Niall by the hand, led him away. Massig waved cheerfully to him and called: "I'll see you later."

Another sloping corridor led to what were evidently the living quarters. Niall expected a large room; instead, he found a wide chamber with other corridors leading off it. What impressed Niall was the straightness of the walls and the neat right-angles of the doorways. It all struck him as unimaginably sophisticated and marvelous.

Sefna halted in front of a door in a side corridor; two steps led down into a large, square room with rushes on the floor. There were seats, made of sliced logs of wood, and a low table that consisted of one great round of wood, three feet in diameter. Through a low door in the wall, a dark-haired girl looked into the room. Sefna said: "Dona, come and meet your cousin Niall." The girl came in and shyly accepted his handclasp; she had large brown eyes and an olive complexion. Niall judged her age to be about twelve.

In spite of Niall's protests that he was not hungry, Sefna began to prepare food. Suddenly, Niall was very tired—so tired that he could scarcely keep his eyes open; this, after all, was normally the time of the afternoon when the travelers had slept. And his last sleep had been in the great fortress on the plateau. He relaxed on the couch of leaves and rushes and tried to answer Dona's questions. Periodically, other children looked into the room from the corridor, but Dona shooed them away imperiously. It dawned on Niall that he was an object of general curiosity, and that Dona was the center of some envy because he was her guest. In the pleasure of proprietorship, Dona soon lost her shyness, and Niall found himself treating her as if she were an older version of his sister Runa, teasing her and telling stories; she was so enthralled by his account of the country of the ants that he had to repeat the whole thing twice.

When the food arrived he found he was hungry after all, perhaps because it was hot—an unusual luxury. As he ate, he did his best to answer Sefna's questions, but sheer fatigue made his eyelids droop. He was relieved when his father arrived, accompanied by Kazak, and he ceased to be the center of attention. He dozed through much of the conversation that followed. Finally, he and his father were shown into a smaller chamber with grass couches that were covered with woven cloth; it was luxuriously soft, and he soon fell into a dreamless sleep.

When he woke up, he found Dona sitting by his bed, patiently waiting for him to open his eyes. She told him that in an hour's time, Kazak was giving a feast in honor of his guests. In the meantime, she would show him where to wash and then take him on a tour of the "palace" (which its inhabitants referred to as the "shelter").

He was impressed to learn that there was another level beneath this one. They had dug down to the water table, thirty feet below, and excavated a series of basements. In these there were the communal wells, and rooms in which the men and women could perform their ablutions. There were also astonishing sanitary arrangements, and an army of dung beetles disposed of the human waste.

The people of Dira had also domesticated ants and grey spiders. The ants were of the aphid-tending variety; they had cut galleries deep into the walls in which they had built their nests; in these nests they tended the greenfly larvae until they were large enough to be taken into the outer world; there, in the greenery by the shores of the lake, they were farmed like cattle, and milked of their honeydew several times a day; the honeydew was one of the most important food sources in the "palace." The spiders were kept for their silk, which was treated by some process that removed its stickiness and then woven into cloth. There were workshops in which the women wove cloth from cotton and spider silk, and workshops in which stonemasons worked on large chunks of stones, transported from many miles away on rollers, and lined new galleries and corridors. This underground city was in a perpetual ferment of activity, like an ants' nest. But this was not simply because such activity was necessary to keep everyone fed and clothed. It was because, as Niall knew only too well, one of the chief problems of life underground was boredom. Only a small percentage of the human beings in Dira went outside more than once a month, and even then, it was only for an hour at a time. The spiders knew there were human beings somewhere in the area of the salt lake; many years ago, they had captured hundreds of them in a great raid. (Niall's grandfather Jomar had been among the captives.) But in those days, the humans had lived in caves near a ruined city, a dozen miles away on the shores of the lake. After the raid, the survivors had scattered into the desert; many had died. Then Kazak had reorganized them and, with the aid of fire, had driven a colony of leaf-cutter ants out of their underground city on the edge of the desert. This city became the "shelter." In twenty years, Kazak's people had turned it into a palace and an impregnable fortress. The purpose of the massive slabs of stone that covered the walls was not simply to prevent the earth from collapsing; it was to prevent insects from tunneling into the palace.

Niall learned more of the history of Kazak's people at the feast that took place that night. They ate at low tables made of slices of tree-trunk. The floor was covered with rugs made of animal pelts, some of them consisting of dozens of skins of small rodents sewn together with artistry and skill. Ulf sat beside Kazak, with Niall on his other side, and since Kazak's voice was deep and impressive, Niall could hear every word. Kazak described how they had discovered tools in the great fortress on the plateau—metal axe-heads and saws, hammers and pincers—and how paintings on the walls of tombs had taught them to use these. The slabs of stone had to be moved by night, because of spider patrols; even the "shepherds" who looked after the ants had to take them out an hour before dawn and bring them back after dark.

At first, the greatest problem for the inhabitants of the underground city had been lighting. Although there was an abundance of the green "copper beetle," from which oil could be obtained, there were not enough of them to provide oil for the whole community. Then one of the men who had explored on the far side of the lake told of a black, tarry substance that bubbled to the surface in a remote inlet, and whose smell resembled that of burning beetle oil. Kazak dispatched two men to fetch samples. And he discovered—as he expected—that this black, sticky oil burned with a smoky flame. And if the flame was kept small enough, there was no smoke. From then on, the black oil was mixed with the oil of the copper beetle, and the underground city had its own street lighting system. Teams of men took turns to bring the oil from the other side of the lake—a six-day journey—while women and teenage girls had the job of replenishing the oil lamps and trimming the wicks to avoid smoking.

Niall listened to all this as he ate his way through course after course. He had never seen such an abundance of food, and much of it was completely new to him. Jomar had told him about fish, but he had never tasted any; now he ate three different varieties, caught in the river that ran into the salt lake. There was also a great deal of meat, most of it heavily salted. (Kazak spoke with pride of their food store, which—he claimed—was so large that they could sustain a six-month siege.) Niall was particularly delighted with a tiny mouse, hardly bigger than the tip of his finger, which was skinned and roasted with some kind of seed; he ate a whole bowlful to himself. The drink was either honeydew diluted with water or fermented fruit juice. This juice was far more intoxicating than the kind he had tasted at home, and he observed with sly amusement that Ingeld drank far too much of it, and became increasingly talkative. She also made no secret of her interest in Hamna, and in Hamna's younger brother Corvig, stroking Corvig's shoulder-length yellow hair and squeezing Hamna's biceps. Halfway through the meal, the attractive girl who was serving the guests tripped on the rug, and emptied a bowl of an oily salad over Ingeld's head. She apologized profusely; but Niall, who had seen exactly what happened, was aware that it was no accident; he caught the girl's eye and smiled, and she smiled back demurely. Ingeld, trying to conceal her fury, had to retreat to the dwelling that had been assigned to her to wipe the oil out of her hair. But she was back half an hour later, her hair tied back with a ribbon, and was soon as talkative and demonstrative as ever.

Kazak was an impressive figure of a man, in spite of his double chin and fleshy nose. But he obviously enjoyed exercising his authority, snapping orders at the serving maids and generally treating his subjects as though they were unruly children. Everyone showed him the greatest respect, and agreed with everything he said. After his third cup of wine, Kazak became boastful, and told stories that illustrated his wisdom and foresight. There could be no doubt that these

101

stories were basically true; but Niall still felt that it was unnecessary for such a great chieftain to proclaim his own virtues.

At the end of the feast Kazak stood and proposed a toast to the guests. Everyone stood up and drank to them. Then Kazak slapped Ulf on the shoulder and suggested that he should bring his family and come and live with the people of Dira. Niall was thrilled and delighted at the idea; the thought of living permanently in this magnificent palace struck him as too good to be true. Yet he knew his father well enough to realize that he was altogether less enthusiastic; he could tell this by the way Ulf nodded slowly, keeping his eyes averted. He resolved to use all his powers of persuasion to try to change Ulf's mind.

After the toast, Kazak asked his daughter Merlew to sing. Niall found the idea puzzling and rather embarrassing. His mother used to sing him to sleep as a child, and she still sang lullabies to his sisters. But the notion of singing as a public entertainment struck him as altogether incongruous.

His doubts vanished when Merlew opened her mouth. Her voice was sweet and pure. The song she sang was about a girl whose fisherman lover was drowned in the lake, and there was something about its simplicity that made Niall want to cry. When the song was over, everyone applauded by banging their clenched fists on the tables; Niall applauded loudest of all. Now he knew beyond all doubt: he was not simply in love with Merlew; he regarded her as a goddess, someone who deserved to be worshipped. Everything about her intoxicated him, from her slender figure to her coppergold hair and her brilliant smile. Merely to look at her made him feel as if he were dissolving inside. It would have been ecstasy to die for her.

Merlew sang two more songs: one a lament of a queen for a warrior killed in battle, and one a light-hearted ballad about a girl who fell in love with a big, shiny fish. Again, Niall laughed and applauded louder than anyone else, and then was suddenly stricken with embarrassment when she looked across at him and smiled. He sat there with his heart pounding against his ribs, aware that his face was red, and hoping that Ingeld had not noticed. The thought that Merlew had not only noticed him, but also smiled at him, filled him with bursting happiness.

After Merlew sat down, Hamna stood up and recited a stirring ballad about a king marching to war against overwhelming odds. It was Niall's first experience of poetry, and again he felt moved to the point of tears. He also felt relieved that Hamna was Merlew's brother; he was so handsome, and recited so impressively that Niall was sure no woman could resist him. When Hamna sat down, Ingeld took his hand and kissed it, and Hamna looked embarrassed.

After this, there were many more songs and many more poems. For Niall, it was a magical experience; each song and each ballad seemed to carry him away into another land, so that when it was over, he felt as if he had been on a long journey. The tales of heroic deeds made him feel proud to be a human being; at the same time, he felt sad that his own life had been so devoid of heroism. He resolved that, at the first opportunity, he would do something to prove his own courage. He kept glancing cautiously sideways, hoping that Merlew would smile at him again; but it was obvious that she had forgotten he was there. On the other hand, he frequently glanced across to the opposite table and found Dona watching him. Her obvious admiration flattered him; but he accepted it as his due, as he accepted the admiration of his sister Runa. If he had been told that Dona's feelings about him were exactly the same as his own about Merlew, he would have been embarrassed but indifferent.

A point came when a boy whispered something in Kazak's ear. The chieftain stood up, raised his arm for silence—a quite unnecessary gesture, since there was instant silence when he rose—and announced that it was time for the herdsmen to take out the ants to the lakeside. Half a dozen young men stood and went out, halting at the door to bow to Kazak. This seemed to be taken as a signal that the feast was at an end. Merlew also went out, terminating Niall's interest in the proceedings. Kazak beckoned to Ingeld to come and take her place, patting the seat beside him, and she did so obediently. Other people began to drift out, all making a bow to Kazak as they left the hall; he was too absorbed in Ingeld to notice them.

Niall asked Hamna: "How can you tell what time it is when you live underground?"

"We have clocks."

"What is a clock?"

"A bucket of water, with a small hole in the bottom. It takes exactly half a day for the bucket to empty."

Now, suddenly, Niall understood the purpose of the bucket in Dona's house, suspended from the ceiling and dripping incessantly into another; he marveled at the ingenuity of Kazak's people and again longed to be one of them.

Hamna said: "Are you tired?"

"No, wide awake."

"Would you like to go out with the herdsmen?"

"Very much."

"I will have to ask the king for permission. No one is allowed out without a pass." He went and bowed before Kazak, who looked annoyed to be interrupted, nodded his head and gestured impatiently. Hamna came back looking pleased with himself.

"Let's go before he changes his mind."

They left by an exit at the far end of the palace; Hamna had to assure the sentry that they had Kazak's permission to leave, and he handed them both a small wooden tally. Hamna placed these in a leathern wallet he carried at his waist. "If we lose these, we shan't be allowed in again."

Niall was puzzled. "Why are they so strict?"

"Safety. Only the king is allowed in and out without formal permission. You see, with so many of us in the shelter, it would be a disaster if someone went out without permission and was seen by a spider patrol. We have to be strict."

"But why does that apply to you?"

"Why not?"

"You're the king's son."

Hamna shrugged. "We are all the king's sons."

It was a clear, starry night, and dawn was showing in the eastern sky. A cool breeze blew from the lake. Niall was surprised how glad he was to feel the wind on his face again.

Ahead of them, a herdsman was walking, half a dozen ants following at his heels like dogs. Hamna fell in step beside him and they began to talk about the aphids, which were exceptionally abundant this year. Niall was glad to be left to his own thoughts; he was dreaming about Merlew, and about the songs and stories he had been listening to. They filled him with an almost painful excitement. As the sky gradually grew paler, and the grey light was reflected in the waters of the lake, he tried to imagine what the world would be like without the menace of the spiders—a world in which men could live openly above ground and travel anywhere they liked. When the herdsman had turned off down a path into the bushes by the stream, Niall asked Hamna:

"What do you think would happen if the spiders found out about your shelter?"

"Life would become very dangerous. But we'd put up a good fight."

"But could you win?"

"I think we might. You see, we've tried to make the shelter impregnable. There are only two entrances, and they're so narrow they could each be defended by one man. So they'd have to besiege us and hope to starve us into surrender. But we've got stocks of food to last for six months—perhaps more. I'm told the spiders don't like the heat, and this place becomes a furnace in the summer. So I think we'd stand a good chance."

"So you're not afraid of the spiders?"

"Oh, no. We're not afraid of them." His voice sounded so confident that Niall believed him.

They had reached the shore of the lake. On the far side, directly opposite, there were low hills rising to mountains as high as the plateau. At this point, the lake was about ten miles wide; Niall found its silver-grey expanse disturbingly beautiful. But as usual, his eyes scanned the eastern sky for spider balloons; he had come to associate beauty with danger. The sky was clear, already turning blue.

Hamna said: "Aha!" and quickly stripped off his tunic. In three steps, he was swimming in the lake. A moment later, he returned to the shore holding a large fish.

"These swim down the river, but they can't live in the salt water. The birds usually eat them, unless we can get there first."

Hamna made a cairn of stones and hid the fish underneath it. Then he ran back towards the water.

"Come on."

"I can't swim."

"Yes, you can. Anybody can swim in this water."

And, to Niall's astonishment, this proved to be true. When he advanced into the lake up to his chest, he felt himself being lifted off the bottom. A moment later, he was propelling himself forward with his shoulders out of the water. Hamna taught him how to move his arms and legs in rhythm, and he was soon gliding through the water. It had an unpleasant taste, like the water in the depths of the burrow, but stronger. He bumped into something and cried out in alarm. Hamna swam alongside him, reached down and found another fish. During the next half hour, they found half a dozen.

Then they waded ashore, wrapped all the fishes in a piece of cloth Hamna carried in his wallet and walked along the sandy beach to the point where the river flowed into the lake. By that time, the water had dried on them, and Niall found that it left an unpleasant stickiness behind. But this was soon washed away in the river. After that, they lay down on the sand in the shade of a palm tree and dozed in the warm air.

Niall was still full of questions. "Why did you say that you are all the king's sons?"

"Because in our city, we all have equal rights. Besides, the king has many children."

"How many?"

"Perhaps . . . oh, fifty."

"But how many wives does he have?"

Hamna thought carefully. "About a hundred and eighty."

Niall was bewildered. "And where do they all live?"

"With their husbands, mostly."

"But you said the king was their husband."

Hamna said patiently, as if explaining to a child: "They have husbands, of course. But they are also the king's property—just as we all are. He can choose anyone he likes."

This idea astounded Niall. "But don't the husbands object?"

"Of course not. If they wanted to, they could leave us and go and live elsewhere. But they prefer to stay."

Niall thought about this. "And if we came to live with you, would my mother also become the king's wife?"

"I suppose so. If he liked her."

Niall's heart sank. He suddenly knew, beyond all shadow of doubt, that his father would never agree to live here. He asked the question that had been troubling him since they arrived.

"Does the princess Merlew have a husband?"

"Not yet. She's only seventeen. Besides, she's too busy. Since her mother died, she's been mistress of the royal household."

That, at any rate, was a relief.

Hamna sat up, yawning. "We'd better get back. The spiders should be over soon."

"Do they come every day?"

"Oh, no—particularly at this time of the year. This is the season for sandstorms."

Back in the shelter, it seemed very dark. In the corridors, only a few lamps were lit—Niall learned that this was the usual state of affairs. Yesterday, the king had ordered all the lamps to be lit in honor of the guests; now things were back to normal.

In Sefna's dwelling, Dona was sewing by the light of a single lamp. Sefna, apparently, was at work in the weaving sheds. Everyone above the age of twelve had to work for a few hours every day. When Dona saw Niall, she brightened and asked him if he felt like playing a game.

"What is a game?"

She took out a pot containing a number of colored stones and demonstrated various games of skill—resting the stones on the palm of the hand, tossing them into the air and trying to catch them all on the back of the hand, then introducing many additional complications. After this they played guessing games, each trying to outguess the other about the number of stones they kept concealed in the hand. Then Dona glanced at the water clock and asked: "Would you like to go and play with the others in the big hall?"

Niall was feeling sleepy. "I think I'd like to rest. What do you do?"

"The children play games after the tenth hour—hide and seek, blind man's buff, wrestling."

"Wouldn't I be too old?"

"Oh, no. Merlew often joins in, and she's seventeen."

"All right." He managed to sound so casual that he surprised himself.

There were thirty or forty children in the big hall, their ages ranging from about ten to fifteen. To Niall's disappointment, the princess was not among them. A mischievous-looking lad called Eirek seemed to be in charge, and since he looked only about eleven, Niall found this puzzling, until Dona explained that they chose a different play-group leader every week. It was an attempt to develop leadership qualities. When they were introduced, Eirek clasped Niall's forearm and asked: "How old are you?"

"Sixteen."

"You're not very big for sixteen. Kles there is bigger than you and he's only fourteen."

"Where I live, we aren't as well fed as you."

Eirek sighed. "Here there's nothing much to do except eat."

The observation made Niall thoughtful.

Eirek clapped his hands. "All right, we'll start with the flute game. Dona, you play the flute. The rest of you sit down." They sat in rows on the floor, Dona a few yards away with her back turned. Niall, sitting at the end of the front row, was handed a smooth wooden stick about six inches long.

"We pass the tally from hand to hand while the flute is playing," Eirek explained. "When the flute stops, whoever is holding it has to kiss the person next in line. And he's out of the game." Niall was sitting next to a blue-eyed little girl of ten, who gave him a demure sideways glance.

As Dona started to play, Eirek called: "Stop. Merlew, are you going to join in?" Niall's heart skipped; the princess had entered from behind him. She was wearing a single garment made of spotted fur which left her arms and her long legs bare.

"I'm sorry I'm late," she said.

Eirek accepted her apology with a nod. "All right. Sit there on the front row." Niall took care not to look at her as she sat beside him. He could feel the warmth radiating from her body against his bare arm.

Dona started to play again, and Niall was impressed by her skill; she played a merry dance tune that repeated itself over and over again. Everyone passed the tally at top speed. Periodically, Dona stopped; then there was much laughter as the person holding the tally had to kiss the next person along. Gaps left in their ranks by the children who dropped out of the game meant that boys often had to kiss boys, and this occasioned shouts of mirth and some embarrassed blushes. Niall laughed as loudly as the rest. After a few minutes, there were only a dozen left in the game, and Eirek ordered them to form a circle. Now the tally passed round at great speed, and Dona deliberately made her solos longer, to increase the tension. Every time it reached Merlew, Niall willed the music to stop. And after a few minutes, it happened; she was just about to put the tally into his hand when the flute ceased.

Niall smiled broadly in an attempt to disguise the beating of his heart; Merlew leaned sideways, quite coolly took hold of Niall's head in her hands, and planted a firm kiss on his lips; everyone laughed approvingly. For a moment, her eyes met his; they seemed calm and mocking. Then she stood up and joined the others. The next time round, Niall found himself holding the tally when the music stopped. The small girl held up her face to him, and her lips held his for a moment longer than necessary. There were mocking "Oohs," and as Niall retreated from the game, the girl blushed rosily.

For Niall, the remainder of the morning passed far too quickly. It dawned on him, with delighted astonishment, that he was an object of curiosity, particularly to the female sex, and that the boys were disposed to admire rather than resent him. When the girls were told to choose partners for a three-legged race, four tried to seize Niall simultaneously; the winner was a rather heavily-built, dark-haired girl called Nyris, and the two of them won the race, just ahead of Merlew and her partner. After this, the younger children sat down to rest, and Eirek announced that the last game of the morning would be a wrestling contest for everyone over the age of thirteen. Niall was surprised but far from displeased to learn that the girls were expected to take part. Soft mattresses stuffed with grass were laid on the floor. The girls were again allowed to choose, and Niall found himself partnered with Nyris.

Each bout commenced with the two adversaries facing one another, arms raised with forearm resting against forearm and fingers interlocked. At a given signal, they braced their feet and began to push, each trying to drive the other backwards. When they slipped and lost contact, they interlocked arms and legs, each trying to wrestle the other to the ground. Then, on the ground, they struggled until one was able to sit astride the other and press the hands back against the mattress. There were points given by judges—the younger children—for each stage.

Nyris, being heavier than Niall, easily won the first stage of the contest. But when it came to wrestling, her weight was no match for his sinewy strength, and he was soon sitting astride her, pressing the backs of her hands against the floor. As he stood up, he observed to his relief that Merlew had beaten her opponent, a broad-shouldered but clumsy youth whom she immobilized by pinning him to the ground with her full weight. It was clear that she was a great deal stronger than she looked.

Niall's next two opponents were male, and both were bigger and heavier than he was. But, like Nyris, they lacked agility, and Niall had no difficulty in beating them both.

Now, as he had hoped, he found that he and Merlew were the two finalists. Both were panting, and before they started, Eirek allowed them to recover their breath. Then they faced each other and locked forearms. Her hair, damp with sweat, was clinging to her forehead, and Niall found her enchanting.

Eirek gave the signal to start. Quite suddenly, Merlew braced herself and pushed with all her might; Niall reeled backwards and everyone applauded. She was on him immediately, trying to fling him to the ground before he had a chance to recover. But Niall was not to be caught out a second time; their arms interlocked, their legs intertwined, and each tried to upset the other's balance. Her face was pressed against his, and she was breathing heavily in his ear; the sensation was so pleasant, that he stopped trying to unbalance her and simply allowed himself to enjoy the consciousness of feeling her in his arms. She tried to upset his equilibrium by relaxing, but he only took advantage of it to press her further backwards.

At that moment he realized there were two more spectators: Kazak had emerged from his dwelling, which opened onto the hall, and Ingeld was standing beside him. For a moment, Niall wondered if the king would be angry to see his daughter clasped in the arms of his guest, and relaxed his grip; with a fierce twist of her body, Merlew threw him to the ground and landed on top of him. They struggled, panting, for several minutes, until she forced one of his hands back against the floor. Now he tried the trick that she had used against him a moment ago; he suddenly allowed himself to relax, as if surrendering. Automatically, she relaxed too. With a violent twist of his hips, he threw her sideways, twisted her arm to the ground and lay across her. She hissed: "Cheat!" But his weight pinned her to the ground. Cautiously, he moved sideways, so their bodies were parallel and, holding down her head with his own, he tried to force back her wrists. Her breath was warm against his ear. They seemed to be locked in a position in which neither had the advantage, and although he could have subdued her by brute strength, he felt this would be a triumph of force rather than skill.

At that moment, he felt her lips against his ear, as if she were about to whisper; then they parted, and her teeth gently bit into the lobe of his ear. The sensation was at once erotic and disturbing, and he became still. Before he was aware of what was happening, she had twisted from under him and wrenched her hands free. A moment later, she was gripping his wrists and forcing them back.

He chuckled: "Cheat."

She whispered: "That makes two of us."

Still laughing, he allowed her to push the backs of his hands against the mattress. To underline her triumph, she struggled on top of him and sat astride his hips. The spectators burst into loud cheers. Ingeld, he noticed, wore a mocking smile.

Kazak came forward and patted his daughter lightly on the head. Merlew sprang lightly to her feet without giving Niall a second glance. Kazak turned to Ingeld. "You see why I made her mistress of the household?"

Ingeld's smile was inscrutable. "She is indeed a remarkable young lady."

Merlew gave Niall a gentle kick in the ribs with her bare foot. "Come on, boy, get up." The "boy" was at once patronizing and affectionate.

Later, as Niall and Dona walked back towards her home, she said: "You shouldn't have let her beat you."

"I couldn't help it."

"I saw what she did. She bit your ear." She reached up and touched the lobe of his ear. "Did it hurt?"

He said modestly: "No, not much."

Dona said with conviction: "She's a dreadful cheat."

Her tone made Niall feel guilty. "Perhaps I am too."

"No, you're not!" She took hold of his arm, and laid her cheek on his shoulder.

That evening, as he and Ulf were on the point of going to bed, Ulf said: "We're leaving tomorrow."

"Tomorrow!" Niall could not keep the dismay out of his voice.

"Don't you want to go home?"

"Yes, of course." His voice lacked conviction. "But couldn't we stay for just a few days more?"

Ulf laid his hand on Niall's head. "Do you think you'd be ready to go then?"

Niall said doubtfully: "Yes."

Ulf stared at him with furrowed brows, then shook his head. "Would you like to live here?"

"Yes, of course." He could not keep the eagerness out of his voice. "If we all lived here."

Ulf shook his head. "That's impossible."

"But why, father? Don't you like it here?"

"Oh, yes, I like it here. But I don't think I could live here."

"Why not?"

"It's too complicated to explain." He climbed onto the mattress and pulled the blanket round his shoulders. "But if you want to stay here, I could go back alone."

He said with dismay: "Oh, no, you couldn't do that."

"Why not? I know the way back. Hamna wants to come with me to the far side of the plateau. I'd be almost home by then."

"And leave me here?"

"We could fetch you later. Sefna says she'd like you to stay."

It was very tempting—to stay in the same house as Dona, who was like an adoring young sister, and be able to see Merlew every day. . . .

"What about the king?"

"It was Kazak who suggested it."

"And what do you think?"

"I want you to make up your own mind."

A few minutes later, Ulf's regular breathing revealed that he was asleep. But all Niall's desire for sleep had vanished. From the next room, the tiny light of a single lamp percolated past the curtain that hung in the doorway, making a moving shadow on the ceiling. From outside, in the corridor, he could hear voices, the comforting sound of human beings going about their business—it was still two hours to midnight, and the palace of Kazak never fell silent until the early hours of the morning. (Absence of daylight meant that it was easy to lose the habit of sleeping at night.)

The temptation to stay here was enormous. His presence was not needed in the burrow. Since Veig had domesticated the ants and the pepsis wasp, hunting had become a sport rather than a necessity. There was food in plenty within five miles of the burrow. And he could—as Ulf said—go home any time he wanted. Why not stay here for a few weeks, a few months, longer? . . .

Niall badly wanted to convince himself. But the thought of deserting his family touched his conscience, and made him question his own motives. The chief motive, he was well aware, was Merlew. He thought of the cool touch of her lips, of her small white teeth biting his ear, of her slim legs locked around his own, and a feeling of enormous joy made his heart expand. He allowed himself to daydream of becoming Merlew's husband, perhaps of taking Kazak's place as king. And it was then that he suddenly began to experience the cold finger of doubt. He remembered Eirek's comment: "There's nothing much to do here except eat. . . ." and tried to imagine what it would be like to be cooped underground for year after year. At home, at least, he was free to come and go as he wished. There was a whole world to be explored, a world full of marvels like the country of the ants and the great fortress on the plateau. Here, they spent their lives hiding from the spiders.

Now he saw the problem with great clarity. If he lived here, life would be pleasant and safe. But it would also be predictable. A child could be born here, grow up here, die here, without once experiencing the excitement of discovery. Why did Dona question him endlessly about his life in the burrow and his journey to the country of the ants? Because for her, it represented a world that was at once dangerous and full of fascinating possibilities. For the children of this underground city, life was a matter of repetition, of *habit*.

And this, he suddenly realized, was the heart of the problem. Habit. Habit was a stifling, warm blanket that threatened you with suffocation and lulled the mind into a state of perpetual nagging dissatisfaction. Habit meant the inability to escape from yourself, to change and develop. . . .

He was distracted by the sound of laughter from outside; two children were chasing along the corridor. It brought back the memory of the games in the great hall, and the thought of Merlew. All his certainty vanished. How could he ever become bored when he could see Merlew every day?

He had been lying awake for more than an hour and still felt no desire to sleep. He began thinking of Kazak. Why had the king asked his father if he could stay? Could it have been Merlew who suggested it? If only he could talk it over with someone instead of lying there with his head full of unanswered questions. . . . Perhaps Sefna was still awake?

Very slowly, so as not to awaken his father, he slipped from under the cover and tiptoed to the door. But the room next door was empty. He tiptoed across it, and listened against the curtain of the room where Sefna and Dona slept; the sound of steady breathing told him they were also asleep. He went to the main door and peered out into the corridor. Hamna's younger brother, Corvig, was strolling by, his arm around a girl.

"Hello, Niall. What are you doing?" he said.

"Nothing. I couldn't sleep."

"Sleep! It's too early to sleep. We're going to Nyris's house to play a game of brads. Why don't you come along?"

He said apologetically: "I don't think I'd better. We may leave in the morning and I ought to get a good night's sleep." He was disappointed that Corvig had a companion; he would have liked to ask his advice.

Corvig tucked his arm through Niall's. "Well, walk along with us anyway."

The girl, who had large, attractive eyes, asked him: "Why do you have to leave so soon?"

"My father wants to get back. I wish I could persuade him to stay a few days longer." He turned to Corvig. "Couldn't you ask your father to talk to him?"

They had emerged into the main thoroughfare, the one that led to the great hall.

"He's over there," Corvig said. "Why don't you ask him yourself?"

The king was walking alone, looking at a roll of parchment which he held within a few inches of his nose. Passers-by acknowledged him respectfully, but he paid them no attention. Corvig approached him, bowed his head, and said: "Father . . ." Kazak glanced up irritably, then saw Niall and smiled.

"Excuse me, sir, but Niall wants to ask you something," Corvig said.

"Yes, yes, he's very welcome." He took Niall's arm. "What is it, my boy?"

"It's about leaving tomorrow, sir . . ."

Kazak frowned. "Tomorrow? As soon as that! Why can't you stay longer?"

"That's what I wanted to talk to you about. Couldn't you ask my father?"

Kazak shrugged irritably. "I've asked him already. He says he's worried about his family. But that's no reason why you shouldn't stay."

"I'd like to sir."

"You would? Good!" A guard approached them and saluted the king. Kazak said: "Look, I'm busy at the moment, but why don't you go and talk to Merlew. You'll probably find her alone."

"Thank you, sir!"

The king's dwelling was two stories high, the main door approached by a short flight of steps. The guard who was standing in the doorway stood aside to allow Niall to enter. He found himself in a wide entrance hall supported by pillars of stone; the walls were covered with dyed curtains in royal green. A dozen lamps made it almost as bright as day.

There seemed to be no one about. He crossed to a curtained doorway and peeped in. The large, comfortable room had rushes on the floor and wooden carved furniture; it was also lit by many lamps. But there was no one there.

To the right of the entrance hall was a flight of stairs. Standing at the bottom of these, Niall thought he could hear voices. He hesitated—it seemed wrong to walk around someone's house like this—then remembered that he had the king's permission. His bare feet made no sound on the stone steps. He found himself in a low, well-lit corridor, with several curtained doorways to the right and left. From behind one of these came the sound of women's voices. Niall approached it hesitantly, and was about to call: "Is anybody there?" when he heard the sound of a woman's laugh. He recognized it immediately; it was Ingeld's voice. Again, he was tempted to retreat. But as he turned away, he heard the sound of his own name. As he hesitated, Ingeld went on: "It wasn't his fault. I blame his father and brother."

Merlew's voice asked: "How did it happen?"

"I don't know. They wouldn't tell me. That's what makes me suspicious. You'd think they'd tell a woman how her husband and son met their deaths."

"Perhaps they didn't want to upset you."

"Upset me!" Ingeld's voice was incredulous. "Do you think they'd care! I'll tell you something. They almost left me to die in that fortress on the top of the plateau."

"Oh, no! What happened?"

"I can't stand heights, and when I looked down all those steps, I felt dizzy. So they just turned their backs on me and walked off."

"That's disgraceful! And what did you do?"

"I just had to close my eyes and follow them. They were already out of sight and I couldn't bear the thought of all those horrible spiders."

Merlew sounded genuinely angry. "They shouldn't treat a woman like that."

Ingeld snorted. "They don't know how to treat a woman! They're savages."

There was a brooding silence, and Niall felt it was time to withdraw. He was already ashamed at having overheard so much. But as he turned away, he heard Ingeld say:

"You seem to like the boy."

"What makes you say that?"

"The way you were wrestling with him this morning."

Merlew's voice said coldly: "I don't know what you mean. Wrestling is one of our customs."

"The king thought you found him attractive."

"Attractive! That skinny boy! You must be joking!"

"The others all seem to like him."

"Of course, they do. Because he's a stranger. But the novelty will soon wear off."

His cheeks burning, Niall tiptoed away. There was a strange, leaden feeling inside his chest, the same feeling he had experienced when he heard that Thorg and Hrolf were dead. He was tingling with humiliation. As he passed the soldier at the door, he felt that his face must be revealing everything he felt. But the man merely nodded in a friendly manner. He made his way back down the main thoroughfare, deliberately walking in the shadows in case someone spoke to him. Inside his brain, Merlew's voice repeated again and again: "Attractive! That skinny boy! You must be joking!" It was true. He could see it now. To a king's daughter, he was bound to look underfed and undersized. And he had imagined that she found him attractive. The thought made him writhe with embarrassment.

Yet when he thought back on this morning, he could have no doubt that she had been flirting with him. Why had she bitten his ear? Why had she given him that secret smile as he said goodbye to her? Had she merely been playing with him? His misery turned to a dull rage and he decided that he hated her. That, at least, was better than the emotional turmoil that made him feel like bursting into tears.

As he entered the sleeping chamber, Ulf's voice said: "Where have you been?"

"I couldn't sleep, so I went outside."

He settled himself down on the grass couch and pulled the blanket up to his chin. After a silence, he said:

"I've been thinking about tomorrow. I'll come with you."

Ulf grunted. "You'd better get some sleep. I want to set out early."

But Niall knew his father well enough to detect the note of gladness in his voice.

They left the city an hour before dawn, at the same time as the ant herds. Hamna and Corvig, who had obtained special permission from the king, accompanied them. Kazak himself walked with them as far as the entrance and embraced them both, kissing them on their foreheads and cheeks. To Niall's relief, the king expressed no curiosity about why he had changed his mind. The streets of the underground city were deserted at this hour, and Niall had to swallow back a feeling of intense regret as he looked on it for the last time.

"Remember," Kazak said, "you have my permission to return here with your family." He added reflectively: "I haven't seen Siris since she was a little girl."

Ulf bowed respectfully. "I'll discuss it with her, Sire." But Niall knew that he had no such intention.

"Do that," said Kazak, and hurried back inside again; it was evident that he found the dawn wind too cold.

The eastern sky showed a streak of grey, but the sky overhead was still black. Ahead, the salt lake reflected the stars. It looked so beautiful that for a moment, Niall forgot his bitterness about Merlew. Then he recalled her comment about "that skinny boy," and relapsed into somber brooding. And for the next half hour or so, he daydreamed pleasantly of various situations in which he made her pay for the insult. She had been captured by the death spiders and carried off to their city. Niall was her only hope. . . .

Ulf said: "We've decided to avoid the plateau. Kazak says it would be quicker to cross the mountains to the northwest."

Hamna said: "I cannot advise you, because I've never been that far. But I am told that the land on the other side of the mountains is easy to cross. There has been much rainfall in the past ten years."

Now they had reached the shores of the lake and were traveling due west. They were more heavily laden than when they had left the burrow a week earlier—Kazak was generous with food supplies—but their loads felt lighter because they had been provided with panniers, held on the back with straps around the shoulders and waist.

As the sky lightened, Niall glanced back over his shoulder, and saw the spider balloons reflecting the rising sun. There were two of them, high up and moving in a direction that would carry them over the salt lake. He warned the others and they took cover in the undergrowth, under the twisted branches of a thorn tree. It was unlikely that the spiders would have seen them in any case; the light was still poor, and the balloons were at least two hundred feet up. Hamna and Corvig, he observed, did not seem to be in the least troubled or anxious. They produced fruit, bread, and meat from their packs and sat eating as cheerfully as if on a picnic excursion.

When the balloons had vanished over the horizon and they were again marching along the shore of the lake, Niall said: "You don't seem worried by the spiders."

Hamna shrugged. "We've learned to live with them."

"But . . ." Niall caught a warning glance from his father and relapsed into silence.

With the dawn, the wind rose and changed direction until it was blowing from the west. As the morning advanced, it became stronger, and acquired a dry, hot taste until it seemed like the breath of a furnace. Finally, it turned into a half-gale, carrying dust and grains of sharp sand that made their eyes smart. Hamna and Corvig looked increasingly depressed as their excursion turned into a test of endurance. They wrapped their mantles round their heads so that only a small slit remained, and plodded on obstinately. After half an hour of this, Ulf advised them to turn back. At first they refused, feeling it was a matter of honor to accompany the travelers on the first day of their journey. Ulf pointed out that the purpose of companionship was conversation, and that in weather like this, conversation was almost impossible. Hamna allowed himself to be convinced; they embraced, exchanged promises to meet again soon, and separated. Hamna and Corvig turned their backs on the wind with evident relief.

Now Ulf found himself wondering whether it was wise to choose the route over the mountains. It was longer than the route over the plateau, although less arduous. But in this cutting wind, which dried their mouths and chapped their faces, the advantage was neutralized. Leaning into the wind, peering out through the flapping slits in their headcloths, they plodded forward at a rate of about five miles an hour. Niall looked longingly at the choppy waters of the salt lake; but he knew that bathing would be impractical. With no river to wash off the salt water, the aftermath would be even more discomfort.

By the time the sun stood directly overhead, both were exhausted. They decided to take advantage of the first clump of trees or bushes to halt for the midday meal. But for the next two miles, there was no sign of even a single tree. Half an hour later, they realized they were at the western end of the lake, heading out into the desert, towards a country of broken foothills and dry wadis.

At this point, Niall saw an object like a large rock a few hundred yards to their right. He tapped his father on the shoulder and pointed. Ulf nodded, and they hurried towards it. Another fifty yards made it clear that this was no rock, but the remains of a building. Most of it was buried in the sand; all that remained were the broken profiles of walls against the sky.

On the western side of the building, the blown sand formed a ramp. They scrambled up it to the lowest point in the ruined wall and found themselves looking down into a sand-filled courtyard. On the far side, a flight of badly eroded steps led up the side of a broken tower. They were looking at a smaller—and more decrepit—version of the fortress on the plateau. But it was a shelter from the wind. As they landed on the soft sand inside the walls, they experienced immense relief to be in a haven of stillness.

They were so tired that for the next half hour they sat in the shade, backs against the wall, luxuriating in the pleasure of no longer having to move their limbs. The wind seemed to be howling with frustration as it tried to reach them. As he sat there, his eyes closed, Niall felt his heartbeat slow down to normal, and waves of relaxation carried him into a realm of freedom from all anxiety.

Ulf touched his arm, and he realized he must have fallen asleep. He looked up at the sky to check the position of the sun, and was surprised to see only dark clouds. The wind had risen to a shriek, and although they were still sheltered from it, the sand on the far side of the courtyard was being blown into clouds. The sky became darker; then, suddenly, they were in complete blackness, surrounded by flying grains of sand. The wind was now so powerful that Niall was afraid it would tear down the wall that gave them shelter.

From their panniers they unpacked the covers of spider silk and wrapped themselves inside them. The wind now seemed to be blowing from all directions at once, as if determined to reach them, and sand blew over the broken wall behind them like water surging over a harbor breakwater. Niall thought of Hamna and Corvig, and hoped they had reached the shelter before the storm began. It seemed to him providential that they had discovered this ruined fort at exactly the right time. If necessary, they could remain here all night.

Gradually, the wind died down. The sky cleared, and the returning light was like day breaking. Then, quite abruptly, the wind died away altogether, and sunlight beat down on them. The sun was still high above them—it must have been about two hours into the afternoon. They were both covered in sand up to their necks. On the opposite side of the courtyard, it had piled up against the wall in a ramp. Niall rose unsteadily to his feet, his legs painfully stiff, and stretched. He tried to peer over the wall behind him but it was a few inches too high. With his feet sinking into the soft sand, he walked across the courtyard and scrambled up the sand to the top of the wall.

What he saw made him gasp. A broken city lay below him. Its ruined buildings were all at least twenty feet lower than the wall he was standing on, and they had now been uncovered by the gale. Facing him was a building with tall columns—not square columns like those in the fortress on the plateau, but slim cylindrical columns, some of them still supporting fragments of lintels and walls. And in the midst of the empty space in the center of these columns, there was an object that glittered dazzlingly in the sunlight. Niall shouted: "Father, come and look."

A moment later, Ulf joined him. "Ah, yes, I should have known," he said. "This is the city that was ruled by Kazak's father Beyrak."

"You mean they lived above ground?"

"Until the spiders drove them out."

"And was this place built by Beyrak?"

"No. It's been here for as long as anyone can remember. They say it was built by some ancient people called the Latina."

"And what do you think that is?" Niall pointed to the glittering object.

Ulf shrugged. "I don't know. Whatever it is, it's made of metal."

It took them ten minutes to find a way down to the sand below, scrambling over the uneven walls. From outside, they could see that the fortress was a square building of carved blocks, the walls partly covered by cement. There were tall, narrow windows, and the door that faced the city was also tall and narrow, with strange unknown symbols carved into the wall above; this door was completely blocked with fallen masonry and sand. Leading from this doorway towards the ruined city was a double row of columns, most of them merely stumps, while broken fragments of column lay on the road. The tops of some were carved with imitation leaves and vines.

Most of the houses were little more than broken walls, although a few had the remains of upper stories; they were built of a mixture of baked mud and brick. The rooms seemed very tiny, some no more than a few feet square.

While Ulf explored the ruined houses, Niall wandered in the building with the columns, which lay at the end of the causeway. Underfoot were slabs of stone set in some kind of cement. Between the columns were a number of immense rectangular boxes, carved out of stone. When Niall concentrated, and then allowed himself to relax, he received a strong impression that these boxes were somehow associated with the dead.

The causeway ended with a flight of steps, each one twelve feet wide, leading up to the remains of a gateway. Of the temple to which this gateway had once afforded admittance, there was nothing but a great circle of columns, each one standing on a six-foot cube of granite and most surmounted by lintels. Niall was astonished to see that the pavement underfoot was made of small squares of colored stone, forming pictures of birds and animals. And in the center of this mosaic pavement stood the glittering object that had so intrigued him. As he approached it, he was amazed to realize that he could see his own reflection in the curved metal surface. But it was frighteningly distorted, and changed as he came closer. The thing looked a little like a huge beetle supported on metal legs, with glass eyes around the front of its head. But it was obvious to Niall that these straight legs, braced apart at an angle, would be useless for walking.

Niall tried to grasp something of its purpose by relaxing his mind and attempting to absorb impressions; but such faint impressions as he received were so confusing that they meant nothing; it was like trying to read the unknown symbols above the door of the fort. Whoever had made this glittering monster, with its mirror-like surface, was quite unlike the men he knew. Yet there was something man-like about this structure; only a human being could have made it. But for what purpose? Could this metal insect have been made to carry men across the desert on its segmented legs?

In the curved side, just below and behind the "eyes," there was a structure that was unmistakably a door. Niall knew this from an instinct derived from racial memory, without ever having seen a real door. He touched it; the metal was hot from the sun, yet not so hot as he might have expected. On one side of this door there was a curved metal handle. Niall grasped it, pushed it, pulled it, twisted it, even banged it with the heel of his hand. This, he knew instinctively, was the key to entering this bizarre insect. But the door behind did not even vibrate. Then, as he grabbed the handle impatiently, something yielded to his fingers, and he staggered as the door slid open. He jumped back in alarm; the door had behaved exactly as if an invisible man had pulled it open. But there was no sign of anyone inside. Cautiously, Niall peered through the doorway, then climbed in. It was only then that he realized that the "eyes" of this insect were made of some transparent substance, like white sand when it was fused by a hot fire, and that they admitted the daylight.

He was in a small "room" in which there was space for very little but the leather-covered seats. Everything else in this room struck him as magical yet totally confusing. There was nothing in his experience with which he could compare the control panel, with its gauges and dials, or the steering columns in front of one of the seats. All that he knew was that this metal insect had been created with a precision and delicacy that staggered his imagination. Having no concepts that would enable him to interpret his impressions, Niall found himself overwhelmed by a feeling of awe which convinced him that this incomprehensible device had been created for purposes of religious worship.

He sat down cautiously on the sun-warmed seat, and delicately prodded the control panel with his finger. Nothing yielded; it defied his curiosity like a blank wall. But underneath the panel there was an open compartment containing a number of objects, which he examined one by one. When he pressed the handle of an oil can, the oil squirted out into his face and made him jump; he tasted it with his tongue, found it unpleasant, and wiped his face with his hand. Wrenches, screwdrivers, and box spanners all failed to yield up their secrets. He had never felt so completely bewildered and baffled. One short, cylindrical piece of metal, about half an inch in diameter and a foot long, intrigued him because of its weight; it was heavier than solid granite. He decided instantly that, no matter what happened, this was now his own property; neither father nor brother—not even King Kazak himself—could persuade him to part with it. He smacked it into the palm of his other hand and reflected with satisfaction that it would kill an ant at one blow, and stun the most heavily-armored beetle. With this in his hand, he would not be afraid even of a crater insect.

He examined it more closely. The ends were made up of concentric circles, and close to one end, on the curved surface, there was a finely etched circle about half an inch in diameter. He put the cylinder between his teeth and tried biting it. To his astonishment it proceeded to elongate itself, stretching itself out of his mouth like a telescopic cigar. The other end struck a button on the control panel; instantly, there was a strange high pitched hum and the seat began to vibrate beneath him. With one single bound, he was out of the doorway and on solid ground, looking with horror at the machine that was now throbbing with life.

His father heard the noise and came running towards him. Niall realized that he had left his newly found weapon behind; his fear of the noise was overruled by his determination not to lose it, and he reached in and grabbed the telescopic rod, which was now about five feet long.

Ulf said: "What happened?"

"I don't know." A green light flashed on the control panel, then the humming noise stopped.

They walked around the device, tried to rock it, walked underneath it, and finally decided that it was not worth any further effort. When Ulf asked to see the telescopic rod, Niall handed it to him with reluctance. Ulf examined it carefully, swished it through the air, and then, to Niall's relief, handed it back.

As Niall took it from him, grasping it by the broad end, there was a click and the rod contracted, and once more became a short, heavy cylinder.

Studying it closely, Niall realized that the secret lay in the finely etched circle on the curved surface. When he pressed this, the metal yielded slightly, and the cylinder expanded into a rod with a pointed tip. As he held it in his hand, balancing it gently and trying to fathom its purpose, he observed a curious tingling sensation in his fingers. If he held both ends of the rod, stretching out his arms to their full extent, it became stronger.

He pressed the circle again; there was a click, and the rod contracted again into a cylinder. The mechanism baffled him; he spent five minutes, making it expand and contract, and finally decided it was beyond his comprehension. Yet the tingling sensation he experienced when it was fully extended was somehow oddly familiar.

Time was passing; it was now the middle of the afternoon, and they had to think of moving. Back at the fort, they scrambled up the sloping ramp of sand, and Ulf jumped down into the courtyard and handed up their panniers. It was while Niall was reaching down for the second pannier that the first one unbalanced and rolled down the slope. Niall made no attempt to stop it; its closed flap would prevent the contents from escaping. But as he helped Ulf back up on to the wall, he seemed to detect some movement at the foot of the slope. He stared hard and decided that the pannier must have slid under its own weight. Slowly, he made his way down the ramp, staring intently at the pannier; once more it seemed to him that he detected some slight movement. Cautiously, Niall reached out and grabbed the strap. As he took the pannier's weight, the sand underneath seemed to crumble. Then, to Niall's incredulous horror, a hairy, segmented foreleg broke through the surface. Another one followed. A moment later he was looking into the eyes of a big spider, as it tried to scramble from the sand that entombed it. His reaction was immediate and instinctive; he raised the telescopic rod and drove it with all his force into the hairy, strangely expressionless face. The spider hissed with pain, and Niall recoiled as he experienced the almost physical force of its will, striking out at him like a poisoned sting. He knew with total certainty that if the spider pulled itself clear of the sand, it would be upon him with a single bound, holding him pinioned with its forelegs as it sank its fangs into his flesh. He pulled the rod free, and struck again and again—into the mouth, the eyes, the soft body behind the head. The willpower of the creature seemed to hold him at bay like an arm; his own will, nerved by terror, resisted it. Then, suddenly, its resistance ceased; he was aware that its awareness was dissolving into death. His father was standing above them, looking down in horror. Then, when he saw that the spider was motionless, he circled round it and stood beside Niall.

The spider's body was halfway out of the sand, and they could see that it was bigger than the grey spiders they had encountered in the fortress on the plateau. This one was about the size of the trapdoor spider on which the pepsis wasp had laid its egg. The double-segmented fangs, with a channel for poison, showed that it belonged to the tarantula species. But while the tarantula's hairy body was brown, sometimes with patches of yellow, this spider was jet black. Instead of the double row of eyes in the front of the head, this had a single row that seemed to extend in a continuous band around the head.

The same thought struck them both together. This was not some primitive desert spider that lived in the empty rooms of the fort; it was a death spider.

Then Niall remembered the two spider balloons that had drifted overhead before the wind changed direction. He used his telescopic rod as a lever to force the black body out of the sand. Underneath it, he could see the silk of the balloon.

Ulf looked nervously over his shoulder.

"The other one must be somewhere round here. We'd better go."

"What about the spider? If the other one finds it, they'll know it's been killed." Suddenly, he remembered the story of the execution of the rebel humans who had killed a death spider—the slow, cruel torment lasting many days—and shivered.

"Yes. We'll bury it."

It took only a few minutes to cover the spider with sand, and to keep this in place with a number of flat stones. As they walked away, Niall looked back; from ten yards distance nothing betrayed the spot.

Niall walked to the edge of the lake and washed his telescopic spear in the salt water, cleaning off the blood and the white, gluey substance with a handful of grass. After that, he made it contract and stowed it in the bottom of the pannier. They hurried on towards the distant mountains, suddenly oppressed by a sense of danger, as if unknown eyes were scanning the landscape in search of them.

Kazak's advice proved sound. On the far side of the mountains, rainfall had transformed a wilderness into a land of moderate abundance. The landscape was not unlike that in the vicinity of the burrow. So although the detour cost them an extra day's travel, it was nevertheless far less arduous than the journey across the plateau. It was more than ten years since Ulf had been in this region, and he remembered it as a rocky desert. Now some climatic freak was transforming it into a habitable area. This also meant there was more danger from tiger beetles, scorpions, and other night predators. So in spite of the heat, they traveled by day and spent the night in improvised shelters.

On the morning of the third day, Niall woke up in a shelter built of rocks and thorn bushes and smelt an odor that was strange to him. It was not unlike the smell of caterpillar hide when set to dry in the sun. The wind was blowing from the northwest. When he asked his father about it, Ulf shrugged and said: "It's the smell of the delta." It was the odor of decaying vegetation, mixed with a sweeter, slightly nauseating smell. Niall observed that Ulf seemed depressed until the wind changed.

On the morning of the fourth day, Ulf met with an accident that could have been serious. While they were sheltering under a tree in the heat of the day, they both noticed a movement in some bushes about fifty yards away. A large, tailless rodent was standing on its hind legs, trying to reach some edible berries. Because Ulf and Niall were resting, it had not noticed their presence. Ulf seized his spear and moved carefully out of its range of vision, then began to move cautiously towards it, taking advantage of the shelter of creosote bushes. Niall quietly took his telescopic spear from the pannier and pressed the button to make it expand. At that moment, he heard a shout of pain, and the rodent took fright and vanished.

Ulf was on one knee, and his right foot and the lower part of the leg seemed to be in a hole. For a moment, Niall assumed he had simply stumbled into a crack in the dry ground. Then Ulf dragged the foot out, and Niall saw that a dark, hairy creature, not unlike a caterpillar, was clinging on to it. Without hesitation, he rushed forward and drove the end of the spear through the creature's body. Even that failed to make it let go. A convulsive contraction of its body almost dragged Ulf's leg back into the hole. Then Ulf was free, although he was no longer wearing his sandal, and the blood ran from his ankle.

Niall drove his spear down the hole until the creature stopped moving. "What was it?"

Ulf was sitting down, examining his foot. "A lion beetle larva. They're like trapdoor spiders—they hide in a hole."

It took an hour to dress the cuts—a number of deep parallel scratches, obviously made by sharp teeth or mandibles. Ulf was carrying an ointment made of the root of the devil plant, and he smeared this on strips of cloth and bandaged the ankle and foot. It seemed a pity to make such use of the cloth—a present from Sefna for Siris—but it was a necessity. With spare sandals, presented to him by Hamna, on his feet, he limped forward vigorously for the rest of the day.

By evening, they were in country they recognized, about twenty miles from the burrow. Again they slept in an improvised shelter of rocks and bushes. But in the morning, Ulf's foot was badly swollen and beginning to turn blue. Niall took Ulf's pannier and marched awkwardly with one on either shoulder, while Ulf used a crutch made of a branch of a tree. Both were aware that it was now a matter of urgent necessity to reach the burrow before nightfall; by the following day, Ulf's foot would probably be too poisoned to walk. So they staggered on, covering less than ten miles during the heat of the day. Then they paused in the shadow of a rock, and ate and drank; Ulf slept a little. The foot was now so swollen that he could not rest his weight on it; the crutch had to take the full weight of his right side as they moved forward a dozen yards at a time, halting for frequent rests. Then, as the sun dipped towards the horizon, Ulf seemed to call reserves of strength from somewhere and began to swing forward at a steady pace. The great red rocks became visible on their right, then the cactus grove. They were now so exhausted that they would have been an easy prey for any scorpion, tiger beetle, or trapdoor spider. Niall clutched his telescopic spear, using it as a staff, and staggered unevenly as the panniers swung on his back.

Suddenly Veig and Siris were running towards them across the sand, with Runa trotting behind. Niall was relieved of his packs and felt at once absurdly light, as if about to float off the ground. Siris put her arm round her husband's waist and supported him across the last fifty yards to the burrow. As he stood waiting for them to go in first, Niall looked out across the desert at the distant plateau and felt a kind of incredulity at the thought that he had been so far away from home. Even the thought of Merlew seemed slightly unreal.

There was only one cause for sadness in the relief of homecoming. Jomar was too feeble even to rise from his bed to meet them. In the light of the oil lamps—they lit all six as a celebration—it was obvious that he was dying. In the two weeks since they had seen him, his face had become very thin, and his eyes were sunken. Siris told them that he had only just recovered from a fever. But the real fever was weariness, a sense that he had seen all there was to see, and that life held no more interest for him. Now that Thorg and Hrolf and Ingeld were gone, and he was unable to walk more than a few yards beyond the entrance to the burrow, Jomar had lost his delight in being alive. He listened with apparent interest to the description of Kazak's underground city, but when he asked, "Are there still rats among the ruins?" it was obvious that he had not taken it in.

Niall could understand his apathy. After Kazak's palace, life at home seemed unbearably dull. Although he had been in Dira for only two days, it had taught him the meaning of living in a community, of consorting with others of his own age and exchanging ideas and feelings. In retrospect he idealized it; everything about Dira now seemed charming and exciting. He envied Ingeld for being able to live there for the rest of her days. He often thought fondly about Dona, and was saddened by the thought that he had left without saying goodbye— she had been asleep at the time. Only the recollection of Merlew made him wince.

The burrow seemed strangely empty without Thorg and Hrolf and Ingeld, and the realization that Jomar was dying brought an oppressive feeling of loss, a sense that something was coming to an end. They had moved the old man into an inner chamber of the burrow, so that he could sleep undisturbed. Every morning, they helped him out into the daylight; there he sat until the sun became too hot, dozing and listening to the hum of flies. Sometimes, if there was no wind, they moved him into the shade of the euphorbia; Niall sat on guard, his spear close at hand in case of attack by some predator. He noticed that when the old man asked to be taken back inside, his hands were as cold as if they had only just emerged into the daylight.

During these final weeks, Mara played an important part in keeping the old man's mind alert. She had changed greatly. The juice of the ortis plant had transformed her from a nervous, fretful baby into a lively child who was interested in everything. She spent a great deal of time sitting on her grandfather's knee and asking questions; if he failed to answer she drummed on his chest and said: "Tell me, tell me." Jomar told her stories about his childhood, and legends of the great hunters of the past. And Niall sat in the corner, hands clasped round his knees, and tried to memorize everything the old man said. He had always loved stories; but since the trip to Dira, he had a consuming desire to know about the past.

One day, when Mara had fallen asleep on Jomar's knee, Niall asked him about the ruined city. Jomar had been born a few miles away, in the foothills, and had played there during his childhood. Birds and rodents lived there, and Jomar had often set traps for them.

Niall asked him about the building with the tall columns; Jomar said it had once been a temple to the gods. But when Niall asked about the strange boxes carved out of solid stone, Jomar confessed that he had never seen them. And his description made it clear that the city had then been covered in sand to a depth of about ten feet. This explained why he had never seen the stone boxes, or the shining metallic monster in the midst of the temple.

Niall asked: "How old were you when the spiders carried you off to their city?"

The old man was silent; Niall assumed he was unwilling to speak of it. But after a long pause, Jomar said: "It must have been— when I was eighteen summers. Eighteen or thereabouts. . . . It was a black day for the men of Dira."

"What happened?"

"They came on us in the dawn. There must have been hundreds of them. I knew they were there as soon as I woke up."

"How?"

"I couldn't move in my bed. I tried to sit up, but it was as if I had a big rock on my chest. Then I tried to move my arms. They'd gone dead, as if I'd been lying on them."

"But what had happened?"

"They'd pinned us down. We were all the same."

"But how?"

"With willpower."

Niall felt the roots of his hair stirring. He was thinking of Kazak's city. "What happened then?"

"Nothing until they found us."

"Found you?" Niall was bewildered. "Didn't they know where you were?"

"Not exactly. They knew we were in there somewhere."

"But if they pinned you down, surely they must have known where you were?"

"No. They kept us pinned down until they found us."

"What happened then?"

Jomar moved Mara from his knee, and carefully laid her on the bed; it was as if he did not want to be in contact with her while he remembered.

"They killed all those who resisted. They killed my father, and our chief Hallad."

"Did they try to attack the spiders?"

"Not physically. But they tried to fight back with their wills. The spiders didn't like that. Hallad was a strong-willed man."

Jomar described how the spiders had kept them prisoners in the caves all through that day. The spiders disliked the heat; they preferred to travel by night. During the course of the day, the spiders ate the men they had killed. Unlike human jaws, the chelicerae of the death spiders move sideways. Jomar could not bear to watch as his father was eaten by four spiders; he turned his eyes away. But he could still hear the sound of tearing flesh.

With time to spare, the spiders preferred to soften their prey by injections of venom, and eat when it was a few days old. But there was no time now; they wanted to return to the spider city. That evening, as the sun set, they began the long journey back. Some of them took advantage of the change in the direction of the wind to travel by balloon; these carried the children with them. But adult humans were too heavy for the balloons; they had to march. It was a long journey of many weeks, for they had to make a great detour round the intervening sea. And the spiders were in no hurry; they were determined to bring back all their captives alive.

But why, Niall wanted to know, were the spiders so keen to preserve their prisoners? He was anxious to discover some less terrifying aspect of the spiders, something that would enable him to feel less afraid. But Jomar's answer brought him no comfort.

"They wanted them for breeding—especially the women." Jomar's breathing was hoarse; the effort of talking had exhausted him. "The men weren't so important. One man could father a lot of children. But they never had enough women."

Mara began making whimpering noises in her sleep. Niall realized immediately that it was his fault; his fear and loathing had communicated itself to her. Jomar reached out and laid his hand on her forehead; she sighed and became quiet. Jomar said sadly: "No, never enough women."

"How did you escape, Grandfather?"

The old man smiled. It took him several moments to summon the energy to speak. "In a balloon. We took balloons." Niall waited. Jomar said finally: "The other two worked for the bombardier beetles. It was their idea. They were intelligent—not like the men in the spider city. The spiders killed all the clever ones. They wanted us fat and stupid. But the beetles didn't care. All they wanted was explosions. . . ."

"Explosions?"

"They liked big bangs—the bigger the better. That's why they wanted human beings—explosives experts. These two decided to escape—Jebil and Theag. They found out how to make a gas to fill the balloons—hydrogen it was called. They asked me to help. That was the day I found out the spiders meant to kill me. So I had nothing to lose. I showed them where the women made the balloons. . . ."

"Women made them?"

"Yes. Under the supervision of the spiders. They had a store-house with hundreds of balloons. We just walked in and helped our-selves. The guards didn't try to stop us. They thought we'd been ordered to fetch the balloons. Why should they think otherwise? . . . No human being had ever tried to escape that way. They simply let us walk out." He laughed, but even his laugh revealed his exhaus-tion. Five minutes went past, and Niall assumed the old man was asleep. Then Jomar began to speak again. "The other two died. One of them came down in the sea, the other in the delta. Their balloons must have been faulty. But mine carried me to the mountains near the lake. I landed fifty miles from where I'd been captured."

"Did they come looking for you?"

The old man laughed dryly. "They've been looking for me ever since."

Mara began to whimper again. Jomar said: "Hush," and again laid his hand on her head. A few minutes later, his own regular breathing revealed he was asleep.

Two days later, Jomar died. Runa came in early, while they were all asleep, and said: "Grandfather won't talk." And suddenly, they all knew he was dead; it was the kind of instantaneous certainty they all took for granted. Jomar was lying face down on the floor, his hands spread out about his head, as if he had fallen from a great height. But when they turned him over his face was peaceful. It was clear that his last moments had not been haunted by fear of the spiders.

Ulf, Veig, and Niall spent all that day digging his grave, at the foot of the euphorbia; they dug deep to try to preserve the body from insects. But when Niall looked at the grave a few days later, it was full of the characteristic holes of the scarab beetle. In the desert, food was seldom allowed to waste.

On the evening of Jomar's death, Siris tried to make contact with her sister in Dira. She used the inner room—the room where Jomar had died—and the rest of them sat in the next room in total silence, listening to her breathing and waiting for that change of rhythm that would indicate success. They sat there for perhaps half an hour; then she sighed and rejoined them. During the meal that followed, she was obviously worried.

"What is the point of fretting?" Ulf said finally. "In Kazak's city, only the ant herds know when it is sundown. The rest of them lose all sense of time."

Siris nodded, but said nothing.

She tried again at dawn the next day, hoping to awaken Sefna from her sleep. Again, there was no result. Listening to her breathing, Niall understood what she must be feeling. The first stage of an attempted contact was to clearly picture the other person, and to send out thought-waves. It was easiest if both communicators made the attempt at the same time. But this was not essential; if the two shared a certain basic sympathy, then the sender could attract the attention of the other person, who would suddenly experience a nagging feeling of anxiety. Then, as contact was established, both parties would experience a strong sense of the other's presence, exactly as in a normal conversation.

If the sender failed to make contact, then a grey and unresponding space developed, with its own peculiar variety of silence—a silence often broken by the echoes of other voices. This usually indicated that the contactee was preoccupied, perhaps involved in some activity. Yet even after the sender had abandoned the attempt to make contact, the other person might suddenly become aware that the attempt had been made. This often happened between the two sisters, and on such occasions each would remain receptive for as long as possible in case the other "called back."

This is why Siris was worried. Staring into that grey, empty space, with its hint of other voices, she had had a foreboding that something was wrong. And as the days passed without contact, the foreboding became a certainty.

Niall himself was oppressed by a presentiment of evil. Neither he nor Ulf had spoken about the killing of the death spider, but it had never been far from their thoughts. They remembered Jomar's story of the ritual execution of the small band of desert dwellers who had killed a death spider. And they also remembered that, on the day of the sandstorm, two spider balloons had passed overhead. From the moment Niall had looked into the eyes of the death spider until the moment he watched the life drain out of its jointed limbs, only a short time had elapsed—perhaps half a minute. But that was time enough for the dying animal to send out its message of alarm to its companion.

Kazak believed his city to be impregnable. Niall knew this was wishful thinking. He had experienced the power of the spider's will as it tried to paralyze him into immobility. Jomar's story of his own capture told how that power could be used.

A week after the death of Jomar, Niall's foreboding was confirmed. That was the morning when, drinking the dew out of the waru plant, he became aware of the spider balloon bearing down on him. And in the hours that followed, as the armadas of balloons drifted overhead and the fear-probes invaded the burrow, he tried not to allow himself to reflect that he was responsible for this misfortune. Instead, he comforted himself with the thought that, since the spiders were mounting this large-scale search, they could have no clear idea where their quarry was hiding.

Then, as he was falling asleep that night, a sudden thought shocked him into wakefulness. If Ingeld had been captured by the spiders, she could tell them precisely where to look. . . .

Ulf had been struck by the same thought. The next day, as they were eating, he said: "We must leave this place and return to our old home at the foot of the plateau."

Siris, whose eyes were dull with lack of sleep, said: "When?"

"Tonight at dusk. It would be stupid to delay. They will keep coming back until they find us."

Niall looked down at his father's foot, which was still swollen. "Do you think you can walk that far?"

"There is no alternative."

"We need the leaves of the gereth plant," Veig said.

The gereth bush grew on the edge of the desert; its leaves had powerful medicinal properties; mixed into a poultice, they could reduce most swellings within hours.

Niall said: "I saw one when we came back from Dira."

"Where?"

"Not far—perhaps two hours away."

"I will come with you."

Ulf shook his head. "We shall need you here, Veig. There is much to be done if we intend to leave tonight. Niall is old enough to go alone."

So Niall set out as soon as he had finished eating. He carried a woven basket for the leaves, a small gourd of water, and his metal spear. This, fully extended, served as a staff. The sensation of its weight in his right hand gave him a feeling of confidence. With this, he could defend himself against most predators.

There were still at least five hours before midday. If he encountered no problems, he should be home before then.

Niall maintained constant vigilance throughout the ten-mile walk, surveying the ground for the convex hump that indicated the lair of the trapdoor spider, and the sky for spider balloons. He also made a wide detour around large rocks, knowing that scorpions liked to make their homes underneath them. Periodically he concentrated his mind, checking for subconscious warnings of danger. When he was fully alert, a sixth sense would warn him of most dangers in advance. But he encountered nothing more menacing than a big camel spider, which came close enough to see whether he was a rodent or a lizard, decided he was neither, and went on its way. Niall had never understood why solifugids were uninterested in human beings.

A mile beyond the clump of trees where they had once encountered the saga insect, Niall found the gereth bush he had noticed earlier. It stood about four feet high, and its broad, shiny leaves had small red shoots at the upper end, shoots that would turn into pointed flowers. To Niall's surprise, the whole bush was now covered in a silken web, fastened round it like a tent. Peering inside, through the close-woven mesh, he saw dozens of baby spiders, each no more than an inch in diameter. When he touched the web gently with the point of his spear, the mother spider came out of concealment to see what was happening. She was light brown in color and had a big, fat body and very long forelegs, covered with small bristles that looked like thorns. She was about a foot in diameter, and had tiny black eyes that seemed to look at Niall with a kind of intelligence.

Niall had never encountered the tent spider before, and had no idea whether they were poisonous. In order to get at the leaves, he would have to cut the web with his knife. A mother spider defending her young might well decide to attack.

They contemplated each other for several minutes; then the tent spider lost interest and retreated behind one of the broad leaves. Niall sat down where he could see the tip of the forelegs protruding and emptied his mind. It took him only a few seconds to clear his mind of thought and induce the sense of timelessness that was so important to this type of contact. When this happened, he felt for a moment as if he was looking down on the spider from a great height. Then, suddenly, he had become the spider.

This surprised him. When he had attempted to attune his mind to that of the grey desert spiders, he had been aware of them as separate identities. It was as if they had some kind of instinctive defense against his probing. The tent spider seemed to lack such defense. It was as if she recognized no difference between his mind and her own. His consciousness blended naturally with hers. With the grey spiders, there was no blending; they were like oil and water. And with the death spider, there had been active rejection, an attempt to penetrate his mind.

He found this fascinating. It meant that his relation to the tent spider was like the relation of the death spider to himself.

There was a whining sound as a dew fly plunged past his head and into the web. It was attracted by the scent of the red flowers and failed to see the thin, clear strands of web. Instantly, the tent spider was in motion, and Niall became aware that she was hungry. The last few insects that had blundered into her web had escaped, being too large and powerful. But the dew fly, shiny and black, was no more than three inches long, and its feet were entangled in the sticky droplets. In two bounds, the tent spider had approached the fly from the other side of the web and struck with her fangs. The venom was a quick acting nerve poison, and within seconds the fly had begun to struggle in slow motion. With her long forelegs, the tent spider reached through her web and hauled him inside. By this time, she had totally forgotten the intruder watching her; Niall was too big for her to take in. Her mandibles crunched into the soft underbelly of the dew fly, which was still alive but unable to react.

For Niall, it was a disgusting sensation—to be inside the spider's mind as she wolfed down the living flesh. It made him feel sick. Yet he continued to be fascinated by the clarity of the sensations. He was aware of the spider's visual field, which extended all the way round her head, and of her satisfaction as she filled her stomach with the first meal in a day. He had to look at his own arms to convince himself that they were not long legs covered with spiky bristles. He even felt a protective warmth for the baby spiders which clambered around among the leaves and looked for a hole in the web through which they could investigate the blinding sunlit world outside.

He was also aware of a certain instinctive conflict that was taking place inside the spider. She was hungry, and while she was protecting her young, she was unable to hunt for food. (Niall was aware that this primitive spider hunted her prey, lying in wait for passing insects rather than using a web to trap them.) She was also a mother, and knew her children were hungry; she ought to offer them the remains of her feast. But her own hunger overruled the desire to feed her children. She had no real choice; she was wholly ruled by instinct.

Niall deliberately controlled her will, to make her stop eating. Then he made her drop the remains of the dew fly down to her children, who instantly swarmed over it, biting one another in their anxiety to get at the flesh. And, as he felt the mother's unappeased hunger, Niall felt a pang of regret for the joke he had played on her.

It was the strangest—and in some ways the most exciting sensation he had ever known: to be in control of the will of another creature. He felt a strong affection for this spider who had, in a sense, become a part of himself. At the same time he recognized that this was akin to the emotion he had experienced towards Merlew—this desire to mingle his mind with hers and take possession of her will. This, he realized, was why he had found it so exciting when she had kissed him, and when she had nibbled his ear: it had seemed to be an admission that she was willing to subjugate her will to his. That was why he was so shocked and angry to hear himself described as "that skinny boy." He felt that she had set out to cheat him, merely for the pleasure of feeling that his will was subjugated to hers. . . .

His emotions were troubling the tent spider, which had never experienced jealousy, and found it a bewildering and frightening sensation. In spite of her venom and her predilection for eating living creatures, she was fundamentally innocent and vulnerable. This was perhaps the strangest realization of all. He was experiencing a sensation like love for a creature that lived by eating live insects.

Niall carefully parted the strands of the web at the top of the bush and began to gather the leaves. The smallest and thickest made the best medicinal poultices. He was so preoccupied with the sensations of the spider, wondering what was happening to her web, that he failed to notice the shadow that floated past a few feet away. His attention was attracted by the next one, which was like the shadow of a small, swiftly moving cloud. But the sky was cloudless and there was only a light breeze. That was why the spider balloons were drifting past so slowly, and so close to the ground.

As on the previous day, his total absorption allowed him to suppress the fear-reaction before it began. The balloons were so low that it seemed inevitable that he would be seen within moments, and he accepted this with the calm of a man who sees there is no escape. He was standing in the open, with no concealment. He made no movement, looking down on the bush, and allowing his consciousness to merge with that of the spider. They were aware of his presence; of that he was certain. They were aware of the life-field of every living thing on the ground below them. Five minutes passed, and he raised his eyes. The last of the balloons was already floating away from him; he could see clearly the outline of the spider in the semi-transparent bag underneath, its legs folded into a knot.

Now the danger was past, he had to make an effort to prevent a delayed reaction of fear and relief. He sat down on the ground and stared after them. In the distance, to the northwest, he could see the pinnacles of red rock on the horizon. Directly south of these lay the burrow. The spiders were drifting directly towards it. And Niall had no possible doubt that this was their objective.

He was flooded with anguish, a sense of being totally overwhelmed by events. He was, after all, little more than a child; his whole life had been spent under the protection of his family. Now, quite suddenly, it seemed that his world had been shattered. The first reaction was a reversion to childhood, a sense of helplessness that threatened to drown him in terror and self-pity. Then something of his new-found manhood reasserted itself. At the same time, he realized it might still be possible to warn his family. Crossing his legs and bowing his head, he sent out an urgent thought message to his mother. He continued to do this for several minutes, until his concentration wavered and he felt mentally exhausted. He tried again, trying to force his mind to be calm, but his sense of urgency made this impossible. He was totally unable to relax into the receptive state of timelessness in which he could establish contact.

It was a long time before he was able to fight off the feeling of weakness induced by dejection. But the increasing heat made him aware that it would be pointless to sit there any longer. Once he began to walk back in the direction of the burrow, he felt better. He also experienced a certain grim pride in the fact that he was indifferent to the heat. He noted the weariness of his body, the sweat that ran down his sides, with a sense of detachment, as if experiencing someone else's discomfort.

When he came within sight of the organ-pipe cacti, he felt a glow of hope; everything looked normal enough. But while still a hundred yards from the burrow, he knew something was wrong. The large stone and the thorny bush that normally concealed the entrance had been dragged aside; the bush lay ten feet away. Now, suddenly, his misery became so acute that it seemed to burst his chest; it was as sharp as physical pain. He shouted as he ran the last few yards, and his own voice shocked him into a sense of reality.

The body of a man lay upward across the threshold. He could tell it was a man because the naked breast was exposed. For a moment he experienced relief, for the black, swollen face was that of a stranger. Then he recognized the bracelet on the upper arm and knew he was looking at the body of his father. The combination of spider poison and heat had already started the process of decay.

Three oil lamps were still burning. On their last day in the burrow, they had evidently decided that they could afford the extravagance. Baskets containing food and water had been neatly arranged against the wall, and the roll of cloth Niall had brought back from Dira was tied in a bundle. There was no sign of a struggle. The spears stood in their usual place near the door, and a bowl of ant porridge lay, half eaten, on Runa's bed. If it had not been for the decaying corpse across the threshold, Niall could have believed that the family had gone outside for a moment.

He took an oil lamp and searched the rest of the burrow. There was no one there; even the ants had gone.

He had ceased to feel any emotion. The weight of reality seemed to crush his feelings. Even the corpse of his father seemed too real to arouse a response.

He sat on his bed, staring blankly into space, trying to adjust to this new and empty reality. Then his eyes fell on the bowl of porridge, reminding him that Runa and Mara were probably still alive. This stirred him out of his apathy. He went outside and examined the ground. It was dry and hard, but to his trained eye, the few marks on its dusty surface left no doubt of the direction the spiders had taken. They were headed northwest, towards the sea.

Back in the burrow, he nerved himself to move the corpse, pulling it by its clothing onto his father's bed. The face was now so bloated that it looked like a monstrous statue, the teeth showing yellow between the black lips. Niall kept his eyes averted from it. He covered Ulf's body with the cloth from Dira—out of a desire not to look at it rather than any feeling of respect. Then he packed food from the baskets into one of the panniers. He also packed his telescopic spear.

At this point he had no definite plan of action—only a desire to escape his sense of inner desolation by forcing himself to move. If his father's body had not been there, filling the air with an increasingly nauseating stench of decay, he might have stayed in the burrow indefinitely.

As he left, he dragged the stone across the doorway, then spent half an hour sealing it with smaller rocks. The sun was now directly overhead, but he was indifferent to the heat. His intention was to make sure that the burrow should remain impenetrable to insects. The place that had been their home for the past ten years was now Ulf's tomb. He wanted his father to sleep undisturbed until his children could return and give him a warrior's burial.

PART TWO

The Tower

It was fortunate for Niall that he encountered no predators that afternoon. He was in a state of shock and rebellion against fate. He felt that he had been pushed too far, his emotional resources drained dry. If a scorpion or tiger beetle had blocked his path, he would have stared at it with a kind of bored disgust, as if it had somehow come too late. It was pleasant, but a little frightening, to be totally without fear.

He moved fast, following the marks in the sand. The spiders were so light footed that they left little sign of their passage; it was impossible to guess how many there were. The footprints of Veig and Siris were quite clear; from their depth in the soft sand, he could tell that they were carrying burdens—probably Runa and Mara. Yet although he continually strained his eyes towards the horizon, he caught no glimpse of them.

The route lay along the western edge of the rocky wilderness between the burrow and the country of the ants. The main vegetation was thorn and tamarisk; the sand was strewn with black volcanic pebbles. The countryside rose gradually to a range of mountains in the distance; to the east lay the black peaks of spent volcanoes. It was a bare and inhospitable country, and the westerly wind, that had blown over miles of hot grey rock, dried the sweat as fast as it formed on his body. He took pleasure in his feeling of grim indifference to these discomforts. The thought of Ulf's bloated corpse made him feel that physical pain was a boring triviality.

He had lost all sense of time, and was mildly surprised to notice that the sun was not far above the western horizon. The hills were now closer. The earth underfoot was red in color, and there were red rocks stretching into the distance, some of them tall pillars more than a hundred feet high. It was time to look for a place to sleep. But in this bleak land, no spot seemed preferable to any other. Eventually, he came upon a great slab of red stone, buried in the earth at an angle of about thirty degrees. A thorn bush had grown in its shelter. Niall spent half an hour hacking it out of the ground, then smoothing the place where it had grown. Then he ate his evening meal—dried meat and cactus fruit. The taste of the bitter spring water from the depths of the burrow brought a feeling of nostalgia, and a sudden desire to burst into tears. He fought it back, clenching his teeth, and began gathering rocks to make his shelter impregnable to night predators. In this barren land it seemed an unnecessary precaution, but the activity helped him to suppress the increasing feeling of sorrow forcing its way through the numbness.

In the early hours of the morning, he was glad of his precaution. He was awakened by the sound of movement on the other side of the thorn bush. There was now a faint moon, and he could see the outline of some large creature, probably a scorpion. It had detected his presence, perhaps by some involuntary movement in his sleep. His hand reached out and gripped the metal cylinder. He could hear the scraping noise of the creature's armored body on the stones. Then the thorn bush moved. He gripped the nearest branch in both hands, and resisted the pull. Aware of this resistance, the creature began to circle the bush, looking for a point of access. Niall forced himself into a half-sitting position, his head pressed against the sloping rock above; hearing his movements, the creature redoubled its efforts. The moon was reflected briefly from a multifaceted eye. It was attempting to force a gap between the piled rocks and the top of the thorn bush, using its armored shoulders as a wedge. Niall felt the light touch of a feeler against his foot. Leaning forward, he pressed hard on the side of the cylinder; with a click, it slid open; at the same time, Niall jabbed with all his strength. There was a hiss of pain, and the thorn bush was pulled several feet. Expecting at any moment to feel jaws closing on his flesh, Niall again jabbed into the darkness with his spear. It connected again, sinking into something soft. Then the creature turned, and he saw the glint of moonlight on its scaly back as it scuttled off. Whatever it was, it had decided that its intended prey had a dangerous sting. Niall dragged the bush back into position, then lay down again, the spear beside him. When he opened his eyes again, it was dawn. He lay and watched the sun rise, shivering in the chilly air, then ate some dried meat, washed it down with water, and set off once more towards the hills.

As the ground rose, the air was cooler; the atmosphere was warm and hazy. Although the ground was too hard to show traces of footprints, he was certain that his family had already passed this way; the worn, overgrown track had once been an ancient road, and was the obvious route to the main pass across the hills. In one place where it descended into a narrow valley, dust had accumulated, and he could once again discern clearly the footprints of Siris and Veig, and the lighter marks made by the spiders.

A few miles farther on, he came upon a cistern by the side of the road. It had been made of large slabs of granite, evidently transported from elsewhere; it was about two feet wide, its top half covered with a large, flat stone. The water was very clear, and there was green lichen clinging to the walls below the surface. Niall took his cup from his pack—it had been carved out of wood by Jomar—and dipped it into the water; it was startlingly cold. After drinking his fill, Niall poured water over his head and shoulders, laughing aloud with relief and delight as the cold water made channels through the dust on his skin.

There were also clear signs that his mother and brother had halted there; he recognized the mark of a sandal they had brought as a present from Sefna to her sister. Yet although he searched the ground minutely, he could find no sign of the footprints of the children.

As he stared into the water, and at the moss-covered stones that had fallen into it, he experienced a glow of awakening energy, immediately extinguished by the thought of his dead father. But it was the first time in two days that he had felt that spontaneous upsurge of pure joy in being alive. He stared into the water, allowing his mind to relax as if sinking into the cool depths, with their green-shaded lights. He felt as if he were relaxing into a comfortable bed; yet his mind remained as wide awake as ever. Part of his consciousness was aware of his wet hair, of the sun beating down on his back, of the hardness of the ground against his knees; another part was floating in the shadowy coolness, drifting peacefully as if time had come to a stop.

Then, suddenly, the water had disappeared, and he was looking at his brother Veig. Veig was lying on his back, his eyes closed, his head propped against the roots of a tree. He was obviously exhausted, for his mouth hung open and his face looked grey and lifeless. But he was not dead, for his chest was heaving. Perched close to his head, a few inches away, was the pepsis wasp. It seemed to be guarding him in his sleep.

His mother was seated nearby, drinking water in tiny sips from a gourd. She also looked tired, and her face was covered with black streaks where perspiration had mixed with the dust of travel.

Without being aware of how he knew it, Niall realized that this scene was taking place at this moment. He noted there was no sign of the two children, and that the four spiders who were stretched out in the sunlight were brown and not black. By merely transferring his attention, he was able to examine them as carefully as if he were standing beside them. Their bodies were covered with brown, velvety hair. Their faces, seen from in front, looked oddly human, for they had two enormous black eyes under a kind of forehead. Under these there was a curved row of smaller eyes, and under these, a protuberance that looked like a flat nose. The chelicerae with their folded fangs resembled a beard. Both the front legs and the chelicerae looked very powerful. The abdominal section was smaller and slimmer than in most spiders. When one of them heaved itself to its feet to turn its face into the glare of the sun, it conveyed an impression of muscular strength and athleticism. These creatures actually seemed to enjoy the sunlight.

Niall had never seen a wolf spider before, but it was obvious to him that these were hunting spiders, who captured their prey by sheer speed. He also observed that there were two more large, black eyes at the back of the head, giving them all-around vision.

The countryside around them was not unlike the country of the ants: a green plain with trees and bushes; he could see red berries on the nearest bush. There were also palm trees and tall cedars. But his vision was limited to the area in the immediate vicinity of the spiders.

Niall was also interested to observe that he was aware of what was taking place in the minds of the drowsing wolf spiders. Because they hunted their prey, rather than waiting for it to blunder into a trap, their mental outlook seemed closer to that of human beings rather than to that of web-building spiders, and their thought processes were somehow active rather than passive. This velvet-brown spider whose face was now receiving the force of the midday sun was thinking about how many days it would take to get back home again. Niall tried to grasp what it meant by "home," and glimpsed a bewildering picture of an immense city full of towers— incredible square towers, full of windows. Between these towers stretched spider webs, their strands as thick as his grass rope. And in one of these strange towers lurked a being whose name filled everyone with fear. When Niall tried to grasp the source of this fear, he seemed to find himself in a vast, dark hall across which stretched hundreds of grey cobwebs. And from somewhere in its darkest corner, down a tunnel of cobwebs, black eyes were watching him with the cold curiosity of a death spider.

Now, suddenly, Niall began to experience a disquietude that made his flesh crawl. Until this moment, he had felt himself a detached observer, bodiless and therefore invulnerable. Now, staring into the eyes that watched him from among the cobwebs, he felt for the first time as if he were actually there in the dark hall, being studied by a totally merciless intelligence. As the disquietude hardened into dread, Niall instinctively closed his eyes; the vision immediately vanished, and he found himself looking once more into the clear water of the cistern, and at the slimy green moss that had grown on its sides.

He looked round nervously, and was relieved to find himself alone. In spite of the heat of the day, his body felt icy cold. And although he was now back in the country of barren red sandstone, he continued to feel that the black eyes were watching him from amid the tangle of cobwebs. It took several minutes for this impression to fade.

As his skin began to absorb the sun's heat, he realized with surprise that he was hungry. In the stress and misery of the past two days he had felt little or no desire for food. Now his appetite was back again. He ate slowly, crunching some of the dry, biscuit-like bread they had brought from Dira, and enjoying the luxury of washing it down with draughts of cold water.

When he had refilled the gourd with spring water, he relaxed in the shade of a thorn tree—first jabbing between the roots with his spear to make sure there were no centipedes. Lying there, staring at the milky blue sky through the branches, he became aware that his natural optimism had returned with his appetite. It was plain to him now that, since his father's death, a cloud had descended on his mind and turned him into a sleepwalker. Now it was as if he was awake again, and his powers of reason had begun to reassert themselves.

Ever since he had left the burrow, his energies had been directed to a single purpose: to join his family. Without thinking about it clearly, he had accepted that this would involve allowing himself to become a captive of the spiders.

But then he had made the natural assumption that his family was in the hands of the death spiders. Now he knew this was not so, the situation looked altogether less hopeless. If he allowed himself to be taken prisoner, the brown hunting spiders would be in a position to watch his every movement. But while he was free, he could watch them—and watch for an opportunity to free his family. . . .

Before he could do that, he had to catch up with them. Reluctantly—for his body still ached with tiredness—he heaved himself to his feet, pulled on his pack, and resumed the climb to the top of the pass.

The road wound upward between columns of weatherworn sandstone, which in places lay across the road as if hurled there by an earthquake. The higher he climbed, the steeper the path became. From this height, he could look back on the route he had traveled; on the far horizon lay the great plateau, surrounded by desert. He seemed to be the only creature alive in this immense, empty landscape. For a long time he stared at it—the land in which his whole life had so far been spent. Then he turned and forced his aching legs to climb the last thousand feet to the summit.

Suddenly he felt the breeze blowing cool against the sweat on his body; it was being channelled between high sandstone cliffs, and it carried a smell that he had never encountered before—a sharp, clean scent that made his heart lift. Ten minutes later, he was looking down on a strip of green plain, beyond which lay the immense expanse of the sea. Even at this distance, the strong, sharp wind carried the smell of salt spray. An enormous exultation made his heart expand. He felt that he was looking at a land that he had known in the remote past, at a time long before spiders were lords of the earth.

It was already late afternoon; if he wanted to reach the plain before dusk, he would have to start now. He raised the gourd to his mouth, to moisten his throat before beginning the long descent. As he did so, a voice in his ear said clearly: "Niall, be careful."

The shock almost made him drop the gourd; the water he was drinking went down the wrong way and made him choke. He had expected to see his mother standing behind him; but there was no one. Neither was there any cover where someone could hide. He was standing in the middle of the road, the sheer cliffs rising on either side.

He felt so shaken that he sat down on the nearest rock. It was only then, trying to reconstruct the sensation, that he decided that the voice had not spoken in his ear, but inside his head.

He stared down at the flat green plain below, with its trees and bushes. He could see no sign of living creatures. Yet somewhere down there, Siris was watching him. She must have seen him outlined against the skyline. And if she had been watching for him, he could be certain that the brown hunting spiders had also been watching.

As he gazed at the plain, trying to guess where the hidden eyes were concealed, her voice spoke again. "Go back. Go back." This time it was undoubtedly inside his chest, and it seemed to be an impulse rather than a verbal message.

He looked behind him, over the path he had traveled, and knew it was pointless to tell him to go back. There was nowhere to go. He might succeed in hiding in a cave or gulley for a few hours. But discovery would be inevitable. This bare landscape offered no concealment.

He was left with two choices: to stay where he was, or to go forward. He chose without hesitation. It was better to act than to do nothing. He swung the pannier onto his shoulders, and started on the long downhill road to the plain.

As soon as he began to move, he felt surprisingly light-hearted. Niall was too young and inexperienced to know real fear. Faced with the same choice, his father or grandfather would unhesitatingly have chosen flight and concealment—not out of fear, but out of recognition that a man who allowed himself to fall into the hands of the spiders had virtually condemned himself to life imprisonment. It was Niall's ignorance that enabled him to march towards captivity without deep misgivings. Because the future was unknown, it seemed full of promise.

The downhill road was straighter, and therefore steeper, than the southern approach to the pass; it made the calves of his legs ache. As he descended towards the plain, the sea disappeared beyond the horizon, and some of the lightness went out of his heart. But he was excited at the thought of seeing his mother and brother again, and strained his eyes continually for any sign of movement on the green expanse below. There were many locations where the spiders might have lain in concealment, and as he approached such places, his heart contracted with tension. But when, after two hours, the road became less steep, and the nearest trees were only a few hundred yards ahead, he began to wonder if he was mistaken to believe the spiders knew of his presence. The thought brought a twinge of disappointment. Now there were no large rocks ahead, not even a bush that was large enough to conceal a grasshopper. . . .

This thought was passing through his mind as his eye caught a blur of movement at the edge of his vision. Then he was hurled forward onto the ground with such force that the breath was knocked from his body. Powerful forelegs seized him and turned him over; his arms pressed to his sides, he was lifted clear of the ground. He screamed as he found himself looking into black, featureless eyes, while unfolded fangs were raised to strike. Instinctively, he froze, hoping to disarm the aggression by immobility. Then claws seized him from behind; he felt the pannier removed from his back, and a loop of sticky silk passed around his body, pinioning his arms.

When the first shock had passed, he became oddly calm. It may have been the humanoid look of the faces that reassured him. They might have been intelligent lobsters, with the faces of old men. At close quarters, the hunting spiders had a peculiar, musky smell which was not unpleasant. When unfolded, their fangs were terrifying; but when folded into the chelicerae, they looked not unlike two elaborately curled bunches of hair at the end of a beard. After those first few terrifying seconds, when Niall expected to be injected with poison, he understood that they had no intention of harming him, and allowed them to see, by his passivity, that he had no intention of trying to escape.

The spider that held him raised his body clear of the ground so the other spider could tie his ankles. While moist, the silk had an elastic, pliable quality; yet although scarcely thicker than a blade of marram grass, it seemed virtually unbreakable. Niall's ankles felt glued together.

When his arms and legs had been secured, Niall was swung over onto the spider's back, and held there by its pedipalps—the nearest thing a spider possesses to a pair of arms—and then, suddenly, they were in motion, flying over the hard ground at a speed that made his head whirl. The spider ran with a loping motion, so Niall bounced up and down with every long stride. When, periodically, he seemed about to fall sideways off the velvety back, the spider reached up with its forelegs, without breaking its stride, and readjusted his position. Behind them ran the other wolf spider, carrying Niall's pack.

Niall had often seen the camel spider—or solifugid—traveling across the desert at this speed, looking like a ball of windblown grass; he had never expected to look down on the ground as it flashed past his eyes at fifty miles an hour. He tried turning his head sideways and focusing his eyes on the horizon; this made him feel less dizzy, but the bumping of his head against the spider's back made it impossible to keep his gaze fixed for more than a few moments at a time. Finally he closed his eyes, gritting his teeth, and concentrated on enduring the jerky motion that made the blood roar in his ears.

Then, quite suddenly, he was lying on the ground, and there was a face looking down at him. A moment later, he recognized the familiar smell of his mother's hair as she held him tight against her and kissed his face. Then Veig helped him into a sitting position and held a cup with water to his lips. His mouth felt dry, and his throat was full of dust, so he coughed violently when he tried to swallow. He realized that his hands and legs were now free, although the skin was torn where the sticky web had been pulled away.

His senses cleared; he realized he must have fainted. The spider on whose back he had traveled—the largest of the four, and obviously the leader was standing there, looking at him with its featureless black eyes; the line between its mouth and the folded chelicerae looked like a pair of downturned lips, pursed in disapproval, while the row of smaller eyes below the main ones looked like some curious disfigurement, a row of shiny, black warts. It was not even breathing heavily.

Veig said: "Do you feel strong enough to walk?"

"I think so." He stood up unsteadily. Siris began to cry.

"They say we have to move on," Veig said.

The contents of his pack, he saw, had been emptied out on the ground, and one of the spiders was examining them one by one, prodding them with its foreleg or with a pedipalp. It picked up the metal tube, looked at it briefly, and tossed it down among the prickly pears and dried bread. At the same time, Niall felt the mind of the big spider probing his own. It was trying to observe his reaction to this search of his belongings. But its insight was crude and uncomprehending. It probed his mind as clumsily as the other spider was examining the contents of his pack, as if prodding with a blunt finger.

Then its attention was distracted; the other spider was looking with interest at the folded sheet of spider silk Niall used as a sleeping bag. The big spider went and examined it carefully, and Niall could feel the impulses of communication that passed between them. Their language was not verbal; it consisted of a series of feelings and intuitions. Neither of them could say: "I wonder where this came from?" but what passed between them was a questioning impulse, accompanied by an image of the death spider that had vanished in the desert. Simultaneously—their minds seemed to work in concert—both spiders recognized that this silk was too old to be the death spider's balloon, and they immediately lost interest in it.

Suddenly both spiders became alert. Niall could see no obvious reason for this sudden vigilance. The big spider hurried off to a nearby thorn tree. When Niall looked more closely, he could see that they had spun a web between the lower branches and the trunk. A big grasshopper had jumped straight into it and was struggling frantically. It made no sound—the spiders in any case were deaf—but the vibrations of its panic had instantly communicated themselves.

While they watched, the big spider paralyzed the grasshopper with one swift jab of its fang, detached it from the web by biting through its strands, then proceeded to eat it. It was obviously hungry.

Niall took the opportunity to ask the question that had been constantly on his mind. "Where are Runa and Mara?"

"They took them off in balloons."

"And the wasp and the ants?"

Veig nodded towards the spiders. "Inside them," he said drily.

A moment later, a violent blow knocked him forward on his face. One of the spiders was standing over him, its fangs extended ready to strike. When Veig tried to sit up, it pushed him down again with a blow of its powerful foreleg. Veig lay passively, looking up at the exposed fang that hovered threateningly over his face. Once again, Niall felt his own mind probed by the leader, which had now finished its meal. It wanted to gauge his reaction to the threat to his brother. Niall was glad that his chief emotion was anxiety; he felt intuitively that any sign of anger or aggression would have been punished instantly.

When it had made its point—that talking was not allowed—the spider moved away and allowed Veig to sit up. Then it prodded Niall with its pedipalp and indicated the contents of his pack; it was clearly an order to replace them. As Niall did this, he again felt the mind of the leader probing his own. He observed with satisfaction that he was able to keep his mind empty and passive, and that the spider seemed satisfied.

Five minutes later they were on the move again. Siris looked weary and drained of emotion. Niall could sense that she was still in a state of shock at the death of her husband, and separation from the girls. He could also sense that her delight in seeing him again was neutralized by a feeling of despair that he was now a prisoner. She seemed to feel guilty, as if this was her fault. Niall longed to talk to her; but under the continual surveillance of the spiders, this was impossible.

The spiders moved fast, and they expected their prisoners to keep up with them. Now, at last, Niall could understand how they had covered so much ground. For them, human walking speed was an unbearably slow crawl. So the prisoners were forced to move at a trot, while the spiders marched alongside at what was, for them, a leisurely walking pace. At first Niall was hampered by the pack on his back, which bounced up and down. When the leader noticed this, it took it from him, and one of the others was made to carry it. It was a relief to be free of the burden.

With more leisure for observation, Niall would have enjoyed the countryside through which they were now passing. He had never seen anywhere so green. This fertile coastal plain had once been rich farmland—they passed more than one half-ruined farmhouse—and had now been allowed to return to its natural state, with many varieties of trees and tangled grass underfoot. Insects hummed past them—flies, wasps, dragonflies—and grasshoppers chirped in the undergrowth. To Niall it appeared a kind of paradise, and it seemed ironic that he should be seeing it for the first time as a prisoner.

An hour later, with the sun sinking behind the mountains, they halted for the night. The humans were all exhausted; they flung themselves on the ground, their faces turned to the sky, breathing deeply. One of the spiders began to spin a web under the nearest low tree, while the others basked in the evening sunlight. As the pounding of Niall's heart subsided, he drifted off into a pleasant state of relaxation. Momentarily, he felt the mind of the leader probe his own; but it was obviously a matter of routine, and he could sense its lack of interest. In a semi-dreamlike state, he tuned in to the minds of the spiders. It was rather like overhearing their conversation, except that he was also aware of their physical sensations. At the moment, their chief concern was hunger. Spiders, he now realized, ate only living food, so could not carry their rations with them when they were traveling. It was not simply that they preferred the taste of fresh meat; there was something else—something about the life-force itself—that they enjoyed and absorbed.

It also became clear to Niall that, compared to human beings, these creatures were almost entirely the slaves of instinct. For millions of years they had been little more than food-catching machines whose whole lives centered on seizing their prey and injecting it with venom. They had no other interest in life. Niall could enjoy the scenery and think about distant places, use his imagination. The wolf spiders were indifferent to the scenery, except as a possible source of food, and totally lacked anything that might be called imagination.

Fortunately, they were surrounded by an abundance of food. Before the light had faded, the web had caught half a dozen meat flies, two wasps and a butterfly, and these had immediately been paralyzed and handed to the spiders in order of rank. As they ate their living prey, their minds became a glow of immense satisfaction. Niall realized with alarm that part of their hostility towards human beings was that they regarded them as potential food; when they were hungry, it seemed a waste to be escorting these prisoners instead of eating them. But as soon as they had satisfied their appetite, this irritability disappeared. They made no attempt to prevent the prisoners from gathering fruit from the bushes, and watched with tolerance as Niall climbed a coconut palm and tossed down the green coconuts into Veig's waiting hands. The humans found the slightly astringent milk deliciously refreshing, ideal for washing down the dried rodent flesh and stale bread. With a good meal inside them, their spirits began to revive. A curious atmosphere of mutual tolerance built up between the humans and the spiders. Niall became aware that these huge, immensely powerful creatures were the slaves of the death spiders; their attitude towards their masters was one of respect, but with an undertone of fear and resentment. They disliked obeying orders and would have preferred to be free to lie in the sun and catch insects. Even web-building was not natural to them. They did it because it was the simplest way of catching food; but their natural inclination was to catch their prey with swiftness and strength. Hunting gave them the deepest satisfaction they knew.

He was so tired that he slept that night without a covering, on a makeshift bed of grass and leaves. When he opened his eyes again it was dawn, and one of the spiders was already devouring a flying beetle that had been caught in the web. The other spiders were dozing in the sun; unlike the death spiders, these hunters had no love for the hours of darkness, and the return of daylight filled them with a drowsy satisfaction. Observing their lazy, slow-moving minds, Niall was reminded of the ants. It filled him with a peculiar excitement, this ability to understand the minds of his captors. All his life, he had been terrified of the spiders. Now some deep intuition told him that this conquest of fear was the beginning of a far greater conquest.

They ate a breakfast of fruit and dried meat, washed down again with the milk of the green coconut. The spiders had by this time eaten their fill—as the sun rose, an abundance of flying insects blundered into their web. When he came close to this web, Niall observed that it had a pleasant, sweetish smell; this was obviously what attracted the insects.

Veig whispered: "I wonder what we're waiting for?"

Niall said: "They're waiting." He hesitated, unable to finish the sentence.

"I *know* that. But what for?"

"For . . . for someone. For . . . people."

Veig and Siris both looked at him curiously.

"How did you know that?"

Niall shrugged and shook his head. It was a subject he was not willing to discuss in front of the spiders.

Half an hour went by. The sun was hot, but there was a pleasant breeze from the north. The humans moved into the shade of a thorn tree, while the spiders continued to doze in the sun; they seemed to be able to absorb a degree of heat that would have given a human being sunstroke. One of them rolled on its back, exposing its grey, soft underbelly to the warmth. The spiders were so confident of their ability to read the minds of human beings that they felt no need to take precautions.

Niall decided to try an experiment. He was curious to know how far the spiders would respond to purely mental danger signals. He imagined taking the metal tube out of his pannier, making it expand into a spear, and driving it into the spider's exposed belly. The spider showed no reaction. Next, Niall imagined picking up a large, flat stone that lay nearby, and bringing it down with all his strength on the head of the dozing spider. Once again, there was no reaction. He was aware that this was because he was merely toying with the idea, with no intention of putting it into practice. So he deliberately made a powerful effort of imagination, and tried to envisage what it would be like to stroll over to the flat stone, then to raise it above his head and dash it down on the upturned belly. This time, the spider became uncomfortable; it moved its head so its eyes could see in all directions, and rolled over onto its stomach. It glanced suspiciously at the human beings, and Niall felt the clumsy probe of its mind. He relaxed his own mind into drowsy immobility, deliberately creating a mental wave-length of a tent spider. The spider's vigilance relaxed, and after a few seconds, its mind again fell into the soothing, repetitive rhythm of physical pleasure.

Then, suddenly, the leader became alert; it sprang to its feet—Niall again had an opportunity to observe the swiftness of its reactions—and stared intently towards the north. Niall listened, but could hear nothing but the normal sounds of the morning. It was at least another minute before he was able to detect the sound of movement in the bushes. Again, he marveled at the acuteness of the spider's senses.

A moment later, he was amazed to see the figure of a man emerging from among the trees. At the same instant, the reaction of the spiders told him that this was what they had been waiting for.

The man who now marched confidently towards them was a magnificent specimen, well over six feet tall, with powerful shoulders and a deep chest. He wore a woven tunic, and his shoulder-length blond hair was held round his head with a circlet of metal. For a brief moment, Niall thought he was looking at Hamna, then, as the man came closer, knew he was a stranger.

Ten feet away, the man came to a halt, fell on one knee, and made a gesture of obeisance to the spiders. The leader sent out a brusque impulse of acknowledgement that also contained an element of impatience, as if to ask: "Where have you been?" The man's attitude expressed total subservience. The spider transmitted a mental order that signified: "Very well, let's go," and the man again inclined his head.

Niall expected the newcomer to greet them, or at least, to exchange a glance of sympathy. In fact, he ignored them. In response to a gesture from the leader, he picked up Niall's pannier and slung it on his back, then stood there, waiting for the next order. Niall studied his face with interest. The eyes were mild and blue, and there was a hint of weakness in the downturned mouth and unassertive chin. He moved with a precision that Niall at first took to be self-assurance, but which he soon recognized as the indifference of a well-trained animal.

When Siris stood up, and used a short length of grass-rope to tie back her long hair, the man eyed her with momentary interest. But it lasted only a fraction of a second. Then he looked back at the spiders, waiting for orders. It was obvious that he felt no fellow-feeling for the captives.

The big spider gave the order to march, and the man set off towards the north, walking with long, swift strides. Niall, Siris, and Veig were made to follow, all three obliged to break into a trot to keep up with the newcomer. The spiders walked behind at their own leisurely pace; Niall could sense their relief that the main part of their journey was over.

Once he had established that the spiders were communicating amongst themselves, Niall tried to tune in to the mind of the man in front. He found it a frustrating exercise. His mind seemed as blank and indifferent as that of a grey desert spider. But, unlike the desert spiders, he seemed totally unaware that Niall was trying to probe his thoughts and feelings. This was not because his mind was attentive and vigilant, but because his attention was directed solely at the outside world. He was indifferent to everything else.

Because the newcomer set the pace, the journey was less exhausting than on the previous day. They were refreshed after a good night's sleep, and the cool breeze was pleasant. Niall found the smell of sun-warmed vegetation intoxicating. Soon he heard a sound that was new to him: the cry of seagulls. His blood tingled with excitement. And when, ten minutes later, they reached the top of a low rise and looked down on the sea, he experienced a surge of exultation that made him want to laugh aloud. This was quite unlike the salt lake of Thellam. It was a deeper blue, and it stretched as far as the eye could see. Waves crashed onto the beach where three small craft were waiting, and salt spray blew against his face like rain. This great expanse of salt water, with its white-capped waves, seemed the most beautiful thing he had ever seen.

There were people lying on the sand; when the big man shouted, they scrambled hastily to their feet and stood to attention. Then, when they saw the spiders, they all dropped on one knee and made gestures of obeisance. The big man shouted an order, and they again stood to attention. Niall was surprised to realize that there were women among them: strong, big-breasted women with hair even longer than his mother's. They stared straight in front of them, their arms down by their sides, while the breeze whipped their hair round their faces. Even when Niall and Veig stood directly in front of them, their eyes did not waver. Niall, who was totally unacquainted with military discipline, found it bizarre and rather disquieting. These human beings were trying to pretend that they were trees or stones.

The men, he saw, were as well built as their guide, and all had the same muscular arms and thighs. But their faces, while handsome and impressive, somehow lacked individuality. The women—there were three of them—were all beautiful, with slim, strong bodies and well-shaped features. Like the men, they wore no covering on the upper part of their bodies, and their bare breasts were suntanned. Veig surveyed them with incredulous delight, like a hungry man presented with a good meal.

The big man shouted an order in a language Niall found incomprehensible; the men and women broke ranks, and began to haul the ships into the water. Each of these craft was about thirty feet long, and had a curved prow and stern. Once they were afloat, the spiders approached the shoreline and halted within ten feet of the breaking waves. They folded their legs underneath them; then two men approached each one, lifted them, and carried them into the boats, holding them well clear of the waves. After this, the women clambered in, one to each boat. Niall, Veig, and Siris were also ordered to separate, one to each craft; Niall found himself sharing a boat with the big spider and one of his subordinates.

These long, graceful vessels were of the type that had once carried Vikings over northern seas, built of overlapping planks, with a deep keel. The center of the ship broadened, then narrowed again towards the stern, giving it an outline that resembled a swan. In the middle of the boat was a canvas tent, in which the big spider had been housed; its subordinate was in a kind of basket sheltered by the prow. Niall could sense that both were deeply uneasy; travel by sea ran counter to their strongest instincts.

Niall was fascinated by everything about the long ships. To the men who traveled in them, they were cramped and uncomfortable, but for Niall they were miracles of mysterious craftsmanship. They had no decks and—apart from the canvas tent—no shelter. Wooden seats ran along either side, and each side of the ship had seven oar-holes with rowlocks. The central space was reserved for the mast, which was lying flat in the bottom, and for barrels and ropes. Niall was ordered into a seat in the stern. His pack was handed to him. There he sat, trying to be inconspicuous, absorbing everything that went on around him. The men sat facing him on their benches and unshipped their oars. The woman stood on a low wooden platform with a supporting rail, facing the rowers. A man with a long pole pushed out the ship until it was a dozen yards from the shore and well clear of the other two craft. Then, at an order from the woman, the men leaned forward and heaved on their oars. The woman began a rhythmic chant, beating time with her hands; the oarsmen rowed perfectly in time. Niall felt so exhilarated as they surged forward into the waves that he felt like shouting for joy.

Not all the men were rowing; half of them sat on benches between the oars, or strolled up and down the gangway, talking amongst themselves. Niall also stood up and looked over the side, and no one seemed to object. The sight of the waves breaking against the prow of the boat struck him as unutterably beautiful.

Listening carefully to the men, he now realized that they were not speaking some foreign tongue. Their language was recognizably the same as his own, but strangely accented, so he had to strain his attention to understand it. And when the woman shouted orders in the same language, it again became incomprehensible.

The woman, he soon recognized, was the most important person on board. In all the men he sensed an attitude of respect, even of worship. This was understandable—she was tall, and had corn-colored hair and perfect teeth—but Niall sensed that it was not her beauty they admired so much. When, after half an hour or so, she beckoned one of the men and ordered him to take her place on the platform, he dropped onto one knee and kissed her hand, then remained in that position until she stepped down. As she walked down the central aisle of the boat, the seamen hastened to make way for her. When she snapped her fingers, one of them handed her a garment of some animal skin with which she covered her shoulders. The wind was becoming chilly. A little later, the woman strolled over to Niall who was now sitting, trying to keep warm—and looked down at him with an expression of mingled curiosity and contempt. He found it easy to read her mind. She was thinking—although without words—"This one won't be of much use." Something in her contemptuous gaze reminded him of the princess Merlew, and the memory of humiliation still made him wince.

The spiders had relapsed into a state of miserable passivity, and the woman seemed to know this. On this boat, she, not the spiders, was the supreme commander. When Niall turned his attention to the big spider in his canvas tent, he was surprised at the depth of its fear and anxiety. It was afloat on an element over which it had no control; every heave or roll of the ship made it feel sick. It was totally indifferent to everything except its nausea and desire to be back on dry land.

When they had been at sea for about two hours, another relay of oarsmen took over; they did this by sitting beside an oarsman and allowing him to slip away, so that not a stroke was lost. The men who had been relieved flung themselves flat in the center aisle and gave themselves up to the bliss of relaxation; this was so strong that Niall could feel it flowing around him in waves, producing a delicious light-heartedness.

Towards midday, the wind dropped, then changed round to the southeast. The woman shouted an order. The sailors who had been drowsing in the sun leapt to their feet and raised the mast. This fitted into a receptacle made from a hollowed tree trunk. Then a triangular sail was raised. Niall was curious to see how the ship could continue to sail due north when the wind was blowing from the southeast, and was fascinated by the movable boom that allowed the sail to be moved around to catch the wind at the right angle. His ability to read the minds of the sailors made it possible for him to understand exactly what they were doing.

Now the ship was under sail, the oarsmen could relax. Food was served, and Niall was handed a plate. He was very hungry, and the food seemed exquisite—soft white bread, nuts, and a creamy white drink that he had never tasted before—it was, in fact, cow's milk. A man came and sat beside him, and tried to make conversation, but Niall found his accent impossible to follow. When he tried to understand by tuning in to the man's mind, he found this equally frustrating—it seemed to be almost a blank, a mere response to his physical sensations. The man soon gave up and moved off to talk to someone else. Niall was relieved to be left alone. It seemed strange that such magnificent physical specimens should have such oddly feeble minds.

The food made him sleepy, and he lay on the floor and dozed, his head on his pack. But after a pleasant and peaceful sleep, he began to experience a nightmare in which he seemed to be choking and feeling sick. As his senses returned, he became aware that his mind was picking up the acute mental distress of the two spiders. The reason, he soon realized, was that the ship was plunging up and down with increased violence; the wind had risen so that it took three men to control the sail. The sky was full of dark clouds. He stood up and looked over the side. The other two boats were in sight, about half a mile away, and the wind was driving them forward at tremendous speed. But it was also becoming stronger by the moment. A wave suddenly broke over the side of the ship, covering them all with spray. Yet the sailors seemed unconcerned. They had sailed in worse weather than this and had total confidence in their ship.

When another gust of wind seemed to threaten to turn the ship on its side, the commander ordered the men to lower the sail. Oarsmen again took their places on the benches. At that moment, the rain began to fall; but Niall could hardly distinguish it from the salt spray. He experienced a tremendous feeling of exhilaration, the sheer joy of a desert dweller for whom water has always represented the rarest of blessings.

Another wave burst over the side, and some of the rowers were swept off their benches. It made no difference; others took their places immediately, and continued to heave rhythmically, their powerful bodies shiny with the spray. Others seized wooden vessels and began bailing out the water that now surged up and down the gangway. When the ship almost stood on end on its stern, the water flooded into the canvas tent; a moment later, the flaps parted, and the big spider looked out. The velvety fur was plastered flat with water, and it seemed to radiate misery and helplessness. The woman saw it, and immediately pushed it back into the tent, pulling the flaps closed. The spider in the prow was lying in the bottom of its basket, from which the water ran in streams, its legs tightly bunched beneath it; only a movement in the black eyes betrayed that it was alive.

Looking over the side to see how the other ships were faring, Niall saw the big wave coming and braced himself to meet it, ducking his head. For a moment, the ship seemed to be full of water, and about to turn over. Then, miraculously, it righted itself. Niall felt something touching his icy flesh; looking down, he saw the forelegs of the spider locked round his waist; it had been washed out onto the deck. He could sense that it was mindless with fear, and would strike at him with his fangs if he tried to make it release its grip. So he stood there, clinging to the side, while the water flooded around his waist. Suddenly, the spider released its grip and was swept down the gangway as the ship plunged into another deep trough in the waves.

Niall's instinct was to respond to its misery and despair. He was feeling curiously unconcerned about the water that surged around him and threatened to knock him down. He had seen the ship survive one tremendous wave, and realized that it was buoyant as a cork. Even if filled with water, it would still not sink. And the wide, flat bottom and the deep keel meant that it would be almost impossible to turn over. All Niall had to do was to make sure that he was not swept overboard. And when a coil of rope almost knocked his feet from under him, he seized the opportunity to tie one end round his waist and the other to the wooden capstan that held the anchor rope.

When the spider was washed back towards him, and seemed in danger of being swept over the side, Niall grabbed it by its forelegs and pulled it against him. It recognized this as a gesture of assistance and tried to wind its other legs around him. Since the spider was bigger than he was, this was impossible, and the next plunge of the boat almost wrenched it away again. The problem seemed to be that its body was more buoyant than Niall's, so each surge of water threatened to throw it the length of the ship. And, unlike human hands, the claws at the end of its legs were pathetically inadequate for taking a grip on the sides of the boat.

It was obvious to Niall that it needed something it could cling to. The safest place, quite obviously, was the basket, which was firmly attached to its place inside the great curving hollow of the prow. When the ship rode up a wave, this hollow filled with water; but at least it offered a kind of security. Niall staggered forward, hampered by the spider—whose fangs were still extended in instinctive response to terror—and steadied himself against the curving upright of the prow, which reared above him like a striking snake. For a few moments, the ship was level as it reached the bottom of a wave. Deliberately using his mind, Niall tried to make the spider understand that it should return to its place in the prow, and cling to the woven sides of the basket, whose lattice-like projections offered a grip for its claws. As another wave almost forced him to release his grip, the spider seemed to grasp what he was trying to convey; it released his body and, like some huge cat, heaved itself back into its basket. A moment later, another wave almost threw Niall on top of it; the prow filled with water; but when it subsided a moment later, the spider was still clinging to the sides of the basket.

Someone tapped him on the shoulder; it was the commander. She offered Niall a wooden bucket, and in sign language told him to start bailing. Niall tried to obey, but found it difficult; since he was at least a foot shorter than most of the sailors, he had to raise the full bucket above his head, and most of the water blew back on him. He sat down and clung to the bench.

There was a ripping sound, and Niall suddenly found himself engulfed in wet canvas; the wind had snapped two of the ropes holding the tent, tearing it from top to bottom. Now it was flapping like some huge sail. The spider inside it was hurled like a stone from a sling against one of the oarsmen, and knocked him backwards off his bench; then Niall found himself sharing his own bench with the struggling spider. He tried to extricate himself; as he did so, the ship lurched on to its side. The canvas struck him a violent blow on the shoulder. With a strange sense of slow motion, Niall found himself being carried over the side.

It all happened so quickly that there was no time for alarm. The wave carried him backwards, plunged him down to a depth of six feet, then brought him, blinded and gasping, back to the surface. As his gaze cleared, he saw the ship righting itself. The rope jerked at his waist, almost lifting him out of the water. In the momentarily calm sea, he grabbed it with both hands and tried to heave himself towards the ship. At that moment, he felt an arm groping at his back, trying to pull him down, and for an instant experienced total, blind panic. A hairy foreleg tried to wrap itself round his neck. Automatically, he lashed out with his feet, trying to kick himself free. The sea did the rest; the spider's grip was broken and it was swept away from him.

As this happened, Niall found himself staring for a moment into the expressionless black eyes, and he experienced its sense of despair and hopelessness as clearly as if it had called out to him. Quite suddenly, his own fear vanished. The spider was asking for aid, fully aware that Niall held the key to its life or death. Niall's instinctive response was to release his grip on the rope and launch himself towards the spider. Immediately, it ceased to struggle. Niall reached it a moment later and had to fight panic as the legs wound themselves round him. Then he remembered the rope. He grabbed it with both hands and tried to heave himself back towards the boat. A wave submerged him, but he continued to cling to the rope. Then he bumped against the boat's wooden side; arms were reaching down for him. The spider was still clinging tightly as they were both hauled out of the water. Hands grasped him under the shoulders and dragged him over the side. The sailors who were lifting him fell backwards, and Niall fell on top of them, the spider's legs still wrapped around him. He felt one of them snap as they struck the bench.

His lungs seemed to be full of water; he knelt there, his head on the bench, coughing and vomiting. Yet in spite of the lurching of the ship, which made the water surge around his waist, he felt a deep sense of relief and security to be able to cling once more to a solid object.

He was still clinging to the bench half an hour later, when the storm subsided. It seemed to happen quite suddenly; one moment he was being heaved up and down; the next, everything was still. He looked up and saw a patch of blue sky overhead. The wind became a mere breeze, and the water in the bottom of the ship ceased to surge back and forth and was suddenly as still as a pond. Sunlight warmed his bare back, and he felt he had never experienced such a wholly delightful sensation.

The ship was in chaos. Everything seemed to be afloat; ropes, barrels, sea chests, oars. Niall stood up and peered over the side; neither of the other two boats was visible. He waded to the other side and looked over; the sea was empty. But on the northern horizon he caught his first glimpse of land.

The sail was raised, and the tiller tied in position. Then everyone aboard helped to bail the ship. Within half an hour, there was only a narrow strip of water down the central aisle. Niall himself lent a hand, using a wooden ladle, and as he did so, experienced a glowing sensation of happiness to be working alongside the brawny sailors, playing his own small part in clearing up the chaos left behind by the storm. Now the danger was past, everyone was smiling and relaxed, and he was pleased to observe that they no longer ignored him but treated him as one of themselves.

One of the sailors handed him his pack. All the food in it, with the exception of the prickly pears, was ruined. But the heavy metal tube was still there; its weight had prevented the pack from being swept away.

The storm now seemed like a dream. The sun was beating down from an electric blue sky, and soon no trace of dampness remained on the boards. The two spiders were lying there absorbing the heat, one at either end of the ship. The spider Niall had rescued had lost its front claw as they struck the bench, and a trickle of blood ran from the broken leg. Niall observed that the sailors took care not to approach too close; not, obviously, out of fear, but out of respect and solicitude. They seemed to have an almost religious veneration for the spiders.

He was standing on a bench, straining his eyes towards the approaching land, when someone tapped him on the shoulder. It was the commander, and she was holding a metal goblet in both hands. As she held it out towards him he saw that it contained a golden liquid that sparkled in the sun. He accepted with a smile of gratitude—the sea water had given him a raging thirst—and raised it to his lips with both hands. It was a sweet, fermented liquor, not unlike the drink brewed by his father, but richer and far more pleasant. The woman took the cup from him, looking into his eyes, and drank from the other side of the rim. Niall suddenly noticed that the sailors had ceased their work, and were all looking at him. He realized that the drink was not simply a friendly gesture, but some kind of ceremony. But what was its meaning? Then, as he looked past her to the big spider, which lay sprawled in the sun, one of its legs bent at an unnatural angle, he guessed the answer. It was a gesture of thanks for saving its life.

When she had drained the goblet, the commander smiled at him, then turned it upside down and allowed its last drop to fall onto the boards. She turned away, and the sailors resumed their work.

The drink induced a pleasant light-headedness, and a sensation of warmth in his veins. His weariness vanished. At the same time, he realized that his mind was in tune with the minds of the sailors; he could feel their joy that the storm was over, and that the ship was approaching land. But what surprised him was that he was still unable to perceive their thoughts as individuals. When he tried to look into the mind of any one of the sailors, it was as if he was looking *through* it, into someone else's mind, and then through that, and into someone else's, in a kind of infinite regress. It reminded him of looking into the minds of the ants. They seemed to share one another's identity.

The only exception to this was the commander. She seemed to have her own confidence and individuality, the recognition that she had to make decisions and take on responsibilities. Yet even here, there was not the kind of individuality he had become accustomed to in his mother and Ingeld, and nothing remotely like the self-assurance of Merlew. It was as if a part of her mind were transparent, like clear water, totally unclouded by reflection or self-awareness.

One of the sailors gave a shout and pointed over the starboard side. Niall jumped to his feet and stared out across the smooth sea. In the blue haze of the distance, he could see the other two boats. It was all that was needed to complete his sense of happiness.

The shore was now close, and Niall could make out a rocky coastline, with undulating cliffs, needles and pinnacles of sea-worn granite, and green fields sloping to the sea. The wind was a gentle breeze that carried them smoothly towards the land, as if to make up for its previous violence. As they came closer, he could see trees and yellow gorse, and a large bee zoomed past his ear. But there was no sign of people, or of human habitation.

The oarsmen began to row as the commander beat time. The ship followed the coastline in a westerly direction for perhaps two miles. Then, as they rounded a peninsula, Niall saw the first evidence of human handiwork—a harbor of white stone that reflected back the sun. Now the breeze dropped, and the heat increased. They passed a rocky islet on which were the remains of a tower; but most of its carved granite blocks lay around its base.

The harbor itself was the most impressive sight he had seen since the castle on the plateau: the great curving wall, twenty feet thick, built out into the sea, the massive dressed stones of the jetty, the strange wooden machine that towered into the air on the end of the quay, the fleet of boats moored inside the harbor; once again, Niall experienced a peculiar excitement at the thought that men like himself had once built this immense structure. Only at close quarters was it apparent that all this had been built a long time ago, and had been allowed to fall into semi-ruin.

Once inside the harbor bar, the rowers ceased to pull, and the boat glided across the still water under its own momentum. From the quay, a man threw down two of the thickest ropes Niall had ever seen, and these were secured to the prow and the stern. A gangplank was lowered. The commander was the first to cross. Then she knelt, her head bowed, as the two spiders followed her.

Workers on the quay assumed the same attitude of homage, and remained in this position until the spiders had passed.

A sailor touched Niall on the elbow and indicated that he was to go next. He assumed he was to be escorted ashore as a prisoner, and was surprised to realize that he was expected to go alone, and embarrassed that the sailors stood to attention as he passed. The commander put out a hand to steady him as he stepped off the gang-plank.

"What is your name?" It was the first time she had spoken to him.

"Niall."

"A name of good fortune."

Niall failed to understand her. "Why?"

"You have earned the favor of the spiders. There can be no greater good fortune."

She took his arm and led him along the quay. The dock workers continued to stand to attention as they passed. They were, he observed, even bigger and more powerful than the sailors; he had never seen such muscles.

He asked diffidently: "Where are we going?" She looked so stern and purposeful that he half-expected her to ignore him. But she seemed to accept his right to question her.

"To the harbor master's."

She indicated the square, grey stone building at the end of the quay. Like the quay itself, this was in a poor state of repair, and its windows had been bricked up. The commander knocked on the door. In a moment, it was opened by one of the wolf spiders, which stood aside for them to enter. After the glare of the sunlight, it took Niall's eyes a few minutes to adjust to the darkness. He seemed to be in a large, empty room that smelt of damp and decay. Only a little light was admitted through cracks in the roof. He almost stumbled into the big wolf spider.

A cobweb sloped down from the rear corners of the room to within a few feet of where they were standing. In the center of this web, looking directly at them, was a black death spider. It was smaller than the wolf spiders, and its black, shiny body was more bulbous than theirs. The single row of black eyes extended round its head like a row of beads. These, and the folded poison fangs, gave the face the same frightening, inscrutable expression he had observed in the spider he had killed.

Niall experienced an uncontrollable rush of fear, which communicated itself instantly to the spider. He could feel its will probing his own—not in the clumsy, inexpert manner of the wolf spiders, but with a subtlety that betrayed a sharp intelligence. What terrified him was the thought that the spider might be able to read his mind, and discover that he had killed a death spider.

His instinctive response to the probing was to become passive, and to blank his mind. The death spider was attempting to enter his brain, exactly as Niall had entered the brain of the tent spider. Since there was no point in resistance, Niall's reaction was to duplicate the mental vibration of the tent spider. In effect, he became the tent spider as naturally as a chameleon changes color.

He could sense that the death spider found this puzzling. It half-recognized the vibration, but found it strange and unfamiliar. Its brain transmitted a communication to the brain of the big wolf spider; it was a single impulse, like a signal, and therefore as easy to interpret as a facial expression. It was saying, in effect: "He seems to be an idiot."

The reply-signal was a dubious gesture of assent, as if it had said: "I'm afraid so."

If this exchange had taken place in words, Niall's feelings would have betrayed him. Both the wolf spiders knew the truth about him. In the crisis of the storm, his mind had communicated directly with theirs, and no dissimulation was possible. But in the swiftness of the exchange of mental impulses, he had no time for fear, or even for relief that the wolf spider had not betrayed him.

The death spider turned its attention to the commander. Its will issued a blunt command: "Take him away." A moment later, Niall was out in the dazzling sunlight, unable to believe that the danger was over.

She noticed that he looked shaken.

"Were you afraid?"

Niall nodded. "Yes."

A gleam of sympathy came into her eyes.

"You don't have to be. They treat their servants well."

Niall wanted to ask more questions, but she cut him short. "I have to report to my captain. You'd better go and wait for your family to arrive."

Niall wandered back to the end of the quay. The sailors had all disembarked, and the ship was empty. No one seemed to pay him any attention. He asked one of the dock workers when they expected the other two ships. The man shrugged and said: "Soon." And since neither was in sight, Niall walked back along the quay. The big wooden tower-like structure now seemed to be in operation, and he was curious to see what it was used for.

He found it in a kind of inner harbor. A ship was being unloaded there. It had a flat bottom and was broader than the ship on which Niall had sailed. It was obviously a cargo vessel, the deck divided into bays to prevent its load from moving around in heavy seas. These were full of sacks of coarse brown cloth. A wheel at the base of the wooden structure made it possible to manipulate it over the ship, and a square platform was then lowered down to the deck on ropes; when it had been loaded with sacks, it was raised again and swung back onto the quay, where the sacks were loaded into a cart. To Niall, it seemed a miracle of engineering, and he sat and watched its movements with fascination.

He was also intrigued by the man who was supervising the unloading. He was much smaller than the brawny dockers who surrounded him, scarcely taller than Niall. He wore a shabby yellow tunic and a hat of peculiar design, with a peak that protected his eyes from the sun. He gave orders in a rapid, sharp voice, but with a strange accent that Niall found incomprehensible.

The man was obviously not a docker; neither did he seem to be one of the sailors. Idly, Niall tuned in to the little man's mind, and knew immediately that his speculation had been correct. This man's thought-vibrations were active and chaotic, quite unlike the disturbing, ant-like passivity of the sailors and dockers.

As he tried probing further, the man looked around uncomfortably, aware of this attempt to invade the privacy of his head—as Niall's own family would have been. A moment later, he glanced up at Niall. For a moment, Niall thought he was about to speak; then a sailor carrying a sack blundered against him, and the little man exploded with impatience. "Look where you're going, you flea-brained oaf!"

But ten minutes later, when the last of the sacks was unloaded, he climbed up the ladder and walked straight up to Niall. Niall, who was sitting on a capstan, looked up at him guilelessly. The man had a sharp, thin face with a large beak of a nose, and an almost bald head. He placed one hand on Niall's shoulder, peered into his face with mock aggression, and said:

"What the 'ell do you think you're playing at?"

Niall said: "I'm afraid I don't understand."

"You understand all right." He sat down on a sack, then said in a friendlier tone: "Where you from?"

Niall pointed. "The great desert."

The little man said: "Oh, you're one o' them, are you?"

Niall asked: "What are you called?"

"Bill."

"That is a strange name."

"No, it's not. Where I come from it's a perfectly normal name. What's yours?"

"Niall."

"That's not a name, that's a river!"

Niall found his conversation as baffling as his accent. From his smile, it was apparent he was joking, but the joke was incomprehensible.

The little man looked at him from under lowered brows, as if trying to make a decision. He stared so long that Niall began to feel uncomfortable. Then the man said: "Who taught you to read minds?"

Niall answered readily: "Nobody taught me."

"Oh, come on!"

Niall found this puzzling. "Come on where?"

The little man decided to try a new line of questioning. "When did you arrive?"

"Half an hour ago. I'm still waiting for my mother and brother. They are out there." He pointed to the sea. As he did so, he saw that both ships were now in sight, about a mile offshore.

Again the little man stared into his eyes for an uncomfortable length of time. Niall was now anxious to get away to meet the ships. He stirred impatiently.

"Do it again," the man said.

"Do what?"

"What you did before."

It seemed easiest to comply, so Niall stared into the man's eyes, tuned in to his thought waves, then deliberately used his own mind as a probe.

The little man looked startled. He shook his head and said quietly: "Well, well, well."

Niall understood that. "Well what?"

"I don't know what the crawlies'll do when they find out."

"Crawlies?"

"The black bastards. The spiders. Creepy crawlies."

"What do you think they'll do?"

The little man placed the ball of his thumb on the palm of his other hand, and gave a violent twist. He meaning was perfectly clear. Niall felt his face grow pale. Now he no longer felt anxious to hurry away.

"Do you think they'll find out?" he asked.

The man shrugged. "I dunno. I've never worked out just what they can do and what they can't." He chewed his lip thoughtfully. "But I've got a feeling they don't know half as much as they'd like us to think."

Niall glanced out to sea. The ships appeared no closer. "Are you a servant of the spiders?"

The man shook his head violently. "No, thank God. I can't stand 'em. They give me the creeps."

"Then what do you do?"

"I work for the bombardiers."

"The beetles?"

"That's right."

"What kind of work?"

The man grinned. "Make bangs. I'm their chief explosives expert." He pointed to the sacks. "That stuff in there's for making gunpowder."

They were interrupted by one of the dockers. He stood to attention, saluted the little man, and said that the cart was ready to leave.

"All right. I'll be with you in a minute. Get ready to start." Waving him away, he waited until the docker was out of hearing, then leaned forward and said in a low voice: "Take my advice. Don't let the crawlies find out."

"All right." Niall tried to look more courageous than he felt.

The little man climbed on top of the sacks. The cart, which had two enormous wheels shod with iron, also had two shafts, each about ten feet long. Four muscular dockers seized each one of these and, at an order from the little man, began to heave. By the time they reached the end of the quay, they were moving at a steady trot. The little man turned and gave a brief wave. Niall waved back, and watched until the cart was out of sight. Then he walked thoughtfully back towards the main dock.

On the way there, he met the commander. She smiled at him— she seemed in a good mood—and gave him a thump with her clenched fist. He was aware that this was a friendly gesture, but he felt it had almost broken his shoulder.

"You need fattening up," she said.

"Fattening?" There was something about the way she said it that made him feel uneasy.

"The masters like us to be strong and healthy. Like that." She pointed to a passing docker whose muscles stood out on his arms like cables.

Niall said without conviction: "Yes, I'd like that."

Staring at her face, trying to read her expression, he found that he had automatically tuned in to her mind. He experienced nervous embarrassment, as if he had inadvertently bumped against her, and instantly withdrew his scrutiny. A moment later, it struck him that she seemed unaware of this contact of minds. Cautiously, prepared for instant withdrawal, he tried again. He at once became aware of why she was so pleased with herself—and with him. Her commanding officer had just congratulated her on bringing the wolf spiders safely back to land. If the spiders had been harmed, she would have been blamed and punished. And although it would not have been her fault, she would have accepted the blame and the punishment. As it was, she had received only praise, and consequently felt well disposed towards Niall.

All this Niall saw instantaneously, simply by tuning in to her feeling-waves. Once he had assured himself that she was unaware of his scrutiny, he continued to probe her mind. It was an odd sensation. By tuning in to her consciousness, Niall felt as if he was inside her head, looking out through her eyes. He was aware of her female body, of the bronzed breasts that bounced as she walked, and the long legs whose stride forced him to hurry to keep up. For the moment, he had ceased to be Niall and become this tall, beautiful woman. He was even aware of her name: Odina.

But why was she unaware that he was inside her head? The answer, he realized, had something to do with that strange blankness that he sensed inside the minds of these people. It was as if a part of their consciousness was anaesthetised.

Then, suddenly, he began to see an outline of the answer. It had to do with the spiders. These people were so accustomed to their minds being probed by the spiders that they took it for granted. Their minds had open doors, so anyone could wander in and out . . . like

173

the pepsis wasp, that was so used to being handled it made no attempt to sting, even when one of the children tried to stroke it.

They had reached the end of the quay. The nearest ship was just passing the outer harbor wall. Niall felt a thrill of delight as he recognized Veig's face looking over the side, and he waved vigorously. Veig waved back. As the ship was hauled against the quay, Niall could see that its port side had been damaged, its upper planks smashed as if by a heavy downward blow.

Five minutes later, the commander came ashore, followed by the wolf spider escort. Behind them came Veig. Niall started to run towards his brother, but was stopped by something that seemed to knock the breath from his body. The wolf spider was glaring balefully at him, and the beam of its will had stopped him like a heavy blow. Then, having made its point, the spider marched on past the kneeling commanders. It was evidently in a thoroughly bad temper.

Odina touched Niall on the shoulder, and raised her finger reproachfully.

"When the masters walk by, the slaves lower their eyes."

Niall said meekly: "I'm sorry."

He and Veig were made to stand to one side as the sailors disembarked. Niall whispered: "Where have you been? What happened?"

"The mast blew down in the storm—almost capsized us. Luckily, the other boat stayed with us. . . ."

The commander of his ship gave him an angry glare.

"Talking among prisoners forbidden."

Veig said: "Sorry."

They stood there silently, watching the other ship approach. Out of the corner of his eye, Niall observed them as they talked. Evidently Odina was telling her colleague what had happened in the storm. The woman stared at Niall with astonishment and disbelief. Then she strode over to them, looked into their faces for a moment, and said: "All right talking permitted." She turned her back and walked off.

Veig said: "What on earth was all that about?"

Niall whispered: "I'll tell you later."

The other ship had been moored farther along the quay. This time, Niall and Veig kept silent, their eyes averted, as the commander came ashore followed by a wolf spider. Behind them came Siris. They waited until the spider was twenty yards away before they rushed to embrace her. She was looking pale and ill. As Veig was hugging her, Niall caught the thought of one of the dockers; he was thinking: "What a skinny woman—I wouldn't like to kiss her. . . ." Niall experienced a flash of protective indignation as he looked at his mother; to him, she seemed slim and beautiful. These slaves of the spiders had a strange idea of beauty.

Odina touched Niall's arm. "Come."

As they followed her along the quay, they heard one of the commanders ask, with no attempt to lower her voice: "Why are they coming with us?"

"The master's orders," Odina said.

Beyond the quays, they crossed a wide area of waste ground, covered with damaged boats, broken carts, and piles of litter. The walls that surrounded the docks had been allowed to fall into a state of ruin. Evidently this had once been a large and flourishing port; now it had shrunk to a small harbor. Only the road underfoot seemed in a good state of repair; it was made of some hard, smooth substance like a continuous sheet of marble.

Beyond the dock wall, they came upon a row of hand carts, similar in design to the one Niall had already seen, but smaller. A dozen or so bored-looking men were standing around. When Odina snapped her fingers, six came running and bowed in front of her. Odina and the two commanders climbed into one of the carts; two men seized each of its shafts, and stood waiting for further orders. Odina pointed to another cart, and then signalled Niall, Veig, and Siris to climb in. As they did so, one of the men who took the shafts exclaimed: "Niall!"

"Massig!" Niall recognized him immediately as one of the group that had come to escort him to Kazak's underground city.

They locked forearms, but as they did so, one of the commanders snapped: "That's enough!" Massig went pale and hastily stood to attention. Odina gave an order. Her own four men went off at a sharp trot; the other cart followed them. Niall looked with concern and astonishment at the back of Massig's head. The hair, which had once been so beautifully washed and groomed, was now tangled and dirty.

The landscape around them was flat and desolate. There were ruined houses on both sides of the road, most of them only a few feet high. Ahead the road ran straight as an arrow to the top of a range of low hills. Outside the ruined town, the scenery improved, with green fields and trees, but remained oddly depressing. With its tangle of weeds and undergrowth, with the occasional ruined wall or barn, it looked as if it had survived some terrible disaster.

The runners proceeded at a steady jog-trot so long as the road was level; but when it began to slope gently upwards towards the hills, their pace slowed. Niall could tell from Massig's movements that he was tiring, and the thought distressed him; yet there was obviously nothing he could do about it. Finally, when the slope became so steep that the men had to slow to a walk, he leaned forward and tapped the nearest man on the shoulder.

"Would you like us to get out and walk?"

The man was so astonished that he stopped, and the others had to stop too.

"Walk?" The man shook his head in bewilderment. "Why?"

"So as not to tire you."

He shook his head. "Oh, no. We'd get into terrible trouble if you did that."

"Why?"

"Because it's our job to pull you. If we didn't, the masters'd want to know why." He turned his back again, and began to heave. Massig shot Niall a sympathetic glance, as if to say: Thanks for trying anyway.

Half an hour later, the cart reached the top of the hill. Below them, enclosed in the hollow bowl of the hills, lay the spider city he had seen in his vision by the well. It was a city of tall square towers—towers that, in reality, were even greater than in his vision. And even at this distance, he could see the enormous cobwebs that stretched between them. Most of the towers were grey; a few were almost black. Many were obviously little more than ruins, yet even the ruins were taller than the great columns of twisted rock near their home in the desert. Niall had never seen anything so breathtaking; it was like a city built by giants.

And in the center of this grimy city, standing alone in its own green space, stood the white tower. It was not as tall as many of the surrounding buildings, but it stood out from them in its pure, blinding whiteness. In the sunlight, it sparkled as if lit from within by its own dazzling sun. Unlike the other towers, this tower was cylindrical, although the top was slightly narrower than its base. It might have been a slender white finger, pointing at the sky.

Niall looked at the faces of his mother and brother, and saw their feelings were the same as his own. It was a strange moment.

For many days now, they had known that this was their destination. Yet the city of the spiders had remained a dream. They were not even afraid of it, because it seemed an unreality. Now suddenly it was real, and the sensation was like waking from a dream. It was far more real and frightening than Niall had imagined; its stained towers somehow resembled ruined teeth in the face of a skull. Even without the giant cobwebs it would have been ugly and menacing. Yet the white tower, in its square green space, seemed indifferent to the ugliness and menace. It aroused in Niall a curious spark of pure joy, and he sensed that Veig and Siris also felt this. It seemed oddly familiar, as if he had often seen it in dreams.

The runners, who had paused to regain their breath, now began the descent to the city. Although steeper than the uphill route, this was less difficult, for the cart had brakes that the runners operated from the shafts, so they could check its forward rush. Relieved of his anxiety about Massig—who was now walking at a comfortable pace—Niall was able to relax and pay more attention to his surroundings. What surprised him here was the beauty of the scenery. It had evidently been raining—black clouds still hung over the distant hills—and the grass and bushes glistened with it. Halfway down the slope, the road plunged into woodland, and the sun vanished. These were not the bare, hardy trees of the desert; some of them had trunks five feet in diameter, while their branches over-arched the road and formed a green tunnel; others stretched up so high that he could not see the sky through the maze of branches. The grass between the trees was so green that it looked like the weed in the bottom of a slow-flowing stream. When they passed between two high banks, Niall was able to pluck a few blades and chew them; they were sweet and succulent, and their taste seemed to bring a vision of endless forests.

Then, suddenly, they were out of the woods, their eyes dazzled again by the evening sunlight, and the black and grey city was directly ahead. The contrast was strange and somehow unbelievable, as if either the woods or the city must be an illusion. The fields on either side of the road were now cultivated, and they could see a few men working in them. Then the road which remained as smooth as marble ran along by the side of a river whose waters looked deep and black. Half a mile later, they were crossing a bridge, its iron towers half rusted away. Underneath the bridge was a 50-foot cobweb;

lurking in its corner, in the darkness of rust-stained masonry, he caught a glimpse of black eyes peering out at them.

Then they were in the spider city, and the great towers formed solid ranks on either side. They were so tall that Niall had to tilt back his head to see the strip of blue evening sky above. Many were ruined; he could see through their empty windows into bare rooms with collapsing walls. At street level, steps often descended down behind rusting iron railings to invisible rooms below, and men and women seemed to use these constantly. The sheer number of people took his breath away; they seemed to be hurrying in all directions like the ants beyond the rocky wilderness. The majority were men—all tall, powerful, and muscular—but there were also a number of women and girls. Most of these wore tunics that covered their breasts but left their arms bare; a few, he noticed, wore dresses that also covered their arms. One tall, bare-breasted woman who crossed the road in front of them was so like Odina, that Niall had to peer into the distance to make sure the three commanders were still in their vehicle, which was now about a quarter of a mile ahead of theirs.

Evening was drawing on, and the towering buildings excluded the sunlight. As the streets grew darker, the people disappeared. When their cart finally came to a halt, the streets were almost deserted. Their runners placed the shafts on the ground and helped them to descend. Odina came out of the darkness, placed her hand on Niall's shoulder and pointed.

"They will show you where you are to sleep. You are to live with the charioteers."

Niall said: "Thank you," because he could think of nothing else to say.

"Don't thank me. Thank Krol."

"But who is Krol?"

"The master you saved."

"The spider who . . ."

"Ssshh!" She placed her hand fiercely over his mouth and glanced up into the air. "Never use that word! Here they are the masters. If one of them approaches, bow down before him. Otherwise you'll soon find yourself in the great happy land."

"Great happy land?"

"Don't ask so many questions. Curiosity killed the bat." She turned to one of the runners. "What is your name?"

"Daraul."

"Daraul, I give them into your charge. Your life for theirs." The man made a gesture of homage. "You will receive your orders in the morning." She seized Niall's ear and gave it a friendly twist that made his eyes water. "Sleep well, little savage."

"Thank you."

She strode off into the darkness.

The man called Daraul was the one to whom Niall had made the suggestion about walking. Now he had seen Niall treated with some degree of familiarity by the commander, his attitude became more friendly. "Follow me, all of you. Be careful of the steps—they're broken."

Massig took Niall's arm. "I'll help you."

They descended the steps into the dark basement area. Someone pushed open a creaking door. The smell of burning oil met them, and they entered a large, dimly lit room. It seemed to be full of men, many of them lying or sitting on low bunks or beds. When Siris came into the room, some of them stood to attention, and one started to sink onto one knee.

"There's no need for that," Daraul said. "These are only savages from the desert." He said it without contempt, merely stating a fact.

One of the men said: "Then what are they doing here?"

"I don't know. It's orders from above."

As if relieved of some burden on their attention, the men turned away and ignored the newcomers. Some were eating food from bowls, others were sewing or repairing sandals. The room was warm from the heat of their bodies and smelt of sweat.

Massig touched Daraul's arm. "If you like, I'll look after them and find them somewhere to sleep."

Daraul looked at him with the same blank incomprehension that he had shown when Niall offered to get out of the cart. Massig put his hand on Niall's shoulder. "He's a friend of mine. We'd like to talk."

"What about?" Daraul asked.

"Oh, all kinds of things—how we got here, for example."

Daraul shrugged, still looking baffled. "Oh, all right."

It struck Niall that Daraul, like most of the other men in the room, was of a low degree of intelligence, but in no way hostile.

During the next half hour, Massig found beds for them. They had to carry oil lamps and walk along a black corridor to some remote part of the basement. In a big, musty-smelling room there were dozens of beds in various states of disrepair. Fortunately, their legs seemed interchangeable, fixing into wooden sockets, so they were able to assemble three relatively undamaged frames. These they carried back to the main room, Massig helping Siris with hers. Another dusty room revealed piles of ancient mattresses stuffed with fragments of rag, while another was filled with blankets, many rotting with damp. Niall was too tired to care. Siris yawned so much that they left her lying on Massig's bed while they went in search of pillows—these were made of wood and covered with a thin layer of leather; when they returned, she was fast asleep.

Next Massig took them to the communal kitchen; this was uncomfortably hot, due to a huge iron stove which had been stoked with firewood. There seemed to be an abundance of vegetables, and even a big metal bowl filled to the top with some dubious-looking meat. Niall was too tired to cook; he settled for a bowl of a green colored soup from a tureen on the stove, with a chunk of hard brown bread. This tasted far better than it looked—in fact, was so full of interesting flavors that he went back for a second helping. Their beds were erected in a corner of the basement room, and they sat and ate with their backs propped against the wall. The man in the bed next to Niall looked at him in a friendly way and said: "You're too thin. We'll soon fatten you up." It was a remark he was to hear constantly during the course of the next day or so. It was not simply a jocular comment, intended to make conversation, but a serious observation, stated with deep conviction. Among the charioteers, eating seemed almost a religion.

While they ate, Niall listened to the conversation that went on around them. He was hoping to achieve some insight into the minds of the human inhabitants of the spider city. But he soon grew bored. The men seemed obsessed by various games—many of them played a game that involved a handful of carved wooden sticks—and talked endlessly about a long-awaited match between the charioteers and the food gatherers in two days' time, involving some kind of ball. There were times when Niall had the hallucinatory feeling that he had accidentally tuned in to the collective mind of the ants. Yet for all their obvious lack of intelligence, these men seemed good natured and kindly enough, and once they had become accustomed to the presence of Niall and his companions, treated them as if they were

all part of a large family group. After a lifetime of reliance on himself and his small family, Niall found this sense of communal identity rather pleasant and relaxing.

As they ate, Massig described how Kazak's city had been overrun. The story was soon told. Two days after Ulf and Niall had left for home, the ant herds had failed to return in the evening. A search party, led by Hamna, had also failed to return. The next morning, when Massig woke up, he found himself unable to move. . . . Niall could already guess the rest of the story. The spiders marched straight into the city, led by one of the ant herders, who was terrified out of his wits. No one stood a chance. Many men were killed. In Massig's opinion, this was not because they showed signs of resistance, but simply because the spiders were hungry. A number of children were also killed and eaten. The rest had been taken away, and were now here in the spider city under the care of nurses.

There seemed to be hordes of spiders—hundreds of them, mostly the brown wolf spiders (whom Massig called soldiers). It was they who organized the long march to the sea. Massig admitted that this was less of an ordeal than he expected. They were well fed, and when anyone showed signs of exhaustion, the spiders either allowed them to rest or ordered them to be carried on improvised stretchers. When the prisoners arrived in the spider city, all were in relatively good health.

Massig described how they were paraded in the main square, in front of the white tower, and the mothers reunited with their children. But this was not to last. The men were divided into groups and assigned to various tasks. Some became food gatherers, some agricultural workers, some city workers, some—like Massig—charioteers. The women were not separated; they were taken, all together, to the central part of the city reserved for women. For, Massig explained, women were revered in the city of the spiders. Among spiders, the female is more important than the male—she often eats him after courtship. The spiders found the human system of treating women as household slaves deeply offensive to their natural instincts. So women were trained to be the masters, men the servants. Since the women of Kazak's city had become accustomed to domination by the males, they would have to be reeducated. Until they learned to assume their new role as masters, they would be kept segregated from their husbands.

Niall asked: "And what about the children?" He was thinking of his sisters.

"They're kept in a nursery not far from the women. But the women won't be allowed to see them until they've been reeducated."

Massig had now been here about a month. The work was hard but he had no serious complaints. Every morning the charioteers had to report to the square at the center of the Women's Section; their job was to take the overseers to work—some to the fields, some to the docks, some to other parts of the city. It was not a bad job, especially if you could get the city run. The dock run was the hardest, and Massig suspected he had been assigned to it as a punishment; one of the women had overheard him referring to—here Massig looked nervously around and lowered his voice—referring to the masters as "spiders."

Niall was puzzled. "But what's wrong with that?"

"They say it's disrespectful—talking about them as if they're insects."

"But I met a man in the docks who called them crawlies," Niall said.

"Sshh!" Massig looked round in alarm, but no one was listening. "Who on earth was that?"

"A man with a funny name—Bill, I think he said."

"Oh, he's not one of us. He works for the beetles. His name's Bill Doggins." He said it with contempt, and Niall was secretly amused at the way Massig had already learned to identify with his fellow workers.

"Billdoggins?"

"Bill Doggins. He's got two names for some reason. The men who work for the beetles say it's an old tradition."

Veig leaned forward and asked in a low voice: "Do you think there's any chance of escaping from here?"

Massig looked horrified. "No! Not the slightest. Where would you escape to? They'd simply hunt you down. But why should you want to escape? It's not a bad life here."

"Well to begin with, I don't want to be a slave."

"Slave? But we're not slaves."

Veig asked ironically: "No? What are you?"

"We're servants. That's quite different. The real slaves live on the other side of the river. They're all idiots."

"Why, what's wrong with them?"

"I've told you—they're idiots, quite literally. They look like monsters." Massig did an imitation of a man with a slack jaw, glazed eyes, and blubber lips.

"Why do they want slaves if they've got servants?" Niall asked.

"Oh, for the really nasty jobs, like cleaning the sewers. They also get eaten."

Niall and Veig said together: "Eaten?" They said it so loud that Siris opened her eyes for a moment.

"Yes. The spiders breed them for food."

Niall was fascinated and horrified. "Do *they* know that?"

Massig shrugged. "I think so. They just take it for granted. They're about as intelligent as ants."

Niall glanced around at the men who surrounded them, but said nothing.

"What about the . . . servants. Do they ever get eaten?" Veig asked.

Massig shook his head emphatically. "Oh, no. At least, only under very unusual circumstances."

"Such as?"

"Well, for example, no one is allowed out after dark. There's a general rule that the spiders can eat anyone they catch out at night." He added quickly: "But of course, it never happens because no one is stupid enough to go out at night."

"But why don't they want people to go out after dark?"

"I suppose they want to stop husbands sneaking off to see their wives, or mothers trying to see their children."

Veig said scornfully: "And you mean to say you like it here?"

Massig looked defensive. "Well, I didn't say I liked it, but . . . well, I suppose it could be worse. At least we get plenty of sunlight. In Dira, we were lucky if we saw the outside world once a month. And the food here is quite good—they like to keep you well fed. And we're allowed to play games every Saturday afternoon. We can apply to change jobs once a year—I'm going to try to be a sailor next year. And of course, we retire at forty."

"Retire? What's that?"

"We don't have to work any more. Instead, we go to the great happy land."

"The what?"

Before Massig could reply, there was a strange booming sound from outside; it made Niall's hair prickle on his scalp. It was repeated several times—a sound like the moaning of some gigantic creature in pain.

"My God, what's that?" Veig exclaimed.

"That means it's time for lights out. We have to get to sleep fairly early because we have to be awake at dawn."

The men in the room began extinguishing their oil lamps and climbing into bed. Only one lamp was left burning. All conversation died away.

"What's the great happy land?" Niall whispered to Massig.

Massig whispered: "Ssshh! We're not allowed to talk after lights out."

"Why?"

"I'll explain in the morning. Good night."

He turned his back on Niall and pulled the coverlet round his shoulders. The room was now quiet except for the sound of heavy breathing. It was oddly comforting to be among so many human beings. Within a few minutes, Niall had fallen into a deep and peaceful sleep.

It seemed that he had hardly closed his eyes when he was awakened by the sound of movements around him. One by one, the lamps were lit. Veig, always an early riser, was already out of bed. Siris, her long hair tangled with sleep, sat up and yawned. A man passing by the end of her bed made her a low bow.

Massig opened his eyes, peered around sleepily and pulled the blanket over his face. A moment later, he began to snore softly.

Then, to Niall's surprise, all the men in the room dropped to one knee in an attitude of obeisance. It took several moments before he noticed that a woman was standing inside the door. She looked like Odina—but then, all the commanders seemed to look alike.

In a clear, precise voice, she said: "The strangers will report to the parade ground with everyone else." Then she turned and went out. The room returned to its normal activity. And Massig, who had been awakened by her voice, threw back the coverlet and scrambled out of bed. He was looking pale and shaken.

"Do you think she noticed me?" he asked Niall.

"No, I'm certain she didn't."

Massig breathed a sigh of relief. "They're pretty strict about sluggards."

"Sluggards?" Niall had never heard the word.

"People who can't get up in the morning." He groaned. "That's the one thing I don't like about this place—they make you get up so early. In Dira, we never slept for less than twelve hours. And after an all-night party, I once slept right round the clock and missed a day. . . ."

Niall asked: "What do we do now?"

"We eat. We're due on parade in an hour."

He led them into the kitchen, where vessels of food steamed on the stove. The cooks had been working since an hour before dawn. Massig helped himself to a bowl of the green soup and a plate piled with vegetables and meat. Niall and Siris took smaller quantities. Next to the kitchen there was a large dining hall, with long wooden tables. Veig was already seated, a full plate in front of him. He waved his spoon at them.

"This meat is very good. What's it called?"

"Rabbit."

"What's that?"

"A kind of rat with long ears. But they breed quicker than rats."

After that, Massig settled down to the serious business of eating, and only grunted in reply to their questions.

Niall observed that there was very little conversation in the rest of the room—only the sound of spoons on wooden platters, and the champing of jaws.

Even Siris ate well. After her long night's sleep, her cheeks had regained their color. It would have been impossible for her not to notice the admiring glances cast at her as men passed their table, and although she kept her eyes on her plate, Niall could tell that she enjoyed it. For the past twenty years, the only men Siris had seen had been members of her own family; it must have been a strange experience to feel herself admired by a roomful of muscular and handsome males.

After they had finished eating, Massig showed them the washing arrangements. A nearby room was full of dozens of wooden buckets, each filled to the brim with water. They were instructed to take one of these into the next room, a large, bare chamber whose stone floor was covered with narrow channels. There Niall and Veig were invited to remove their travel-stained clothes, and to pour the water over themselves. Siris was conducted to a smaller room nearby. Massig handed them lumps of a grey-colored root, and showed them how to dip it in the water, then rub it on the skin. The result was a sappy-smelling froth which seemed to dissolve the dirt away. They were allowed to help themselves to as many buckets of water as they wanted. To desert dwellers, this seemed an unbelievable and delightful extravagance. So did the method of drying to which Massig introduced them—rubbing themselves all over with large rectangles of a rough and absorbent cloth.

When Siris emerged from her own private washroom with her skin glowing and her hair soaked with water, Niall thought he had never seen his mother looking so beautiful. He contemplated his own shining skin and clean hands and feet with a certain complacent satisfaction; he was beginning to understand why Massig liked this place.

Ten minutes later, they were assembled in the street outside. Now he could see it in broad daylight, Niall found it at once frightening and rather exciting. The tall grey buildings towered above them like cliffs, and cobwebs with strands like ropes stretched between them, some of them flat, some almost vertical. Many of the webs had obviously been there for years, for they were thick and furry with an accumulation of dust. A huge fly, its body as large as a man's head, smacked into one of these webs and sent down a shower of assorted debris, including wings of long-dead flies. The fly rebounded, soared upwards, and encountered another web, this one almost invisible, in which it buzzed frantically. Almost instantaneously, a black spider scurried across the web and leapt on the fly; a second later, the buzzing had ceased, and the fly hung limply as the spider swathed it in silk. Now Niall understood why the spiders left their old webs hanging there, instead of re-absorbing them into their bodies in the frugal manner of most spiders. Flying creatures took care to avoid the old webs, which were conspicuous, and blundered into the new ones, which were almost transparent.

At an order from Daraul, the men stood to attention; at another barked command, they began to march down the center of the street. At the next intersection, they turned right into a wider avenue. Niall experienced an upsurge of joy as he saw, in the distance, the white tower outlined against the blue morning sky.

They passed another platoon of men, traveling in the opposite direction. Niall could tell at a glance that these were the slaves of whom Massig had spoken. They wore drab grey smocks and were

shambling rather than marching; their faces were blank, with drool-
ing mouths and eyes that seemed incapable of focusing properly;
their limbs often seemed to be crooked and distorted.

"Where are they going?" Niall whispered to Massig.

He shrugged. "To work. They're either the latrine squad or the
sewer squad."

This wide avenue was in a better state of repair than the narrower streets. Some of its buildings were breathtaking, stretching up
to such heights that Niall had to bend his head right back to see the
rooftops. Some of them had elaborate domes on top. One vast, square
building seemed to be built of green marble and had columns like the
ruined temple in the desert. Others had large ground-floor windows
made of some clear, transparent substance that reflected the light.
Another seemed to be built entirely of this transparent substance, and
its strange, curving planes were full of distorted reflections of the surrounding buildings. Niall tried to imagine what the original inhabitants of this extraordinary city must have been like, but found the
task beyond his narrow experience. He could only suppose that they
must have been a race of giants, or very great magicians. But in that
case, how did the spiders defeat them?

The avenue was longer than it looked. It was half an hour before
they emerged into a great open space directly opposite the white
tower. There was a wide plaza, paved with the smooth, marble-like
substance, and on the far side of this the broad space of emerald
green grass that surrounded the white tower. Facing the tower, at the
end of the avenue, there was an even taller building whose lower
stories were faced with black marble and whose upper part seemed
in an excellent state of repair. This soared above all the other buildings in the plaza. And it differed from these buildings in another
respect; it had no windows. Closer inspection revealed that its windows had all been sealed up with some white substance so that they
showed up as faint squares against the surrounding grey. Facing the
white tower across the great open space, it created the inescapable
impression of presenting it with a deliberate challenge.

Daraul made them line up in two ranks, facing the black facade.
Then he ordered Niall, Veig, and Siris to stand to one side. A few minutes later, a woman came out of the building. For a moment, Niall
thought it was Odina, then realized that this woman was taller. She was
dressed in a uniform of a black, shiny substance that left her arms bare.

"Stand to attention," Daraul muttered. "Chins up."

The woman marched across to them and surveyed the men with a hard, piercing gaze. They stared in front of them as if made of wood. Halfway down the line, she paused before a man who stood half a head taller than the rest. He had immense biceps and a chin like a rock.

"Your eyes moved," she said.

Still staring straight in front of him, the man said: "I'm sorry, commander."

The woman raised her hand as if to slap his face; the man tensed to receive the blow. Then, suddenly, she seemed to change her mind. Her fist clenched and hit him with tremendous force in the solar plexus. The man gasped and doubled up. The woman stepped back, and kicked him in the face. He was so heavy that the blow failed to make him reel backwards; instead, he sank onto his knees; the woman drew back her boot and dealt him another kick under the chin. With a groan, the man collapsed, his arms outspread, and a trickle of blood ran onto the marble. None of the other men stirred an inch. The commander glanced quickly up and down the line to make sure that no one had moved, then marched on and finished her inspection. Finally, she turned to Daraul.

"Very well, you can assign their duties." She came and stood in front of Niall, Veig, and Siris; all were attempting to maintain an unflinching stare. Niall observed that she had a faint, ironic smile.

"Which of you is Niall?"

Hardly daring to move his lips, Niall said: "I am."

"Oh." She looked surprised. She stood in front of Veig for a long time and felt his muscles, then gave him a gentle blow in the stomach with her fist. "You're stronger than you look."

Veig stared straight in front of him, unmoving.

She looked contemptuously at Siris, felt her arm, then ran her hand down over her body; Niall could sense that his mother was trying hard not to flinch.

"You look strong enough," the woman said, "but you need fattening up. And we'll have to do something about your breasts." She turned on her heel and snapped: "Follow me." She marched back towards the black-fronted building. Niall and Veig glanced at each other, then followed her. Behind them, Daraul began giving orders.

The double doors of the building were at least ten feet high and proportionately wide. Outside, in the shade of the portico, two big wolf spiders stood on guard. They were evidently of a lowly rank, for the woman ignored them. Niall, Veig, and Siris followed her into a dimly lit hallway; it took time for their eyes to become accustomed to its gloom after the dazzling morning sunlight. To their right was a wide marble staircase; two more wolf spiders stood guard at its foot. Although his sun-dazzled eyes could scarcely see them in the semi-darkness, Niall was interested to observe that they seemed to regard him with curiosity; he could sense the impulse that passed between them.

They followed her to the next floor, where she paused to speak to a woman dressed in the same black uniform, and who might, in the dim light, have been her twin sister. Here Niall sensed powerful will-vibrations which seemed to be issuing from an open door. He peered in and saw a large hall full of wolf spiders. They were standing in orderly ranks, and on a raised platform, facing them, a large black death spider was shouting orders—or what, in human language, would have been orders. The telepathic will vibrations were so strong that even Veig appeared to notice them. They were apparently beyond Siris's psychic range, although when a particularly furious shout echoed through the building, she gave a start of surprise.

The woman finished her conversation and beckoned them to follow her again. She led them up three more flights of stairs, each guarded by two wolf spiders. The third flight was covered with a heavy carpet which yielded softly under their feet. The two guards who stood at the top of this flight were black death spiders. The woman spoke to them.

"The prisoners are here to see the Death Lord."

Niall observed that she spoke in a loud, clear voice as if addressing someone slightly deaf. And the spiders, who could sense the vibrations of her voice without being able to hear it, responded directly to her meaning. One of them sent back a message that meant "pass." And the woman was sufficiently attuned to its thought vibration to understand the order. It was the first instance Niall had observed of direct communication between a human being and a spider.

She beckoned to them. Suddenly, for the first time since he had been in this city, Niall experienced a rush of panic. He was remembering Jomar's stories of Cheb of the Hundred Eyes, and the legend of the Great Betrayal, when Prince Hallat taught Cheb to understand the secrets of the human soul.

This sense of unease swept upon him so quickly that it was like a sudden storm. The more he tried to subdue it, the more the waves of panic battered against his defenses. What if the Spider Lord realized that he was responsible for the death of the spider in the desert? For one insane moment, he contemplated confessing everything, and flinging himself on the Spider Lord's mercy. He experienced a momentary gleam of hope, then thought of the swollen body of his father and knew it was an illusion.

The black door that faced him was cushioned with the same shiny material as the woman's uniform, and studded with nails that gleamed yellow in the half-light. The two death spiders who stood guard there seemed to be awaiting an order. Niall stared at it, frozen with misery and terror. Then he noticed that their escort was also nervous, and for some reason this observation brought him a spark of comfort. It was partly malicious satisfaction that the bully who had kicked a man in the face should herself be subject to fear. But there was also some deeper cause for satisfaction that eluded him.

By some process of association, he found himself thinking of the castle on the plateau. This was the image that enabled him to begin to fight the panic. It was the thought that it had been built by men, and that men had once been the lords of the earth, that provided the rallying point for his scattered resources of courage. He concentrated hard; it was difficult to maintain in the face of the panic, but he persisted. Then, suddenly, the light seemed to glow inside his skull, a single pinpoint of control and optimism. In the state of calm that followed, he realized suddenly that they were not waiting to be taken into the presence of the Death Lord. They were already in his presence. It was the Death Lord who was sending out this vibration of panic that had almost destroyed his control.

The door swung open. Their escort prostrated herself on the floor. Then, at an order from the guard, she entered the room on her hands and knees. She was so nervous that she had forgotten to beckon them to follow. Siris reached out and took the hands of her two sons; it was she who took the first step across the threshold of the Death Lord.

With a shock, Niall realized that this dark hall was familiar. So were the invisible eyes that watched him from a tunnel of grey cobwebs. This was the place that he had seen as he stared into the well in the country of red sandstone.

The will of the invisible presence issued an order; the woman crawled to the side of the room and remained kneeling. From the shadows, the eyes contemplated the three prisoners and tried to read their minds. Nothing was visible among the cobwebs, not even a stir of movement. And Niall was also still, for he felt that the slightest movement, either of his body or of his mind, would expose them all to danger.

It was a strange sensation: facing this maze of cobwebs, and recognizing the presence of a personality that stared out at them from the darkness. As a child, Niall had often been aware when someone was looking at the back of his head. This was much the same feeling, but a hundred times as strong. Before this moment, King Kazak had been the strongest personality he had ever encountered. But Kazak seemed a child to the will that now probed his own.

Niall made no attempt to simulate the mind-vibrations of the tent spider; an instinct told him that it would be pointless. He was dealing with an intelligence that was, in most respects, far greater than his own, and that would see through the deception. Instead, he merely closed his mind, while appearing to remain open and passive.

A violent blow struck him in the chest and hurled him backwards. He landed on the wooden floor with a crash that drove all the breath out of his body. Siris, who had heard and felt nothing, looked round in astonishment, then ran to help him. Another invisible blow caught her across the shoulders and knocked her spinning, so she fell on one knee. Veig, bewildered and uncertain, stared at them and wondered what was happening; to him it looked as if his family had suddenly flung themselves into random motion.

A voice inside Niall's chest said clearly: "Get up." The instruction was so clear it was as if it had been whispered in his ear. Niall's impulse to obey was instantly checked by some deeper impulse that told him to ignore it. This impulse was like a countercommand, and it overruled his fear.

Again, the voice said: "Get up." Niall pushed himself into a sitting position, then staggered to his feet. His shoulder was bruised, and the back of his head throbbed from contact with the floor. Yet the physical pain had its advantages. It enabled him to avert his mind from the relentless will that tried to force him to reveal himself.

He felt the force close round his body like a gigantic fist, squeezing his breath away. It was trying to show him that it could, if it so desired, crush him into a pulp. Niall was aware that this was true; yet, oddly enough, it failed to intimidate him. An intuitive logic told him that his invisible tormentor would not be trying to frighten him if it intended to destroy him.

To Veig and Siris, it looked as if Niall had floated clear of the ground and was hovering in the air. Then Veig saw the pain on his brother's face and rushed forward. His hands encountered Niall's shoulders, which were pinched and constricted, and tried to pull him down to Earth again. The force struck Veig, and sent him hurtling across the room so that he crashed into the wall. Siris screamed and ran to help him; this time, she was allowed to reach him. At the same moment, Niall was suddenly released and fell to his knees.

Their guard had leapt to her feet as Veig struck the wall within a few feet of her. Now she screamed: "Stand to attention!" But Niall was aware that the order came, not from her, but from the watcher in the shadows.

They obeyed her automatically. All three stood there, staring into the darkness, waiting for what would happen next. Of the three, only Niall was aware that the Death Lord was wondering whether to kill them immediately. He was also aware of an incredible fact: that this powerful being who now faced them was self-divided and troubled. The nature of the conflict eluded him. He was only aware that the Death Lord wanted to kill them, and at the same time recognized that this would solve nothing.

He was not afraid that his life hung in the balance; there was no time to be afraid. Neither was he relieved when he realized, a moment later, that their lives were to be spared.

The voice in his chest said: "You can go." For a moment, Niall was almost tricked into moving. Again, a deeper impulse stopped him. It was as if a third person were present inside him. He stood there, waiting, as the minutes passed. The room was completely silent. There was not the slightest stir among the cobwebs.

He felt the command before it was transmitted by their guard. She shouted: "All right, turn round!" And, when they obeyed her, "Follow me!" She opened the door, stood aside for them to pass, then made a low obeisance before closing it again. Niall was aware that the invisible watcher continued to observe him as they followed her down the stairs. It ceased only as he stepped out into the sunlight.

Veig and Siris looked badly shaken. Both had believed themselves on the point of death; even now, they were not sure the danger was over.

Their guard was aware that something strange had taken place, and that Niall was somehow responsible for this. She looked at him oddly, trying to understand why this slim, brown-skinned youth, with his blue eyes and clean-cut features, should be of interest to the Lord who controlled so many destinies.

Niall could have answered her question. He had known the answer ever since he heard the voice of the Spider Lord inside his chest and felt the immense power of his will crushing his body.

The two of them had met before. Their minds had confronted one another as Niall gazed into the cistern in the red desert. Ever since then, the Death Lord had been consumed with curiosity to know more of this human creature whose mind could leap across the barriers of space. He wanted to know whether Niall understood the nature of his own powers, and whether he knew how to control them.

And now, after seeing Niall, he knew as little as ever. The questions remained unanswered. But he was capable of waiting. The patience of a spider has no limits.

On the low wall that surrounded the building, a man was sitting with his head in his hands. As their guard approached, he jumped to his feet and stood to attention. Niall recognized him as the man she had kicked in the face. One of his cheeks was swollen grotesquely, and there was a cut across the bridge of his nose; one eye was turning black.

"Take these people to the supervisor," the woman said.

The man nodded smartly. She turned on her heel and went back into the building.

"Come on." The man led them across the square to a two-wheeled cart parked on the grass. He raised its shafts and indicated that they were to get in. Siris, looking sympathetically at his battered face, said: "We don't mind walking. Just tell us where to go."

The man shook his head, as Niall had known he would. "Sorry. Got to obey orders." Unwillingly, they climbed into the cart.

Now, for the first time, Niall noticed men at the base of the white tower, and that one of them was wearing a yellow tunic. He tapped the man on the shoulder.

"What are they doing?"

He glanced across the grass without interest. "They're beetle-men. We're not allowed to speak to them."

"Why not?"

"Don't know. We don't ask questions." He broke into a jog-trot, jerking them backwards in their seats. Niall looked back curiously towards the tower. The men were carrying barrels from four-wheeled carts and placing them at the base of the tower. The little man in the yellow tunic seemed to be giving the orders.

Their charioteer trotted briskly along the wide avenue, apparently without effort. Except for a few wolf spiders, and a platoon of slaves marching in the distance, it was almost deserted. Niall leaned forward and asked their charioteer:

"Where are all the people?"

The man said laconically: "Working."

Niall tuned in to the charioteer's mind and observed with surprise that he felt no resentment towards the woman who had kicked him. He felt that it was his own fault and that he deserved his punishment. Niall found such an attitude incomprehensible.

In front of a green building with columns like the ruined temple the charioteer lowered the shafts to the ground and helped them out.

"This way."

He led them up a flight of badly worn steps to a pair of elaborately decorated bronze doors, one of which he pushed open. Inside, they found themselves in a large hall with a grey marble floor; around the wall at intervals were marble benches. Huge windows filled the place with sunlight.

A woman was walking up the wide staircase. The charioteer cleared his throat and said: "Pardon me . . ."

The woman turned round and said: "Good God, Siris! What on Earth are you doing here?"

Siris recognized the voice; it took her a moment longer to associate it with the face. Then she cried: "Ingeld!" and ran to embrace her. For a few moments, both women laughed aloud, and Ingeld swung Siris clear of the ground. Then she noticed the charioteer, who was kneeling on one knee.

"Where are you taking them?" she asked.

"To the supervisor, m'lady."

"That's all right. I'll take them. You wait down here." She turned to Niall and Veig. "So they captured you too. I thought they would."

Siris asked: "Are you a prisoner?"

Ingeld smiled and raised her eyebrows.

"Not exactly . . ."

Veig was looking at her stomach. "I thought you were pregnant?"

Ingeld said casually: "Fortunately, it was a false alarm."

Niall and Veig exchanged glances. Niall knew what his brother was thinking: that Ingeld had invented her pregnancy to persuade Ulf to escort her back to Dira.

"Come and see Kazak." Ingeld slipped her arm round Siris's waist.

"Kazak?" Siris knew the name well.

"Yes, he's the supervisor."

She beckoned to them and led them up the stairs.

Ingeld had changed a great deal since they last saw her. To begin with, her black hair was now beautifully arranged, piled on top of her head, and held in place with a gold circlet. She had also gained weight, so that her figure was now statuesque. She was wearing a gleaming white tunic that showed off her shapely bronzed legs, and white sandals. Her full lips seemed redder than when Niall had last seen her. She was undoubtedly looking prosperous and healthy. By the side of her, Siris looked thin and rather drab.

The next floor was something of a disappointment for a palace. There was simply a wide corridor, with identical wooden doors all the way along. Outside a door at the far end stood two guards whom Niall recognized from the underground city. Instead of giving Niall a friendly smile—as he had expected—they stared woodenly in front of them and straightened their backs as Ingeld went past.

It was the most magnificent room Niall had ever seen. The floor was covered with a royal green carpet, and the walls hung with heavy green curtains. The ceiling was gold, and two immense chandeliers suspended from it sparkled with crystal. There was no furniture, but the floor was covered with cushions. At the far end Kazak was reclining on a pile of these while two women agitated the air around him with fans made of ostrich feathers. A shade of annoyance crossed his face as he saw the strangers who followed Ingeld, then changed to astonishment as he saw Niall. He started to stand, and the two women hastened to help him.

"My dear boy! This is amazing. Why did no one tell me you were here?" Niall blushed at this effusive welcome. "And can this be Siris?

Yes, of course it is! You look just like your sister. Welcome, my dear. Well, well. And you are? . . ."

"Veig."

"Yes, Veig, of course. And where is . . ." for a moment he tried to recollect the name—"where is Ulf?"

Siris said: "He was killed by the spiders."

Kazak shook his head, and his double chin also shook. "How dreadful! I'm so sorry. Please come and sit down." He turned to one of the women. "Bring us something to drink. Yes, that's right, my dear, sit there." Niall observed the gleam of interest in his eye as he looked at Siris. "Sit down, Niall. And you . . ." He had obviously already forgotten Veig's name. "Yes, I'm so sorry to hear about Ulf. But of course, he killed a spider, didn't he? That's why we're all here."

Niall was on the point of telling him the truth, then changed his mind. The fewer people who knew, the better.

Siris asked: "Where is Sefna?"

"She's in the women's quarters. You'll be able to join her later."

"And my children, Runa and Mara—shall I be able to see them?"

"Oh, yes, I'm sure that can be arranged."

The girl came back bringing a tray with tall metal cups. The golden drink was sweet and cool and had a lemony flavor. Kazak's was in a silver cup decorated with precious stones. He said, "Thank you, my dear," and patted the girl's thigh. Then he smiled at Siris. "I drink to your health, my dear." Out of the corner of his eye, Niall glimpsed the shade of vexation that crossed Ingeld's face.

Kazak asked: "Who sent you here?"

"A woman dressed in shiny black."

Kazak raised his eyebrows. "One of the servants of the Death Lord. How did you come to meet her?"

"She took us to see him."

Kazak was obviously perplexed. "And you've seen the Great Lord himself? But why?"

Niall let Veig and Siris describe what happened. Kazak listened intently, and his eyes took on a curious, brooding expression. When they had finished, he looked at Niall.

"Do you understand what this is all about?"

Niall said awkwardly: "I suppose it's something to do with the killing of the spider."

Kazak asked quickly: "Did he ask you about it?"

"No."

"Then it couldn't be." He gave Niall a penetrating glance from under his hooded lids, and Niall was aware of the force of his personality. "Are you sure you've no idea? You can be quite frank with me. You're among friends."

Any impulse Niall had to tell the truth was countered by the same deep impulse that had checked him in the presence of the Spider Lord. He shook his head firmly: "I've no idea."

"Mmmm." Kazak drank meditatively. "Very odd." And for the next ten minutes he questioned them carefully, getting them to describe everything that had happened since they were captured. Niall contented himself with a precise, factual account, but he was aware that Kazak was unsatisfied. The king's intuition told him that the solution of this riddle lay in Niall himself; he could not make up his mind whether Niall was withholding something or not. Again and again, Niall felt the king's penetrating glance trying to pierce through to his secret.

Ingeld was becoming bored and restive. When Kazak paused to sip his drink, she asked: "Shall I take Siris to see the women's quarters?"

Kazak shrugged. "Yes, I suppose so. And you'd better take her to see her children." He smiled at Siris. "It's against the rules, but since it's you . . ."

"But shan't I be allowed to stay with them?" Siris asked.

He shook his head. "Quite impossible, my dear. Ingeld will explain why. But don't fret. I'm sure we can arrange something." He touched her lightly under the chin. "I'll talk to you about it later."

He stood up and escorted them across the room, one hand on Siris's shoulder. At the door he turned to Niall and Veig. "You two will have to work, of course. That's the rule here. Everyone has to work. Even I have to. But you needn't start until tomorrow." He patted them on the shoulder, then turned his back, dismissing them.

In the corridor, Veig asked Ingeld: "What work does he do?"

"Work? He's the king!"

"And they still let him be king, even here?"

"Oh, yes. In fact, he's in charge of all the people here." She was evidently glad to explain it to them. "As soon as the Spider Lord saw him, he realized that Kazak was exactly what he needed. You see, the people here are so stupid. They need someone to keep them organized."

Niall said: "I thought the commanders did that."

"Yes, but that's the whole point. All the commanders are equal, so they can't appoint one above the others."

"Couldn't they appoint a spider?"

"Oh, no, that wouldn't do. To begin with, they don't really understand human beings. And of course, they can't talk." She glanced over her shoulder. "By the way, we're not supposed to call them spiders—they don't like it. We're supposed to refer to them as Masters."

They were crossing the hall downstairs when a woman came in through the door. Niall's heart turned a somersault as he recognized Merlew. Ingeld called to her: "Look who's arrived."

Merlew looked at Niall with pleased astonishment. "Well, it's the young wrestler!" Niall blushed.

Merlew had acquired a suntan. In her short white robe, she looked dazzlingly beautiful. With a sinking of the heart he realized that he found her more alluring than ever. When she gave Veig a warm smile, Niall experienced a pang of jealousy.

Merlew asked: "Where are you going?"

"I'm taking them to the nursery. Why don't you come?"

"No thanks. I've some dressmaking to do. But why not invite them to dinner this evening?"

It was clear that this idea did not appeal to Ingeld. "I'll have to ask your father first."

Merlew said smartly: "Nonsense. I'm mistress of this household. I'm inviting them."

Ingeld flushed. "Very well. You can take the responsibility."

"I will." She smiled at them. "I'll see you tonight."

Niall observed the expression on Veig's face as he stared after her. Merlew had made another conquest.

Outside, their charioteer leapt to his feet, but Ingeld surveyed the two-wheeled cart with disfavor. "It looks horribly uncomfortable. I think we'll take ours." She waved dismissively at the charioteer. "You can go." She led them back through the building and out into a paved courtyard. Here two charioteers were sitting in the shade playing the game with carved wooden sticks. When Ingeld snapped her fingers, they leapt to their feet. Niall glimpsed her fleeting smile of pleasure; she evidently enjoyed being able to exhibit her power in front of her relatives.

Niall could see why she preferred her own transport. This two-wheeled cart was large enough for half a dozen, and the seats were comfortably padded. It was made of a light yellow wood, and its wheels were large and elegant. When they were seated, Ingeld said: "To the women's quarters," and the charioteers pulled them out through a rear entrance.

Siris turned to Ingeld. "Do you have to work?"

Ingeld raised her eyebrows. "Oh, no. In this city, the men do most of the work. They seem to regard women as a superior species. It's rather pleasant." She smiled complacently at Niall and Veig. "But I wouldn't work anyway. I suppose you might say that I'm the queen."

"You're married to Kazak?"

"Oh, no, not exactly. But I'm in charge of his household."

Niall said: "I thought Merlew was."

"We share the work." Her voice was cool.

As they approached the white tower, Niall saw that the main square was swarming with activity. It seemed full of large green insects. He asked Ingeld: "What are they?"

She wrinkled her nose with disgust. "They're the beetles. I can't imagine what they're doing." She leaned forward and asked the charioteers: "Do you know what's going on?"

One of them said: "I should think they're going to 'ave another go at blowin' up the tower."

"Ah. This should be worth watching. Stop where we've got a good view."

They halted at the edge of the square, next to the building that housed the Spider Lord. The square seemed an almost solid mass of green-backed beetles. They had long powerful forelegs, yellow heads, and, at the rear, a short, tail-like appendage. They were very large—the largest probably more than six feet long—and their big bodies crashed against one another as they pushed and jostled. When Niall tuned in to their minds, he immediately experienced a sense of effervescent excitement that made him want to laugh aloud. It was totally unlike the watchful vigilance of the spiders, or the strange collective consciousness of the ants. These creatures seemed to be endowed with an excess of high spirits. If they had been human they would have slapped one another on the back and nudged one another in the ribs. As it was, they deliberately bumped against one another out of sheer exuberance.

Some of the black spiders had emerged from the building, but they stayed in the shadow of the portico. Niall sensed in them an attitude of contemptuous dislike for the beetles, mingled with a caution that seemed to contain an element of fear.

At the foot of the white tower, the men had piled barrels in a double row. Then they dragged away the empty carts and pulled them to the far side of the square, where they took up positions behind them. Only the little man in the yellow tunic was left near the tower. He picked up a small barrel and proceeded to lay a powder trail across the turf, halting at the low wall that divided the grass surrounding the tower from the main square. The beetles suddenly became still as the man struck a light with a tinder box; a moment later, a wisp of white smoke rose from the end of the powder trail and raced across the grass. The little man lay down behind the wall, and covered his ears with his hands. Something about the tension in his arms aroused in Niall an intuition of danger. He grabbed Veig and Siris by the arm.

"Quick!"

They responded to the urgency in his voice and followed him as he scrambled out of the cart. Ingeld hesitated, perhaps feeling that it would be beneath her dignity to hurry, but finally followed them. As her foot touched the ground, there was a crashing roar like a thousand thunderclaps and a blinding burst of light. A moment later, Niall felt himself caught by a tremendous wind that threw him backwards. Fortunately, the cart took most of the blast and was turned over on its side. Niall's skull exploded into stars as he was spun round and thrown against the wall of the building. Something struck him in the back and knocked the breath out of his lungs. When his vision cleared, he saw that it was Veig, who was now sprawled on the ground. Siris lay a few feet away. Ingeld, caught upright by the blast, and without the shelter of the cart, had been hurled twenty feet into the middle of the avenue. So were the two charioteers. The white tower was blackened but obviously undamaged.

There was chaos in the square, a struggling mass of beetles, many upside down, their legs waving in the air. Some of them had been picked up by the blast and hurled against the wall of the building behind them, where they had landed on top of the spiders.

The air was full of a horrible, pungent stench that made Niall cough and brought tears to his eyes. It took him a few moments to realize that the source of these choking fumes was not the explosion but the beetles themselves. One of the black spiders, trying to drag itself out from under the body of a struggling beetle, struck out with its fangs, which glanced off the green armor plating. There was the sound of an explosion, and the spider was instantly surrounded by a cloud of poisonous green gas discharged from the beetle's tail-like appendage. They were close enough for Niall to feel the heat that accompanied the cloud. The spider dragged itself clear, leaving behind the end segment of one of its legs, and hastened to remove itself from the vicinity of the choking fumes.

As order was restored, it became clear that no one had been badly hurt. Ingeld was standing up, her white tunic torn and stained with blood; but when Niall ran to help her, he discovered that the blood came from a nosebleed; her cheek was scratched, and so were her hands and knees; otherwise she seemed undamaged. Veig and Siris looked dazed, but were unhurt. The charioteers had been less fortunate; one had done a somersault over the cart and seemed to have a broken leg; the other was bleeding from a dozen cuts on his head and shoulders. Niall's intuition of danger had been sound. If they had remained in the cart, they would have been picked up and hurled backwards. Now he understood why the men had dragged their own carts so far across the square.

The little man in the yellow tunic was making his way towards them. Niall saw that it was Bill Doggins and that he was avoiding the jostling of the beetles with a skill that suggested long practice. Ingeld rushed at him screaming "Idiot!" then doubled up with coughing.

"Sorry about that," he said.

"What happened?" Niall asked.

"We used a bit too much gunpowder, that's what. Mind, it wasn't my fault. Orders from 'is 'ighness 'imself." He nodded in the direction of the headquarters of the Death Lord.

Ingeld, who was still choking, gasped: "You're a dangerous lunatic. I'm going to report you to the king."

The little man shrugged. "Report me to who you like."

She glowered at him. "I will." She turned to Siris. "I'm going back to change." She walked away with a slight limp.

Siris hardly seemed to notice her departure; she was regarding the little man with an expression of awe.

"How do you do it? Are you a magician?"

He snorted with laughter. "I wouldn't say that. I'm what used to be called a sapper. That's someone who blows things up." He held out his hand. "My name's Bill Doggins, by the way. What's yours?"

When the introductions were over, Doggins said: "Ah, well, better get on with the job. Let's go and see if we've managed to knock a few chips off it."

They followed him across the grass. His workmen had already gathered round the foot of the tower. He called: "Any luck?"

One of the men shook his head. "Not a bloody crack." He dipped a cloth in a bucket of water and wiped it across the black soot left by the explosion. "Just look at that!" The wet cloth left a spotlessly white mark behind it. "It hasn't even stuck to it!"

At close quarters, Niall could see that the tower was not pure white; there was a slight tinge of blue-grey which may have been due to the fact that it seemed partly transparent. To stare at it was a strange sensation, a little like staring into deep water. Niall felt that his eyes should be able to see through its surface, if only he tried hard enough; yet the harder he tried, the more he became aware of the reflection of his own face looking back at him. The effort seemed to make him slightly dizzy. He was reminded of the occasion when his father had taught him to dowse for water with a forked twig; at a certain point, the twig had writhed in his hands, as if it had suddenly come to life, and he had experienced this same curious dizziness as if falling slowly into a deep pit.

He reached out and wiped the black gunpowder stain with his finger; it came off on his fingertip, leaving the surface smooth and shiny. But he noticed the faint electrical tingle as he touched the tower. He pressed the flat of his hand against the spot that had already been wiped clean and the sensation seemed stronger. At the same time, he experienced an indescribable sensation in his head. It was like smelling some sharp, metallic odor, completely unlike the sulphurous smell the gunpowder had left behind. It happened again when he pressed his hand against the surface a second time and was even stronger when he used both hands.

Doggins was staring up towards the top of the tower, his face twisted into a grimace of puzzlement.

"Why'd you suppose they built it if they don't want anybody to get inside?"

Veig said: "Perhaps it's solid."

Doggins looked at Niall. "Do you think so?"

Niall thought about it, then shook his head.

"No, do you?"

"No."

"Why not?"

Doggins shrugged. "Same reason as you. I just don't."

A number of bombardier beetles had joined them. Niall could sense their disappointment as they searched the white surface for any trace of a crack. One approached Doggins and seemed to be rubbing its feelers together. To Niall's surprise, Doggins raised his hands in front of his face and made similar movements with his fingers, occasionally touching both hands together. The beetle made more movements with its feelers.

Veig whispered incredulously: "I think they're talking."

Doggins, who overheard the remark, grinned. "Of course, we're talking." He made more signals with his fingers. The beetle replied, then turned and walked away. For a creature of such size, it moved with remarkable lightness.

Niall asked: "What was he saying?"

"He says we ought to dig a trench round the foot of the tower and try to get the gunpowder underneath it."

Siris said: "But why do they want to blow it up? It's so beautiful."

"*They* don't care one way or the other. It's them bleedin' crawlies who want to blow it up."

"But why?"

Doggins sighed. "I dunno. They just don't like anything they can't understand." He glanced sideways at a number of death spiders who, together with a group of commanders, were approaching the tower. "But I don't think they're going to succeed. Not with gunpowder anyway. Now if we could get hold of a bit of dynamite or TNT . . ."

Niall walked slowly round the tower, peering hard at its surface, trying to detect any sign of an entrance. There was not even a crack in the smooth alabaster surface. He continued to experience a curious, tingling sensation, and the sharp, metallic odor.

A voice behind him said: "What are you doing here?"

He started as if awakened from a dream. Odina was standing so close that he bumped into her as he turned.

"I . . . we're . . . looking at the tower."

"You know it is forbidden for servants to approach it?"

"No, I didn't."

"Well, it is. And in this city, ignorance is no excuse. If it happens again you will be punished."

"I'm sorry."

Her stern gaze softened. "What are you doing here? Why are you not working?"

"King Kazak said we could start tomorrow."

"King Kazak?" For a moment she was puzzled. "Ah, the new supervisor. Well, he is subject to the law, like the rest of us. Idleness is against the law."

Niall said: "We were on our way to see the women's quarters and nursery. But our guide was hurt by the explosion."

"Wait here."

She left him and went back to the group of commanders who were peering into the crater left by the explosion. She talked earnestly for a while, and several of the women glanced curiously at Niall, then at Siris and Veig. After a few minutes she returned.

"Come, I will escort you." She went up to Veig, who was talking to Doggins, and tapped him briskly on the shoulder.

"Follow me."

He was startled, but obeyed her. As Siris turned to follow, Doggins gave her a solemn wink.

Odina shook her head at Veig. "Servants are not allowed to speak to slaves of the beetles."

"Why not?"

The question seemed to irritate her. "Because that is the law. We must all obey the law. And servants are not allowed to ask questions."

"I'm sorry."

His apology seemed to mollify her. She beckoned imperiously to a group of charioteers sitting on the wall that surrounded the square; they all snapped to attention. "Take us to the women's quarters." Four men pulled a cart over to them and stood at attention as they climbed in. It was only just large enough for four, and Veig and Niall were squeezed on either side of Odina. Niall found the contact of bare arms and thighs curiously disturbing. He observed that, under her bronzed suntan, Odina's face had colored.

The charioteers took a side street out of the square. The buildings towered above them, cutting out the sunlight.

Odina said: "You may ask me questions."

Veig, who disliked taking orders, replied: "But you told us we weren't to ask questions."

"I have now given you permission." Her voice was as wooden as her expression.

There was silence as they tried to think of something to ask. Then Siris spoke: "Who built this city?"

"I cannot answer that question."

Veig said: "Why aren't we allowed to speak to the servants of the beetles?"

"I cannot answer that question."

Niall said: "Where is the great happy land?"

"I cannot answer that question."

"Because you don't know the answer, or because you're not allowed to tell us?" Veig asked.

"Because I don't know the answer."

Niall said: "What is the great happy land?"

"It is a land over the sea where the faithful servants of the masters go to live out their lives in peace."

Niall said: "Can I ask you another question?"

"Yes."

"Last night, when I called the masters 'spiders,' you told me not to use that word or I'd find myself in the great happy land. What did you mean?"

She smiled. "We also use it to denote the land where the soul goes after death."

Veig said: "But the servants don't have to die before they can go there?"

She looked scandalized. "Of course, not! They go there as a reward for faithful service."

The cart had crossed two broad avenues. Ahead, the street now seemed to be blocked by a high wall. Then, as they came closer, Niall realized that the wall ran down the center of an avenue. At close quarters it was impressive: enormous carved grey blocks, each more than two feet long and cut so accurately that no mortar was required to hold them together. A row of iron spikes ran along the top. A few hundred yards along the avenue, the wall was pierced by a small gateway, whose iron gate was closed. Two wolf spiders stood on either side of it. As they approached, a woman in a black commander's uniform came out of a small stone building beside the gate. Odina called:

"These are newly arrived prisoners. I am taking the woman to her quarters."

The commander glared at Niall and Veig with obvious contempt. "Then why are the men going too?"

"They are her sons. They are going to visit their sisters in the nursery."

The woman shrugged and unlocked the gate with a huge iron key, then stood aside to allow them through. Niall and Veig kept their eyes averted from her scornful gaze. Niall asked Odina:

"Why did she seem so angry?" He meant "bad tempered" but felt it would be tactless to say so.

"Men are not allowed in this part of the city. To be caught here without permission means death."

The streets here seemed totally deserted. There were no platoons of slaves, no wolf spiders, no charioteers waiting for passengers. Even the spider webs stretched across the streets seemed dusty and old, as if abandoned long ago. Many of the windows were broken, and they could see through into empty rooms whose walls were often in a state of collapse.

At the end of another long, narrow street, they emerged suddenly into a large square. In its center was a tall column surrounded by lawns and flower beds. After the uniform grey of the buildings, the colors were dazzling. Odina said:

"This is where the women live."

The buildings that surrounded the square were all in an excellent state of preservation; their windows gleamed in the sunlight.

Many of them had impressive columns in front of the main door. On a lawn at the far end of the square, a group of women were being drilled by a commander clad in black. Other women, dressed in identical white tunics, were kneeling in the flowerbeds or pushing wheelbarrows. Odina pointed to a building with a pink facade.

"That is the hostel for newly arrived women prisoners." She tapped one of the charioteers on the shoulder. "Stop here." She explained to Niall and Veig: "Men are not allowed to approach within a hundred paces on pain of death." The cart halted in the middle of the square. She and Siris climbed out. Niall watched them cross the lawn and disappear into the pink building.

The charioteers stood at attention, holding the shafts of the cart. Niall and Veig sat there in the sunshine, staring with appreciation at the flower beds. He had never seen so many colors in such proximity: reds and purples, blues and yellows, all surrounded by the soothing green of the lawns. There were also bushes, many covered with tiny red flowers, or with magnificent purple blossoms.

They soon realized that they were also an object of curiosity. Women broke off their work to stare at them. Then a tall blonde woman who had been working nearby, trimming the edges of the grass with a small sickle, came over to them. Niall smiled at her and said hello, but she ignored him. She was looking with interest at Veig. Then she reached out and felt the muscles of his upper arm. Veig blushed. The woman smiled at him invitingly, then reached up and touched his cheek.

Niall became aware that a girl standing by the edge of the flower bed was signalling to him. When he stared at her, she beckoned imperiously and called: "Slave!" When Niall pointed to himself, she nodded, and again beckoned to him. Niall looked towards the charioteers for advice, but they were staring straight ahead. Finally, since the girl seemed to be growing impatient, Niall climbed out of the cart and went across to her. She was a pretty, dark-haired girl with a snub nose and firm chin; something about her reminded him of Merlew.

"What is your name?"

"Niall."

"Come here, Niall." The girl turned and walked away from him. Slightly mystified, he followed her towards the bushes that formed the centerpiece of the flower bed. When they were within their shade she turned to him and said imperiously: "Kiss me."

Niall gaped; it was the last thing he had expected. The girl grew tired of his hesitation, pulled him towards her and wound her arms round his neck. A moment later, her body was pressed tightly against his own while her lips kissed him swiftly and repeatedly. After his initial surprise, Niall found the sensation delicious, and abandoned himself to its pleasure.

After a few moments, the girl gave a sigh of delight and drew back to look at him. "Now kiss me," she said. Niall obeyed without hesitation. The soft lips parted, and she placed both her hands behind his head to hold their faces together. They clung together for so long that he became slightly breathless.

The girl pulled away from him, gently released herself, and peeped round the edge of the bush. Satisfied that they were unobserved, she took him by the hand and said: "Come over here." Her voice was trembling and breathless. Niall allowed her to lead him to a patch of long, unmown grass. She dropped down in it and held out her arms. Niall was puzzled. He could see no advantage in kissing horizontally rather than vertically. Nevertheless, he obeyed, and allowed himself to be pulled down beside her. A moment later, her hands were once again locked behind his head, while her lips moved so urgently against his own he felt as if she were drinking him.

A tremendous blow on the ear made his head explode with light. He looked up and saw Odina bending over them, prepared to hit him again. His head ringing, he scrambled to his feet. Odina's eyes were blazing with anger. She gave the girl a violent kick with her boot. "Get up, you slut." She turned on Niall, and he had to dodge another blow.

The girl seemed quite unafraid; the main expression on her face was of regret. When Odina drew back her foot to kick her again, a dangerous expression came into her eyes, and Odina changed her mind.

"Get back to work! I'll deal with you later." She turned on Niall. "You, get back in the cart."

The cart was empty; the four men at the shafts looked stolidly ahead, like patient horses. Odina strode past them, into the clump of flowering shrubs in the center of the next flowerbed. Niall considered whether to shout a warning to his brother, then remembered Odina's furious eyes and decided against it. There was a cry of pain, and a few moments later, Odina stormed out of the shrubbery, dragging Veig by the ear. Niall could not prevent himself from laughing, but an angry glare from Odina checked his mirth. The blonde woman followed them, looking cowed. Odina pointed silently to the cart. Veig came and joined Niall there. Without giving them another glance, Odina strode back into the pink-fronted building. The women went on with their work as if nothing had happened. From the far end of the square, they could hear the sound of feet marching in unison.

Veig said: "Do you think she is very angry?"

"She looks furious. But it wasn't my fault. I thought that girl wanted to show me something."

Veig chuckled: "She did."

A quarter of an hour went past. Finally, Odina came back, followed by Siris. She snapped an order at the charioteers, and they launched into simultaneous motion. Odina looked from Veig to Niall, but they avoided her gaze. She said: "You're lucky it was me and not some other commander. The penalty for unlawful bundling is fifty lashes."

"Bundling?"

Siris was mystified. "What have you been doing?"

"She asked me to help her move a heavy wheelbarrow," Veig said. "When we got into the bushes, she leapt on me. I thought she was going to eat me."

Odina looked sternly at Niall. "I suppose that dark haired girl asked you to go and help her?"

"No. She did this with her finger, and I went to see what she wanted."

"You're a couple of fools. Don't you realize that the women's section is forbidden territory to men? If I reported this you'd lose both your ears." But her tone had a note of protectiveness.

Niall said: "But what's wrong with kissing? Why is it against the law?"

Odina took a deep breath; for a moment, it looked as if she might get angry again. Then she shook her head pityingly.

"You have much to learn. There is nothing wrong with kissing, provided the right people are doing it. But sometimes the wrong people do it."

"Who are the wrong people?"

"Have you seen any of the slaves yet?"

"Yes, we passed some of them this morning."

"You saw how horrible they looked?"

"Yes."

"That is because their parents were the wrong people. You see how strong and healthy I am?" She stretched out her shapely arm and flexed the muscle.

"Yes."

"That is because my parents were the right people." She smiled at them with genuine kindness, as if she had explained everything.

They absorbed this in silence for a moment. Then Niall asked: "What sort of people were your parents?"

She looked surprised. "I don't know."

They all stared at her in astonishment. "You don't know?"

"Of course not."

Niall said: "But I know who my parents are."

Odina nodded. "But you are savages. You leave reproduction and breeding to chance. Why do you suppose all the commanders look so strong and healthy? Because their parents were carefully chosen. Why are all our men so tall and handsome? Because we do not leave their breeding to chance."

"But are all your babies born strong and healthy?" Siris asked.

"Of course not. But if they are weak and unhealthy, they are not allowed to live."

Siris asked mildly: "Isn't that rather cruel?"

"No. It would be cruel if we let them live, for their children might also be unhealthy. By not allowing them to live, we make sure that our whole race remains strong and healthy."

Veig asked: "But what about the slaves?"

"The slaves are an inferior class. We keep them because we need someone to do the unpleasant jobs. And of course, the spiders . . ." she quickly corrected herself, "the masters need them for their banquets."

Niall asked, with misgivings: "As servants?"

"No. No." She seemed mildly impatient. "As the main dish. They love human flesh. Of course, we also breed cows and horses and sheep. But they say human flesh tastes best of all."

This left them feeling slightly shaken. After a long pause, Veig asked: "Doesn't that . . . worry you?"

She shook her head vigorously. "Of course not. They never eat their servants—unless, of course, they go out after dark. Or break the law in some other way. Like trying to get into the women's section." She said this with a note of warning, glancing at them from under lowered eyelids.

For the past ten minutes, the cart had been traveling along the same broad avenue in the direction of the river; now, as the charioteers struggled to prevent the cart from running away on a downhill slope, it lay directly ahead of them, a wide expanse of water glittering in the sunlight. The immense bridge that had once arched across it was now broken in the middle; the rusty iron girders were twisted and bent. The charioteers were ordered to halt. Odina pointed to a low white building on the other side of the water.

"There is the nursery."

Siris asked anxiously: "But how can we get across?"

For answer, Odina pointed to a boat that lay on the foreshore at the bottom of a flight of steps. She tapped two of the charioteers on the shoulder. "You can take us across. You two wait here."

A few minutes later, they were in the middle of the river; the boat, which was like a smaller version of a Viking craft, shot forward smoothly with every stroke of the oars.

Niall asked: "How did the bridge become broken?"

"The servants of the beetles blew it up. It is to prevent the mothers from trying to see their children."

Siris asked: "But aren't the mothers *ever* allowed to see their children?"

"Of course, twice a year. Then, if they wish, they can spend a whole day together. But of course, many of them prefer not to bother. I have not seen my own children since birth."

"You have children?"

She corrected her. "I have borne children, I do not have them."

Siris asked: "But didn't you want to see them?"

She shrugged. "I missed them a little for the first week, then the feeling went away. I knew they were well cared for."

"And who is your . . . who is their father?" Siris asked.

"One was called Brucis, one was called Mardak, and one was called Kryphon."

She asked timidly: "And . . . do you still see them?"

Odina sighed; she obviously found Siris's questions naive. "I have passed them occasionally in the street. But it would be impolite to show that we knew each other. You see, they are only servants. Their business is to father children. They would be embarrassed if I spoke to them."

"But don't you *feel* anything for them?"

"Why should I? Would you expect me to feel something for these men"—she gestured at the charioteers—"because they are rowing us across the river?"

Niall glanced cautiously at the two men, wondering whether they might be upset by her remark; but they were staring straight ahead and showed no sign of having heard.

The boat bumped to a halt against a flight of steps; one of the men leapt out and secured it to a ring, then helped Odina to step ashore.

At the top of the steps they encountered a tall, powerfully-built woman dressed entirely in blue; like most of the commanders, she resembled Odina so much that she might have been her sister. She was carrying an axe that was taller than she was; a spike protruded from the back of the blade. She saluted Odina, then glanced down at Siris's stomach.

"How many months?"

"She is not pregnant," Odina said. "She is here to visit her children, who arrived a few days ago."

The woman said: "I hope you can control her." She stood to attention as they went past.

"What did she mean?" Siris asked in a whisper.

Odina shrugged. "Some of the mothers refuse to leave their children. Only last week, she had to kill one of them."

"Kill her!"

"Yes, she had to chop off her head."

Veig said: "Couldn't she just have knocked her unconscious?"

Odina shook her head decisively. "No. She was suffering from emotional disease. She might have infected others."

"Emotional disease?"

"That is what we call it when people refuse to control themselves. And of course, such a woman might produce tainted children. That is why they must be killed."

They were crossing a pleasant lawn with a large flowerbed. Ahead was a long, white building, its windows shielded by brightly colored awnings. Many women in various states of pregnancy wandered about the lawns, or sat in the shade of trees. A few women in blue uniforms could also be seen; each of these carried a small hand axe suspended from her belt.

Odina pointed to a wooden bench on the edge of the lawn. "You two will have to wait there. No men are allowed in the children's quarters. But make sure you stay there until we come back. The guards have orders to kill any man who wanders around here without permission."

Niall and Veig sat on the sun-warmed bench—it was, in fact, uncomfortably hot—and watched Siris and Odina disappear round the corner of the building. Niall could hear a strange hissing sound, and the trickle of running water; by leaning backwards and peering around an intervening tree, he could see a fountain that hurled a spray of water high into the air. It fascinated him, and he would have liked to go and investigate; but one of the women in blue was standing on the edge of the lawn and eyeing them with an open disapproval that made him nervous. He could imagine her severing his head with one fierce swing of the axe.

"What do you think about all this?" Veig indicated the women and the nursery buildings.

"It's very beautiful." To the eye of a desert dweller, it might have been the Garden of Eden.

"It's beautiful, but it makes me shiver. It's like that woman who brought us here . . ."

"What do you mean?"

"She's so pretty, and she seems so nice, yet she says such horrible things. I felt quite sick when she told us about that woman having her head chopped off—just for wanting to stay with her baby."

"Sshh!" Niall said. He suspected they could be overheard by the woman in blue and that Odina might return to find two headless bodies.

"I don't see why I should be quiet." Nevertheless Veig lowered his voice.

Niall said: "I'll tell you what puzzles me. If they go to so much trouble to make sure the babies are all strong and healthy, why are they all so *stupid*?"

Veig was struck by this. "Yes, you're right. They are stupid, aren't they?" He thought about it. "Perhaps it's because their jobs are all so boring."

Niall shook his head. "No, it's more than that. I've got a feeling . . ."

Before he could put it into words they were interrupted by an excited shout; a moment later, Runa had flung her arms round them and was trying to hug and kiss them both at the same time. Behind her came Siris, carrying Mara. And behind Siris, walking with Odina, was a slim girl dressed in a blue tunic. To his delight, Niall recognized

Dona. He freed himself from Runa and jumped to his feet; Dona ran towards him, holding out her hands. Her eyes were shining with excitement. Niall hugged her round the waist and swung her round, lifting her feet off the ground. This was too much for the blue-clad guard, who stepped forward angrily and said: "That's enough of this bundling! If you're not careful, you'll both lose your ears."

Niall put her down guiltily, and Dona turned away, abashed. Then, to Niall's surprise, Odina said: "You're quite right, commander. But these people are savages who haven't seen one another for a long time. I'll make sure they behave themselves." She gave her a winning smile. The guard shrugged ill-humoredly and turned away.

"I'll bundle you later when there's no one around," Niall whispered to Dona.

She blushed rosily, and Niall's heart turned a somersault. In the semi-darkness of Kazak's underground city, he had never noticed how pretty she was. In the months since he had last seen her, the thin child's body had filled out, and the shapely arms and shoulders were tanned.

Runa and Mara also looked sunburned and healthy; and both were distinctly plumper. When Runa asked "Where's Daddy?" Niall realized that she was unaware of her father's death. Fortunately, Mara changed the subject by asking Veig to tell her a story. Niall and Dona sat at the end of the bench and looked at each other. He felt grateful to Odina when she wandered across the lawn to talk to the guard.

"Why are you wearing that blue dress?" he asked.

"I'm one of the nursemaids. I help take care of the children. I've been given Runa and Mara to look after."

"Do you like it here?"

"Oh, yes, I love the children. But it's a bit lonely without Mummy."

"I'm going to see Kazak tonight. Would you like me to ask him if you could go and work for him? He lives in a beautiful palace."

Her eyes lit up for a moment. "Will you be there?"

"No. I have to start to work tomorrow."

Her face became sad. They looked at each other and realized that it might be a long time before they met again. Suddenly, he wanted more than anything in the world to hug and kiss her. Looking into her eyes, he was aware that she shared his desire. But in the presence of the guard—who kept glancing suspiciously towards them—it was impossible. Instead, they cautiously allowed their hands to touch.

Niall was interested to observe how far their minds seemed to be in tune. He was not making any conscious effort to read her thoughts, yet was as aware of them as if they were inside his own head. It was as if, in the excitement of rediscovering one another, their mental lives were interpenetrating.

The guard changed her position so she could observe them over Odina's shoulder. Curious to know the cause of her hostility, Niall tried tuning in to her mind. It was unexpectedly difficult, and for a moment Niall suspected that she was aware of his efforts and was deliberately blocking them. Yet her face, as she listened to Odina, seemed to betray no such awareness. He tried again and was suddenly struck by a strange suspicion: that the woman's mind was inaccessible because it was not functioning on the normal human level. A moment later, his efforts succeeded, and he realized with a shock that he had been correct. This was not the blankness he had observed so often in the inhabitants of the spider city, which was almost a form of absent-mindedness. This was the strange, watchful passivity of a spider waiting for its prey to fly into the web. Incredible as it seemed, he was looking at a human being whose mind functioned like that of a spider.

Dona, he noticed, was looking at him curiously, aware that something unusual was taking place. Yet because their minds were in harmony, she made no attempt to gain his attention; she was curious to know what was fascinating him so much.

Now, suddenly, Niall could see exactly why the guard was watching them with so much hostility. She detested savages, regarding them with contemptuous superiority. The sight of Niall and Veig filled her with antagonism. But Odina was her superior in rank; so unless Niall or Veig broke the rules, she had no right to object. The force of her dislike was so strong that Niall felt himself coloring with anger.

She seemed totally unaware that Niall was observing her mind. Something about her attitude reminded him of the tent spider, although the force of her vitality was far stronger. Impelled partly by malice, partly by curiosity, Niall tried the experiment of implanting an idea in her mind; he tried to make her feel that someone was staring at her out of a window of the nursery building. For a few seconds, nothing happened; the woman continued to listen to Odina, nodding her head and keeping Niall and Dona under observation. Then, as if she could stand it no longer, she turned abruptly and stared towards the nursery. Niall was astonished by the success of his experiment. He tried willing her to raise her hand and scratch her nose. This time she obeyed without hesitation. Niall found it almost unbelievable. She was obeying his will without even being aware of it. He made her shift from one foot to the other, fiddle with the axe at her belt, reach round to scratch the small of her back. Finally, he made her look intently towards the nursery building, trying to identify the source of her vague discomfort. While she did this, he took the opportunity to lean forward and snatch a kiss from Dona. When the guard looked back again, they had just separated.

A few minutes later, Odina turned and made a signal to Dona. It had evidently been prearranged.

"I have to go now," Dona whispered. "I've got to distract your sisters so they won't cry when you go." She glanced round to make sure the guard was looking the other way, then reached up and briefly caressed Niall's cheek. Then she stood up and took Mara by the hand. "How about a game of hide and seek? Come on—you and Runa run and hide, and I'll come and find you."

A moment later, Runa and Mara were almost out of sight among the bushes and Odina signaled that it was time to leave. Niall tried to catch Dona's eye for the last time, but she was already hurrying away across the lawn.

As he climbed back into the boat, Niall's mind was a seething ferment of questions and insights. Unaccustomed to sustained rational thinking, he felt as if his head was going to burst.

One thing seemed very clear. The nursery guard was not a spider; she was a human being. So if her mind resembled that of a spider, it must be because it had been shaped and molded by the spiders—molded from such an early age that it had taken the imprint of the spider mentality. After all, Veig had "molded" the pepsis wasp and the ants until they were, in some respects, almost human. . . .

This seemed to explain how the spiders controlled their servants. Unlike the bombardier beetles, they seemed to have no obvious form of communication. That was because it was unnecessary; they merely had to implant an idea, a suggestion. Every one of the servants of the Death Lord contained a "second self"; and that second self was a spider. . . .

So long as the spiders controlled this second self, they were the undisputed masters of their human slaves. But what they had not anticipated was that another human mind might take advantage of their training and achieve direct control of their slaves.

And now, for the first time, Niall was suddenly aware of why the Death Lord was so anxious to uncover his secret. If human beings could master the techniques of mind control, then the days of spider supremacy were numbered. Like a tame insect, the slave-mind was a lock that could be opened by more than one key.

As these thoughts struggled to find expression in words, Niall was studying Odina. Compared to the nursery guard, she was indisputably a true human being. Yet even in her, Niall could detect that curious blankness, as if a part of her mind had been put to sleep. That blankness, he now recognized, was a sign that her mind had been violated by the spiders. Her mental privacy had been stolen, and she was not even aware of it.

At the moment, for example, she was wondering what to do with the "savages." Her present situation made her vaguely unhappy. She was accustomed to living her days according to a strict routine. Although the routine varied, its rules were inflexible; for every problem, the rules had an answer. But now she was not sure which of the rules applied. She had offered to take charge of the savages because it was obviously incorrect for them to be wandering around alone. Now she had done her duty, she was not sure what to do next. At the moment, she intended to take Siris back to the women's quarters. But that would still leave the problem of what to do with Veig and Niall. . . .

The thought of being separated from his mother made Niall decide to try to implant a suggestion in Odina's mind. The boat was close to the opposite shore; time was running short. He stared at her profile, and concentrated on the suggestion that she should take them all back to Kazak's palace. It was hard to assess her reaction. As the prow of the boat gently nudged the bank, he asked: "Where are we going now?"

"I'm taking you back to the new supervisor." Her voice was clear and decisive. He could sense that she was pleased with herself for thinking of this convenient solution. It made him feel guilty, but when he looked at his mother's sad face—she was still thinking of her children—the guilt was outweighed by satisfaction at winning her this temporary reprieve.

It was mid-afternoon when they arrived back in the main square. Niall felt sorry for the charioteers; Odina had ordered them to return via a lengthy detour along the river bank, and they were exhausted. She seemed completely indifferent to their misery and often shouted at them to go faster. It occurred to Niall that this was not a matter of cruelty or callousness; her imagination simply failed to grasp them as fellow creatures. This was what disturbed him about her; she seemed pleasant, kindly, and well meaning, yet she was totally devoid of imagination.

A group of slaves was pulling a cartload of earth across the square, while others pushed behind. At the foot of the tower, more slaves were filling in the crater. Among these were a number of men whose size and muscular development proclaimed them servants rather than members of the slave class. Niall asked: "Why are those men working with the slaves?"

"They are being punished. Servants who are disobedient or lazy can be sentenced to become slaves." She added with satisfaction: "It is one of the best ways of maintaining discipline. Most servants would die rather than become a slave."

Veig asked: "Does that mean they might be eaten?"

"Of course. They lose all their privileges."

"What kind of disobedience?"

She shrugged. "Failing to show proper respect to a commander. Even staying in bed too long in the mornings."

Now Niall understood why Massig had been so nervous this morning.

Two black-clad commanders were standing on guard at the main entrance of Kazak's headquarters. Behind them, through the open door, Niall caught a glimpse of a death spider. His heart contracted with sudden apprehension as their charioteers turned into the side street and took the rear entrance that led into the courtyard. Two wolf spiders were lounging in the sun, and two more commanders stood on either side of the entrance to the building. Odina climbed out of the cart, made an obeisance to the spiders, and saluted the commanders.

"I am delivering the savages back to Supervisor Kazak."

The woman stared contemptuously at Niall and Veig.

"I will inform the supervisor. Leave them here."

Odina saluted, climbed back into the cart, and barked an order at the charioteers. She left without a backward glance.

The commander kept them waiting for ten minutes, ignoring them as though they were invisible. Staring at her, Niall found himself tuning in naturally to her emotional vibrations. What he saw made him flush with anger. She regarded "savages" as a contemptible form of animal life and was convinced they had an unpleasant smell. But most of her contempt was reserved for Siris, whom she saw as repulsively skinny and unfeminine. For a moment, Niall actually saw his mother through her eyes; it was a disturbing experience, as if Siris had been physically transformed into a kind of ape.

From somewhere inside the building, a door slammed and a woman's voice shouted an order. Their guard turned and vanished into the building. She was away for about ten minutes. The other guard gazed stolidly in front of her; her way of overcoming her disgust towards savages was to try to pretend they were not there.

The door opened; the guard snapped: "Follow me."

Even before he entered, Niall sensed the hostility that awaited him inside. What he had not expected was to find the hall full of black death spiders, so many that there was scarcely room to move between them. Niall had to fight a powerful urge to turn and run. The nearest spiders were watching him as if ready to pounce and sink their fangs into his bare flesh. For a brief moment of panic, he felt the end had come, and tensed himself to fight. But the impenetrable black eyes merely watched as he followed the guard. He could sense in them a mixture of fear and loathing, as if he were some noxious poison insect. With a detached part of his mind, he also noted that this battery of hostile willpower produced an actual sensation of physical cold, like an icy wind. When he followed the guard up the stairs, it was confined to his back. As they turned the corner, it vanished. It was impossible to doubt that the gaze of the spiders carried some negative charge.

They passed the corridor leading to Kazak's chamber and continued up the stairs; after the fourth floor, these became narrower, and Niall realized they were being taken to the top of the building. At the end of every corridor, wolf spiders stood on guard, although this part of the building seemed deserted. It was in a poor state of repair; the walls were disfigured by black and green mold, and slabs of plaster had fallen off, exposing the lath underneath.

They turned into a badly-lit corridor whose wooden floor creaked and yielded ominously under their feet. The guard opened a door and beckoned to Siris.

"You will remain in there until you are needed."

The room inside seemed to be bare, except for a bed and a wooden chair. Siris said "Thank you." Her lips were very pale. The guard slammed the door behind her and pushed a bolt into place.

Two doors farther along, she beckoned to Veig, and pointed. The door was bolted behind him.

Niall was taken to the far end of the corridor. The door was already open. She gestured for him to enter. He asked: "Are we prisoners?"

"You will speak only when you are spoken to." She stood back as he went in as if to avoid contamination from the slightest contact. The door slammed and the bolt slid into place. He heard her footsteps retreating over the creaking boards.

This room was so badly lit that it took him a few moments to see that it was entirely bare except for a few cushions scattered on the floor. There was a smell of dust and decay. The only light came from a high window which was opaque with grime.

He bent down and picked up a cushion. It was damp and smelt of mold. Quite suddenly, he felt an overwhelming desire to fling himself on the floor and burst into tears. Ever since he had discovered the bloated body of his father, Niall had carried a burden of misery; now it seemed to rise up inside him like a storm, sweeping away all attempts at resistance. Yet some final remnant of pride held him back from his surrender. He sat down in a corner on the damp cushion, pressing his forehead against his knees. At that moment he felt more alone than he had ever been in his life.

Only one explanation seemed to fit the facts: that they had somehow discovered that he was responsible for the death of the spider in the desert. In that case, there could be only one outcome: public execution for all three of them. . . . The thought of bringing so much misery on his mother and Veig made him feel like groaning aloud.

But how could they have discovered his secret? He could imagine only one possibility: that he had been betrayed by the expanding metal spear. He had wiped it carefully afterwards, to remove all traces of the spider's blood. But it might still be detectable by senses keener than his own. He cursed his own stupidity for bringing the spear with him instead of leaving it behind in the burrow.

A curious feeling of being observed made him look up and stare intently towards the door. It was made of wooden planks and looked solid enough to withstand a battering ram. When he examined it more closely, there was no sign of any crack or chink through which he might be watched. He decided that his nerves were playing tricks and sat down again. But whenever he closed his eyes, resting his forehead on his knees, the uncomfortable sense of being observed persisted. If he leaned his head back against the wall and looked straight at the door, it seemed to vanish.

Time seemed to hang in suspension. His mind slipped into a dull passivity; occasionally, his eyelids drooped and he was jerked into wakefulness as his head slid sideways. He felt that time had come to a halt. After what seemed a very long time—perhaps two hours—a faint sound made him alert. It was the squeak of a door. He listened intently, but heard nothing more. Finally, after another long silence, he heard the creak of a floorboard. He crossed to the door and placed his ear against it. There was no further sound.

That could mean only one thing: it was not a human being who had retreated along the corridor. In that silence, any human being, no matter how light, would have been audible. But a spider, with its wide leg span, could tread on the solid boards on either side of the corridor. The creak of the door indicated that it had been in the next room.

Now, suddenly, he understood that feeling of being observed. It was not of eyes watching him through some crack in the door, but of a mind tuning in to his own. Because of his fatigue and despair, he had made no attempt to shield his thoughts. He cast his mind back, trying to recall every mood and thought since he had heard the guard's retreating footsteps. Then, with a kind of mental shrug, decided it was pointless. It was too late to do anything about it.

Once again, time seemed to hang suspended. It must now be mid-evening; soon it would be dark. He was hungry and thirsty, but these sensations hardly seemed important.

A creak in the corridor galvanized him into alertness. Soft foot-steps were approaching, the steps of someone with bare feet. They stopped outside his door, and the bolt began to move.

Whoever was trying to pull it back was having difficulty. Then the door opened a few inches. A woman's voice called his name.

"Merlew!"

"Sshh!" She tiptoed into the room and closed the door behind her. "Where are you?"

"Here, in the corner." He was so glad to see her that he wanted to hug her, but was afraid of her reaction.

Merlew was peering around with distaste. "What a horrible place. Isn't there anything to sit on?"

"Some cushions."

"Oh, well, they'll have to do." Her voice was restoring him to a sense of normality; there was something very down-to-earth about Merlew. She tossed a cushion against the wall and delicately lowered herself onto it.

Niall sat beside her. "Why have you come here?"

"To see what's happening to you."

"Why?"

"Because I was worried, of course!"

His heart suddenly became so light that the miseries of the past hours seemed unimportant.

"Why have they locked us up like this?"

"Sshh! Not so loud." She placed her hand on his lips; it was soft and had a scented smell. Niall resisted the temptation to kiss it. "I can't stay long."

"Does your father know you're here?"

"No, and you must promise not to tell him." She was whispering close to his ear. The feeling of her warm breath, and of her body pressed gently against his, intoxicated him.

"Of course I wouldn't. But why has he locked us up like this?"

"It's not his fault. He has to do what they tell him. This place has been swarming with spiders all afternoon."

"What do they want?"

She whispered: "I don't know. I was hoping you could tell me."

He looked away from her, shaking his head.

After a pause, she said: "Don't you have any idea?"

He said: "I don't know."

Merlew placed her hands on his cheeks, and turned his face towards her. "Do you trust me?"

The question astonished him. "Of course, I do!"

"And you want me to help you?"

"So long as it's not dangerous for you."

Suddenly, he knew she wanted to be kissed. It was only necessary for him to lean forward for their lips to touch. She moved one hand from his cheek to the back of his head and pressed her face tightly against his. Niall's arms went round her and pulled her against him.

She was the first to disengage. Their position was uncomfortable, with bare shoulders pressed against the cold wall. He felt delight and incredulity as he saw that she was arranging the rest of the cushions on the floor. She apparently felt no incongruity in breaking off a kiss for this banal operation. A moment later, she had pulled him down beside her and pressed her body tightly against his.

It seemed so amazing that he found it hard to believe. Ten minutes ago, he had given up hope; now he felt he was holding everything he had ever wanted in his arms. If he had been told that he was to be executed the next morning, it would have left his delight untouched. He was aware of everything about her, of her bare legs pressed against his, of the silky material of the short tunic under his fingertips, of the breasts rising and falling against his chest, of the sweetness of her breath against his face. He kissed her ear, her neck where the hair began, her eyelids, and her forehead; she stroked his hair and kissed his mouth. In the sheer pleasure of physical contact, both would have been happy to lie on the damp cushions for the rest of the night.

Somewhere below, a door slammed. She sat up and listened, then went to the door and peeped out. A moment later, she tiptoed back. Niall was sitting up again, his arm and thigh tingling as the blood flowed back into them. She sat down beside him and for another moment they kissed again. She was the first to break away.

"Listen, I'll try to find out from Daddy what this is all about. But don't you have any idea?"

Niall said: "I killed a spider."

"You what?" She looked at him with incomprehension.

"It was on the way back from your city."

He told her the whole story: of the sandstorm, the finding of the telescopic spear, and of how he had suddenly found himself confronted by the buried death spider as it struggled out of the sand. She shuddered as he described driving the spear into its face. But when he had finished, she shook her head.

"I don't see how they could possibly know about that. They'd naturally assume it was your father."

"But they can read minds."

She shrugged impatiently. "I don't believe that. If they could read my mind, they'd have eaten me a long time ago."

"There was a spider in the next room when they brought me here. I think it was trying to read my mind."

She looked at him keenly. "What makes you think that?"

"I heard the door creak as it went out. And the boards in the corridor."

"Then what makes you think it was watching you?"

"I just had a sort of feeling. . . . You know how you feel when someone's staring at you from behind?"

"Do you often have feelings like that?"

He smiled. "Only when someone's staring at me from behind."

She sighed. "I just don't understand. Are you sure there's nothing else?"

"Don't you think killing a spider would explain it?"

"It might—if they knew. . . ."

She suddenly stood up.

"Where are you going?"

"To talk to my father. I'm going to try and persuade him to talk to you."

"Don't tell him about the spider."

She turned and knelt on the floor beside him. "I've got to tell him. And you've got to trust him."

"But he works for them."

"Of course, he does. He can't do anything else. And he's very lucky to work for them—it's better than cleaning sewers. But he doesn't like them. How could he when he saw them killing so many of our people? They even ate poor Nyris." She shuddered.

"I still don't feel it's a good idea to tell him about the spider. The less people who know, the better. I haven't even told my mother and brother."

She placed her hand round the back of his head.

"You've got to trust me. My father can't help you unless he knows the truth."

With her face so close to his, he found it impossible to object.

"All right. Do as you think best."

She leaned forward and gave him a long kiss. Then she stood up and went out. He heard the bolt slide back into place.

His happiness made it hard for him to think. Instead, he recalled over and over again every detail of the past quarter of an hour. When he remembered how much he had hated her, how often he had daydreamed of punishing her, he felt ashamed. It seemed absurd to be upset because she had called him "that skinny boy." That was simply her nature. She was a forthright person, used to giving orders and getting her own way. Yet she could be marvelously sweet and yielding. The thought of her lips pressed against his made him almost dizzy with pleasure. Her scent still lingered on his arms, and when he closed his eyes, he could imagine her lying beside him.

Suddenly, it was dark. He sat there, hugging his knees and reflecting that the smell of damp and mold would never again strike him as disagreeable; it would always remind him of Merlew. Merely to think of her name was a sensation like music.

He must have fallen asleep. A sudden light made him start in alarm; then Merlew's voice said: "Don't worry. It's only me." She was holding a small oil lamp. "You can come down now. My father wants to see you."

He followed her along the corridor. "What about my mother and Veig?"

"They've already gone. Look." She pushed open the end door; her lamp revealed an empty room.

They went down the stairs. The spider guards were no longer there. The lower floors of the building were brightly lit with the flames of many oil lamps, some of them enormous gold-colored objects with tall glass chimneys. Merlew blew out her own lamp and pushed open a door. "In here."

It was a large room whose walls were covered with blue and gold hangings. The furniture was of the same type he had seen in Kazak's palace in Dira, but more comfortable. Half a dozen girls were seated or lying on couches; one was brushing another's hair.

Merlew clapped her hands. "Berris, Nella." Two of the girls stood up; Niall had seen them that morning, fanning King Kazak. One of them looked at him and laughed.

"What is it?"

She pointed to a metal mirror on the wall, and he saw that the left side of his face was covered with dust; so was the whole left side of his body. The other girls stared at him and began to laugh.

Merlew flushed. "That's enough. Don't waste time!"

But the girls were plainly unimpressed; one was still laughing as she laid her hand on Niall's arm and led him out of the room. He followed her along a corridor and into a large, white tiled room whose atmosphere was heavy with steam and perfume. The floor underfoot was of mosaic tiles, not unlike the ones he had seen in the temple in the desert. In the middle of the floor there was a sunken bath, circular in shape, full of blue-tinged water that steamed gently.

The girls, both of whom were olive-skinned and dark-eyed, led him to the edge of the bath; a flight of steps went down into the scented water. When one of them started to remove his tunic, Niall started nervously and tried to cling on to it. They both laughed.

"Don't be silly! You can't have a bath in your clothes!"

"But I can undress myself . . ." In the burrow, his mother and Ingeld had always undressed in the dark, and the men had averted their eyes.

The taller of the two girls shook her head. "That's our job. You don't have to be shy. We bathe the king every morning."

Niall submitted to being stripped, and the girls held his hands as he descended into the water. It was just as well; one of the top steps was slippery, and he would have lost his balance except for their firm grip.

The water was pleasantly warm, and he recognized the scent he had smelt on Merlew's hair and hands. When he was standing in the water, up to his shoulders, the girls pulled off their own tunics and jumped in beside him; the water surged up and soaked his hair. Then, while one of the girls massaged his face and torso, the other rubbed a green liquid into his hair, then rubbed it into a cloud of foamy lather.

After this, they made him sit on the steps while they poured jugs of water over him. Every time he turned his head and caught a glimpse of naked thighs, he closed his eyes. The girls noticed this and began to tease him, pulling his face against them as they washed his hair. After a few minutes of this, he decided that he looked ridiculous and joined in the laughter.

They made him stand as they dried him with enormous towels, rubbing his hair so vigorously that it made his eyes water. He was led to a couch where they rubbed oil into his body and trimmed his nails and hair. They combed his hair and brushed it, then held it in place with a narrow band of cloth round the forehead. Finally, one of them put on her tunic and went out; when she returned, she was carrying a dark blue tunic and sandals of yellow leather. When they had dressed him in these, one of them wiped the steam off a full-length mirror and showed him his reflection. He had to agree that he had never known himself so clean and so attractive. He no longer looked like a savage, but like one of the young men who had come to greet them as they approached Dira.

The door opened, and Merlew looked in. "Is he ready? Oh, yes! How handsome!"

Niall blushed, but the mirror told him she was telling the truth.

"That blue color suits you. It belonged to Corvig."

"Where is Corvig?"

"Working on the rabbit farm. They wouldn't let Father keep him here." She nodded to the girls. "You can go now." As soon as the door closed behind them, she put her arms round his neck and pulled his face against hers. Then, sighing with reluctance she pushed him away.

"We mustn't keep the king waiting any longer. When you go in there, I want you to do this." She went gracefully on one knee, bowing her head. "Try it."

Niall did so, but felt awkward. "Do I have to? I've never done it before."

She placed her finger on his lip. "Do it for me. I want you to impress my father." She kissed him briefly. "I want him to like you."

"All right." If she had told him to fling himself, fully clothed, into the bath, he would have done it without hesitation.

She took his hand and led him out. The air felt cool to his skin and he felt as if he were treading on a cushion of yielding foam.

She pushed open the door at the end of the corridor; the room inside was lit by so many lamps that it might have been daylight. The king was lounging on a heap of cushions, tended by half a dozen girls; he looked as if he had not moved since that morning.

"Ah, my dear boy. Do come in." As Niall went on one knee and averted his head, Kazak smiled with pleasure. "Well, that was done like a courtier. Excellent!" He stood up, helped by the girls, and crossed the room. "Come and sit down. You must be starving." He placed one hand lightly on Niall's shoulder.

The door clicked; Merlew had gone.

As soon as Niall was seated, a girl handed him a metal goblet and another filled it from a long-necked jug. It was the golden liquid he had drunk with Odina on the boat. Kazak watched with approval as he drained it. The drink seemed unutterably delicious, cooling his burning throat like icy nectar. Almost immediately, Niall experienced the sensation of pleasant light-headedness and the warm glow in his veins.

The girls placed carved wooden bowls of food in front of him, fruits, nuts, soft white bread, and a dish containing small cooked birds, still warm from the oven. When he looked questioningly at Kazak, the king said: "That is all for you. I have eaten already." He gestured to one of the girls. "Krista, play our guest some music to aid his digestion."

She took up a stringed instrument, sat on the floor in front of them and began to sing in a sweet, clear voice. Kazak lay back on his cushions and closed his eyes in an expression of contentment. Niall was too ravenous to pay attention to the music. Yet in spite of his hunger, he ate sparingly. He knew that too much food would make him sleepy, and some intuition told him that he should keep his wits about him. For the same reason, he resisted the temptation to drain the second cup of the honey-colored liquid, and sipped it slowly.

When he had finished eating, one of the girls came forward with a damp, scented cloth and wiped his hands and mouth; another dried him with a soft towel.

The girl ceased playing. Kazak seemed to wake up. He looked at Niall with a benevolent smile.

"Had enough?"

"Yes thank you, Sire."

"Good. Then we can talk." He turned to the girls and clapped his hands. They gathered the food bowls and went out.

Kazak rearranged his cushions closer to Niall and sat on them with his legs crossed. He said: "Well, young man, you seem to be causing us quite an amount of trouble."

Niall blushed. "I'm very sorry. But I don't know why."

Kazak looked Niall direct in the eyes. "Don't you?"

Niall answered truthfully: "No."

Kazak frowned, staring down at his feet; the movement accentuated his double chins. He said finally: "You killed a spider."

Niall had to prevent his voice from trembling as he answered: "Yes."

Kazak stared at him. "How?"

"With a kind of spear . . ."

"This?" From under a cushion, Kazak produced the metal cylinder. "Yes."

The king held it out to him. "Show me how it works."

Niall took it from him, located the concentric circle in the metal, and pressed it; the rod slid open. Kazak watched carefully. Niall pressed again; the rod contracted. Kazak held out his hand, and Niall gave it to him. Kazak located the circle, and pressed it with his thumb. Nothing happened. He pressed again and again. Finally he handed it back to Niall.

"Is there some trick?"

"I don't think so." Niall pressed, and the rod expanded. Kazak took it from him and tried again. Nothing happened. After trying for perhaps a minute, Kazak dropped it on the floor with a motion of irritation.

"Why do you think you can do it and I can't?"

"I don't know." It had never occurred to him for a moment that the mechanism would not work for other people.

"Tell me the story of how you found it."

Obediently, Niall repeated the story of the sandstorm, of the ruined city, and of the glittering machine. Kazak reached behind him and found a bleached board and a piece of charcoal.

"Could you draw it for me?"

Niall made a crude sketch of the machine, realizing, as he did so, that he had forgotten many details. Kazak stared at it for a long time. He asked: "Can the rest of your family open and close the rod?"

"I don't know."

"Why not?"

"I . . . didn't show it to them."

Kazak nodded sympathetically. "Afraid your brother might want to take it from you?"

"Yes."

"All right. Tell me about killing the spider."

Niall repeated the story as he had told it to Merlew. Kazak interrupted to ask: "Were you looking into its face?"

"Yes."

"Yet you were still able to kill it?"

"Yes."

Kazak said: "It is almost impossible for a human being to kill a spider, unless he can take it unaware. They can knock a man down by sheer force of will. Why do you think you were able to kill this one?"

"Perhaps it was dazed from being buried in the sand."

Kazak shook his head. "No. It still had time to send an alarm signal before it died. Did it not try to resist you?"

"Yes."

"With its willpower?"

"Yes."

"Then how were you able to kill it?"

"I don't know." To Niall, the question seemed absurd. It had all happened in the blink of an eyelid, and he had not even thought about it.

Kazak refilled his goblet from the jug and sipped it thoughtfully. He looked at Niall from underneath his bristling eyebrows. "Do you begin to understand why the spiders are so interested in you?"

Niall said: "Because I killed a spider?"

"Not because you killed a spider. Because you were *able* to kill a spider."

Niall shook his head. Kazak said patiently: "I will explain. When the body of the dead spider was found, they discovered that it had been pierced through the brain. It had died instantly. Yet it had had time to send out an alarm signal. That meant that its will was fully awake and active. It should have been impossible for you even to raise that spear." He was staring into Niall's face, watching for some reaction, but Niall could only nod uncomprehendingly.

Kazak went on: "It was the first time in more than two hundred years that a spider had been killed by some other creature. The murder—because that is how they regarded it—caused a sort of panic. It meant that spiders were no longer invulnerable. They felt they had to find the killer at all costs. That is why they invaded the land of Dira. That is why more than fifty of my people died."

Niall said: "I'm sorry."

Kazak sighed. "Regrets are futile. That is also why your father died. It didn't take them long to find out that you and he were near the fortress at the time." He avoided Niall's eyes as he said this. "Now do you begin to understand why they were so anxious to find you?"

Niall averted his eyes. "To kill me?"

He was astonished when Kazak said: "No. Not necessarily to kill you. They think your father killed the spider."

After a long pause, Niall asked: "What then?"

Kazak said: "If you were the only one, it would make sense to kill you. You see, when things like this happen, they often happen to many people at the same time. I don't understand why. It seems to be a law of nature. If they kill you, there may still be dozens—perhaps hundreds—more like you." He stared into Niall's eyes. "But while you are alive, you can be of use to them."

Niall shook his head. "How?"

"Do you think you could recognize others like you?"

Even if Kazak's eyes had not been boring into his own, Niall would have recognized that everything depended on this question. Kazak was asking him to admit that he was different from others, and that he knew he was different. It was a moment when each knew precisely what was in the other's mind. Niall said finally: "I think so."

Kazak's face relaxed into a smile. He leaned forward and slapped Niall on the shoulder. "That's what I wanted to hear." Niall could sense his relief, and it surprised him; there had been no moment when Kazak had not seemed master of the situation.

Kazak moved off the cushions, stretched his legs, then relaxed once more against the wall. "Good, now we can discuss this sensibly." He refilled his goblet and handed the jug to Niall, who refilled his own goblet but took only a small sip. "But first, let us be quite clear about one thing. Would you be willing to work for the spiders?"

"Work for them?" Niall gaped with astonishment.

Kazak said with a touch of impatience: "Help them locate others like you?"

"But how could I?"

Kazak smiled. "It's perfectly simple. The spiders will comb the deserts for savages. In fact, they already know where most of them are located."

"They know?"

"Of course. Why do you think they send out those damn balloons all the time?"

Niall said: "But in that case . . ." He stopped, too bewildered to go on.

"In that case, why don't they capture them all at once? Because they need the free human beings—the savages, as they call them."

Niall was puzzled. "In what way?"

"For breeding." He smiled benevolently at Niall. "That's what most of my people are going to be used for. Haven't you noticed what's wrong with most of the people in this city?" Niall waited. "They're stupid. Most of them are little better than morons. That's because the spiders deliberately breed them for stupidity. If a child seems more intelligent or more enterprising than the others they kill him."

Niall felt his brain was spinning. "But why?"

"Why? Because intelligent human beings are a threat. To begin with, they don't like being eaten. In the days when human beings were masters of this planet, they used to breed cattle for food. Now the spiders breed people for the same purpose."

Niall said: "But only the slaves."

Kazak smiled at him pityingly. "Only the slaves! And what do you suppose happens to the others?"

"They work for the spiders."

"And when they've finished working?"

Already sensing the answer, Niall said: "They are sent to the great happy place."

Kazak laughed brutally. "The slaughterhouse."

Niall shook his head. "You mean they're *all* going to be eaten— all the servants, all the commanders?" He was thinking of Odina.

Kazak nodded. "That's right. Everybody who's not in on the secret." He added reflectively. "I don't think they'll bother to eat me—I'm too tough. Or Merlew."

"Is Merlew in on the secret?"

"Of course."

Niall felt chilled and shocked. It was hard to think of Merlew as an accomplice in this mass deception and murder.

Kazak seemed to read his thoughts. "You have to look at this sensibly. The spiders are the masters. They can do what they like, whether we agree or not. And although you might not believe this, they're not really as bad as you might suppose. Some of them are quite remarkable people. You should think of them as people, by the way, not insects. They can sense our feelings about them and don't like being regarded as insects. So get into the habit of thinking of them as people. And they *are* the masters. They can do what they like. It doesn't bother you to eat a dead bird, does it? Well, it doesn't bother them to eat a dead human. To them, we're only intelligent cattle. Yet I've known people who kept birds as pets—they loved them as much as their own children. The spiders feel the same about human beings. They often get quite fond of us. Now if it's a choice between being eaten and being regarded as a pet, I know exactly where I stand. I prefer to stay alive."

Niall was as much impressed by the king's flow of words as by his reasoning; it was the first time in his life he had heard anyone speak so fluently. Kazak's fine, masculine voice had an amazing range of tones, from caressing intimacy to passionate assertion. Niall found he was listening to it like music, yet at no point did he feel that Kazak was using it simply for effect.

He had to collect his thoughts to ask the question that was troubling him. "If the spiders kill the intelligent children, why do they need the desert people for breeding? We are more intelligent than most of these servants of the spiders."

"A good question." Kazak was like an approving schoolmaster, and Niall experienced a flash of pride. "The spiders spend ten generations reducing their servants to stupidity, and then find their servants turning into imbeciles. Where do you think the slaves come from? They're the tenth generation of people deliberately bred for stupidity. That's why they need new breeding stock—like yourself."

"Like me?" Niall was taken by surprise.

"Of course. Your job will be to father children."

Niall felt himself blushing. "And the women . . . how do they feel about it?"

Kazak said gravely: "They have no objection whatever. Except, of course, frustration at being segregated."

Niall suddenly recalled the snub-nosed girl who had lured him into the bushes; for the first time, he understood what had been happening. The thought made his brain whirl.

Kazak said: "So I think you can begin to see why I chose to cooperate with the spider people. It was not simply a question of my own survival. It was a desire to do the best I can for my people. Of course, the men aren't so badly off. But I don't want to see the women turned into breeding machines—particularly my own daughter. She seems to be rather fond of you, by the way." Niall felt himself flushing with pleasure and avoided Kazak's eyes. "Then, of course, there's your own mother. How would you like to see her penned up in the women's quarters, producing a stranger's baby once a year? Upsetting? You have the power to make sure it doesn't happen."

He drained his goblet and slowly refilled it, giving Niall time to reflect. Niall stared past the king's head, through the window; the full moon was rising in the black night sky.

"Are you sure the spiders . . . the spider people want me to work for them?" he asked finally.

Kazak nodded. "Quite sure."

"When I came in this afternoon, I felt they all wanted to kill me."

"Of course. Because for them you represent a danger. If they were certain"—he emphasized the word—"that you were an ally, they'd soon feel different."

Niall looked at him with polite disbelief. "You think they would?"

"Of course. They need your help."

"But I killed one of their kind."

"They don't know that, and I shan't tell them."

"Won't they guess?"

"Not if you don't allow them to. As far as they're concerned, the man who killed the spider is now dead—your unfortunate father. I was very sorry about that, by the way; I liked him. But we have to look at things practically. You killed a spider, they killed your father. Now you're even, and it's time to forget your grudges and work together."

"What shall I have to do?"

"We'll discuss that tomorrow. Then I shall take you to see the Spider Lord." Niall went pale. "There's nothing to fear. I think you'll find the interview pleasant enough. I shall do most of the talking."

"May I ask you one more question?"

"As many as you like, my dear boy."

"How can you be certain they're not deceiving you?"

Kazak smiled imperturbably. "You mean how can I be certain they won't kill me when I've ceased to be useful? Simple logic. They need me. They need someone to organize all the human beings in this city, someone they can trust. That's the point I'm making, Niall." It was the first time he had called Niall by his name. "They need people they can trust. Why should they eat you or me? They've thousands—hundreds of thousands—of people they can eat whenever they want to. But they've almost no intelligent human beings they can trust. That's what they really need. Besides, they're not savages, you know. They're highly civilized creatures. They have their thinkers and their artists and their statesmen—I've been talking with their leading statesman all afternoon, a spider called Dravig. You'd be amazed how fascinating these people are, once you get to know them." He studied Niall's expression and recognized the shade of doubt. "I know what you're thinking—that it's hard to feel friendly towards people who are eating human beings. I feel the same. But if they trust you, they don't mind you protecting those close to you. They accept that as normal and natural."

"What about my mother and brother? Will you let them into the secret?"

Kazak frowned thoughtfully. "I don't know. Not yet, at any rate. I have to make up my mind that they can be trusted. You see, if they can't be trusted, and we let them into the secret, we're simply endangering their lives. I haven't even let my own sons into the secret. It's better for them not to know it." He looked into Niall's eyes. "And of course, I don't have to emphasize to you how important it is to keep all this to yourself. The spider people are ruthless with those who betray their trust."

Niall nodded. "I know."

"Good." Kazak leaned forward and patted his shoulder. "I think you and I are going to make a good partnership." He clapped his hands. "Now, do you feel like more music?"

The girls came in. Without being bidden, the lute player took up her instrument and began to sing. The other girls joined in softly. Their singing was incredibly skillful and beautiful. But Niall found it difficult to concentrate. The thought of the secret filled him with a mixture of excitement and anxiety. He already knew that Veig would refuse to cooperate. Veig's nature was too straightforward; he would never feel anything but loathing for the spiders. As to his mother, how could she forgive the killers of her husband? If he now refused to cooperate with Kazak, he was condemning them to death. . . .

Kazak touched him on the shoulder. "I'm afraid you're falling asleep." It was true that he had difficulty keeping his eyes open. "Would you like to go to your sleeping chamber?" Niall nodded gratefully. "Mirris, show him to his room—the one opposite Merlew's. . . ." He smiled at Niall. "Sleep as long as you like. You have a long day tomorrow. Don't forget this." He tossed Niall the metal cylinder.

Mirris was one of the two girls who had bathed him. She gave him a mischievous backward glance as she led him up the stairs. "The king seems fond of you."

"Is he?"

"You ought to know!" She led him along a corridor whose carpet deadened their footsteps and flung open a door. He followed her into a bedroom that was so luxurious that for a moment he thought there must be some mistake.

"Are you sure this is mine?"

"Quite sure."

The bed was at least two feet above the floor and covered with a gold-colored cloth. Underfoot, the carpet felt as soft as young grass. The lights burned in tiny crystal vases, emitting a rosy glimmer.

She pulled back the coverlets. "Those are your night clothes." She pointed to a blue garment that hung over the end of the couch. "Shall I help you to undress?"

For a moment he thought she was joking; when he saw her eyes were serious, he smiled. "No, I think I can do it alone."

She gazed up at him and he could feel the radiated warmth of her body.

"But now you live in the palace, you don't have to do things alone. We are here to do things for you. I could be your personal servant. Would you like that?"

"I'm sure the king would object."

"Oh, no, I'm sure he wouldn't. Would you like me to ask him?"

It was then, quite suddenly, that Niall found himself aware of her thoughts. It seemed to happen because he was looking down into her eyes, and there was some natural sympathy between their minds. All at once, he knew that she was offering herself because the king had ordered her to. He also knew that she was delighted to obey—that there was nothing she wanted more than to be his servant. He only had to say the word, and she would regard herself as his property, to do with as he liked.

Then the thought of Merlew crossed his mind. He shook his head. "I don't think that would be a good idea."

Her face clouded with disappointment. "Why not? You need a servant."

"The princess might not agree."

Her face became puzzled. "Why not? I am only a servant. She would have no cause to be jealous."

What Niall glimpsed in her mind perplexed and disturbed him. It was almost as if they were talking about two different Merlews. He was suddenly chilled by a sense of foreboding, of learning something he would prefer not to know.

He forced himself to smile at her. "Let me ask her first."

"All right." Her face became radiant again. "Can I get you something before you go to bed—a drink, something to eat?"

He shook his head. "No, thank you."

She dropped him a curtsy before she went out, and he realized that she already regarded herself as his servant.

He sat down on the edge of the bed, which yielded softly beneath his weight, and stared blankly at his reflection in the mirror on the wall. It was like looking at a stranger. Yet it was not merely his physical appearance, the blue uniform of a king's son, the white braid round the hair, that brought this sense of estrangement. It was the feeling that all his inner certainties had been undermined.

Two hours ago, he had been in a daze of happiness to realize that Merlew found him attractive. It seemed impossible that she could love him; but when she kissed him in the bathroom, he had come to feel that it was incredible but true.

Now that certainty had evaporated. It had happened as the servant girl stared up into his face. Suddenly, he had realized that she was a bribe. Like this bedroom, she was intended to keep him happy. But she had not told him the truth—that Kazak had ordered her to be his servant. She had made it sound as if it was her own idea, and that she would have to ask the king for permission. He had to be flattered into cooperation.

Had Merlew also been ordered to bribe him—with kisses, with implied promises of love? Now, suddenly, he seemed to hear her voice: "What, that skinny boy? You must be joking," and his heart seemed to wither inside him.

The uncertainty was intolerable. He slipped off his sandals and crossed the room. His door opened noiselessly. Facing him across the corridor was a door painted royal green; the handle was shaped like a serpent. As he reached out for it, he hoped for a moment that he would find the door locked; yet even before he touched it, he knew it would be open. The handle yielded, and he pushed the door ajar.

The room was lit with the same rose-colored flames as his own. At a dressing table on the other side of the bed, Merlew was sitting, brushing her hair before the mirror. She was dressed in a long, silky garment of a creamy white color and her feet were bare. Her yellow hair was spread over her shoulders, and she was completely absorbed. If she had moved her eyes a fraction of an inch, she would have seen Niall's face watching her through the open door; but she was gazing into her own eyes, lost in thought.

He opened his mouth to speak to her, then changed his mind. Her beauty seemed to hurt his senses; he was unwilling to expose himself to further misery. Then, as he watched her face, his mind seemed to find her thought-vibration. For a moment, he was quite certain that she would sense his presence and turn round. But her absorption made her oblivious.

Then, quite suddenly, he was inside her body, drifting along with the stream of her feelings and sensations. In that moment, all his misery and jealousy disappeared; since his own identity was merged in hers, jealousy would have been an absurdity. He was aware of her essence, her reality. A few moments before, she had been an imaginary girl, a dream image created by his desire and inexperience. Now, suddenly, she was a real person, and he was ashamed of his stupidity. The girl he was now looking at was the Merlew he had glimpsed through the mind of the servant girl, who had known her since childhood. This reality was at once more complex and more commonplace than his dream image of femininity.

The real Merlew was generous, good natured, and easy to please. She was also imperious and capricious; she regarded having her own way as a law of nature.

At this moment, she was wondering idly what had happened to Niall. She liked Niall. The skinny boy, whom she had found interesting but slightly ridiculous, had improved greatly in the months since she had last seen him. He was taller and stronger, and some experience had made him more mature. Although she had been carrying out her father's orders, it had been a pleasure to make Niall fall in love with her. He was a good-looking young man, and she liked good-looking young men. At home she had been surrounded by them; here in the spider city, she felt deprived. Of course, Niall was shy and awkward, with no experience of lovemaking; but she could soon remedy that. In fact, she was looking forward to becoming his teacher; it gave her pleasure to teach men the rudiments of lovemaking. . . .

Niall closed the door silently and went back to his own room. He felt like laughing aloud. It seemed incredible that so much misery and jealousy could evaporate so quickly and so completely. He still found Merlew beautiful and desirable, but the feeling was unadulterated with illusions; he felt as though he had been married to her for ten years. He also felt as though he had aged ten years. It was not an unpleasant sensation.

All desire to sleep had vanished. He went to the window and looked out; the main avenue outside was bathed in moonlight. It looked totally deserted. By standing at an angle, he could see the white tower; it seemed to be shining in the moonlight with a milky glow. At the same time, he experienced an inexpressible sense of longing which was somehow amplified by his new feeling of freedom. Like the moon, the tower seemed remote and untouchable. Now he no longer dreamed of Merlew; the tower seemed to have become the focus of his deepest desire.

He picked up the metal cylinder from the chair where he had dropped it, and touched the button that made it expand, observing as he did so that it was not necessary to exert any pressure. The end of the rod caused a tingling in his fingers; it was the same sensation that he had experienced that morning, pressing his hands against the tower.

He went out into the corridor and closed the door behind him. At the far end, someone went past, mounting the stairs; it was one of the servant girls. He stood until she was gone, then went to the head of the stairs. As he began to descend, he heard the sound of a door closing softly. Merlew was standing in the corridor. As he watched, she knocked gently on his own door, then turned the handle and entered. Niall went on down the stairs.

The hallway was empty. He tried the main door; it was locked. But the door into the rear courtyard was open. So was the gateway into the street. Niall made no attempt at concealment; he was aware that the spiders hunted by will, not by sight, and his strange inner-calm gave him a sense of invulnerability.

The sight of the tower at the end of the avenue released a sense of serene exultancy. Even among these towering buildings, it looked enormous, and the moonlight seemed to magnify its size. His eyes remained fixed on it as he walked along the avenue. When he reached the square, he observed two wolf spider guards standing outside the entrance of the building with the black facade. They watched him without curiosity as he crossed the square; anyone who walked so casually in the moonlight must have an official reason for being abroad.

Near the tower, the smell of explosive still lingered in the air. The earth underfoot was soft where the crater had been filled in.

Niall walked slowly round the foot of the tower, staring at its milky surface. At close quarters, the glow seemed stronger than the moonlight, as if it came from inside. And as he stared at it, a curious sense of anticipation swept through his body. The rod in his hand was now tingling, prickling against the damp skin as if emitting tiny points of light. It was the sensation he had experienced in the past when dowsing for water, and it seemed to draw him towards a particular spot on the northern side of the tower. As he approached, the sense of inner certainty became stronger. He took the ends of the rod in both hands, and as soon as he did so, experienced a dizzying sensation that made him feel the ground was swaying. He looked up, and the tower seemed immense, stretching up as far as the eye could see. The metal contacted its surface, and the dizziness became a sudden acute nausea; for a moment, he was choking. His knees were buckling, and he was staggering forward into a whirlpool of darkness. Then his senses cleared, and the darkness changed into light. He was standing inside the tower.

This impression lasted only as long as it took his eyes to refocus. Then, with a shock that made him feel breathless, he found himself standing on a beach. For a moment, he felt he was dreaming. But there could be no doubting the reality of the waves breaking a few yards from his feet, or of the slimy, weed-covered rocks that stretched into the sea.

Niall had no doubt what had happened. His grandfather had told him too many tales of magic for him not to recognize an example of the enchanter's art. He stared up at the pale blue sky overhead, at the immense line of cliffs that extended into the distance, and sought some clue to his present situation. The coolness of the breeze, and the presence of drifting white clouds in the sky, argued that he was far from the desert. The trees on the clifftop were unlike any he had ever seen; they were taller, and of a darker green. The sea itself looked more grey and cold than the sea he had crossed two days ago.

It was when he was looking along the beach for the second time that he saw the old man sitting on a rock. The sight made him start; he was certain the beach had been empty a few moments ago. Now he had no doubt that he was in the presence of the magician.

When the old man raised his head, Niall received another shock; it was his grandfather Jomar. It was only as he approached closer that he began to experience doubts. This man was taller, and there was a completely different quality about his gaze. Yet the resemblance was remarkable; he might have been Jomar's brother.

As Niall came closer, the man stood up. His garments struck Niall as completely outlandish. They were of a uniform shade of pale grey, and covered his entire body from his neck to his feet. The trouser legs terminated in polished black shoes.

Niall raised his hand, palm outward, in the desert salute. Because the man was older, it would have been impolite to speak first.

The old man smiled; his eyes were of a pale blue. "Your name is Niall." It was a statement, not a question.

"Yes, Sire."

"You needn't call me sire. My name is Steeg. At least, that's what you'd better call me. How do you do?" But when Niall reached out to clasp arms, he drew back. "I don't think you'd better try to touch me." His smile made it plain this was not a rebuke. He pointed to a rock. "Would you like to sit down?"

Niall sat on the weed-covered boulder; the old man re-seated himself on his rock. He looked at Niall for several moments without speaking, then asked: "Do you know where you are?"

"Inside . . . I was inside the white tower."

"You are inside the white tower. Close your eyes." Niall obeyed. "Now feel the rock you are sitting on." Niall did so, and was astonished to realize that it had a smooth, flat surface. He opened his eyes and looked down at the green weed and the sea-worn granite. When he touched it, he could see that it was an illusion; his fingertips encountered something more like smooth wood.

The old man said: "Take off your shoes and feel the sand." Niall did so, and found that his feet were now resting on a hard, flat surface. When walking across it, it had never occurred to him to doubt that it was sand because it looked like sand.

Niall said: "You must be a great magician."

The man shook his head. "I am not any kind of a magician." He pointed to the beach. "And this is not a magical illusion. It is what used to be called a panoramic hologram. When men were still on Earth, holograms used to be the main attraction of children's amusement parks."

Niall asked eagerly: "Do you know about the time when men were lords of the earth?"

"I know everything about it."

"And are you one of those ancient men?"

The old man shook his head. "No. In fact, I am not really here at all, as you'll see if you try to touch me." He held out his hand; when Niall tried to touch it, his fingers passed through it. He felt totally unalarmed. The old man's smile was so pleasant, and his manner so casual and intimate, that it was obvious there was no cause for fear.

"But you must be very old."

"No. I am far younger than you. In fact, I am only a few minutes old." He smiled at Niall's bewilderment. "Don't worry. Everything will be explained in due course. But before we begin, I think we'd better move upstairs."

Niall glanced in bewilderment at the sky. As he did so, it vanished, and he found himself looking at a white, luminous ceiling. In place of the cliffs and the distant horizons there were the curved white walls of the tower. He was not seated on a weed-covered rock, but on a kind of solid stool made of pale wood; the old man sat on an identical stool. This circular room otherwise seemed to be empty, except for a central column stretching from floor to ceiling. But its surface seemed somehow unstable, as if it were in continuous slow motion, like smoke.

The old man stood up. "Would you like to follow me?" He walked towards the column and vanished into it, disappearing completely. But his voice issued from the smoky white surface. "Step into it, as I did."

When Niall obeyed, he found himself surrounded by a kind of white fog. Then he was floating upwards. A moment later, he stopped with a slight jerk.

"Step forward again," the old man said.

For a moment, Niall thought he was under the night sky. He could see the moon and stars overhead; the spider city lay around them. A few hundred yards away, he could see the black-fronted building of the Spider Lord. He could even see the wolf spiders standing on guard before its door. But when he stepped forward, his outstretched hand encountered glass. It was so transparent that it reflected none of the light that filled the room.

He pointed to the spider guards. "But can't they see us?"

"No. The light can enter the walls but cannot leave again."

This room was comfortably furnished with furniture not unlike that of Kazak's palace. The chairs and the couch were covered with a black substance like leather. There was a soft black carpet on the floor. The only unusual item was a device like a tall black box which stood against the glass wall; on its sloping upper surface was a panel of opaque white glass. A row of control buttons underneath it reminded Niall of the strange machine in the desert.

"What is that?" he asked.

"That is the most valuable object in this place. It cost more than this whole city to make."

"But what does it do?"

"To begin with, it creates me."

Niall recalled the creation myths his mother had told him as a child. "Is it a god?" he asked with awe.

"Oh, no, just a machine."

"But I thought only a god could create."

"That is untrue. You see, you are also creating me."

That sounded so absurd that Niall could only stare. The old man said: "I am reacting to your questions and your responses. Even my appearance is borrowed from your memory."

It took Niall some time to absorb this. "And this tower?"

"This tower was created by men before they left the earth. It was intended to be a museum—a place in which the history of the earth would be stored. When it was almost completed, men realized that the earth would pass through the tail of an immense radioactive comet."

"What is a comet?"

"I will show you. Look."

As he spoke, the sky overhead changed. The full moon became a crescent, hanging above the rooftops. The buildings of the city were suddenly transformed; their windows filled with lights, and searchlight beams illuminated the facades of the buildings in the square. And in the southern sky, directly above the great avenue, there hung a dazzling trail of white vapor, terminating at its lower end in a mass of blue-green light. It looked like a giant version of the falling stars Niall had seen so often in the desert, except that instead of moving, it hung motionless.

"This is the comet Opik," the old man said. "Its head is twelve thousand miles in diameter, and the coma—the shell surrounding the nucleus—is fifty thousand miles across. The tail is more than seven million miles long.

"It is not as frightening as it looks. This head is full of tiny particles, most of them not much bigger than a grain of sand. Even if it had struck the earth directly, it would not have destroyed it. But Opik came from somewhere beyond the solar system, and was powerfully radioactive—that means it contained substances that would destroy most animals. Men had less than a year to prepare to evacuate the earth. More than a hundred million people—most of the earth's population—escaped in giant space transporters. But before leaving, they completed this tower, for the days when men would return."

Niall shook his head. "I don't understand."

"That is why they built this tower—so the men of the future would understand."

Niall said sadly: "I am afraid I am too stupid."

"That is untrue. Your intelligence is equal to that of the man who built this machine—Torwald Steeg. But Steeg died a long time ago, and you find his language difficult to understand."

"But you said your name was Steeg."

The old man smiled. "I have a right to the name. I am all that remains of Steeg's mind." He pointed to the black box. "You see, I am not really here. I am inside that computer. And you are not really speaking to me—you are speaking to that computer."

"What is a . . . computer?"

"All your questions will be answered. But it will take a long time. Are you willing to stay here until you are satisfied?"

"Yes . . . of course. But . . ."

"But you are worried about your mother and brother."

Niall experienced a flash of superstitious fear; it was unnerving to feel that not even his thoughts were private.

"How did you know?"

"I became aware of you—or rather, the Steegmaster became aware of you"—he pointed to the computer—"when you activated the flying machine in the desert. Ever since then, we have been observing you. It was the Steegmaster that summoned you here tonight."

"Why?"

"That question will also be answered. But first, there are many other things you must know. Are you ready to begin now? Or would you prefer to sleep?"

"I don't feel like sleep. And besides . . ."

"You are worried about your mother and brother."

"Yes. I am afraid of what Kazak will do to them when he finds I am gone."

"He will do nothing to them. He will not dare to tell the Spider Lord that he allowed you to walk out. So he will pretend that he is keeping you under observation in his palace. And he will treat your mother and brother like honored guests, because he knows that as long as he holds them in his palace, you will want to return."

"How do you know this? Can you read his mind?"

"No, not as you can. But we have also been observing Kazak for a long time. We can predict how he will react. For all his cunning, he is not a difficult man to understand."

"And the Spider Lord? Can you understand his mind?"

"Very easily. You see, he has only one desire—to remain master of the earth. At the moment, his chief desire is to persuade you to help him."

"Why?"

"Because he is afraid there are others of your kind. He wants to find them all, to destroy them. When he has done that, he will destroy you and all your family."

This was something that Niall had suspected; but to hear it expressed so bluntly made his heart sink.

"Can he be defeated?"

"If he could not be defeated, he would not be afraid of you."

He asked quickly: "How can it be done?"

The old man shook his head. "You are trying to learn too fast. We must begin at the beginning. Come with me."

As he passed Niall, his clothing brushed Niall's bare arm, but Niall felt nothing; yet he observed that the garments made rustling noises, and that his footfalls were audible on the carpet.

He followed the old man into the column, and was again surrounded by white mist. His body sank gently, as if it had become a feather.

As soon as he stepped into the room, he knew it was one of Steeg's magical illusions; it was far too large to be accommodated in the tower. It was a broad gallery, about a hundred feet long, whose walls were covered with a rich brocade of blue and gold and with many pictures. At regular intervals there were pedestals with busts and statues. Crystal chandeliers hung from the decorated ceiling.

Through the windows, Niall caught glimpses of an unknown city. It was smaller than the spider city—hardly more than a small town—and the houses were only two or three stories high. It was divided by a river—the tower stood on its bank—crossed by several bridges of arched stone, and seemed to be surrounded by a wall with square towers at regular intervals. Beyond the city there were green hills with terraces. People in bright-colored clothes were going about their business through the streets and squares.

Niall was fascinated by the pictures on the walls. It was the first time he had ever seen a painting, and he was astounded that human faces could be rendered with such accuracy. He found the art of perspective even more incredible. He could see clearly that he was looking at a flat surface, yet streets and landscapes looked as if they were part of a view from a window.

"Where are we?"

"In a city that no longer exists. It was called Florence, and it was once the intellectual center of the western world."

Niall shook his head. "I cannot understand your words. What is an intellectual center? And what is the western world?"

"You will soon understand all these things. But first, your mind has to be prepared to receive the knowledge. I want you to lie down here."

In the center of the gallery there was a machine of blue-colored metal; its lower part consisted of a bed or couch above which was suspended a metal canopy whose lower face was covered by opaque glass.

"What is it for?"

"We call it the peace machine. Its purpose is to remove all tensions from the body and mind. After that, you will be ready to begin the process of absorption."

"Absorption?"

"The real name for learning. What you learn is absorbed by your mind as food is absorbed by the body, and becomes a part of you."

The surface of the bed was so soft that Niall sank into it as if it had been made of eiderdown. As soon as he did so, a light came on behind the glass above him and there was a faint humming sound. He immediately experienced a sense of relaxation so deep that it was almost painful. Aches and tensions of which he had not even been aware now became apparent as they were in the process of dissolving away. His head throbbed as a slight headache intensified for a moment, then vanished. It was as if gentle, unseen fingers were penetrating his body and untying knots of frustration. As he sighed deeply, he felt as if he were expelling all the miseries of a lifetime. The peace was like the total security of a baby falling asleep at the breast. Images floated lazily through his brain, like voices from another world. With no attempt to resist, he sank into the warm depths of unconsciousness.

As awareness returned, there were brief memories of dreams and strange events which vanished as he opened his eyes. For a moment, he struggled to remember where he was; it was as if he was awakening from one dream to another. The real world seemed strangely simple and obvious when compared with the complexity of the world of dreams.

He turned his head sideways and found himself looking at the bust of a full-bearded man with a strong nose and firm mouth. The inscription underneath it said: Plato. It took him a moment to realize that he was able to read the word carved into the pedestal. Then he sat up in excitement. He was alone in the gallery; the sun streamed in through the windows. He struggled off the bed and stood in front of the bust. Underneath the inscription there was a printed notice under glass. With a delight that made him feel drunk, he read it aloud: "Plato—real name Aristocles—was born in Athens in 427 B.C. His nickname, Plato, means 'the broad,' and referred to his broad shoulders. Frustrated in his political ambitions, Plato founded the Academy, perhaps the first university . . ." What amazed Niall was that he understood the meaning of the words. He knew that Athens was a city in ancient Greece, that political ambitions meant an attempt to become a statesman, that a university was a school for advanced learning. When he looked out of the window, he knew that he was looking at a town that rose to prominence in mediaeval Italy, that the river was called the Arno, that the tall white building with the red dome was the cathedral, the square, dark building nearby the old palace of the Medicis, in front of which Savonarola had been burned. . . .

He sat down on a chair near the window and stared down at the river. It was difficult to know precisely how much he knew, for he had to formulate a mental question before he knew whether he knew the answer. It was as if he had inherited somebody else's library, and was not sure exactly what books it contained.

The old man stepped out of the white column. "Good morning. Did you sleep well?"

"I think so."

"Are you hungry?"

"Yes." He had been so excited that he had failed to notice it.

"Then before we do anything else, you had better eat. Follow me."

He led Niall to a small room containing a few tables and chairs; out of the window, there was a view of the far side of the river with its grey city wall. Next to the window an oblong metal box stood against the wall; the surface was of a dull silver color.

"This is the food synthesizer. I am afraid we have no fresh food here. But the art of synthesis had reached a remarkable stage of perfection in the last days before men left the planet. You choose what you want by pressing the button, and it will be delivered at the hatch below."

Facing Niall on the wall by the side of the machine was a chart with a list of food and drink: fillet steak, ham and eggs, roast turkey, nut cutlet, apple pie with cream, pecan pie, cheesecake, ice cream. . . . By the side of each item was a picture and a silver button.

The old man said: "If I were you, I should stick to items you can eat with your fingers. The grilled lamb chops are usually excellent. So is the roast duck. And I believe the tomato soup is of unusual quality."

When Niall pressed the buttons he had selected, there was a whirring noise inside the metal box. Two minutes later, a small door opened with a click and three plates and a cup slid out on a metal tray. Niall carried it to the table near the window. One of its frames stood open, and a pleasant breeze blew in. From outside he could hear various sounds: the shouts of boatmen on the river, the splash of oars in the water, the clopping of horses' hooves, and the creaking of carts.

He was surprised when the old man drew back a chair and sat down opposite him.

"How can you do that if your body isn't solid?"

"This is a completely controlled environment. The Steegmaster can do almost anything." He waved his hand and all the chairs in the room began to move in and out under the tables; then the tables floated off the floor and performed a waltz in mid-air before settling down again. Accustomed to wonders, Niall merely smiled.

The food was excellent; Niall had never tasted such flavors. The tomato soup was rich and creamy, with just the right degree of astringency; the lamb chops, with rings of paper around the bone, were lightly browned outside and pink and delicate inside; the cherry flavored cheesecake was of such superlative quality that he was tempted to have a second helping; the pistachio and walnut ice cream struck him as the most amazing food he had ever tasted. Even so, it cost him an effort to swallow the final mouthful. Totally replete, feeling that his stomach was on the point of protest, he sat back in the chair, wiping his sticky fingers on a damp cloth supplied in a sealed packet.

"Men who could eat such food every day must have lived the life of gods."

"An interesting observation. But the life of gods consisted in appreciation of being godlike, and the men who created the food synthesiser were totally preoccupied with trivial problems. They were no more godlike than King Kazak or your own father."

What delighted Niall was that he could understand everything the old man said; a few hours earlier, such a sentence would have been beyond his comprehension. He asked: "How did you teach me to read?"

"A simple technique known as sleep learning. The knowledge was implanted directly in the memory cells of your brain."

"Why did you not teach me about the men who made the synthesizer at the same time?"

"In that case, you would lose all the pleasure of learning for yourself. And the pleasure is the most important part of learning."

Now that he was becoming accustomed to the old man, Niall was beginning to observe that his responses were not as natural and spontaneous as those of a human being. It was not something he would have noticed if he had not been aware that Steeg was a man-made illusion; he would have assumed simply that age had destroyed some of his spontaneity. But now he was beginning to see that Steeg's range of human responses was limited. He smiled at the right moments, he nodded in response to Niall's comments, he moistened his lip with his tongue or scratched his nose with his forefinger; but he was like an absent-minded man whose thoughts are half elsewhere, and who has to take a brief moment to register every question. There were none of the subtle human responses of sympathy that continually pass between two human beings as they converse. And when Niall tried to tune in to his thought waves, there was nothing there. It was an eerie feeling, like talking to a ghost.

The old man sighed. "Yes, it is true that I am a fairly crude device. When men were forced to leave the earth, computers had only been invented for two and a half centuries. No doubt men have now perfected computer holograms that are indistinguishable from real people."

"How can you read my thoughts?"

"The language circuits of your left brain work on simple wave patterns. When you think in words, the Steegmaster can detect them. But it cannot detect your feelings or intuitions. In that respect, it is far inferior to your own brain."

"I wish I could understand everything you say. What is a language circuit?"

"It is simpler to show you than to try to explain. Let us go back."

As he stood up, Steeg pushed back his chair with his legs. Niall was fascinated to observe the precision of his responses; there was nothing to indicate that he was bodiless.

Back in the picture gallery, the sun had risen to a point that indicated mid-morning.

"Is that the real sun?" Niall asked.

"No. If that were the real sun, you would see the spider city by its light. But no more questions. In a few hours, you will be able to answer them all for yourself. Please lie down again."

Niall positioned himself once more on the bed underneath the blue metal canopy; again, the light came on as soon as his body sank into its yielding surface. Then the enormous sense of peace and relaxation once more washed gently through his nervous system, bringing an upsurge of tremendous joy. But this time there was no desire to sleep. He was conscious of some point above his head, like an eye looking down from behind the opaque glass and conveying images directly into his brain. It was a strange process, not unlike dreaming. At the same time, a voice seemed to speak inside his chest, although it was not using human language; instead, it was evoking in him the insights and responses that language would have aroused.

When he closed his eyes, he saw the spider city spread out before him as he had first seen it from the gap in the hills: that city of immense square towers—which he now knew were called skyscrapers—with the great river dividing it into two. Then, as if he were rising vertically into the air, the city was below him. Moments later, he could see the sea, and the harbor with its great stone blocks. Then both the city and the harbor dwindled below him until they were reduced to one single point in a broad green plain. He could see the land on the other side of the ocean, and the red desert beyond the mountains. Somewhere there was the burrow, where his dead father lay. As soon as he tried to see it more clearly, the mental image became static and he was able to trace the contours of the great plateau, and of the great salt lake south of Dira. Then, once more, he was rising, so that he could see the lands to the south of the salt lake and to the north of the spider city. His speed increased until he could see the curve of the earth's surface, and the green lands below began to blend into a light blue, while the sea itself became darker. Soon he could see the earth as a furry ball, turning slowly in space. The stars looked enormous and brilliant, as if made of a kind of crystallized ice that was illuminated from inside. To his right, the sun was a ball of exploding radiance that hurt his eyes, so he had to look away. The moon was now a vast silver globe—it seemed strange to realize that it was a sphere when he had seen it all his life as a flat golden plate floating through the clouds. And although only part of its surface was illuminated by the sun, he could clearly see its darkened areas by the brilliant light of the stars.

Then they were out in space, up above the plane of the solar system, so far that the sun itself was hardly larger than an eyeball. One by one, Niall was made aware of the planets in their elliptical orbits: of Mercury, that tiny ball of red hot iron whose surface is as cracked as a wizened apple; of Venus, swathed in its atmosphere of sulphurous mist; of Mars with its frozen red deserts; of Jupiter, the vast red giant made of bubbling liquid; of the grey wanderer Saturn, whose immense bulk consists mainly of frozen hydrogen; and of Uranus, Neptune, and Pluto, whose temperatures are so low that they are little more than floating balls of ice. Niall felt chilled and overawed by the sheer size of the solar system. From the orbit of its outermost planet, Pluto, the sun looked the size of a pea, while the Earth was an almost invisible pinhead. Yet the nearest stars were still as far away from him as the earth's equator is from its polar caps.

When Niall's attention returned to the present, he realized with a shock that he had forgotten who he was. This experience had absorbed him so completely that his identity seemed slightly absurd. In the past, he had frequently "lost himself" in daydreams, or in stories told by his mother or grandfather. These had ignited his imagination; but compared with this experience, they seemed no more than a spark compared to a bonfire. It left him stunned and breathless, feeling like a man who has suddenly awakened from a dream. Immense forces were stirring inside him. He longed to ask a thousand questions, to be allowed to visit every planet in turn, then to voyage through space to other stars and solar systems. He experienced something like despair at the thought that knowledge was infinite and his own life so short.

As these thoughts disrupted his inner peace like an earthquake, the wordless voice inside him seemed to advise him to be patient. The negative emotions were dissolved away; instead, he experienced a consuming appetite for knowledge, a desire to devote the rest of his life to learning and understanding.

"Ask any questions you like," the old man's voice said. "The Steegmaster contains the sum of all human knowledge. It is for you to decide what you want to know."

"Could you tell me about the earth before the spiders came, and about the men who built this city?"

"For that we need to go back nearly five thousand million years, to the birth of the solar system. . . ."

As he closed his eyes again, the voice was no longer coming from the old man but from inside him. Now he was watching a blinding explosion that seemed to fill all space, and that hurled great spirals of gas away from its center like the arms of an octopus. The explosion seemed to go on forever, sending wave after wave of searing, destructive energy into space. Then, very slowly, it subsided, and its own gravity turned the initial explosion into an implosion. The remaining gases, sucked back together again, began to rotate in an immense whirlpool. Gradually, in the freezing cold of space, it lost its heat until the gases condensed into drops of liquid. Half a billion years later, these droplets had condensed into ten planets. Some, like Mercury, were too hot to retain an atmosphere; some, like Mars, were too small and too cold. Only the Earth, nearly a hundred million miles away from the sun, was neither too hot nor too cold.

The formation of the planet was as violent as its birth. Comets and fragments of planets crashed into it, churning it into a mass of boiling mud. It took two billion years for the earth to cool from a seething inferno into a planet with seas and continents. By then, it had shrunk to about a thousandth of its original size. And the sun had also been shrinking steadily, until it reached a point where nuclear reactions began and it turned from a dark globe into a dull red mass, then into a raging atomic furnace. Its ultraviolet rays penetrated the earth's thin atmosphere mostly of hydrogen and ammonia—and caused violent electrical storms. And as the gases and water vapor were subjected to this bombardment, the first complex molecules began to form—the sugars and amino-acids.

There also appeared a molecule called DNA—deoxyribonucleic acid—which had the peculiar property of duplicating itself. It was DNA that created the first form of life on Earth—the bacteria. The bacteria possessed only one simple instinct—to gobble up the organic compounds floating around them in the warm seas, and so steal their energy. Life began as an energy-vampire.

At this early stage, life was almost destroyed by its own success. Bacteria flourished so abundantly that they had soon eaten up most of the organic compounds in the sea. Life would have vanished as quickly as it started if one of these bacteria had not discovered a new trick: manufacturing its own food by absorbing the energy of the sun. By this process—known as photosynthesis—the bacteria learned to make sugar from carbon dioxide and water. They absorbed the sunlight through a chemical called chlorophyll, and the chlorophyll gave these tiny organisms a green color. Soon, the rocks around Earth's continents—there were four immense continents at this time—were stained with a green, slimy substance, the first algae. And the blue-green algae drank the carbon dioxide from the earth's atmosphere and turned it back into oxygen.

Another immense period of time drifted past, during which the earth's atmosphere became increasingly rich in oxygen. Once more, life was in danger of destroying itself through its own success—for to plants, oxygen is a poison, and an earth that contained only plants would die from lack of carbon dioxide. But before this could happen, a new life form appeared, a form that could absorb oxygen and change it into carbon dioxide. These tiny blobs of swimming jelly were the first animals.

As Niall looked down on the earth of a billion years ago, he saw a peaceful and static planet whose warm seas lapped gently on the shores of the barren continents—or rather, on the shores of the barren continent, for the four continents had now drifted together to form one immense land mass known to geologists as Pangaea. On this placid globe, nothing ever changed. For, oddly enough, there was no death. These primitive amoebas and worms and algae shed their old cells and grew new ones and went on living forever.

And then, somehow, life invented death, and all the amazing complexities of evolution became possible. What happened is that these simple living creatures learned how to reproduce themselves, so the parent could die, and the young take over.

A creature that goes on living for millions of years falls into a lazy rhythm of existence. It knows how to survive, and that is enough. But when a new creature is born, it knows nothing whatever. It has to fight to establish a foothold. And it has to develop the power to *remember* what it has learned. An immortal creature has no need of memory; it learned the basic tricks of survival millions of years ago. . . . A new-born creature has to pack its learning into a very short period, otherwise it will not survive. The ancient, immortal organisms were mere vegetables; the new life forms were fighters and learners.

And with the invention of death, history begins. These new organisms were no longer identical; they had individuality. And their individuality meant that they explored new environments, and so began to change in themselves. New types began to evolve new species. Sometimes, an accidental change in the DNA—some careless piece of duplication that gave the creature an extra eye or a finger—made it better able to adapt to its environment than its brothers and sisters; so it survived while they died out. Blobs of jelly turned into worms and fishes and mollusks. And some of those fishes were so spectacularly successful there was no need for further change. The giant shark arrived on Earth nearly four hundred million years ago, and his descendants resemble him in every particular.

But it is a basic law of life that, in some paradoxical sense, the less successful species are the most successful. For they go on struggling and evolving while the successful ones remain static. At roughly the same time the giant shark appeared on Earth, certain fishes with large fleshy fins made a habit of struggling up onto the beach to escape their enemies and relax in the sunlight. They were not particularly well adapted to life out of water; if the tide went out, their fleshy fins were hardly powerful enough to enable them to struggle back to the sea. And their lungs found a diet of undiluted air painfully difficult to cope with—many of them lost consciousness and suffocated before they could regain the sea. Yet the land was so much safer than the sea—for it had no other living creatures—that these early amphibians preferred to risk exhaustion and death to taking their chance among the sharks. They became the first reptiles. And after another two hundred million years of evolution, the reptiles had become the lords of the earth. The plant-eating dinosaurs were the largest creatures the earth has ever known—the brontosaurus was often twenty-five yards long and weighed thirty tons. The meat-eating dinosaurs—like tyranosaurus—were the fiercest creatures the earth has ever known. And the flying dinosaurs—the archaeopteryx and the pterodactyl—became the most mobile creatures the earth had ever known. For a hundred and fifty million years, the dinosaurs dominated. And then they became the victims of their own success. Some great catastrophe—probably a small asteroid—ploughed into the earth sixty-five million years ago and threw up a cloud of steam that turned the atmosphere into a greenhouse. The temperature soared, and the plant-eating dinosaurs, with their huge bodies, died of excess heat. The flesh-eaters, which lived off the plant-eaters, died of starvation. And, for the first time, the warm-blooded animals had a chance to multiply and flourish. The death of the dinosaurs set the scene for the appearance of man.

Man's earliest mammalian ancestor was a rodent—a tiny tree shrew with a long tail and a flexible spine. Over ten million years or so ago, they developed a flexible thumb opposite their fingers to aid them in climbing trees. The shrew developed into a monkey. Ten million more years, and the monkey had become an ape. And a mere five million years ago the chimpanzee developed into two new types of ape: the gorilla and the ape-man. And the ape-man arrived on Earth in time for a three-million-year drought known as the Pliocene era. As the vegetation decreased, the ape-man came down from his trees to spend an increasing amount of time on the ground, digging for roots and worms. He began to develop his earliest and most interesting talent—walking upright on his hind limbs. And since he could no longer rely on the forest to provide him with food, he had to learn to generalize—to scratch some kind of a living from any environment—desert, woodland, mountains, frozen tundra. And in order to cope with these new problems, he developed the largest brain of any living creature.

When, about three million years ago, the weather changed, the ape-man had become the world's most adaptable animal. Suddenly there were lakes and rivers and vast plains of grass; and on these plains were herds of grass-eating animals. The ape-man had always been capable of cooperation with others of his kind, but there had been little opportunity for it in the drought of the Pliocene. Now cooperation became a necessity. A single man stood no chance against the mammoth, the cave bear, the woolly rhinoceros, the giant red deer, and the saber-toothed tiger; but a group of hunters, lying in ambush with spears and bone clubs, were a match for most animals. The upright posture gave man an immense advantage. And the skill required in hunting developed his brain at an incredible rate. The early ape Ramapithecus had a brain that weighed about four hundred grams. The brain of the hunter was half as big again. And in a mere two million years, *Homo erectus* had a thousand-gram brain. Then, only half a million years ago, it increased its size yet again by fifty percent. This remains the average brain size of modern man.

Homo erectus invented the hand axe for skinning animals, but in a million years he made no attempt to develop this simple tool—for example, to provide it with a handle and use it as a weapon. About three-quarters of a million years ago, a group of *Homo erectus* arrived in Europe from Africa and Asia and evolved into *Homo sapiens*, the species to which modern man belongs. This new type of man did not know how to make fire, but when lightning set the forests alight, he carefully preserved the fire and kept it burning year after year. He used it to set fire to the undergrowth and drive animals into traps or over clifftops; he also used it for cooking. The great ice ages came and he used the fire to keep warm in his caves. It may have been fire that produced the "brain explosion" of half a million years ago, for it obliged man to live in integrated societies and forced him to learn the disciplines of a social animal. A small tribe of twenty or thirty human beings can live as simply as a herd of cattle. But a group of a hundred or two hundred has to learn to organize itself. Laws and customs become necessary. Above all, they have to learn good manners. And the primitive grunts that had once served to communicate had to evolve into a more sophisticated language.

There were two main sub-species of human beings about a hundred and twenty thousand years ago. One looked like modern man and was found mainly in Africa. The other, Neanderthal man, was more primitive and ape-like, yet in many ways, just as intelligent. He invented the bow and arrow, which meant that hunters could kill their prey from a distance. His women decorated themselves with red ocher. Moreover, he worshipped the sun and believed in an afterlife— or at least, we can make this assumption from the fact that he manufactured stone spheres and discs and buried his dead with some form of ritual involving flowers. For more than fifty thousand years, Neanderthal man was the dominant human species. And then, suddenly, he disappeared. And his disappearance corresponds with the sudden rise of his more "human" brother, Cro-Magnon man. It seems probable that our ancestors wiped out their Neanderthal rivals between thirty and forty thousand years ago and took over the continent of Europe for themselves.

Compared to Neanderthal men, Cro-Magnon men were supermen. They learned to communicate by speaking in sentences instead of grunts. Their priests—or shamans—used a kind of magic to aid the hunters, drawing pictures of their prey on the walls of caves and performing certain rituals to induce them to walk into the hunter's ambush. They even developed the first form of writing, scratching marks on bone to enable them to predict the phases of the moon and the march of the seasons. They learned to make boats to cross rivers and were soon using them to cross the seas. Now that they could speak, men who lived hundreds of miles apart could trade with one another, exchanging flints, pottery, and animal skins. They learned to domesticate animals; the wolf (which became the dog), the horse, the goat, and to breed cattle and sheep. About ten thousand years ago, they began to develop agriculture, learning to grow wheat and barley. And it was not long after this that they built the first walled cities, and man embarked on a new stage of his evolution.

"So you see, these early farmers had reached roughly the same stage as the men of today. The spiders have put back the clock of human evolution by ten thousand years."

Niall opened his eyes, unsure of whether it was Steeg who had spoken; but the old man was nowhere to be seen.

It was like waking from a very deep sleep; the room in which he was lying looked totally strange. Then he noticed that the sun was shining through the windows on the other side of the gallery; it was already late afternoon. He calculated that he had been lying there for eight hours. The sense of deep relaxation was the effect of the peace machine; by removing all the physical tensions that normally accumulate during prolonged mental activity, it enabled his mind to remain focused on the dream-like panorama that passed before his inner vision.

At the suggestion of some inner prompting, he made his way back to the food machine and ate a bowl of soup and an apple, noticing only as he swallowed the last mouthful that the apple had no core. He was uninterested in the food; all his being was directed to trying to absorb all he had learned and to grasp its implications.

Half an hour later, still damp from a shower—he had coped with the complexities of the bathroom with the mechanical certainty of a sleepwalker—he returned to the peace machine and lay down under its canopy, closing his eyes.

Without any transition, he found himself standing in a landscape that seemed vaguely familiar. This time, he was actually present, with no sense of his body lying on its couch. He was standing on the seashore looking towards a range of hills in the distance. There were many shrubs and palm trees, and the dry soil had a covering of marram grass. Half a mile away was a walled city. Its buildings were of baked mud, and the wall that surrounded it was a mixture of baked mud and stone. As he stared at the line of hills, he suddenly recognized the place. This was the great salt lake of Dira, and the city stood on the site of the ruined city where Niall had killed the spider.

The voice said: "Why do you suppose the city has a wall?"

"For protection against wild animals?"

"No. For protection against other men. These men who created civilization had also learned that it is easier to steal your neighbor's corn and cattle than to raise your own. That is why they needed walls. Crime and civilization were born at the same time."

The comment troubled Niall; it seemed somehow illogical. Civilization seemed momentous and significant, man's greatest single step towards control over his own life. By comparison crime seemed trivial and insignificant. Why was the voice speaking about them as if they were equally important?

"Because crime is far more important than you realize—not in itself, but as a symptom of mankind's greatest problem. Think of what it meant for men to live in cities. It was no longer necessary for every man to be a hunter or a farmer, or for every woman to be a mother and a housekeeper. Because there were so many people living together, each one could perform a different task. There were builders and farmers and weavers and toolmakers and priests. Each one had to narrow down his sights to a single specialized job. You have spent your life in the desert, struggling to find food and drink. Therefore you regarded Kazak's city as a kind of paradise. But what about the people who had been living there all their lives? Did they regard it as a paradise?"

"No."

"Why not?"

"Because they were used to it."

"Quite. And that soon became the problem of these early city dwellers. It had taken man two hundred million years to evolve from a tree shrew, and he often came close to extinction. He had battled against every kind of danger and natural catastrophe just to stay alive. And then, in the mere blink of an eyelid, he had comfort and security . . . and specialization. It happened much too fast. He couldn't change the habits of millions of years in a single lifetime. So he kept reverting back to his older self—the hunter-warrior. That is why he went to war with his neighbors. It made him feel alive again."

"But wasn't he simply destroying everything he had fought for?"

"No. Because the need for comfort and security is even stronger than the need for excitement and adventure. We want security first, *then* adventure—not the other way round. Besides, mere war and excitement failed to satisfy his most powerful appetite—his intelligence. It was a deeper urge than the craving for excitement that led him to invent the hoe and the plough, the wheel and the sail. . . ."

The words faded, and once again Niall found himself watching an inner-panorama of history and understanding it without the need for explanations. He saw the building of the first cities in Mesopotamia and Egypt and China, the rise of the warrior kings, the construction of stone temples and pyramids, the discovery of bronze, then of iron. He witnessed the rise and fall of empires: the Sumerians, the Egyptians, the Minoans, the Chaldeans, and the Assyrians. He also witnessed cruelties that left him feeling shaken and physically sick. He was spared nothing of the destruction of cities and the torture and murder of their inhabitants. The steles of the Assyrians came to life, and he watched them flogging their prisoners, beheading them, burning them alive, and impaling them on stakes. It made him burn with rage, and he watched the downfall and extinction of the Assyrian warlords with malicious satisfaction. But when it was over, he felt tainted by his own anger and hatred.

Then the scene changed to ancient Greece, and his disgust vanished as he witnessed the story of the rise of Hellenic civilization, the birth of democracy and philosophy, the invention of the drama, the discovery of geometry and experimental science. Once again he experienced that sense of enormous excitement at the widening of man's evolutionary horizons, and a sense of pride at belonging to the human species.

In spite of the soothing effects of the peace machine, the strain of absorbing so much knowledge was exhausting. While he was watching the story of the war between Athens and Sparta, the pictures began to blend together and then dissolved into a dream. He woke a few hours later to find himself in darkness and covered with a blanket. Through the window, he could see the dome of the cathedral outlined against the stars. And when he woke again it was already mid-morning, and he could hear the cry of the boatmen, and the vendors in the market place. Once again, he found the food machine and went through the automatic process of eating and drinking; food and drink seemed unimportant in comparison with his craving to learn the remainder of the story of mankind. Then he hurried back and lay down once more under the frosted glass screen.

This time, the dream showed him the story of ancient Rome. He witnessed the age of democratic government, the wars against

Carthage, the rise of the dictator emperors: Marius and Sulla, Julius Caesar, Augustus, Tiberius, Caligula, Claudius, Nero. Once again, he was appalled and morbidly fascinated by this endless tale of bloodshed and stupidity. The story of the birth of Christianity engendered a mood of hope; this doctrine of love and universal brotherhood seemed the most promising development since the birth of civilization. The history of the Church's rise to power under the emperor Constantine made him realize that his optimism had been premature. These Christians showed even less tolerance of their religious opponents than the Romans had done; they even murdered one another over obscure doctrinal points. After witnessing the downfall of Rome under the onslaught of the barbarians, Niall experienced a certain weary resignation. As the picture faded and he again became conscious of his surroundings, he asked:

"Does it go on like this? Is all human history so depressing?"

The voice inside him said: "Not entirely. The next thousand years are depressing because the Church tried to maintain its grip on the minds of men and killed anyone who tried to think for himself. But all that began to change at about the time Brunelleschi built the dome of that cathedral out there." Niall sat up, massaging his eyes. "The change began with a series of great wars called the Crusades, when men began to travel instead of staying in the same place all the time. That broadened their minds, and they built ships and began to explore the world. Then a man called John Gooseflesh invented printing, and someone else learned how to make cheap paper, and suddenly there were millions of books. Then the Church began to lose the battle to prevent people from thinking for themselves. . . ."

Niall's fatigue suddenly vanished; he lay down again and closed his eyes.

"Show me."

This new installment of the tale was the most absorbing so far. He witnessed the story of the Reformation, then how an amateur astronomer named Copernicus realized that the earth traveled round the sun. He saw the invention of the telescope and the great battle between Galileo and Pope Paul V about whether the earth was really the center of the universe. He witnessed the discoveries of Sir Isaac Newton and the foundation of the Royal Society, and watched with delight as the voice of the Age of Reason refused to be silenced by the threats of the Church. He began to feel that at last humanity had discovered the secret of peace and greatness. He even applauded the storming of the Bastille and the execution of Louis XVI—for surely the execution of a few tyrants was excusable in the name of freedom and the brotherhood of man?

The nineteenth century seemed to justify his excitement. With its invention of the railway, the steamship, the telegraph, electric light, it seemed to promise the emergence of a new kind of man. But even as these thoughts filled him with optimism—and perhaps as a response to his optimism—the scene changed to a panorama of nineteenth-century wars and revolutions: the Napoleonic Wars, the revolutions of 1848, the Crimean War, the Indian mutiny, the American Civil War, the Franco-Prussian War, the Russo-Turkish War, and once again he felt himself slipping into depression. It seemed incredible that his own species should be capable of so much greatness and so much stupidity. But as he stirred restively, the voice said:

"Be patient for a while. There are still interesting developments to come."

So Niall closed his eyes again, and tried to suspend his judgement as he witnessed the history of the twentieth century: the Great War, the Russian Revolution, the rise of the Fascists and the Nazis, the Sino-Japanese War, the Second World War, the invention of the atomic and hydrogen bombs, and the uneasy armed peace that these brought about. The scale of human achievement continued to excite him: the aeroplane, radio and television, the computer, the exploration of space. But by now he had become aware of the basic pattern, and had begun to fear that nothing could change it. It seemed depressingly obvious that man had grown into an intellectual giant while remaining an emotional pygmy.

The voice read his thoughts. "Yes, it is true that the history of the human race seems to point towards catastrophe. But that is because I am forced to oversimplify. If you could spend six months here, studying everything in more detail, you would find more cause for hope. Man really has remarkable powers of adaptation."

"But did they go on behaving so stupidly until the comet forced them to leave the earth?"

"For some time, yes. Although atomic weapons forced them to stop fighting world wars, they made up for it with hundreds of minor wars. And meanwhile, their crime rate became so appalling that people were forced to turn their houses into fortresses. In spite of all attempts to prevent it, the world's population continued to rise until the cities were like overcrowded ant hills where it was dangerous to walk the streets. Early in the twenty-first century, they invented a weapon that made war more fascinating and devastating than ever— the Reaper. It was a kind of machine-gun that fired a beam of atomic energy, so that it could be used to cut down a tree or demolish a whole street full of houses. Man found it impossible to resist using anything so magnificently destructive; it became the favorite weapon of terrorists—people who try to achieve their political ends through violence— and governments found it practically impossible to control them.

"And then, in the middle of the twenty-first century, two doctors—a great physiologist and a great psychologist—built the first peace machine. This was one of the most important inventions in the history of the human race. Suddenly, man had a simple method of releasing all the tensions that had made him so destructive. In the past, they had invented various drugs that had a similar effect, but men became addicted to them and wasted their lives. The peace machine was not addictive—it simply left them relaxed and full of energy and courage. Mental illness almost disappeared. So did violent crime. Wars also became increasingly rare. For a while, men congratulated themselves on having solved their greatest problem, and the two scientists—Chater and Takahashi—were regarded almost as saints. Takahashi became president of the Federated Afro-European States. The population rate also began to fall, so that by the year 2100, there were less human beings on Earth than in 1900.

"Yet by that time it had become clear that the greatest of all problems remained. Man had not solved the secret of happiness. In spite of the low crime rate and the freedom from stress, men still felt strangely unfulfilled. They felt that life should be something more than a peaceful, pleasant routine, and that man needed new worlds to conquer. And since they knew there were no such worlds in their own solar system, they began to experiment with space craft in an effort to reach the stars. They had received signals from space that told them there was intelligent life in the star cluster called Alpha Centauri. But even the light from Centauri takes five years to reach the earth. Their fastest space craft would take centuries to reach the nearest star. They decided that the answer was to build space craft that were like miniature planets, containing gardens and rivers—even mountains. The first of these was launched in the year 2100 and set out for the planetary system of Proxima Centauri. Twenty years later, it was overtaken by the first of a new type of space craft with laser drive—an energy that enabled them to reach half the speed of light. The first craft to reach the Centauri system arrived in the year 2130 and established a small colony called New Earth. But most of its inhabitants became homesick and spent another ten years returning.

"Back on Earth, the situation remained much as before. The crime rate had started to rise again, because people were beginning to commit crimes out of boredom. But at least men were intelligent enough to understand the nature of the problem. It was simply that man had evolved much too fast. It had taken him more than a million years to change from a cave dweller into a city dweller, but a mere seven thousand years—less than three hundred generations—to change from a city dweller into a space explorer. Even his body was not ready for the change. It was made for hard work and effort, not for sitting in office chairs. All his instincts were directed towards struggle, and he felt suffocated by his comfortable, peaceful civilization. Men even began to look back nostalgically on the days when war and crime made life more dangerous. A famous biologist wrote a book asserting that the human race would finally die of boredom.

"At that point men suddenly learned that life was in danger of being destroyed by a radioactive comet. It was like a great awakening. Now they had one single aim—to avert the catastrophe. At first they thought of destroying the comet, or trying to divert it, but it was simply too big—fifty thousand miles in diameter. When it became obvious that the collision was inevitable, and that it would occur in less than five years, they began to devote their immense technical resources to building more than a thousand giant space transports. Other scientists began a race to find ways of making human beings immune to radioactivity, by studying the scorpions who are able to absorb hundreds of times as much radiation as animals. They thought they had probably discovered the solution, but few human beings were willing to try it. In the year 2175, the earth was finally evacuated. Six weeks later, the comet passed close to Earth and brushed it with its tail. It destroyed nine-tenths of all animal life, including most of the human beings who stayed behind.

"The last of the space transports left the solar system a few weeks later. An astronomer on board took the last photographs of the comet as it swung around the sun and headed out into space. And he saw something that baffled him. The tail of a comet always points away from the sun, because it is created by the pressure of sunlight on the light gases. Yet as Opik began to leave the solar system, its tail was apparently still pointing backwards. Most scientists refused to accept the evidence of the photographs, because they said it was impossible. But a few began to wonder whether the collision between the comet and the earth was really the million to one chance they had all supposed. . . .

"This tower, and forty-nine more like it, were built in various parts of the earth. This was the first to be built. It was originally intended to be a museum—or time capsule, as they called it—containing the sum of all human knowledge. It was also designed to gather information about what happened on Earth after the great exodus."

"But how can you gather information without leaving the tower?"

"From the minds of human beings. Thought-reading machines were invented late in the twenty-first century, as a by-product of research into sleep-learning. When men learned how to feed knowledge directly into the human memory circuits, they also discovered how to decipher what was already stored in those circuits."

Niall found the thought disquieting. "So you can read everything that goes on in my mind?"

"No. I said thought-reading machines, not mind-reading machines. Your thoughts are only the topmost layer of your mind. They operate on a series of coded signals that can be detected like radio waves. A powerful thought-reading machine can decipher most of the contents of your long-term memory. But it has no power to detect your feelings or intuitions—or the decisions of your will. We collect most of our information from the brains of human beings while they are asleep."

"But what do you want it for?"

"So the men of New Earth can stay in touch with what is happening on Earth."

Niall's heart leapt. "You are able to speak to them?"

"All the information gathered by the Steegmaster is transmitted directly to New Earth."

"So they already know about me?"

"Not yet. It takes five years for the radio signals to reach them."

"But they know about the spiders?"

"Of course."

Niall said eagerly: "Do you think they might come back to Earth and help us fight them?"

"No. Why should they?"

The bluntness startled and dismayed him. He answered lamely: "Because . . . because they are human beings too."

"True. But it would take them ten years to reach the earth, even after they had received your message. Why should they go to so much trouble to help you when you could help yourself?"

The answer rekindled his feeling of hope. "Do you believe we could do it ourselves?"

"If you cannot, then you do not deserve to be free. The law of life is the survival of the fittest. If you cannot defeat the spiders, then you are not fit to survive, and they would deserve to remain the masters of the earth."

This made Niall thoughtful. He said finally: "When I first came here, you promised you would show me how to defeat the spiders. Could you do that?"

"I could."

"But will you?"

"I am afraid it is not permitted."

Niall's heart sank. "Why not?"

There was a pause, then the voice said: "I will make a bargain with you. If you can tell me why not, then I will try to help you."

Niall shook his head in bewilderment. "Is it some kind of riddle?"

"No. Just a bargain."

"But . . . how long can I have to think about it?"

"As far as I am concerned, it is a matter of indifference. But I would not advise you to take too long."

"Why not?"

"Because the longer you stay, the more difficult you will find it to escape. The spiders are still unaware that you are missing. When they find out, it will not take them long to guess where you are hiding. When that happens, there will be an army of spiders to prevent you leaving the tower."

"But how will they guess where I am?"

"You were seen coming towards the tower—have you forgotten?"

Niall remembered the wolf spiders who had been guarding the headquarters of the Death Lord.

"Why haven't they raised the alarm?"

"Because no one knows you are missing yet."

Niall found himself automatically looking out of the window; it was frustrating to see the citizens of Florence going placidly about their business. He asked: "Do you know what is happening to my mother and brother?"

"Yes."

"Can you tell me?"

The voice said: "Close your eyes."

As soon as Niall's eyelids closed, he found himself in Kazak's palace. There was nothing dreamlike about the experience. He was standing in a corner of the room in which he had last spoken to Kazak. There were four people in the room: Kazak, Veig, his mother, and the black-clad guard who had locked him up. The woman was standing to attention, staring straight in front of her. Siris was seated on a pile of cushions; her face looked set and exhausted. The king was standing with his back to the room, looking out of the window. Veig was also standing; Niall thought he looked unhappy and unsure of himself.

"We know he must be hiding somewhere in this city," Kazak said. "If you want to see him alive again, we have to find him before the spiders do."

Veig shook his head. "If we could understand why he ran away —I . . ."

Kazak said irritably: "I've told you, I don't know. It was a stupid thing to do. Everything seemed to be going so well. . . ."

Veig said: "I think he's trying to get back to the nursery."

Siris gave a startled cry; she was staring at Niall. It made Kazak start convulsively. He said angrily: "What the devil are you . . ." Then he also saw Niall. His face expressed astonishment and relief.

"Thank God for that! Where on earth have you been?"

When Niall tried to reply, he found he had no voice. It was a nightmarish sensation; his lips moved, but no sound came out. Then he felt the scene fading. When he opened his eyes, he was still standing by the open window, looking down at the Arno. The old man was standing a few feet away, regarding him with an ironic smile. The whole experience had taken only a few seconds.

He asked: "What happened?"

"You broke the contact."

Niall was feeling so dizzy that he had to sit down on the nearest bench. His heart was pounding violently, and perspiration was running down his face. For a moment he thought he was about to faint. Then the sickness passed, and his vision cleared. He felt very tired.

"They saw me."

"Your mother saw you. So did Kazak."

"Not the other two?" It had all happened so quickly that he had not noticed.

"No."

He buried his face in his hands; it made him feel better.

"Why is my head so strange?"

"You tried to speak, and drained all your psychic energy."

"But they saw me. I was there."

"They saw you with their minds, not their eyes."

After a minute, his heart ceased to pound. His throat felt dry and parched.

"I'm going to get a drink."

He made his way along the corridor to the food machine. It was no surprise to find Steeg there already, seated at the table by the window. Niall pressed one of the "drink" buttons at random; half a minute later, a glass of cold orange juice emerged from the chute; tiny petals of orange were floating on its surface. Niall drank it thirstily. He sat down opposite the old man. He asked: "What will happen now?"

"Now Kazak will be more determined than ever to find you. He believes you possess supernatural powers. He cannot afford to lose you."

The memory of his mother's pale face filled Niall with a sense of guilt. For a moment he contemplated returning to Kazak's palace.

Steeg shook his head. "That would be stupid. This time they would never let you out of their sight."

Niall stared somberly out of the window. "Where can I go?"

The old man smiled. "First, you must complete your side of the bargain."

"The riddle?"

"Not a riddle. A simple question."

Niall buried his face in his hands, but it did nothing to clarify his thoughts.

"You want me to tell you . . . why you can't help me to destroy the spiders."

"Not quite. You asked me if I could tell you how to defeat the spiders. I told you that it was not permitted. But I didn't refuse to help you."

"But you want me to think it out for myself?"

He nodded. "You are beginning to understand."

Niall said slowly: "You can't tell me how to destroy the spiders . . . because"—he groped for words—"because that would be too easy. Men have to find their own freedom . . . or they won't appreciate what it is to be free." He looked at the old man. "Is that the answer to your riddle?"

"It is a part of the answer."

Niall shook his head; his brain still felt weary. "I can't think of any more."

"Then it will serve for the time being."

Niall asked quickly: "Then you'll help me?"

"First of all, let me ask you another question. Why do you want to destroy the spiders?"

"Because they are our enemies."

"But they are not my enemy. I want to know why you think they deserve to be destroyed and man deserves to survive. Is man so much better than the spiders?"

The question troubled Niall; he suspected a logical trap. He said finally: "Men built this city, and the spiders never built cities. They live in the cities left behind by men."

"But they are masters of the earth. Does that not prove they are superior to men?"

"No. They have stronger wills, that's all. That doesn't make them better."

"Why not?"

Niall thought about it and shook his head. "I can't explain. But I *feel* it's true."

The old man said gently: "If you intend to fight the spiders, you need to know *why* it is true."

"Can you tell me?"

"I can do better than that. I can show you. Come."

Niall followed him out of the room, down the corridor and back into the gallery. He was expecting to be taken to the peace machine. But the old man went past it and stepped into the white column. Niall followed. He felt himself rising. When he stepped forward again, they were in the room at the top of the tower with the view over the city. It seemed strange to see it again. The illusion of Florence had been so complete that he felt as though he had been away. The sun was close to the western horizon.

Steeg pointed to the black leather couch. "Lie down there."

Beside the couch on a table of black glass lay a device made of curved strips of metal: it might have been a rudimentary hat. It was connected to the Steegmaster by a length of wire.

"Place it on your head," Steeg said.

His order was accompanied by a mental image. Niall did as he was told. Small felt-covered pads pressed against his forehead and his temples.

"Lie down comfortably and place your head on the pillow. Are you ready?"

Niall nodded. He experienced a faint electrical tingle where the pads touched his skin. He closed his eyes.

He had been expecting to receive some kind of mental image, perhaps accompanied by a wordless flow of insight. In fact, the electrical tingling merely increased until it tickled the skin. This was accompanied by a pleasant sensation as if he had become bodiless and was floating free, like a balloon. The tingling sensation was now flowing from his head to his feet, and the pleasure became steadily more intense. He was completely unprepared for anything so inexpressibly delightful; the tingling seemed to turn into a kind of white light that suffused his whole body as if he had become transparent. It was not unlike the pleasure he had experienced as he pressed Merlew's body against his, but raised to a far higher degree.

Quite suddenly, it seemed as if a higher note of intensity sounded inside the white light, a note that was itself an intenser form of light. It rose higher and higher, and the light became as blinding as the sun at midday. All this was the prelude to an experience that lasted for perhaps five seconds.

So far, he had accepted all that had happened passively, with immense gratitude. But a point came where he became aware that these sensations were not being imposed upon him from outside. They were only a reflection of something that was happening inside. It was as if the sun were rising from below some horizon of his inner being. And then, for a few seconds, there was a sensation of raw power—a tremendous, overwhelming power rising from his own depths. It was accompanied by an insight that, for some reason made him want to laugh. The tower, the Steegmaster, the old man, even the spiders, all seemed a tremendous joke. And he, Niall, was also a joke, for he was aware that Niall was an impostor. In fact, he was an absurdity, for the truth was that he did not really exist.

Then the light faded, the sense of power diminished until it became merely a sense of pleasure, and he felt as if he was being lowered gently onto a beach by some powerful receding wave. Yet the insight remained. He knew now that the power came from inside himself.

The pads that pressed against his skin were no longer tingling. The whole room seemed transformed. He was looking at it as if he had created it. Nothing in it seemed strange or alien.

He remained perfectly still for several minutes, listening to a diminishing echo of the sound that had carried him outside his personality. Then he sighed deeply and removed the device from his head, replacing it on the table. He felt very languid and tired, but totally serene.

The old man was no longer there but the voice inside his chest said: "Now you understand."

There was no point in replying. For the first time, he grasped clearly that the voice was merely the voice of a machine, programmed to respond to his own questions. He had known this before, yet because the machine behaved and sounded like a person, some deeper level of his mind had refused to accept it. Now he knew it was true.

For the moment, he wanted to lie still and absorb what he had just learned.

The prime fact was power.

Yet although this was so simple and obvious, it was also bewildering. The source of power was inside him. He used it every time he raised his hand or lowered his eyelids. Yet it was also strong enough to change the universe. Why did men know so little about their inner power? Why did they make so little use of it? The answer was now clear. Because in order to make use of this power, man has to summon it. And to do this, he has to descend inside himself, and contract his mind to a point. But the process of falling asleep begins in the same way, with that withdrawal from the physical world and descent into the mind. So man seldom becomes aware of the power because he usually falls asleep before he reaches it. . . .

Niall contracted his forehead, summoning all his energy in an act of concentration. He immediately experienced a brief flash of power. It was pale and feeble compared to the intensity of a few moments ago; but this was unimportant. What was important was that he *could* induce it—no matter how dimly—by an act of will.

And now he could understand why the spiders had never progressed beyond a certain point. Throughout millions of years of their evolution, they had remained passive. This had enabled them to grasp an important secret—a secret unknown to men—that willpower is a physical force. Man had never discovered this because he was too busy using his brain and muscles—the instruments of his will. When a spider lured a fly into its web by the force of its will, it knew that force can be exerted without the use of any physical intermediary. So when the spiders became giants, they developed a giant willpower.

Yet even this was a step in the wrong direction. They learned to use the will as men learned to use their muscles; to make reality do their bidding. They directed it *outward*, towards other creatures. But because they had never learned to make active use of their brains, they failed to ask themselves about the source of this power. So they remained unaware of the immense power that lay hidden deep inside themselves. That was why they would be superseded by men. That was why they knew they would be superseded. That was why the Spider Lord was afraid of men.

He crossed to the transparent wall that faced north. On the other side of the lawn that surrounded the tower, the broad avenue continued in a straight line for perhaps another half mile. Beyond that, between half-ruined buildings, he could glimpse the river. Since the avenue appeared to continue without a break, it was clear there must be a bridge.

He asked: "Do you have a plan of the spider city?"

The room was immediately plunged into darkness as its walls became opaque. On the wall facing Niall, projected as if by a beam of light, there appeared an enormous map whose buildings were drawn in perspective, as if photographed at an angle from the air.

The city, he could now see, had been designed in the form of a circle, with the great main avenue running from north to south, and the river serving as its east-west diameter. The women's quarters occupied the southwestern segment, with the central dividing wall running far beyond the city's southern limit.

By far the largest section was the semicircle to the north of the river. This was labelled "slave quarter," and the foreshortened drawings revealed that many of its buildings were ruins. Like the southern section, this also contained a large central square, occupied by a domed building surrounded by lawns.

Niall asked: "What is this?"

"It was once the city's administrative center—the City Hall. Now it is used as a silk factory."

"For spider balloons?"

"For that and other purposes."

"Are the balloons made here?"

"No. The silk is transported to the city of the bombardier beetles, five miles to the north."

"Why not here?"

"Because the servants of the spiders lack the manual dexterity. Balloon making is a highly skilled job, and the servants of the beetles are more intelligent and more skillful."

"If the spiders are afraid of human intelligence, why do they allow the beetles to keep intelligent servants?"

"They have no choice. The beetles are immune to spider poison, and they can be dangerous when aroused."

"But why do the beetles want intelligent servants?"

"Because, unlike the spiders, they are fascinated by human achievement. They are also fascinated by human destructiveness. It is, you see, an evolutionary heritage. They have always defended themselves by producing explosions—therefore, to them, explosions are beautiful. The chief business of their servants is to devise tremendous explosions. To do this, they need a fairly high degree of intelligence."

"That must worry the spiders."

"It did before the beetles and spiders reached an agreement. Now they operate a slave-exchange system. Intelligent beetle menservants are exchanged for attractive females from the spider city."

"Doesn't that anger the servants of the beetles—to see their men sold into slavery?"

"No. They are glad to have a choice of beautiful women. Besides, the servants of the beetles regard it is an enviable job—they are used for breeding."

Niall studied the map for a long time.

"Where would be the best place for me to hide?"

"Anywhere in the slave quarter. They would accept your presence without question."

"But are there no spiders there?"

"Many. But to them, one human being looks exactly like another. You only need to observe a reasonable degree of caution."

Niall suddenly experienced a pang of dread. Inside this tower, he was comfortable and safe. Now he was about to venture into unknown dangers, he experienced a child's overwhelming craving for peace and security. All the knowledge and insight he had acquired during the past two days seemed unimportant. For a moment, he felt something like despair.

The Steegmaster seemed unaware of this inner conflict. The voice said: "Before you leave, it would be advisable to commit the plan to memory."

"That would take a long time." He tried to keep the weariness out of his voice.

"Not as long as you think. Look in the cabinet beside the Steegmaster."

Niall opened the door of the grey metal cabinet and found himself looking at his own face. Its rear wall consisted of a mirror. Meeting his own eyes, he could see the misery and uncertainty reflected in them.

Hanging over the mirror, suspended on a tiny gold hook, there was a fine metal chain, on the end of which was a small circular disc slightly more than an inch in diameter.

The voice said: "Take it and hang it around your neck. It is a thought mirror."

Niall unhooked it and looked at it carefully. The disc was slightly concave, and of a browny-gold color. Now he looked more closely, he could see that it was not an exact circle; the shape was closer to a diamond with curved sides. The surface looked too dull to be a mirror; his face, golden and distorted, looked back at him as if through a cloud of mist.

As he hung it round his neck, the voice said: "No, the other way."

He turned it round so that the concave surface lay against his chest, resting slightly above the solar plexus. He immediately experienced a peculiar and indescribable sensation, as if some shock had caused his heart to contract. His eyes once again met his reflection in the mirror and he saw that the uncertainty had vanished.

The voice said: "The thought mirror was perfected by an ancient civilization called the Aztecs; their shamans used it in meditation before performing a human sacrifice. The secret was rediscovered by paranormal researchers in the late twenty-first century. It has the power to coordinate mental vibrations from the brain, the heart, and the solar plexus. Now try to memorize the map."

Niall stared intently at the map. To his surprise, it no longer cost him a mental effort to grasp it as a whole. It was as if his powers of concentration were somehow aided and amplified by the mirror hanging on his chest. Five minutes earlier, the map had seemed too complicated and undigestible; now, suddenly, it was as if his mind was absorbing it hungrily, as his stomach might absorb food. In less than a minute, he knew it by heart.

He asked: "What is the Fortress?"

"It used to be the main barracks of this city. A barracks is a building that houses soldiers."

"And what is an arsenal?"

"A place where weapons are kept."

He pointed to the map. "Is the bridge guarded?"

"Yes. Last week, one of the commanders was caught as she tried to wade across—she wanted to get to the nursery to see her baby. Now wolf spiders guard both ends."

"What happened to her?"

"She was publicly executed and eaten."

"Is there any other point where it is possible to cross the river?"

"The bridge is still the best. The river is at its shallowest there."

"When would be the best time to attempt it?"

"At dawn, when the guard is changed."

Niall studied the map again. It would obviously be suicidal to try and approach the bridge down the main avenue. But the map showed flights of steps descending to the river at intervals of about half a mile along its embankment. If Niall could gain access to the river near the wall that divided the city, it should be possible to make his way to the bridge along the lower bank.

"Where should I look for shelter in the slave quarter?" he asked.

"Many of the buildings have lost their upper stories. The spiders prefer not to use these for web-building. You would be safest in one of those."

Niall experienced a twinge of pain behind the eyes; when he massaged his cheeks and forehead with his hands, it went away.

The voice said: "The pain is due to the thought mirror. You are not accustomed to using it, and unless you keep your attention concentrated, it will cause headaches. When that happens, turn it round the other way."

Niall turned the mirror so that it faced away from his chest. As soon as he did this, the sense of strain vanished. But he observed that he now felt curiously fatigued. The blood tingled in his cheeks. He lay down on the couch and closed his eyes. A pleasant drowsiness began to steal over him.

The voice said: "It would not be advisable to sleep now. The Spider Lord has just sent a message to Kazak, asking him to bring you to his presence. When Kazak admits you have gone, every spider in the city will be searching for you."

Niall sat up, his fatigue vanishing instantly. Once again, he had to control the fear that trickled into his bloodstream. He had to keep his voice steady as he asked: "What will he do to Kazak?"

"Nothing. The Spider Lord is a realist. But you must leave now."

"Yes." An effort of concentration subdued his fear and renewed his determination. "Shall I be able to keep in touch with you?"

"Yes. Through the telescopic rod. It is attuned to the thought pattern of the Steegmaster. But use it sparingly. Many of the spiders will be able to detect its energies. So whenever you use it, you will be in danger of discovery."

The old man suddenly appeared, standing by the white column. "Before you leave, I would advise you to eat. You have a long night before you."

"I don't feel like eating." His appetite had vanished.

"Then take food with you. You must also change into the uniform of the slaves. Follow me. There is now no time to lose."

Niall stepped into the column and felt himself descending; this time the feather-like sensation was unpleasant, underlining his nervous tension.

They were in the room with the white curved walls. On one of the stools—the one that Niall had mistaken for a weed-covered rock on the seashore—lay the telescopic rod and the coarse grey uniform of a slave. As he slipped it on over his own clothes, his nose wrinkled in disgust; it smelt of stale sweat.

Unlike his own garments, the slave uniform had two wide pockets. There was something in both of them. He investigated and found that one contained a small wooden box. In the other was a light grey tube, about six inches long and an inch in diameter. In the box, under a layer of cotton wool, were a number of tiny brown tablets. The old man said: "These are food tablets—a type developed by men to sustain them on long journeys in space."

"And this?"

"A lightweight garment, also developed for use in space. Touch the disc at the end."

When Niall pressed the end of the tube with his thumb, it elongated to twice its length, then unrolled. It was a baggy garment of dull metallic grey, and looked big enough for a man twice Niall's size. He asked: "Is this necessary?"

"Take it. You may be grateful for it. When you press the end it will re-fold itself." Niall watched with amusement as it converted itself into a neat grey tube, and was surprised that it did this so silently without any of the rustling noise he would have expected.

"Now go, otherwise all the preparation will have been wasted."

He vanished. Niall felt disconcerted by the abruptness of the leave-taking, but it emphasized the sense of urgency.

As soon as he picked up the metal rod, he experienced a tingling sensation in his fingers; when he reached out and touched the wall with its end, his legs felt weak and he was overcome by sudden dizziness. He stepped forward and felt again as if he had fallen into whirlpool. For a moment there was acute nausea; then his senses cleared and he was standing on the grass outside the tower.

PART THREE

The Fortress

The cold wind against his face restored him to a sense of normality. He was in almost total darkness. A few moments later, the moon emerged briefly from behind flying black clouds, so that he could take his bearings. The grass underfoot was wet and slippery; it had evidently been raining heavily. He had to walk carefully to avoid losing his footing. He held the metal rod by its narrow end, using it as a staff, and a few minutes later felt the hard pavement under his feet. The clouds parted again, and the moon revealed the avenue that stretched northward towards the bridge. He turned left and walked in the direction of the women's quarter of the city.

As he crossed to the far side of the square, the wind was so powerful that he had to lean into it. It was a relief to be in the shelter of tall buildings. According to his map, this section of the city was deserted, forming a kind of no-man's-land between the southern part and the slave quarter. He paused in a doorway to shelter from the wind, which made his teeth chatter, and to wait for the moon to emerge. When it did so, he saw something that made his heart contract with fear. The white tower was gleaming in the moonlight, looking as if it was shining with its own inner phosphorescence. And around its base, clearly visible against its whiteness, there was a movement of heaving black shadows. For a moment, he convinced himself that they were cloud shadows; then, as the moon was isolated for a moment in a calm space of unclouded blue, the light strengthened, and he knew they were living creatures. As the light dimmed again, the shadows seemed to be moving across the grass towards him.

His immediate response was to run, but he knew at once that this would be an error. He was already using all his self-discipline to repress the panic; fleeing would amplify it beyond his control. His next impulse was to take refuge in the nearest building. This he also rejected; sooner or later, every building in the city would be searched. The spiders possessed the thoroughness of endless patience. His hiding place would soon become a prison. The correct solution was to keep on the move and hope that the darkness and the wind would delay the search.

He began moving westward, towards the women's quarter, but turned north at each intersection so that he was also moving towards the river. In these narrow, man-built canyons, the darkness was so complete that he had to walk like a blind man, the metal rod stretched out as a feeler, the other hand groping at railings or the walls of buildings. The pavements were cracked and uneven. At one street corner—he could tell it was a corner because the wind converged from two directions—he stumbled over the curbstone into the gutter, and the rod shot out of his hand. As he groped around on all fours, he had to wrestle with rising panic; the thought of losing the rod filled him with despair. Then he recollected the thought mirror. He reached inside his shirt and turned it on his chest, then sat down in the roaring darkness and concentrated his attention. There was a momentary pain in the back of his skull; then he experienced the sense of power and control. He stood up and spread out his hands within a foot of the ground, walking forward slowly. A tingling feeling in the fingertips of his right hand guided him to the object of his search. Now his mind was calm; it was as if he was able to pick up some faint signal from the metal rod. A moment later, he found it lying in the gutter. He turned the disc again away from his chest, aware of how much this kind of concentration drained his energy.

When the moon came out again, he saw that he had reached a broad avenue. His memory of the map told him that the river was two blocks to the north. He stopped in a doorway and scanned the avenue for moving shadows; it seemed empty. Overhead, a vast spiderweb heaved up and down in the wind; but in such a gale the spider would be crouched in the shelter of some windowless room. Niall hurried on up the avenue; now that his eyes were becoming accustomed to the darkness he could move more quickly. In the freezing wind, his face and bare arms were beginning to feel numb. But the cold also brought him comfort; he knew the spiders disliked it even more than he did.

While still a block away from the river, he halted on a street corner to rest. Overhead an immense black cloud covered the moon; he judged that it would take at least ten minutes to pass.

He was unwilling to venture on to the embankment in total darkness; if the spiders were guarding the bridge, then it also seemed likely they would be patroling the river.

He sat on the pavement with his back against the railings of a basement area. Something yielded, and he realized he was leaning against a gate. The thought of sheltering from the wind, even for a few moments, was tempting. He pushed the gate, and it opened with a creak of rusty hinges. Groping on his knees, he felt worn stone steps, slippery with rain. He descended cautiously until he was below street level. There was an unpleasant smell, like rotting vegetation, but at least he was sheltered from the wind. Now his skin was no longer exposed, he experienced an illusion of warmth. He sat there shivering, his arms folded round his knees, and wondered why the smell of decaying vegetable matter seemed to grow stronger.

There was a light touch on his arm, and he started with fear. Since his first assumption was that a spider's fangs were poised to plunge into his bare flesh, he became immobile. The touch groped upward to his shoulder and, at the same time, something brushed the calf of his left leg. As he sprang to his feet, a cold softness closed round his ankle, and the stench of decay was suddenly nauseating. He tore his foot free and felt the same cold softness groping at his arm. Then, as he shrank away, it closed round his upper arm, pulling him against the railing.

In spite of the fear and nausea, it was a relief to know he was not dealing with a spider. These cold, damp feelers moved slowly and deliberately; another was slipping between his legs and winding round his right knee. When he reached down, his hand encountered something cold, soft, and slimy; as he squeezed, it seemed to ooze between his fingers. It might have been a cold-blooded worm.

Another of the wormlike fingers tried to pull the metal rod out of his right hand. Niall gripped it tightly and thrust between the railings; he felt it plunge into something soft. Again and again he thrust with all his strength; each time he felt it sink home. Yet the feelers continued to move, groping round his body with unhurried deliberation.

As he felt a cold touch against his face, his loathing turned to cold fury; once again he gripped the end of the rod and thrust between the bars to the full extent of his arm. His hatred seemed to convulse his brain like a shock, and he felt its power rippling through the muscles of his arm and into the rod. He gripped tighter, clenching his teeth, and again felt the shock run down his arm. Suddenly, the feelers released their hold. Niall staggered back against the wall, then clawed his way up the steps and fell out into the street.

Coughing and retching, he stumbled forward across the road, then recovered his balance and ran. The cold wind was as welcome as a caress.

Before he had run a dozen yards, self control returned. He withdrew into a doorway and stood there, eyes closed, resting the back of his head against the wall until his heartbeat returned to normal. His flesh felt sore where the tentacles had gripped him. Finally, to assist his concentration, he again turned the thought mirror on his chest. The pain in the back of his head made him feel sick for a moment; then it passed, and he experienced once more the satisfying sense of being in control of his body and mind.

If the spiders were advancing towards the river, there was no time to lose. He approached the embankment with caution and waited for the moon to emerge. When it did so, it revealed that the great arch of the bridge was surprisingly close, the road that led towards it empty. He waited for the moon to disappear behind the clouds, then crossed the road. A low stone wall, about four feet high, ran along the embankment. He groped his way along this until he encountered a gap. The metal rod, used like a blind man's stick, revealed a recess with a flight of descending steps. He crouched behind the wall until another interval of moonlight enabled him to take his bearings and revealed that the steps were unguarded, then made his way down to the path that ran by the river. Here he became aware of the need for haste. If there were guards on the bridge, a sudden shaft of moonlight could betray him. He hurried forward until the moon showed through a break in the cloud, then halted and pressed himself tightly against the wall; as soon as darkness returned, he went on. Advancing in this way, it took him more than half an hour to reach the bridge. While still fifty yards away, he took refuge behind a buttress and waited until a longer interval of moonlight allowed him to study it carefully. There was no sign of spider guards; but at either end of the bridge were rectangular structures that might have been some form of sentry box. About to move from his hiding place, he obeyed some instinct that urged him to stay still. After a long interval of darkness, moonlight flooded the river, and illuminated the nearest rectangle; it enabled him to see a square window that looked out towards him. And, as he watched, there was an unmistakable movement behind it. A moment later, it was blank. But it had told him what he wanted to know: the spider guards commanded a clear view along the river, as well as along the avenue that led to the white tower.

The wind that blew across the river was so cold that he was no longer able to feel his hands or feet. If he remained there much longer, he would probably be unable to move. So as soon as a particularly dark cloud crossed the moon he ran, crouching, until he found himself under the shelter of the bridge. There, concealed by its black shadow, he was finally able to sink down with his back against the wall, huddled into a recess that gave some shelter from the wind, and clasp his knees tightly against his chest in an effort to keep out the cold.

Now, at last, he was able to allow the metal rod to contract, and stow it away in one of the pockets of the grey smock. As he did so, he felt the tube that contained the baggy, metallic garment and experienced a glow of gratitude towards the Steegmaster. This, at least, should provide some kind of defense against the wind. Very cautiously, he extracted it and pressed the end with his thumb. As it unrolled, the wind caught it and tried to tear it out of his hands, making a loud, flapping sound. Quickly, he thrust it under his body and sat on it. For the next ten minutes, he groped in the darkness, flattening the garment against the ground, holding it down flat with his frozen feet while his numb fingers tried to unfold it. Eventually, his fingers located a slide fastener and he realized, to his relief, that he understood its purpose—the sleep-learning device had stocked his memory with many such useful items of information. He opened the front of the garment down to the waist, then slipped his feet inside. A few moments later, his arms were encased in the strangely thin material, and the slide fastener had been pulled up under his chin. The effect was astonishing. Although the wind continued to press the material against his bare flesh, none of its cold seemed to penetrate. He might have been wearing a garment of thick animal fur. Now only his hands, feet, and head were exposed, and the arms and legs were sufficiently long for him to be able to retract his hands and feet. Investigation of a lump at the back of his neck revealed a tightly-rolled hood; when his fingers had learned the secret of unrolling it, he discovered that it covered his head completely, and that a drawstring enabled him to close it until only his nose and eyes remained exposed. Further investigation revealed similar rolls at the wrist and ankles, but he decided to leave examination of these until the daylight. It was easier to exclude the wind by holding the ends of the sleeves with his fingers and folding the last six inches of the legs under his feet.

When he once again turned the thought mirror away from his chest, he was overwhelmed by a wave of fatigue which was transformed into a delicious weariness by the warmth that now encased him. Even the wall behind him failed to communicate its coldness through the paper-thin material. A few drops of water pattered against the suit and made him aware that it was raining; when the moon came out again, he could see the rain falling steadily onto the dark moving surface of the water. But his eyes were unable to focus for more than a few seconds. His eyelids closed and his consciousness merged with the darkness.

When he awoke, the sky over the eastern reach of the river was turning grey. His neck felt stiff where his cheek had pressed against the wall; but the recess had kept him from rolling sideways. In spite of the awkwardness of his position, he felt relaxed and rested. The only discomfort was a cramp in his right leg and the stinging sensations where the tentacles had gripped his flesh.

His stomach was rumbling with hunger; he was just beginning to regret his failure to provide himself with food when he recalled the brown tablets; he unzipped the garment—letting in a wave of cold air—and extracted the box from his pocket. The tablets looked pathetically small, and he was tempted to swallow a handful. He took one and placed it on his tongue. It had an agreeable lemony flavor and quickly dissolved as he sucked it, creating a pleasant sensation of warmth. As he swallowed, the warmth increased until it ran down his throat like liquid fire. A few moments later it reached his stomach; suddenly, the hunger vanished and was replaced by a glowing sensation that felt exactly as if he had eaten a hot meal. He was now glad that he had resisted the temptation to swallow several; more than one would undoubtedly have made him feel sick.

Now it was time to take his bearings. First, he removed the metallic garment, shivering in the dawn wind that blew up the river. He carefully flattened it on the ground, then folded it lengthwise, a touch on the button made it roll itself up into a tube that felt as hard as solid metal. Niall slipped it into the pocket of the grey smock.

Next, he tiptoed cautiously to the west side of the bridge and looked upward. From that position he could see the rectangular guard box; but without moving farther from the bridge, it was impossible to obtain a clear view through its window. He decided that the risk of being seen was too great.

On the other side of the bridge, there was no guard box. Here he discovered a flight of steps leading up to street level. He climbed these warily, pausing for at least half a minute on every step. When his head emerged above the top step, he could see across the damaged bridge to the opposite bank. The guard box was a small, open-fronted building which contained only a stone bench; in the days when this city had been inhabited by men, it had evidently been a pedestrian shelter. The wolf spider inside it was crouched against the wall, and was so completely immobile that Niall had some difficulty in detecting its presence. As Niall watched it, he induced in himself a sense of deep calm; he was more likely to betray his presence by the movements of his mind than by those of his body. He deliberately made himself as immobile as the spider, ignoring the cold wind that numbed his arms and legs.

Half an hour later, the sun rose above the eastern horizon; its warmth was as delightful as a caress. As he sighed with relief and pleasure, he experienced an overwhelming sense of pure well-being. It was accompanied by a curious sensation, as if something inside him was dwindling and contracting to a point. As this happened, the pleasure became almost intolerable, and he had to close his eyes to prevent himself from being swept away by it.

As he did this, the feeling of inner contraction came to a halt, leaving him in a condition of deep calm such as he had never experienced in his life. It was then that he became aware of the thought processes of the wolf spider on the other side of the road. Its awareness was also as still as a candle flame on a windless night. A man who stood in that draughty sentry box would experience boredom and impatience. The wolf spider would have regarded such feelings as a kind of mild insanity. It knew that it had to wait there until its relief arrived, and impatience would have been irrelevant. The sun filled it with a drowsy delight; yet its underlying vigilance remained unaffected. To his surprise, Niall realized he experienced no hostility or fear towards the spider; only a friendly sympathy with a strong overtone of admiration.

The warmth caused a pleasant tingling sensation in his bare shoulders and the calves of his legs, and this again seemed to lift his mind like a wave and move it gently towards some deep source of peace. Now it was as if his hearing had suddenly been sharpened a hundredfold, and as if he could hear a kind of whispering sound. For a moment, this puzzled him; then he identified its source. It was coming from a great elm tree standing fifty yards away along the riverbank. With a shock, he realized that the elm was alive: not simply alive in the negative sense of burgeoning wood and leaves, but in the sense of a being of flesh and blood. The tree was waving its arm in welcome to the sun, and exuding a feeling of gladness that had a totally human quality. All its leaves were rippling with pleasure as they absorbed the golden light, as if they were children shouting for joy.

Now that he was aware of the "voice" of the tree, Niall began to recognize a strong undertone of communication. It took him some time to realize that this was coming from the earth beneath his feet. He had to make a mental effort to deepen his inner calm still further; as he did this, he could sense waves of energy rippling past him, like the ripples on a pond when some child has thrown a stone into the water. The tree was receiving this energy and was, in turn, transmitting its own personal response. Suddenly, Niall understood why the city was surrounded by green hills and woods. They focused the waves of energy that flowed through the earth and gave back their own vital response. The result was that this city of concrete and asphalt was pervaded by an aura of living energy. Now he could understand why the wolf spider could wait so patiently for hour after hour. It was not, as he had assumed, simply that spiders are born with the gift of patience; it was because it was aware of itself as a part of this pulsating pattern of vitality.

What intrigued Niall was the sheer intensity of this vital pulse. Now that he had become aware of it, it reminded him of the rhythmic bursts of rain-carrying wind he had experienced in the storm at sea: curtains of rain blowing across the boat in explosive gusts. But unlike the wind, whose gusts were due to the motion of the ship in the waves, these surges of vital energy produced an impression of purpose, as if generated by some intelligent agency. For a moment, he even speculated whether its source might be the Spider Lord himself.

At this point he became aware of a change in the pattern of consciousness of the wolf spider. With a feeling like waking from deep sleep, he returned to his superficial level of everyday awareness. The spider had been stirred into activity by the approach of its relief. Niall noted with interest that the guard was still inside its sentry box, so that its relief was beyond its field of vision; yet without moving out of the box, it was aware of another wolf spider proceeding along the avenue that led to the white tower. By once again relaxing his attention, he became aware of the nature of this awareness. The approaching relief caused small subsidiary "pulses" in the larger pulsation, disturbing its natural rhythm.

Now there was no time to lose. It was broad daylight and further delay would be dangerous. He slipped quietly back down the stairway and under the bridge. The river lay about four feet below the path on which he had spent the night. A bank of grey mud, about six feet wide, shelved down into the water. Niall slipped off his sandals—they were the ones he had brought from Dira—and tucked them into the wide pockets of the smock. Then he lowered himself off the stone ramp and down onto the mud. It was hard, and his feet scarcely made an indentation. A moment later, he was wading slowly into the water.

Here the mud was softer, and had an unpleasant, slimy consistency; unused to wading, Niall experienced a flash of alarm as his feet sank into it. At each step, his feet squelched down into the mud to a depth of almost a foot. Some small living creature writhed between his toes, and he had to suppress a gasp of alarm. He stood still, trying to control the pounding of his heart. What alarmed him was the realization that the bright sunlight would make him visible to any creature on the bank of the river, and that the longer he spent wading across, the greater the chance that he would be noticed. For a moment, he was tempted to return and spend the day hiding in the recess; then he saw that this would be even more dangerous, since he would be clearly visible from the opposite bank. He waded on steadily until the water came up to his armpits. Here the current was stronger than he expected, and he was forced to lean sideways to maintain his balance. Suddenly, the bottom was no longer under his feet, and he was floundering. His first impulse was to try to go back, but he saw this would be pointless; safety lay in going forward. He dog-paddled a few feet, then felt himself sinking; as the water entered his nose and mouth, he panicked for a moment, then struggled to the surface, coughing and choking. What terrified him was the thought that the current might carry him out beyond the shelter of the bridge and leave him totally exposed. He thrashed forward a few yards further, then, with relief, felt the slimy mud under his feet again. He stood there for perhaps a minute, simply to regain his breath and to try to get the panic under control, then again plunged forward towards the bank. A few moments later, he was crossing the hard mud that sloped into the water. But he was aware that he had lost the battle against panic.

He resisted the temptation to pause and regain his breath by leaning on the stone parapet; instead, he scrambled up and made straight for the flight of stairs at the side of the bridge. He had already mounted the first half dozen steps when he became aware that it was too late. The wolf spider was waiting for him at the top, its fangs fully extended. The enormous black eyes were staring down at him without expression.

As he obeyed his impulse to flee, the force of its will struck him in the back, knocking him breathless. He had some vague thought of taking refuge in the river, hoping the spider would not dare to follow him. But even as he reached the edge of the parapet, the spider's fast-moving body struck his own and hurled him down on to the mud. His knees and elbows sank in, making movement impossible. As the spider's weight landed on his back, time seemed to move into a lower gear, and he felt himself struggling in slow motion, observing the terror of his physical being as if watching a stranger. Then his face was pressed into the mud and he felt himself losing consciousness.

He woke as if from a nightmare and realized that he was lying on his back. His eyes were blinded by the sunlight. As he thought of the spider, he flung up his hand to defend his throat, then realized he was alone. He looked up, expecting to see the spider watching him from the parapet; there was no living creature in sight. He struggled to his knees, then to his feet, fighting off waves of nausea. It cost an immense effort to drag himself up on to the stone ramp. Still fighting the desire to retch, he crawled across to the wall and collapsed with his back against it.

It was then that he remembered the thought mirror. He reached inside his shirt and turned it round. The effect was instantaneous: that curious sense of concentration and well-being that was like being *reminded* of something. But by now, he had become sufficiently accustomed to its properties to observe them with a certain precision. First, it was as if his heart contracted with a feeling not unlike fear. Yet because this contraction was accompanied by a feeling of increased control, it produced a flash of joy, of strength. This seemed to spread instantaneously to the viscera, where it blended with a more physical form of energy. Then the brain itself seemed to unite these two, exactly as if it had turned into a hand that was compressing some tough but yielding material. If he was tired, this action of the brain lacked force and he experienced a twinge of pain behind his eyes. This is what now happened. Then the power of the brain—which he recognized as the mind itself—increased its control, and the headache vanished. And now it felt as if three beams of energy, from the heart, the head, and the viscera, were converging on the mirror, which reflected them back again, redoubling their intensity. He could also see—in a brief flash of insight—that the mirror was not necessary. It was merely a mechanical substitute for *self-consciousness*.

As strength and vitality were summoned from his own depths, he tried to understand what had happened. Why was he still alive? Probably because the Death Lord had given orders to capture him alive. Then where was his attacker? Could it have gone to summon the other guard? But he was immediately struck by the absurdity of this explanation. What would be easier than to bind his hands and feet and carry him away on its back?

He stood up and felt the back of his neck. It felt sore and bruised, but there was no puncture mark there. Hope began to dawn. For some reason beyond his comprehension, the wolf spider had left him unharmed. Could it be through the intervention of the Steegmaster?

Cautiously, he mounted the steps again, this time to street level. Wet marks from his previous ascent were still on the stone, revealing that he had been unconscious for only a brief period. He raised his head and peered out across the bridge. It was deserted; so were the streets of the slave quarter. He was about to make a run for the nearest building when he caught a glimpse of the caked mud on his arms and changed his mind. His present state made him too conspicuous. He stood there for perhaps a minute, scanning the street and embankment for any sign of movement; when he had assured himself that they were deserted, he hurried back to the river. There he waded in up to his knees and washed off the mud from his arms, legs, and face.

It was as he was wading back on the foreshore that an absurd idea flashed into his head. He was looking at the marks made by the impact of his own body when he fell from the ramp; the indentations produced by his knees and elbows were clearly visible. Also imprinted in the soft mud were the claw marks of the spider as it had stood above his body. On the left hand side, four marks were visible; on the right, only three. His attacker was a wolf spider with a missing front claw.

With a clarity amounting to a perception, Niall's mind conjured up an image of an exhausted wolf spider lying sprawled in the sunlight, a trickle of pale blood running from its maimed foreleg on to the deck of the ship, and he suddenly knew beyond all doubt that his intuition had found the answer. Pleasure and gratitude rose in him like a bubble. The perception that luck was on his side produced a curious inner calm. He mounted the steps unhurriedly, looked to right and left to make sure that the road was empty, then crossed the street like a man going about his legitimate business.

The houses facing the river had been impressive structures, now crumbling into disrepair; the cracked pavements were covered with a debris of broken glass and decaying concrete. Here also he saw for the first time the disintegrating shells of rusty automobiles, many with helicopter attachments that gave them the appearance of dead winged insects. In the southern part of the city, most windows and doors were still intact; here the window apertures were empty and the doors that remained hung off their hinges. The slave quarter looked as if it had been vandalized by an army of destructive children.

The main avenue, which ran down from the bridge, was overhung with cobwebs, which in places were so thick that they seemed to form a canopy; an instinct warned Niall not to venture beneath them. Instead, he entered a building whose worn facade still carried an inscription: Global Assurance Corporation, and picked his way across a grimy marble floor littered with lath and plaster, and down a series of corridors that led into a narrow street. He peered out cautiously and withdrew his head immediately; about thirty feet above his head, a death spider was repairing its web. He blocked the flash of alarm before it began and retreated into the corridor.

The nearest room contained some broken furniture, and its door had been propped against a cupboard next to the empty window aperture. By moving into the space between the door and the cupboard, Niall was able to command a good view of the street and to watch the spider in its patient work of repair. Half an hour later, he heard the first sounds of life: voices, the sound of footsteps, and the banging of doors. Across the street, he could see people moving about behind the first-floor window aperture. A woman with large breasts and grotesquely thick legs strolled down the street, making soft crooning noises. He noticed that she walked under the spider web with no sign of nervousness.

The noise increased and as the sun rose high enough to penetrate the narrow street, children appeared on the pavements, many of them chewing lumps of grey-colored bread. Some of them shouted, or ran about, laughing; most seemed to be quiet and apathetic. Niall observed the prevalence of low foreheads, flat cheekbones, and narrow, slit-like eyes. One heavily-built boy with a club foot approached a small fat girl and tore her food out of her hand. She began to wail loudly, but no one paid any attention; the boy leaned against the wall a few feet away and ate the bread. Then he approached another child who had just walked into the street, and once again snatched the food from her hands. This child tried to snatch it back; whereupon the boy pushed her in the chest with such force that she staggered across the road. Yet other children sat in doorways or on the edge of the pavement and went on eating stolidly, making no attempt to hide their food.

One small boy ran down the middle of the street, flapping his arms as if he were a bird and making chirping noises. As he ran under the newly-repaired cobweb, he paused and looked up at it. Then, to Niall's astonishment, he bent down, picked up a piece of wood, and hurled it into the air. It curved downward again long before it struck the web. The child threw it again; this time it went slightly higher. Then the boy with the club foot, who had finished eating, picked up the wood and hurled it with all his force into the air. This time it struck the cobweb and stuck there. Then, so quickly that it made Niall start, the spider fell from the sky on its length of thread and pounced on the small child. Niall expected to see the fangs sink into the bare flesh. Instead, the child shrieked with laughter as the spider rolled him on the ground; many other children joined in. And a few moments later, the spider rose into the air on its lifeline of web, while the child jumped up and ran away. Niall found it all totally baffling. The spider had obviously been playing with the child.

Niall's damp clothes were becoming uncomfortable, and when a child peered in through the window and stared at him with curiosity, he decided there was no point in further concealment and walked out into the street. No one paid him the slightest attention. The spider overhead had now started to build another web, apparently oblivious to what was happening below. Only the boy with the club foot gave him a glance that made him feel uneasy—a look that was at once hostile and mocking.

The thought mirror sharpened his senses, making his observation preternaturally keen. He noticed that the slave quarter was full of smells, both pleasant and unpleasant; the smells of cooking mingled with the odor of rotten fruit and sewage. The gutters were full of abandoned scraps of food as well as all kinds of domestic rubbish. There were also, he soon discovered, nonhuman inhabitants of the slave quarter. As a child threw down a large piece of bread, a bird swooped past his head and snatched it up. And in a shadowy, deserted alleyway, he saw a large grey rat feeding on a smashed watermelon. It glanced at him with its sharp little eyes, decided he could be ignored, and went on eating. A fraction of a second later, a spider plunged from the sky and landed squarely on the rat; the animal had time only for a pathetic squeak before the fangs plunged home. A few seconds later, spider and rat had vanished. It had all happened so swiftly that Niall had no time for fear, or even astonishment. He glanced up nervously at the overhanging web, into which the spider had vanished, and hurried on.

Passing an open doorway a few moments later, his nostrils detected a more sinister smell—rotting meat. He paused, hesitated, then stepped into the shadowy interior, treading with caution on broken floorboards. The source of the stench was immediately apparent—a decaying corpse lying in one corner of the room. It was little more than a skeleton, a few disintegrating fragments of grey slave garments covering the rib cage; maggots crawled out of the empty eye sockets. The cause of death—a great block of masonry that had fallen through the ceiling—lay close to the cracked skull. Niall repressed a desire to be sick and hastened back into the street.

The slave quarter was dirty, overcrowded, and apparently totally disorganized. Many buildings were burnt-out shells; others looked as if a vigorous push would bring their walls tumbling down. Inhabited buildings were easy to distinguish because they were in a less dangerous state of disrepair than the others. He strolled into one of these, pushing his way among squabbling children, and was ignored. A doorless room to the right was obviously a bedroom; the floor was covered completely with greasy mattresses. In another room, people sat on the bare floorboards, or on broken furniture, and drank soup out of chipped crockery or gnawed rabbit legs or chunks of grey bread. It was easy to locate the kitchen simply by tracing to its source the pervading smell of burning fat, woodsmoke, garlic, and overripe fruit and vegetables. An enormous saucepan of soup steamed on the wood stove; the cook, a grotesquely fat woman whose forearms were thicker than most men's thighs, was chopping up a mixture of fruit, vegetables, and rabbit meat on a large board; as Niall entered, she poured these into the saucepan, scraping them off with a carving knife. Two late risers came in, yawning and rubbing their eyes. They helped themselves to unwashed dishes piled up in a metal sink and, without the preliminary of washing them, dipped them straight into the cooking pot; neither seemed concerned that their bowls contained a proportion of raw meat and vegetables. They hacked themselves bread from a loaf that was more than four feet long, and dipped this into a wooden bowl of half-melted butter that stood on the windowsill catching the full force of the morning sun. Niall observed that there was a large metal bunker containing various kinds of fruit: apples, oranges, pomegranates, watermelons, and prickly pears. The slaves were obviously kept well fed.

A tall, red-headed man entered the kitchen. Niall guessed he was a member of the servant class condemned to work as a slave. He looked harassed and irritable. Ignoring Niall, he snatched a bowl from the sink, washed it under the tap, and filled it with soup. Unlike the slaves, he took the trouble to dip the ladle to the bottom of the saucepan. Niall tuned in to his mind—he found that the thought mirror made this easier than usual and discovered that the man was entirely preoccupied with the fact that he had overslept, and that in ten minutes' time he had to report for work. The man—whose name was Lorris—hacked a chunk of bread off the loaf and began to eat ravenously. His mood was so sour and hostile that Niall was glad to withdraw his mental probe—the man's state of mind produced an impression exactly like an unpleasant smell.

As he emptied his soup bowl, Lorris seemed to notice Niall for the first time. He asked: "What are you here for?"

Niall thought quickly. "Arguing with a commander. What are you?"

"Constant lateness." He refilled his soup bowl.

Niall said: "I've only just arrived. Is there anyone in charge?"

"Morlag, in building K.2."

"Where is that?"

He gestured. "Along the street and first left."

"Thank you."

Out in the street, he noticed that many slaves were now walking in the same direction. But attempts to probe their minds were frustrating. There seemed to be almost no mental activity in the normal sense. They were living according to a mechanical routine, and each one seemed to regard himself as a mere fragment of a crowd. They moved like sleepwalkers. It was not unlike being among a pack of human ants. As they passed the house where Niall had seen the corpse—the smell of rotting flesh seemed stronger than ever—none of them seemed in the least concerned that one of their number had been killed. Each seemed to feel that it was none of his business. They were totally self-absorbed.

As he made his way through the crowded streets, Niall was struck by the sheer physical variety among the slave class. Unlike the servants and the commanders—who were united by a strong family resemblance—the slaves seemed to be of every shape and size. Many, but by no means all, were physically deformed. Some looked alert and intelligent, some sullen and bored; a few looked dreamily contented. The alert and intelligent ones were usually small and deformed, while taller, more physically attractive slaves often wore a blank, imbecilic smile. Niall noticed the same anomaly among the women, many of whom stood in windows or doorways and watched the men go past; those who looked alert were mostly short and ugly, while tall, attractive women stared blankly into space, apparently hardly conscious of their surroundings. He was struck by the large proportion of women in an advanced stage of pregnancy, and also by the enormous number of children, many of them leaning dangerously out of upstairs windows. The slave quarter seemed to contain more children than adults.

He found himself in a small square in which several platoons of slaves had already lined up. A big, black-bearded man of tremendous physique stood facing them, an expression of grim disgust on his face. The noise was deafening; children shouted and played games, adults screamed at one another, while two very pregnant women fought and rolled in the gutter. Niall approached the black-bearded man.

"I'm looking for Morlag."

"That's me. What do you want?"

"I've been told to report to you."

Morlag suddenly roared "Shut up!" in a voice so deafening that it struck Niall like a physical blow. Instant silence fell on the square, and the squabbling women let go of each other's hair and sat up. Morlag said: "That's better. Any more noise and I'll feed you all to the spiders." He looked down at Niall, whose face was on a level with his chest.

"Why did you get sent here?"

"Arguing with a commander."

Morlag grunted: "Serves you right." The noise had already started up again. "What job do you do?"

"Charioteer."

"All right. Wait there." He pointed to the pavement behind him where four more powerfully-built servants were standing.

A twinge of pain in the back of Niall's skull reminded him that he had been using the thought mirror for too long. He reached cautiously inside his shirt and turned it over. The sense of relaxation was so powerful that for a moment he felt dizzy and had to close his eyes. And even before he opened them, he was once again pervaded by that sense of total calm he had experienced earlier by the river. His own identity seemed to fade away and he became a part of the communal life that surged around him. He was simultaneously inside the minds of all these people in the square, sharing their sense of absurd well-being. He was also aware once more of the rhythmic pulse of life that moved in periodic waves through the earth under his feet, like a rising tide gently breaking on a beach. The slaves were also dimly aware of this pulse, and it intensified their joy in being alive.

Niall's four companions, on the other hand, were totally unaware of it; their minds were entirely preoccupied with which jobs the overseer would assign to each of them. Niall's insight into their minds intrigued him. He could sense that they all regarded it as a humiliation to be condemned to live among slaves, and that this fostered an attitude of resentment towards the spiders. At the same time, each felt that his position had important compensations. Among their fellow servants they were nonentities; here they were regarded almost as gods. They had first choice of the best food, were waited on hand and foot and allowed to take their pick of the most attractive slave women. All this had developed in them a certain spirit of independence; none of them really wanted to be sent back to live among fellow servants. Potentially, such men were allies against the spiders.

At the moment, their attitude towards Niall was unfriendly; he was a stranger, and he might be assigned one of the more desirable jobs. The most coveted assignments were farm work and food gathering, which allowed an unusual degree of freedom. On the other hand, everybody hated street cleaning and sewage work, since these involved working under the direct observation of the spiders. For some reason, working for the bombardier beetles was also regarded with deep distaste.

When Niall turned his attention to Morlag, he realized with dismay that the overseer intended to assign him to take charge of a street cleaning detail. That would be a disaster; he would be recognized as soon as he crossed the bridge. For a moment, he considered the idea of slipping quietly away, then dismissed it; Morlag would want to know what had happened to him. The alternative was to try to influence the overseer's mind, to implant the suggestion that he should be assigned to some other detail.

Niall stared at the back of Morlag's head, at the same time reaching inside his shirt and turning the thought mirror. But even as his fingers touched it, he realized that this was not the answer. The thought mirror reflected his powers back inside himself and so diminished his power to influence other people. It was as he turned it back again that he made another discovery: as the mirror turned, it was as if his focused attention was deflected away from himself in a concentrated beam. Suddenly he understood. When the mirror was turned inward, it intensified his thoughts and feelings. When it was turned outward, it could be used as a reflector, beaming his thoughts and feelings towards other people. He had only to direct his own concentration towards the mirror.

He tried it, staring intently at the back of Morlag's head. The result surpassed his expectation. Morlag was halfway through a sentence, roaring, "Stand to attention and get in line, you stupid . . ."

Then his voice faded, and a blank expression came over his face. He shook his head as if an insect were buzzing around it, and tugged nervously at his beard. Niall's companions gazed at him in astonishment, wondering what had happened. Then Morlag seemed to recollect himself. "Time to get started."

"You . . ." He turned to the nearest servant. "Take this lot to the rabbit farm. You and you, report to the main square for street cleaning." His attention came to rest on Niall. "You . . ." His memory seemed to fail him for a moment, and in that moment, Niall selected from his mind the assignment he preferred. "You, report to the bombardier beetles. You, take this lot to the sewage works. . . ." As he passed on down the line, Niall averted his eyes to conceal his relief.

Five minutes later, Niall was marching north along the main avenue, at the head of a squad of twenty slaves.

The day was bright and cloudless, and the northeast wind had the refreshing coolness of early morning. Accustomed to the hot, dry wind of the desert, Niall found it intoxicating; even the slight dampness of his clothes against his skin gave him pleasure. Ahead of them, the avenue stretched in a straight line towards the green hills in the distance. The sight of them brought a curious elation, a sense that freedom lay on the other side.

Most of the buildings on either side of them were in ruins; some were fire-blackened shells, with trees and tall purple weeds pushing their way out of doors and windows. Overhead, the thick, dusty cobwebs were less dense than in the city center. Niall experienced a continuous sense of observation from unseen eyes; it was as if he were being lightly brushed by beams of intense curiosity. He deliberately kept his mind closed, refusing to allow his consciousness to reflect anything but his immediate surroundings.

A mile or so further on, the scenery changed; ruined skyscrapers and tower blocks gave way to smaller buildings, many surrounded by tangled wildernesses of greenery; this had evidently been a residential area of the city. Soon the webs disappeared as the gaps between buildings became too wide to be bridged with spider silk. Here, at last, Niall felt able to relax, and to give free rein to the thoughts and feelings that filled his being with excitement. Again and again he reached inside his shirt and turned the mirror; each time, he experienced the surge of delight and incredulity as he felt his mind concentrate like a compressed spring, then release its energy in a brief surge of power. It was astonishing to feel that his mind had exactly the same power as his hands: not merely to grasp, but to *change* things.

It was, of course, the same power that the spiders possessed.

And once again he was overwhelmed by that staggeringly simple yet fundamental insight: that men have become slaves of the habit of

300

changing the world with their hands. The spiders had the tremendous advantage of never having formed that habit.

Suddenly, it seemed preposterous that men had been on Earth for so many millions of years without discovering the true use of the mind. And horribly tragic that some of them—like the slaves—had literally lost their minds, like deep sea fish who have lost their eyes. . . .

The thought of the slaves made him look round. They had ceased to march in ranks and were shambling along with bowed shoulders; some stragglers were fifty yards behind. Niall concentrated his will and sent out a beam of command. The result astonished him. The nearest slaves staggered, as if struck by a powerful blast of wind; those farther away jerked frantically to attention. All looked shocked and bewildered. Niall tried again, this time more gently. The slaves immediately closed ranks, threw back their heads and began to march like trained soldiers. Niall himself felt curiously exalted by this response and experienced an answering surge of vitality. For perhaps five minutes—until the attention of the slaves began to waver—he felt as though they were all part of a single organism—perhaps some enormous centipede marching on its multiple army of legs.

Abruptly, the buildings came to an end. From the top of a low rise, they found themselves looking down on open countryside, and on cultivated fields with barley and green vegetables. They passed an orchard where slaves were gathering fruit, tended by an overseer who might have been Odina's sister. Aware of her expectation, Niall saluted her smartly, and made the slaves do the same. Her amazement warned him that this was a mistake, and he made a mental note to avoid flamboyant gestures.

A mile further on, the road entered an area of dense woodland whose emerald green foliage overhung the road. Niall found it so enchanting that he allowed the slaves to break ranks and slow down to a leisurely stroll. There was a point where a small stream ran beneath the road, rippling over lichen-stained pebbles. The slaves ran down into this and splashed through the shallow water; as they did so, Niall's own feet and ankles became almost painfully cold.

As they emerged from the woodland Niall saw, at the foot of the hills to the northwest, a series of red towers like twisted church spires. He turned to the nearest slave, a gangling, cross-eyed youth with a hare lip. "What is that?"

"Crashville."

"Crashville?"

The youth nodded delightedly, and shouted: "Boo-oom!" at the same time waving his arms upwards to simulate an explosion. The other slaves began to chuckle and giggle, repeating "Boo-oom!" in intonations that varied from a low roar to an excited shriek. Crashville must be the slaves' nickname for the city of the bombardier beetles.

Half an hour later, they were met by a tall, bald-headed man who wore a yellow tunic and green eyeshade; his face was red and harassed.

"Where have you been? You're late!"

Niall said: "I'm sorry. They won't walk very fast."

"Where's your whip?"

"I'm afraid I don't have one."

The man groaned, and cast his eyes up to heaven. "Here, borrow mine." From a large pocket of his tunic he pulled a coiled leather whip. The slaves eyed it nervously.

"I don't think I know how to use it," Niall said.

"I'll soon show you." He uncoiled the whip, cracked it, then went behind the slaves and slashed at the ankles of the stragglers. They closed ranks and broke into a trot. The man followed them for a few yards, swearing and cracking the whip, then slowed down to a walk beside Niall.

"See? That's the only way to do it."

Niall said humbly: "I see."

"Why have you only brought nineteen?"

"There were twenty when we set out." Niall had counted them.

The man shrugged. "I suppose a spider got one of them."

Niall was appalled. "You mean one has been eaten?"

The man looked at him pityingly. "You're new at this, aren't you?"

"Er . . . yes."

"You're lucky you didn't get eaten yourself. Oh, well, I suppose we can make do with nineteen."

Now they were entering the city of red towers. Each tower was an immense spiral cone and seemed to be made of a waxy, shiny substance; it was as if some giant had seized each while it was still soft and given it a clockwise twist. Through the door in the base of the nearest tower, Niall could see an ascending ramp. There were window-like apertures in the twisted sides, and from the highest of these, just below the apex of the tower, a bombardier beetle goggled down at them. Around the foot of the tower was a moat about two feet wide, and in this, a small beetle, hardly more than a baby, was floating on its back, its silvery green belly exposed to the sunlight.

This colony of the bombardier beetles consisted of several hundred of these towers, spaced at wide intervals on smooth green turf. Between were low, one-story buildings made of a blue substance like opaque glass, and with small circular windows like portholes; these were evidently the homes of the human servants. Like the towers, the houses were surrounded by neat green lawns, intersected by water channels and by paths of a pink material like marble. Children dressed in yellow tunics broke off their play to stare at them curiously as they passed. Attractive women, many with spinning wheels, sat in the shade of blue glass porches. Most of them wore their hair very long—in some cases, below the waist or piled in coils on the top of the head.

"Who lives there?" Niall asked. He pointed to a tower at least twice as high as the others.

"Nobody. That's the town hall."

They entered the central square, a smooth rectangle of green turf neatly intersected by paths. Niall could now see that the central building consisted of two halves: a blue glass structure surmounted by a red tower. An impressive flight of curved steps ran up to its main entrance.

The slaves, who had evidently been here before, had drawn up in ranks at the foot of the steps. The bombardier beetles who wandered in and out of the building ignored them. As Niall and his companion approached, a man in a shabby yellow tunic emerged from the main entrance and walked down the steps; even at a distance, Niall recognized the spindly legs and beaky nose. He was about to smile and wave when Doggins looked directly into his eyes. To Niall's surprise, he showed no sign of recognition; instead, he looked away and addressed Niall's companion.

"You'd better get a move on or we'll be late starting."

"That's not my fault. This chap"—he glanced pityingly at Niall—"forgot to bring his whip."

"That was careless." Again, Doggins looked at Niall as if he had been a stranger. "All right, get 'em over to the quarry."

"Right, Cap'n." The bald-headed man saluted, then beckoned to Niall. "You, come with me."

Doggins said quickly: "No, I'll be needing him for the next hour or so. You go ahead with this lot. And don't let 'em get near the fireworks." He turned his back on them, saying casually over his shoulder: "You—come this way."

Niall followed him up the steps. They entered a large, dim hall whose cool blue light was welcome after the blaze of the sun. Bombardier beetles and their servants bustled about them, the beetles towering above the humans. Niall sensed about them that same indifferent friendliness he had perceived in the camel spiders of the desert. Without glancing back, Doggins led him across the hall and pushed open a door labelled: Director of Explosives. The room had no windows, but a cool blue light filtered through the walls, creating a curiously soothing effect. Doggins flung himself into an armchair behind a huge desk and glared at Niall.

"Well, you're about the last person I wanted to see."

Niall, who had been hoping for a friendlier welcome, said: "I'm sorry."

"You bleedin' well ought to be. What are we going to do with you?"

Niall said apologetically: "You don't have to do anything with me. I'm supposed to be in charge of the slaves."

"I know that. And where will you go tonight?"

"Back to the slave quarter."

Doggins stared at him incredulously. "You must be crazy. They're all looking for you. We had 'em here first thing this morning."

Niall asked quickly: "What happened?"

"What do you think? We've promised to look out for you and send you back if we catch you."

"And are you going to?"

Doggins shrugged irritably. "Now look, son, you'd better get one thing clear. We've got an agreement with the crawlies—live and let live. If we gave you shelter, and they found out, it'd be war. And we just can't risk that. I shouldn't even be talking to you now."

Niall stood up. "I'm very sorry. I don't want to get you into trouble. I'll go away."

Doggins' glare became less pugnacious. "Where do you think you're going?"

"I'll hide somewhere until it's time to go back."

Doggins grunted. "There's no point. They won't be back looking for you. You'd better stick around here and act normal. And if anybody asks, I don't know you. Right?"

Niall nodded. "Right."

Doggins stared into his eyes for a long time. He said finally: "So they found out."

"Yes."

"I warned you about that." He gnawed his lower lip. "They'll kill you if they find you."

"I know."

There was another long silence. Then Doggins said: "Your only hope is to get back to your own country. We might be able to smuggle you across on one of our boats."

Niall said: "It's very kind of you. But I don't want to go back. I can't leave my mother and brother behind."

"You can't help 'em much if you're dead."

"I'm going to try to hide in the slave quarter."

"They'll find you sooner or later."

"Perhaps. But I can't just give up. I've got to try."

Doggins shook his head with exasperation. "Try what? What are you hoping to achieve?"

Niall met his eyes. "To destroy the spiders."

Doggins smiled pityingly. "And just how do you propose to set about that?"

"The spiders aren't physically stronger than we are—they just have a stronger willpower. And that's no different from having stronger muscles. We could fight them if we used our intelligence."

Doggins regarded him thoughtfully. "Yes, now I can see why they think you're dangerous."

It made Niall realize that, without intending it, he had been concentrating his attention through the thought mirror; the result was that his words struck Doggins with immense conviction. He pressed the advantage.

"You could blow up the whole spider city with your explosives."

"Of course, we could—if we had enough explosive. But we wouldn't, and they know we wouldn't."

"Why?"

"Because we're the servants of the beetles, and the beetles would never order us to do it."

"But why should you be a servant? Men were once lords of the earth."

Doggins gave a snort of laughter. "And a right bleedin' mess they made of it! Do you really want to know why the crawlies don't like human beings? Come with me and I'll show you."

He stood up and led Niall out into the hall. It was totally empty. They climbed a short flight of steps and halted in front of a door made of gold-colored metal. Doggins pulled this open and beckoned Niall to go inside. The room beyond was dark.

A moment later there was a tremendous crash, and a blinding flash of light. Niall jumped backwards and cannoned into Doggins. Doggins gripped his elbow.

"Steady. It's all right. Just stand quietly."

Still trembling with shock, Niall stared with horrified amazement. The opposite wall had turned into a vast expanse of blue sky, with fleecy white clouds, and across this expanse, machines that he recognized as airplanes hurtled with a shrieking roar that deafened him. Suddenly, the view changed; he was looking down from an airplane, watching egg-shaped objects fall towards the ground. They continued to fall until they diminished into dots and disappeared. Then, from the ground below, there was a series of white puffs, one after another, in a straight line. This time the explosions were distant and muffled.

Once his eyes were accustomed to the semi-darkness Niall could see that he was in another large hall. In front of him was an audience of bombardier beetles; he could sense their breathless attention. Now it dawned upon him that the scene he was watching was not some form of magic. A cone of wavering light overhead told him that it was merely an illusion, projected onto a wall-sized screen.

Doggins grasped him by the elbow, steered him into the semi-darkness and indicated a chair. Without taking his eyes from the screen, Niall sat down. He was witnessing a bombing raid on a large city, and the destructiveness took his breath away. He watched tall buildings shudder, then crumble slowly to the ground, sending up a cloud of dust. Fire exploded in clouds of red and yellow, then merged into a whirlpool of black smoke. Firemen directed jets of water into the flames; then another building collapsed and buried them.

Doggins whispered in his ear: "This is just an old movie, not the real thing. The real thing comes later."

Niall said: "It's horrible!"

"Don't let them hear you say that. They think it's marvelous."

The screen went blank for a moment; then there was a burst of loud marching music, and a man's voice announced impressively: "Demolitions!" There was a sibilant stir of applause from the audience; this was clearly a favorite. A semicircular tower block appeared on the screen, photographed from below so that its walls seemed to rear up like the sheer face of a cliff. Then, by some trick of photography, the camera moved slowly into the air and rose towards the roof of the building; the time it took to do this emphasized its enormous height. Finally, the camera was looking down on it from above. It pulled back to a safe distance. Niall held his breath. There was a puff of smoke at one corner of the building, then a second. At the third puff, the walls began to crumble; slowly, the walls cracked and buckled; a cloud of dust went up at the base as the building disintegrated into falling masonry, then subsided into a heap of rubble. Niall had to admit that there was something magnificent about the spectacle.

The remainder of the film followed the same pattern; skyscrapers, building developments, factory chimneys, even cathedrals, all collapsed into the same cloud of smoky dust. And as each one crashed to the ground, there was a sibilant hiss of applause from the beetles—they seemed to make the sound by rubbing their feelers together.

For Niall, this was a shattering experience. By turning the thought mirror towards his chest, he was able to absorb its full impact and appreciate it as a reality. His vision in the white tower had enabled him to grasp something of the extent of human destructiveness. But this unending panorama of violence made him aware that he had not even begun to grasp its enormity. There was old footage of the First World War, showing the artillery bombardments that preceded an attack and disembowelled bodies sprawled on the barbed wire; there were newsreels of the blitzes of the Second World War, and of dive bombers strafing undefended cities. There was archive material of the dropping of the first atom bombs on Japan, then of the testing of the hydrogen bomb on Bikini atoll. As the smoke cloud rose above the ground and revealed that the atoll had ceased to exist, even the beetles seemed too stunned to applaud.

Doggins nudged him in the ribs. "Seen enough?"

"I expect so." But he kept his eyes on the screen until they found themselves outside in the blue daylight; there was something hypnotically fascinating about the violence. It was a strange sensation to find himself out in the empty hall, like waking from a dream.

As they walked into the sunlight, Niall had to shield his eyes. After the cool of the building, it was like stepping into a hot bath.

"How long does that go on?"

"For the rest of the afternoon. We've got about two hundred hours of film footage."

"Haven't they seen it all before?"

"Dozens of times. But they never get tired of it."

The green lawns with their neatly symmetrical buildings seemed somehow unreal. After the unending thunder of explosions, the peace seemed to hover over them like a threat.

They had crossed the square diagonally and were approaching a house that stood on the corner. This was notably larger than those that surrounded it, and a fountain played in the center of the lawn. About a dozen children were dangling their feet in the green water; several of them had the distinctive Doggins nose. When they saw Doggins, half a dozen children rushed across the grass and flung their arms round him, clamoring to be picked up. A pretty, dark-haired girl came out of the house.

"Let Daddy alone. He's busy."

Reluctantly, the children returned to their bathing pool. To Niall's surprise, the girl seized both Doggins' hands and kissed them. Doggins looked embarrassed. "This is my wife Selima."

Niall felt a twinge of envy; the girl was scarcely older than Dona. He held out his hand to clasp forearms and was startled when she dropped onto one knee, seized his hand, and kissed the palm.

Doggins cleared his throat. "Let's have something to eat."

"Yes, Bill." She vanished into the house. Doggins said awkwardly: "Very affectionate girl."

As they entered the house a voice called: "Who is it?"

"It's me, my love."

A large handsome woman with platinum blonde hair looked out of a doorway. She also seized Doggins' hands and kissed them. "This is my wife Lucretia," Doggins said.

The woman gave Niall a brilliant smile; the blue light of the hallway made her teeth look like precious stones. "His first wife," she said.

Niall, slightly taken aback, smiled awkwardly.

Lucretia asked: "What is his name?"

Doggins said: "Er . . . Mr. Rivers."

"Is he a Bill?"

"No, no, just a mister."

"What a pity." She disappeared through the nearest doorway. Niall caught a glimpse of a kitchen, in which several girls were preparing food.

Niall was puzzled. "What did she mean—am I a Bill?"

Doggins chuckled. "I've told 'em that Bill means 'a man of power and magnificence.' She was paying you a compliment."

He led Niall into a large comfortably-furnished room. A slim, bare-armed girl who was sitting on the couch jumped to her feet and kissed his hands. Then, as Doggins sat down, she knelt and pulled off his sandals.

"This is Gisela," Doggins said, "—she's number eight. This is Mr. Rivers, my pet."

The girl glanced shyly at Niall, averted her eyes, and blushed. Niall guessed she was even younger than Dona. She asked her husband: "Shall I wash your feet now?"

"No, pet, just get us some cold beer."

"Yes, Bill." Niall observed that she spoke his name with a certain solemnity, as if saying "lord."

When they were alone, Doggins gave him a roguish grin. "Now you can see why I don't want to get mixed up in any war with the crawlies?"

Niall said sadly: "Yes."

"It's not that I don't want to help you. But you couldn't win anyway." When Niall made no reply, he went on: "I mean, let's be realistic. There's millions of spiders. What can any of us do against that kind of odds?"

Niall shook his head stubbornly. "There must be a way. Otherwise they wouldn't be afraid of us. Why are they afraid of us?"

Doggins shrugged. "Because we're a bloody destructive lot, that's why. You've seen the films."

"Then why aren't they afraid of you? You know the secrets of explosives."

"Why should they be? I'm doing all right. In ten years' time I could even be the General Controller."

The platinum blonde came into the room followed by several girls carrying trays. She moved a low table between Niall and her husband and spread it with a white linen cloth. As she poured the beer, she asked: "Had a good morning, dear?"

"So-so. You know what Boomday's like."

"What did those spiders want?"

"Oh, they were looking for a runaway slave."

"A slave? All those spiders? What had he done?"

Doggins avoided Niall's eyes. "I don't know. They didn't tell me."

The table was now laden with many kinds of food: oysters, mussels, quails' eggs, small roasted birds, and several varieties of salad and vegetables. The beer was dark brown and slightly sweet—and, as Niall realized after drinking down half a glass to quench his thirst, very strong. Before they ate, the girls held out bowls of warm water for them to wash their hands, then dried them on towels that were as soft as eiderdown. After this, the women quietly withdrew.

For the next five minutes both of them devoted their full attention to the food. Niall was experiencing a feeling of romantic melancholy that was not entirely unpleasant; the sight of so many young girls reminded him of Dona, and made him aware that he was missing her.

Doggins was obviously thoughtful. As he ate the quails' eggs with a rich white sauce, he wore an abstracted expression. Periodically, he glanced at Niall from under lowered eyebrows. He said finally: "Look . . . suppose we could make a deal with the spiders? I'm not promising anything, but just suppose we could? Wouldn't that solve your problem?"

"What kind of a deal?"

"Well, suppose they'd agree to let you come and work for us?"

Niall asked cautiously: "What makes you think they'd agree?"

"They owe us a few favors." He bit into a roast lark. "As I see it, they're worried because they're afraid you're a troublemaker. Right? And if we could guarantee"—he laid special emphasis on the word—"that you wouldn't make trouble, it's just possible they might do a deal."

"And I'd live here . . . and work for the beetles?"

"Well, you'd be working for me. I need a new assistant. Do you know anything about explosives?"

"I'm afraid not."

"That doesn't matter. You'd soon learn." Doggins became mellow and expansive. "Gunpowder's easy—saltpeter, sulphur, and charcoal—you just have to get the proportions right. Dynamite's a bit more complicated—my last assistant blew himself up when he was making nitroglycerine. But you wouldn't be doing that. Your first job would be to distill the coal tar products." And, between mouthfuls of food, he began to explain the principles of fractional distillation.

Although Niall appeared to listen attentively, his mind was elsewhere. He found it hard to believe that the spiders would allow him to become a servant of the beetles. Yet Doggins seemed confident enough. The idea was certainly tempting. He could think of nothing more delightful than living with Dona in a house like this. The mere thought was enough to send him into a romantic daydream.

Doggins drained the last of his beer, pushed back his chair, and stood up. He patted Niall on the shoulder. "Don't worry, lad. Doggins the Powerful and Magnificent has a certain amount of influence. Now I'm going to get changed. Help yourself to beer."

Niall was glad to be alone; it gave him a chance to collect his thoughts. What worried him now was what would happen if the spiders learned his whereabouts. If he was recaptured, he would be worse off than before. If they didn't kill him, they would make sure that he never had another chance to escape. So could he risk allowing Doggins to try and negotiate for him?

And even if the spiders allowed him to go free, would he really be so much better off? The beetles were allies of the spiders. To work for them would be almost as bad as working for the spiders.

The more he thought about it, the less he was able to see any solution. He wandered restively around the room, his hands in his pockets, pausing every time he passed the window to stare at the fountain. Now that the children had been called indoors, it looked oddly desolate, its spray rising into the sunlight as if trying to escape into the sky, then curving back to Earth, like his own thoughts. . . .

His attention was attracted by a persistent tingling in the fingers of his right hand; his fingertips had been toying with the telescopic rod. He took it out and weighed it meditatively in the palm of his hand, deriving a curious sense of comfort from its weight. Then, pressing the button that made it expand, he was struck by the intensity of the tingling sensation that communicated itself to his slightly damp skin; the vibration was stronger than he had ever known it. Holding the rod between the thumb and index finger of either hand, he concentrated all his attention on the vibration.

With a clarity that made him jump, the voice of the Steegmaster spoke inside his chest.

"Tell him about the Fortress."

For a moment, Niall's mind was a blank. He asked in bewilderment: "Fortress?" He had already forgotten what the word meant. But even as he spoke, the tingling sensation faded. He stared down at the rod, confused and disappointed, and wondering whether he should try to renew the contact. At that moment, he heard the sound of Doggins' voice in the corridor and pressed the button that made it contract. As Doggins came into the room, he dropped the rod into his pocket.

Doggins looked unexpectedly impressive. Instead of the shabby yellow smock, he wore a black toga, with a gold chain round the waist. The leather sandals were also black, and on his head, in place of the battered green eyeshade, he wore a black peaked hood which gave him a monkish appearance.

"Ready? We'd better get a move on."

Outside in the corridor, the women and children were waiting, all dressed in gaily colored clothes. The only exception was Lucretia, who wore a black linen toga, evidently to emphasize her position as wife number one. As Doggins and Niall marched out into the sunlight, the family walked behind in an orderly crocodile, the tallest at the front, the smallest in the rear.

They crossed the green in front of the town hall and turned into the extension of the main avenue. Every inhabitant of the town seemed to be going in the same direction, the emerald-backed beetles with their bright yellow heads towering above their human servants and conversing among themselves in sibilant squeaks. The humans were excited and boisterous, and if noisy children occasionally cannoned into the legs of the beetles, no one seemed to mind. Niall was struck by the friendly and easy-going relations that seemed to exist between the beetles and the humans; unlike the spiders, these huge, armor-plated creatures seemed to inspire neither fear nor veneration; only affectionate familiarity.

As they left the square, Niall suddenly remembered the word he had been trying to recall. He asked Doggins: "What's a barracks?"

"It's a place where soldiers live. Why?"

"I saw the word on an old map."

Doggins glanced at him quickly. "Of the spider city?"

"Yes."

Doggins asked casually: "It wasn't called the Fortress, by any chance?"

"Yes, it was. How did you know?"

Doggins shrugged. "I've heard rumors about it. Do you think you could describe where it is?"

"I think so. It's in the slave quarter."

They had reached the outskirts of the town, and Niall was interested to see that one of the red towers was under construction, and that a large cloud of golden insects was swarming and buzzing over the unfinished walls. He asked: "What are they doing?"

"Building it."

Niall asked in amazement: "The insects?"

"That's right. They're called glue flies."

As they came level with the truncated tower, the buzzing noise was deafening. Niall shouted above the din: "Are they building it for themselves?"

"Oh, no." Doggins halted and his retinue of wives and children also came to a stop. "They live in nests made of leaves stuck together with glue."

"Then how do you make them build houses?"

"They're specially trained. Watch." He twisted his face into a scowl, wrinkled his forehead, and glowered at the swarming golden insects through narrowed eyes. After a moment, they began to settle on the walls; at the end of thirty seconds, the buzzing noise had ceased, and the insects were crawling over one another's backs. Drops of sweat were standing out on Doggins' face. He gave a gasp and relaxed; instantly, the insects were in flight again. Doggins looked pleased with himself.

"How did you do that?"

"They're trained to respond to mental orders. Why don't you try it?"

Niall stared at the glue flies and concentrated his attention. He was instantly aware of the presence of each individual insect as if they had become a part of his own body, like his fingers or toes. He was even aware of their precise number: eighteen thousand, seven hundred and eighteen. But as he was about to transmit the mental order for them to settle, he recalled his earlier resolve to avoid flamboyant gestures, and changed his mind. "I'm afraid I don't seem to be able to do it."

Doggins smiled sympathetically, but with a trace of satisfaction. "No, it takes a lot of practice."

And now, as they walked on, Niall became aware that the moment of empathy with the glue flies had established a sense of contact with the stream of life that flowed around him. It was

313

astonishingly different from the feeling he had experienced that morning, standing in the square among the slaves. Then he had been conscious of a kind of mindless well-being. Now he was aware of being amongst others like himself, human beings with the same power to think and control their own lives. There was only one difference: they were not aware that they possessed this power.

He asked Doggins casually: "How did you learn to control the glue flies?"

"Oh, it's not difficult. They're used to being controlled by the beetles. I've been with the beetles so long that I suppose I'm on the same mental wavelength, so I can do it too. . . ."

He was wrong, of course. It was nothing to do with mental wavelength; it was purely a matter of will-force. For a moment, Niall felt tempted to explain, then decided that this was neither the time nor place.

Half a mile beyond the edge of the town, the road turned a corner, and Niall suddenly found himself looking down into an immense hole in the earth. It must have been a mile wide and a quarter of a mile deep. The drop made him feel dizzy.

"What is this?"

"An old marble quarry."

"But what made it?"

Doggins grinned. "Human beings."

In its sheer sides, Niall could see the layered geological strata, the broadest of which was the same color as the road under their feet. This was obviously the source of the road-building material.

The road descended into the quarry in the form of a gentle ramp; bombardier beetles and human beings poured down it in a gaily colored stream. On the floor of the quarry he could see dozens of colored tents, one of which—striped in green and white—was far larger than the rest. He could also hear a sound that made his heart lift in sudden gaiety: the noise of brass musical instruments played in unison.

It took them nearly half an hour to descend to the bottom. There were still many large pools of water from last night's rain, and children ran barefoot through these and shrieked with laughter as they splashed one another; other children were gathered around a Punch and Judy show. Pleasant smells of cooking and burnt caramel blew towards them from the colored tents and booths. The members of the brass band, dressed in bright red togas with yellow sashes, stood on a platform of natural rock, and an amphitheater behind them amplified their sounds like a powerful loudspeaker.

This end of the quarry was dominated by a grandstand with perhaps a thousand seats and covered by a transparent dome like a green-tinted bubble.

Doggins said: "If you want a good view of the show, try and get a seat on the top row. It starts in about half an hour. Now I'm going to leave you; I've things to do."

"Thank you." Niall was looking forward to exploring the sideshows.

But a moment later, Doggins was back. He said quietly: "Trouble."

Niall followed the direction of his gaze and felt his heart sink. Among the crowds descending the ramp was a group of bare-breasted women; he recognized them immediately as commanders. For a moment he experienced panic.

"Do you think they're looking for me?"

"No. They often come here on Boomday."

"What shall I do?"

"Don't worry. I don't think they'll recognize you. To them, you're just another slave. But you'd better keep out of sight."

He pointed to the striped marquee that faced the grandstand. "You'll find the slaves working in there. You already know Mostig— he's the bald-headed man you met this morning. Go and ask him if there's anything you can do."

Niall entered the marquee and found it a chaos of activity. Most of the floor space was taken up by an elaborate stage set, which represented an island covered with trees. There was a ship at anchor on imitation blue waves, and nearby a creek ran into the sea. The beach was covered with native straw huts, and a witch doctor with a necklace of skulls was dancing round a cooking pot that contained an unhappy-looking sailor. On closer examination, Niall discovered that the witch doctor, like the island itself, was made of wood and papier-mache, much of it still being painted by the stage hands.

The rear of the marquee, which was open, faced the wall of the quarry, and Niall could see that it was supported by a complex arrangement of ropes and pulleys. Immediately behind the marquee, a cave had been hollowed out of the rock face; in front of this, slaves were loading a cart with barrels. The bald-headed man, looking exhausted and harassed, seemed to be trying to supervise everybody at once. When Niall asked him if there was anything he could do, he snapped irritably: "Just go away." Then he looked closer and said: "Oh, it's you. I could have done with your help a couple of hours ago. Where have you been?"

"Helping Mr. Doggins."

"Well, go and try to make those slaves hurry up. Here, take this." He handed Niall his whip.

Niall made his way into the cave. This sloped back far into the cliff and was packed from floor to ceiling with wooden kegs and ammunition chests. One of the kegs had smashed open on the floor, and the cross-eyed youth was trying to sweep up the gunpowder with an absurdly inadequate broom. Niall could see at once that the problem was not to persuade the slaves to hurry, but to induce them to slow down. They were all wildly excited by the carnival atmosphere, and were rushing backwards and forwards like demented termites, rolling barrels and dragging ammunition cases, then forgetting what they were supposed to do with them and leaving them where other slaves could trip over them. A red-headed youth with knobbly knees, evidently the bald-headed man's assistant, was doing his best to control them but finding it beyond his powers.

Niall introduced himself and ascertained precisely what had to be done. Then he organized the slaves into teams of three and allotted each a separate task. He pretended to make use of his whip; in fact, it was unnecessary. The slaves responded to a concentrated effort of will with a readiness that reminded him of the glue flies. One team fetched kegs from the back of the cave, another loaded them onto small wheelbarrows, while a third wheeled them into the marquee. There they were packed by stage hands into a hollow space underneath the island. Within a quarter of an hour, the work was completed, and the bald-headed man began to look at Niall with a new respect. When Niall asked if there was anything more he could do, he said: "Just keep those bloody slaves out of the way until we're ready to start."

At that moment, Doggins came in through the front entrance of the marquee; as Niall waved to him, he frowned and shook his head imperceptibly. A moment later, Niall understood the reason. Immediately behind Doggins were half a dozen commanders, and the woman walking in the forefront of the group was Odina. Fortunately, her face was turned away from Niall as she spoke to the woman behind her. Niall turned and hurried out of the rear entrance.

The gunpowder cave was now deserted; the broken barrel, with its scattered grey powder, still lay in the middle of the floor. Niall made his way past it to the rear of the cave. Here it was pleasantly cool and smelt of damp fungus. After the turmoil of the marquee, he was glad to relax. He chose a dark corner behind a pile of barrels and sat down on an ammunition case. After a few moments, he allowed his eyes to close and leaned his head back against the wall.

A light touch on his cheek jerked him to wakefulness. He sat up with a gasp of alarm and peered into the shadows. There was a slight movement, and for a moment he thought he was looking at a small millipede. Cautiously, he moved a powder keg to admit the daylight. There was nothing there but a yellowy-green fungoid growth, like a distorted mushroom, growing out of the wall. He took the telescopic rod out of his pocket and poked at it; it seemed quite solid. He wondered if some small creature could be using the fungus as a shelter, and prodded it with his finger. As he did so, a tiny grey pseudopod, like a moist finger, emerged from the edge of the fungus and tried to touch his hand. Instinctively, Niall drew back. Then, since the pseudopod seemed as harmless as a worm, he held out his finger again and allowed the creature to touch it. To Niall's amazement, the pseudopod suddenly became thinner and longer and, with a movement of lightning swiftness, wrapped itself round his finger like a tiny coil of rope. He reached out with his other hand to feel its texture; another pseudopod snaked out from the fungus and gripped his finger. He tugged gently, and felt them tightening their grip. They were trying to tug his hand back towards the fungus. He gave a sudden sharp tug, and pulled his fingers free. Each had a tiny red band where the tentacles had gripped.

This was obviously a smaller version of the creature he had encountered the night before: the same cautious, tentative probing movements that reminded him of the horns of a snail, the same slimy grip that was able to exert a surprising amount of force. He pushed the telescopic rod under the fungus and levered it away from the wall. It seemed to be attached by a central root; but at the base of this root was a circle of tiny orifices, like small hungry mouths. When he pushed the tip of his little finger against one of these mouths, it opened immediately and sucked in the finger, while half a dozen grey pseudopods reached out and tried to grip his hand. They seemed to emerge from the slimy surface of the fungus, as if it was composed of some viscous liquid. When Niall tugged his hand free, the tip of his finger was covered with a slimy substance that stung; he wiped it clean on his smock.

As he stared at the grey pseudopods, he deliberately relaxed and allowed his mind to become totally receptive. He was attempting to discover whether the creature was an animal or a plant. For a moment, his own brain seemed to share its famished and predatory consciousness; then his mind slipped beyond it and he became aware of a sensation of gently pulsating energy, as if he were looking at the creature through the ripples on the surface of a pond.

"What are you doing?"

The voice was as startling as a sudden blow. He had been so intent on the fungus that he had not even noticed Odina as she approached him on bare feet.

She repeated: "What are you doing?"

Niall found his voice. "I'm hiding."

"I can see that. From what?"

His anxiety gave way to a mixture of relief and guilt. The relief was due to the startling recognition that she was glad to see him. The guilt came from his immediate and instinctive violation of her mind. He knew her so well that it seemed completely natural to enter the privacy of her thoughts, yet as he did so, he felt like a thief entering her bedroom.

He made room for her on the ammunition chest, and she sat down beside him; he was not sure whether the suggestion came from his own mind or from hers. He looked into her face for a moment; then, with the same instinctive impulsion, took her in his arms and kissed her lips. Her arms went round his neck and they clung together. It seemed completely natural, and both experienced a feeling of relief and delight that it had finally happened. He also became aware that she had been wanting him to do this since she had caught him kissing the dark-haired girl in the women's quarter.

She was the first to break away; the trained commander in her took over.

"What are you running away from?"

"I had to get away from the city."

"But why?" She was obviously baffled. To her, the spiders were stern but benevolent masters, and it was a privilege to serve them.

318

"They killed my father."

"I know that. It was unfortunate. But he tried to attack one of them."

"I know. But I still find it hard to forgive."

"You *have* to forgive. They are the masters. We have no right to criticize anything they do."

It was strange talking to her like this; he could see her words forming in her mind before she spoke, so there was an odd delayed-action effect as she voiced them. For a moment, Niall was tempted to tell her what Kazak had told him; then he dismissed the idea. It would be unfair to her to allow her to know too much. Her mind was not prepared for such a burden.

She said gently: "You must return with me to the city. They will understand why you ran away and will forgive you." Her arms tightened round his neck so he could no longer see her face. "Then you can become my husband."

It was, Niall realized, an extraordinary offer, like a princess offering to marry a farmhand.

"A commander cannot marry a runaway slave."

She took his face between her hands and looked into his eyes. "A commander can marry anyone she likes—that is her privilege."

She kissed him again, this time very gently, but maintaining the contact for a long time. Something seemed to pass from her lips into him, and from his lips into her—an exchange of vital energy. It was then that Niall realized she had left him without alternatives. It was true that he could easily persuade her to go away and pretend she had never seen him; because she loved him, she would do whatever he asked. But if he did so, he would be turning her into a traitor, and she would feel overwhelmed with guilt. He knew that would be impossible; she filled him with a feeling of protectiveness.

He said: "Very well. I will do as you ask."

This time she tightened her arms round his neck and kissed him hungrily; both abandoned themselves to the pleasure of this exchange of living warmth. Then Niall felt something brush his hair and started with disgust as a pseudopod started to explore his neck. She asked: "What is it?"

He pointed. "What is that?"

She laughed. "Only a squid fungus." She stood up, drew a dagger from her belt and slashed at the fungus. It fell on to the floor. To

Niall's surprise, she bent down, impaled it on her dagger, and dropped it into a leather pouch at her waist.

"What are you going to do with it?"

"They are good to eat." She caressed his hair. "When you are my husband, I will cook them for you." From outside, the brass band played a fanfare. "Now we must go." She took his hand.

"Is it a good idea for us to be seen together?"

She laughed. "Why not? It will make the others jealous."

As she drew him out into the sunlight, Niall experienced a mixture of delight and sadness: delight at being with Odina, sadness at knowing that his attempt to escape had been a failure.

Doggins, who was standing at the rear of the marquee, looked at Niall with astonishment and consternation. Niall avoided his eyes.

The grandstand was now full, the humans tightly packed on benches, the bombardier beetles standing on broad platforms between the rows. Odina led Niall to a bench that was evidently reserved for commanders; she sat down and made a place for Niall at the end. The other commanders glanced at Niall with mild curiosity, and he was interested to observe that none of them seemed to guess his identity. Odina had apparently kept her secret from them.

On the row in front of them, the whole Doggins family stared at the marquee with fascinated absorption, the children all sucking large and brightly colored lollipops. From inside, the green-tinted bubble dome looked blue, its glass so perfectly transparent that it was almost invisible; it seemed to have the property of cutting out the heat of the sun, transforming the midsummer heat into the pale warmth of a winter afternoon.

Odina was talking to the girl sitting next to her. Niall looked at her with a certain pride. With her honey-colored hair, her sunburnt breasts and her white teeth, she was by far the most attractive of the commanders. Happiness had given her an inner glow. Was Niall in love with her? The question was almost irrelevant. He was at the age when everyone wants to fall in love, and would have been willing to consider any girl who showed signs of being susceptible to his attraction. As far as Niall was concerned, the question of whether he was in love with her was secondary to the fact that she seemed to be in love with him.

The band blew another fanfare. There was instant silence, everyone's eyes on the marquee. Slaves were pulling out the pegs that held it against the ground. Bill Doggins stepped forward, bowed to the audience, then turned to the marquee and flung his arms above his head with a gesture of command. The marquee rose slowly into the air, sweeping back towards the cliff on its hidden pulleys, then was lowered over the gunpowder cave to form a backcloth. Cheers and clapping broke out at the sight of the island. Doggins, having established himself as the donor of the entertainment, moved gracefully to one side. Then a black-bearded pirate captain stumped onto the deck of the ship on his wooden leg, glared out ferociously at the audience, and roared: "Avast, ye lubbers, I can see ye watching me! Ye don't frighten Pegleg Pete!" He turned and shouted down below: "Men, there's a crowd of idiots out there staring at us! Let's go and cut 'em to pieces!" At that moment, there was a loud explosion from behind him, and Pegleg Pete leapt into the air like a startled roebuck, losing his hat and telescope in the process. The audience roared with laughter, and the beetles made a curious quivering motion and rubbed their feelers together, making a sound like crickets. Niall, for whom pantomimes were only a distant racial memory, laughed louder than anyone.

The entertainment proceeded. Pegleg Pete and his crew had come to the island in search of buried treasure; Pete said he was hoping to retire on the proceeds and become a hangman in his spare time. But the island was full of murderous cannibals (played by the slaves, with blackened arms and faces). Pete's new Master of Artillery—the last one had been eaten by a shark—was an incompetent who could not strike a match without causing an explosion. When the captain ordered a false distress signal to lure a passing merchantman into an ambush, and the Master of Artillery acquiesced with a cross-eyed leer, all the children shrieked with laughter, knowing the result would be yet another disaster. When the Master of Artillery emerged on deck a moment later with an armful of sky-rockets, the entire crew—including Pegleg Pete dived for cover, and the laughter and stamping of feet was so loud that Niall had to cover his ears. Inevitably, the rockets exploded in all directions, and the Master of Artillery turned a spectacular backward somersault off the deck, escaping injury by a miracle of timing. He was evidently a trained acrobat.

There was a love story, which Niall found even more absorbing than the periodic explosions. The second mate, an honest young fellow who had been captured by the pirates in a skirmish, fell in love with a beautiful lady on the plundered merchantman, and they decided to escape. Seized by cannibals, they were forced to watch from behind prison bars as the natives prepared a feast at which they were to be the main dish. Fortunately, their captors were unaware that the fuel they had gathered for the fire included a bundle of signal rockets. In due course, the fire exploded, the cannibals fled, and the prisoners escaped. Now Niall understood why they were enclosed in the bubble dome; three of the rockets struck it with tremendous impact and exploded without even leaving a mark.

In the third act—the pantomime lasted almost two hours—the mate and his lady love were tied to the masts of the pirate ship, with kegs of gunpowder around them primed to explode, while the captain and crew prepared to escape in the merchantman. The cannibals chose this opportunity to raid the pirate ship. While the hero, with incredible dexterity, cut the bonds of his lady love with a dagger held in his teeth, the cannibals swarmed aboard up a rope ladder. Since the slaves had been insufficiently rehearsed, there was a failure of timing, and the cannibals stood around in a circle, watching the hero's contortions while he did his best to ignore them. Doggins could be seen standing in the wings, waving his arms, but no one paid any attention. Finally, the two principals were freed, and the hero cut the burning fuse with his dagger and tossed the spluttering end over his shoulder. Inevitably, it landed in a bucket of signal rockets, which flew off in all directions, their sparks igniting fireworks which—for unexplained reasons—had been left lying around the deck. This was plainly the build-up to the climax. As the hero and heroine rowed away to safety—pulled by an unseen rope—the ship turned into a spectacular firework display with colored sparks pouring out of its portholes, its hatches, and even the tops of the masts.

At this point, it became clear that the cannibals were not obeying their instructions; they were dancing around joyfully in the showers of sparks, laughing and waving their arms. One of them gave a roar of pain as a rocket soared between his legs, and leapt overboard; but the others seemed to be enjoying themselves too much to be afraid. Doggins finally rushed out from the side of the stage and shouted at them, but his voice was drowned by the crash of fireworks and shrieks of laughter.

It was then that the first explosion occurred; the fo'c'sle of the ship suddenly disintegrated into matchwood. The slaves fell silent and stared with amazement, almost as if they thought it was a joke. In the momentary silence, the voice of Doggins could be heard shouting furiously: "Get out of there you fools!" Then he turned and fled as a tremendous explosion rocked the boat.

Black smoke poured up from the decks and a shower of debris rattled down on the bubble dome. The children in front of Niall were clapping and cheering with excitement, apparently assuming that this was all part of the entertainment. Fireworks were exploding all over the island, and Niall observed with misgivings that the marquee suspended against the cliff had caught fire and was dissolving in an upward surge of flame. The island itself exploded in an ear-splitting roar; as it did so, Niall remembered the gunpowder scattered on the floor of the cave. A second later, the grandstand rocked back and forth as the earth shook, hurling children to the floor. Women began to scream, then to cough and choke as black smoke billowed under the bubble glass dome. The trembling was like an earthquake; fragments of rock pounded down on to the dome like black hail. Some of the seats collapsed; most of them seemed remarkably stable. One huge piece of rock, as large as a man, smashed its way through the bubble glass, splintering the steps below Niall. But most of them caused only star-shaped cracks in the glass, which, in spite of its transparency, was obviously as strong as steel.

Surprisingly, there was no rush to escape; everyone realized they were safer inside. The children below cowered on the floor, staring up at the glass above them as it was darkened with falling rubble. Odina had seized Niall's hand and buried her face against his shoulder. The crashing and shaking gradually receded like thunder, until all was still again.

Niall said: "I'm going to see if Doggins is all right." He made his way down the stairs, clinging onto a rail and skirting the hole that had been made by the falling rock. The smell of dust and sulphur dioxide was choking so that he was unable to swallow. It was like walking through a heavy fog. As the dust settled, and the sunlight revealed what had happened, Niall realized how lucky they had been to be enclosed in the bubble dome. All the tents and sideshows had been blown away. Where the island had been, there was a deep crater in the floor of the quarry. And behind it, the explosives cave had disappeared; the cliff above it had collapsed, and there was only a mountainous pile of rubble.

He found Doggins, looking dusty and angry, staring into the crater. Niall said: "Thank heavens you're all right."

"Oh, I'm all right. But I've lost a hundred bleedin' tons of explosive." He gestured with fury and despair at the pile of rubble.

"What about the slaves?"

Doggins said sourly: "They got what they deserved, bloody idiots. But what am I going to do for explosives for the rest of the year?"

"Hadn't you better go and find your wife? I expect she's worried about you." He could not get used to referring to wives in the plural.

"Yes, I expect so." With a groan of vexation, Doggins turned back towards the grandstand, whose dome was covered with dust and rubble, some of it stained an ominous red. Behind them there was another thunderous crash as a further section of the cliff collapsed.

Mostig, the bald-headed assistant, hurried out from the tunnel under the grandstand; to Niall's surprise he was smiling broadly. He chortled as he patted Doggins on the shoulder.

"Marvelous! You'll get promotion for this!"

Doggins glared at him, evidently suspecting sarcasm. "What are you talking about?"

Mostig lowered his voice. "They think it was all part of the show. I wouldn't tell 'em any different if I was you."

A crowd of bombardier beetles emerged from under the sagging dome and surrounded Doggins. They were waving their feelers and making high-pitched chirping noises, and even Niall could tell they were conveying congratulations. Doggins turned from one to the other with a dazed smile, and waved his fingers with a deprecatory gesture. Niall was puzzled when the largest of the beetles raised his right foreleg and placed it gently on the top of Doggins' head, and Doggins immediately prostrated himself on the ground. He asked Mostig in a whisper: "What does that mean?"

Mostig was staring so intently that Niall had to repeat the question.

"It means . . . it means he's saying they regard Bill as one of themselves," Mostig said finally. He seemed unable to believe his eyes.

"And is that a great compliment?"

"Of course, it is! It's like being . . . made king."

Doggins was being urged to rise to his feet; he did so with an air of broken humility. For a moment, Niall encountered his eyes and was startled by their anguished expression.

Now the smoke was drifting away; beetles and human beings were issuing from the grandstand. Lucretia, brushing the dust from her black toga, looked on the verge of tears, and an air of dejection hung over the rest of the wives and children. When she saw her husband surrounded by beetles, she looked apprehensive; but as she listened to the high-pitched stridulations, her expression changed to delighted astonishment, then to incredulity. The other wives and the children, realizing that something important was happening, also became watchful and silent. Finally, the beetles moved off, and Doggins once more prostrated himself on the ground and remained there until they were out of sight. When he stood up, Lucretia flung her arms round his neck, and the wives and children crowded around him. Mostig muttered in Niall's ear: "Well, some people are born lucky."

Niall was looking for Odina; a moment later he saw her among the crowd that streamed from the grandstand; it was obvious that she was also looking for him. Niall started to push his way towards her. Before he had advanced more than a few yards, someone gripped his arm. It was Doggins.

"Don't go away. I want a word with you."

"All right. But I have to talk to that commander over there." He waved to Odina but she was looking the other way.

Doggins said: "Later." He seized Niall by both arms and steered him firmly in the opposite direction, towards the platform on which the musicians had been playing. Behind this, they were invisible to the crowd.

"That Fortress—can you tell me where it is?"

"Well, yes. But I'd have to draw you a map."

"Never mind the map. Could you take me there?"

Niall stared at him in astonishment; he thought there must be some misunderstanding.

"But it's in the slave quarter of the city."

Doggins nodded impatiently. "I know that. Can you take me?"

"When?" Niall was thinking of Odina.

"Now—tonight."

"I'm sorry, but that's impossible."

"Why?" It was almost a howl of agony.

"Because I've promised to go back to the spiders."

Doggins shook his arm. "What are you talking about, you idiot? I told you I'd handle that."

"But that was before she found me—the commander over there. . . ."

Doggins groaned. "You mean you're under arrest?"

"Not exactly. It's just that I promised her . . ."

"What's going on between you two?" Niall avoided his eyes. "There is something going on, isn't there?"

Niall felt guilty on Odina's behalf; he said finally: "She wants to marry me."

To his surprise, Doggins gave a sigh of relief. "Thank God!" He punched Niall on the shoulder. "So if she wants to marry you, she's not going to turn you over to the crawlies, is she?"

"But she wants me to go back, and I've promised . . ."

"That's all right. You can do that tomorrow." His voice took on a pleading note. "You can persuade her. Tell her you've promised to help me this evening. Tell her what you like. She can stay here overnight and you can both go first thing in the morning."

"But why do you need me to go with you? I could draw you a map."

Doggins shook his head. "That's no good. You brought the slaves here this morning. So you've got to take 'em back this evening. Right?"

Niall was bewildered. "The slaves?"

"That's right. The slaves." He winked.

Suddenly, Niall began to understand what Doggins had in mind, and it startled him. He turned his face away to conceal the hope that made his heart beat faster; Doggins mistook this for hesitation.

"Come on now. It's not much of a favor."

Niall drew a deep breath. "I'll have to speak to Odina first."

Doggins squeezed his arm. "I'll go and get her."

While Doggins was away, Niall's mind was racing. He found it hard to believe his good fortune, yet his relief was tinged with doubt. For the past few hours he had been wondering how to persuade Doggins to become an ally; now it looked as if he had decided to do it of his own accord. What baffled Niall was why he was prepared to take such a risk.

Odina came alone. As soon as he saw her, Niall knew she would do whatever he asked. He reached out to take her hands; then her arms were round his neck.

"Listen, we are going to stay here tonight," he said. "Are you allowed to do that?" She nodded. "Good. I've promised Doggins, and I don't want to break my word." But he could see that explanations were unnecessary; she would accept whatever he said. "Will the other commanders wonder where you are?"

"No. We are allowed to stay where we like."

As she kissed him repeatedly, with tiny, nibbling kisses, he was struck by an oddly inappropriate image: he was reminded of the tiny grey pseudopodia reaching out to grip his finger. Then he dismissed the notion and gave himself up to the physical relief of feeling her pressed against him.

Doggins appeared round the end of the platform, making them both start. "Sorry about that." He smiled apologetically. "It's time we got moving."

There was a light silver mist on the road when they set out, so the rising moon made their shadows seem alive. The air was damp and chilly, and Niall was glad of the inner glow left by the bowl of mulled wine they had shared before they left. He marched in front, while the others followed in two straggling lines. They wore shabby grey smocks, and anyone who passed them on the road would have taken them for an utterly weary band of slaves returning from a long day's work. In fact, the man who marched behind Niall, and who carried his left shoulder higher than his right, was the actor who had played the pirate captain, while the hump-backed youth who shambled beside him was Mostig's assistant, wearing a cushion sewn inside his smock. Most of them were young, having been chosen for smallness of stature.

Progress was slow, for Doggins—who brought up the rear— would not allow them to cover the distance to the spider city at their normal brisk pace; he insisted they should try to think of themselves as tired slaves, and march accordingly. They followed his instructions so conscientiously that it took them almost two hours to cover the distance to the northern outskirts.

Niall, who had at first been doubtful about this venture, began to feel increasingly confident as they approached the city. His main fear had been that these inexperienced youths might betray themselves through anxiety or nervous tension, but he soon realized his mistake. The servants of the beetles had never had reason to be afraid of the spiders, so they regarded this invasion of their stronghold as an amusing adventure. This was why, as he marched through the cold moonlight breathing in the fragrance of leaves and damp earth, Niall experienced the joy that comes from launching into action and knowing that there can be no return.

In fact, the main avenue seemed strangely deserted; the white, broken buildings looked as empty as a desert landscape. This time,

Niall experienced no sense of being observed by unseen eyes. If the spiders were watching them it was without curiosity.

Niall and Doggins had already agreed on their plan. Niall would lead them to the small square in which the slaves had gathered that morning. There they would disband and make their way in groups of twos or threes to the barracks, which was only three blocks away to the northeast. They would take refuge in the nearest inhabited house and wait there until all were gathered together. Then, in the early hours of the morning they would make their attempt. Niall reasoned that when the whole slave quarter was asleep, the spiders would have no reason for vigilance.

It was as they began to approach the river that he experienced his first misgivings. Although oil lamps gleamed from behind the cracked window panes, and cooking smells drifted from open doorways, the streets themselves remained deserted. Niall had taken it for granted that the slave quarter would be as crowded during the evening as it had been at dawn. This silence filled him with foreboding. If the slaves were unafraid of the spiders, why were they all indoors?

Niall turned left off the main avenue and a few minutes later brought his squad to a halt in the square. Although this was deserted, the surrounding houses were full of activity; he could hear babies crying and women and children shouting. For the sake of appearances, Niall called out: "Squad halt! Dismiss!"

Doggins sauntered over, hands in his pockets, and indicated the nearest open doorway with a jerk of his head: "That'll do. Let's find something to eat." The march had made them all hungry.

But as Niall attempted to walk into the house a pregnant woman came rushing towards them, waving her arms and shouting: "No room, no room!" She advanced determinedly and forced them to retreat. The door slammed behind them. Niall and Doggins looked at each other in amused astonishment as Niall said: "What now?"

"Let's try next door."

But the same thing happened there. A pale, hollow-chested man with a goiter was sitting at the bottom of the stairs, eating a bowl of soup; as soon as Niall pushed open the front door, the man shouted: "Sorry, no room. Try somewhere else."

As Niall tried to advance, the man jumped up and firmly blocked the passageway. For a moment, Niall was tempted to push him aside, then decided it would be dangerous to attract attention. Besides, it

329

was clear that the man was telling the truth; he could see that the front room was crowded to overflowing.

Outside, Doggins was becoming anxious. In the deserted square, a group of twenty slaves was conspicuous; it was obviously important to find shelter as soon as possible. But a glance through some of the other lighted windows showed that most of the houses in the square were equally crowded.

The house on the corner bore a rough handpainted sign with the inscription: "K.2." It sounded familiar; then he remembered. This was where he had been told to look for Morlag, the blackbearded overseer. He pushed open the door and was relieved when no one came rushing towards him. But when he stepped into the passageway, a voice from the top of the stairs shouted: "Get out!" A face peered down over the banisters. It was the man called Lorris.

"We've only just got back. Where can we go?"

Lorris recognized him. "Oh, it's you. You can come in. I thought it was a slave."

"But I've got twenty slaves outside. Where can we go?"

Lorris shrugged. "They can go anywhere they like—so long as it's not the same place as last night."

Niall was puzzled. "What do you mean?"

"That's the rule. They're not allowed to spend two nights in the same place."

"Why not?"

Lorris threw up his hands irritably. "How do I know? I didn't make the rule."

"Thanks."

Outside, Niall said: "We'd better move. Let's try the next street."

"Wouldn't it be better to get closer to the barracks?"

"Do you want to risk it?"

"It's better than standing out here." Doggins pointed to an alley at the northeast corner of the square. "Let's go that way."

"It might be better to stick to the main streets."

Doggins shook his head. "Let's take the shortest way. You'd better go first."

Niall decided not to argue. He led them across the square and into the alleyway. But within a dozen yards, the darkness was so complete that they were forced to halt. It was like being surrounded by black velvet curtains. Doggins said: "Hold on a minute while I strike a light."

Another voice, which Niall recognized as that of Mostig's assistant, said: "What's happening?" Niall thought he detected a note of panic.

Then, quite abruptly, he was gripped by a sense of danger so acute that it made the hair stand up on the back of his neck. It was a sense that they were close to some terrible disaster. He gripped Doggins' wrist. "I think we'd better go back."

"What for?"

"Do as I ask."

They obeyed the urgency in his voice. A moment later, they were back in the square. Mostig's assistant said: "Where's Marcus?"

Doggins said: "Marcus?"

There was no reply. It was then that Niall knew the disaster had already happened.

Doggins went back towards the alleyway, calling: "Marcus." Before he could advance into the darkness, Niall seized his arm and held it tight.

"Don't."

Doggins tried to shake himself free. "For God's sake, I can't leave him to die."

Niall leaned forward and spoke in a low voice. "He's already dead." In his mind's eye, he could see the blackened body of his father.

"Oh, Christ!"

Niall could sense his rising panic and grasped the extent of their danger. His own response was to become increasingly focused and controlled. Deliberately using the thought mirror to project the full force of his will, he leaned forward and whispered in Doggins' ear: "Tell them you've found him. Then say we have to move on."

He could feel the command taking effect, the panic subsiding.

Doggins turned back to the others. "All right, we've found him." His voice was brisk and calm. "Now let's go."

Niall said: "Form ranks and follow me."

To his relief, they obeyed without question. If the moon had been visible, the deception would have been impossible; but it was hidden behind tall buildings to the southeast, and the darkness was almost total. A few moments later, they were marching eastward along the center of the narrow street.

Niall was shaken. He had no doubt of what had happened. Marcus had been seized in the dark, probably by a spider that dropped from overhead. Any attempt to scream or struggle had been paralyzed in advance by the brute force of the spider's will. At this moment, he was probably being eaten. And even now, the danger was not over. If any of the others became aware that Marcus was no longer with them, there could still be an explosion of panic that would betray them to the spiders.

It was only when they marched across the next moonlit intersection, and no one glanced to right or left, that Niall knew he could relax. Doggins had said Marcus had been found, and no one thought of doubting his word.

Niall knew precisely where they were; he could see the map of the slave quarter as clearly as if it had been suspended in front of his eyes. Because it had been absorbed in a state of intensified concentration, every detail was sharp and clear. It showed him that the barracks lay two blocks to the north. The simplest approach would have been via that broad avenue that ran from the town hall to the river, but he rejected this as too conspicuous. Instead, he decided to continue along the narrow street and turn left at the next intersection.

On the other side of the broad avenue they entered an area that had at some time been devastated by fire. Most of the houses were empty shells, and there was a smell of burnt wood in the air. To the south, the moonlight shone on piles of rubble, and beyond that he could catch a glimpse of the river. At the next street, Niall ordered a left turn. Here the houses had also been damaged by the fire, but most were still standing. He experienced relief to see that there were no cobwebs overhead. It seemed unlikely that these crumbling buildings would conceal spiders.

Halfway along the street, a twisted tree was growing out of a ruined building, its branches overhanging the road. The house immediately opposite had collapsed, blocking the street with an irregular pile of rubble which at its lowest point was about six feet high. Niall chose this point to scramble across the barrier, leaning forward to test each step with his hands before entrusting it with his full weight. In this way, he reached the far side with nothing worse than a scraped wrist and bruised ankle, and turned to wait for the others. The moon was directly behind them, silvering the branches of the tree, and he observed that its leaves were rustling gently as if in a breeze.

He had time to register this as odd—since the night was windless—when the spider dropped from the darkness. It happened so swiftly that it seemed a flicker of shadow. There was no sound of impact, only the muffled cry of the man on whom it landed, so faint that none of the others seemed to notice it. While Niall stared for a moment, paralyzed by unbelief, he saw the movement of the head that meant the fangs had plunged home. Then he shouted, and the others looked round in alarm. The man attacked had been the hindmost. If Niall had not seen the spider drop no one would even have noticed that he had disappeared. Now he knew what had happened to the missing slave when they were marching to the city of the beetles.

Without thinking about it, Niall began to scramble back up the rubble, knocking someone off balance as he did so. He reached the top in time to see the spider disappearing towards an open doorway, carrying the man's inert body like a large doll.

His reaction was instinctive; he picked up the nearest large brick and hurled it. It made a soft thud as it struck the hairy body. Instantly, the spider stopped—Niall could sense its astonishment—dropped the body, and turned. Even as the stone had left his hand, Niall had realized it was a rash thing to do; now he tried to turn and run. It was impossible; his body had been immobilized, as if the muscles were encased in a block of solid ice. While the others watched in horror, the spider advanced towards him, its fangs extended; in its blank eyes, Niall could sense the intention to kill. He had committed the unthinkable act of attacking a spider.

Then someone screamed, and Niall realized that his body was not entirely paralyzed. The thought mirror was burning his chest as if it had been heated in a fire. As he watched the casually slow movement—the spider seemed to be deliberately taking its time—he experienced a surge of bitter rage at this brutal assumption of total superiority and made a convulsive attempt to tear himself free. The mirror seemed to become painfully hot, so that he was afraid it would blister his chest, and it caused him to intensify the effort. Then, with the suddenness of a snapping cable, the spider's will seemed to rebound on itself, and it flinched. As this happened, it was struck squarely by the concentrated force of Niall's loathing.

It cowered like a dog cringing away from a physical blow. Then its anger overruled its surprise, and Niall again became aware of the full force of its will as it struck back at the control center of his nervous system.

This time he was expecting it, and fought back. Encouraged by his knowledge that the creature was not invincible, he directed his will as if it was a shout of rage. Again he saw it flinch; yet its will continued to hold him at bay, so his efforts were ineffective, like a man trying to hit something beyond reach. He tried to bear down on the spider, leaning forward as if walking into a gale, and felt that its will was crumbling. Then, with a suddenness that made him stagger, it abandoned the fight. For a moment, its legs seemed to buckle; then it turned and fled, seizing the inert body as it went. Niall experienced a surge of wild exultation, perhaps the greatest sense of triumph he had ever experienced in his life. Then, just as suddenly, he was overwhelmed by an immense weariness that passed downward from his shoulders to his feet. For a moment, his knees buckled, but hands prevented him from falling. By the time he was back on the level ground, the weariness had been replaced by a throbbing headache.

Doggins said: "How did you make it go away?"

"I'll explain later." His tongue faltered, as if he were drunk. "We've got to get out of here."

As they hurried on, he could sense their fear and knew that the danger was greater than at any time since they had entered the slave quarter. If there were more spiders in these buildings, they would be attacked before they reached the end of the street. His own exhaustion made him feel helpless, and he was distracted by the burning pain on his chest. It was this actute physical discomfort that led him to reach inside his smock to feel the area with his fingertips; it seemed to be covered with tiny ulcers or blisters. Then, as an experiment, he turned the thought mirror so that its concave side faced inward. Instantly, the pain intensified so that he gasped aloud; Doggins gave him an anxious sideways glance. For perhaps a minute, his brain was like a boat tossed on a choppy sea of agony. Yet this pain finally succeeded in concentrating his will, and he experienced a sense of re-established control. It was intoxicating, almost as exciting as vanquishing the spider. All his life, he had become accustomed to surrendering to a certain degree of pain or exhaustion. Now he had overruled the lifelong habit and for a moment felt like a man standing on a mountain top.

They had reached the end of the street and found themselves looking across another wide avenue, whose time-blackened buildings appeared at once monumental and shabby. Facing them on the opposite corner was a twenty-foot-high wall, its top surmounted by long spikes. The face of the wall was perfectly smooth, as if it had been cut out of solid rock. It looked as unclimbable as a vertical cliff. In the moonlight, the barracks reminded Niall of the citadel on the plateau.

The others were staring at it with dismay. Only Doggins seemed unconcerned. In his expression, Niall detected a gleam of triumph.

Niall asked: "What are you hoping to find in there?"

"Explosives." He gave Niall an odd sideways glance. "And weapons."

"Weapons?"

Doggins said softly: "Yes, weapons." He turned to the others. "All right. Stick close to me, and try and stay in the shadows."

Within fifty yards they found themselves facing the main gates of the Fortress. There were great solid doors, higher than the walls, and also surmounted by spikes that looked as sharp as needles. Beside them, set in the wall, was a smaller door, also made of the same rusting metal. Half a dozen of them tried to force it with their shoulders, but it was as unyielding as the wall itself.

Another fifty yards brought them to the southwestern corner, and to the avenue that ran down to the river. A single glance told them that the west-facing wall was as impregnable as the rest. Unlike the buildings in the avenue, these walls had evidently been built to last for centuries.

Halfway along the north-facing wall, they encountered another entrance. This was a single gate of solid metal, with the usual row of unbroken spikes along its top, and was set between tall pillars, each surmounted by a single spike. Doggins halted and surveyed this with a close attention that Niall found puzzling—it looked as unpromising as any other point of entrance—then said: "Milo, the rope."

One of the men pulled off his grey slave smock; underneath he was wearing the standard yellow tunic of the beetle-servants. From around his waist he uncoiled a length of rope; to Niall's eye it looked dangerously thin. Then from his own pocket Doggins took a metal hook; this unfolded into three separate hooks, forming a grappling iron. He attached it to the end of the rope and tossed it upwards. It caught between the two end spikes of the gate. After pulling it with his full weight to test it, Doggins swarmed up. A moment later, he stood on top of the gate pillar, steadying himself by holding on to the spike. Now Niall could see why he had chosen this spot. Because of the width of the pillar, the gap on either side of the spike was just wide enough to allow a lightly-built man to squeeze through.

Another rope was produced; Doggins tied this to the spike and dropped it down inside the wall. A moment later, he disappeared.

Niall went next. By curving his body upward, he achieved a foothold on top of the gate, then scrambled onto the pillar. The long rooftops of the barrack buildings lay below him in the moonlight. From this point he could also look south to the river, and to the sky-scrapers of the spider city beyond. The white tower shone in the moonlight with its faint green phosphorescence, and immediately beyond it he could see the black bulk of the headquarters of the Spider Lord. Suddenly, he felt very exposed; he squeezed between the spikes and slid down the rope to the ground.

As the others joined them one by one, Niall and Doggins stood looking across the deserted parade ground towards the long, low buildings of the soldiers' quarters. There were no spider webs, and the unbroken window panes gleamed in the moonlight. Something about the place produced in Niall a curious impression of loneliness and sadness. When he spoke to Doggins, he found himself automatically lowering his voice, as if afraid to disturb the silence.

"Why do you suppose the spiders never came here?"

"Why should they? There's nothing here for them."

"So it's been like this ever since men left the earth?"

Doggins gave a crooked smile. "I hope so."

A few yards away to the left, something white gleamed at the foot of the wall. Niall went to investigate and found himself looking at a heap of bones. The skeleton had evidently been there a long time, and weather had made the skull thin and brittle.

He turned to Doggins: "Somebody tried to get in."

Doggins stirred the bones with his foot; some of them fell apart. "I'd like to know why he died there." He looked thoughtfully at the top of the wall.

"Perhaps a spider caught him."

"Perhaps." He sounded unconvinced.

A thin, high wail shocked them both; it was like the cry of some strange bird. Then Niall realized it was coming from the group at the foot of the wall. Doggins called: "What happened?"

"It's Cyprian." A man was writhing on the ground, his body arched in agony.

Doggins dropped on his knees beside him. "Cyprian, what happened?"

The man tried to speak, but the pain convulsed his lips; as he choked, a white foam appeared on his lips. Then, suddenly, he twisted backwards and stopped struggling. His eyes had turned upward, showing only the whites of the eyeballs. Doggins took his pulse, but it was already obvious he was dead. It had all taken less than ten seconds.

Doggins stood up; he looked very pale. "Anyone know what happened?"

They shook their heads; Niall could see they were stunned and close to hysteria.

Doggins raised the dead man's right arm and turned it over. On the underside of the forearm, there was a scratch about an inch long.

"That's what did it. The spikes are poisoned."

The thought of how close they had been to death sobered them all. But Doggins was determined not to allow them time to think about it.

"We've got to get moving. Now listen carefully. One of these buildings is an arsenal. I want you to find out which one it is."

Niall pointed to a building in the northeastern corner. "I think it could be that one."

"Why?"

"It was marked on the map."

Doggins shook his head. "It looks like an office building to me. But let's find out."

Closer examination proved that he was correct. They forced the door by using their shoulders as battering rams, then lit oil lamps and spread throughout the building. Most of the rooms contained desks and filing cabinets. The air smelt stale and dead, like the air in a tomb, and dust blackened their hands whenever they touched anything. When Niall tugged on a curtain, it tore like wet paper.

Doggins was pulling out all the drawers of a desk. When one proved to be locked, he took out a knife and worked it into the crack, twisting the blade impatiently. It snapped, but Doggins gave a grunt of satisfaction as he opened the drawer. He weighed the long-barrelled gun in the palm of his hand.

"What is it?"

"A Flecknoe blaster." He took it to the window and examined it in the moonlight.

"What does it do?"

"Releases pure energy. Watch."

There was a blue flash that made Niall jump, and a thread of twisted light seemed to leap from the barrel; at the same time there was a smell of heated metal and ozone. Through the wall at the side of the window, Niall could now see moonlight. The blaster had made a neat circular hole about six inches in diameter.

"How did you know it would be there?"

"Just a guess—this isn't the first barracks I've been in." He patted the gun. "Now we're ready if we meet a spider."

"Is that what you were hoping to find?"

"One of the things."

Milo appeared in the doorway. "There's nothing here, sir. It's just an office building, as you said."

Doggins asked Niall: "Are you sure this was the location of the arsenal?"

Niall closed his eyes. He had made no special effort to memorize the layout of the barracks—it had seemed unimportant at the time—but he could still see the word "Arsenal" in the northeastern corner of the plan.

"Yes. Quite sure."

Doggins shook his head. "In that case, the map must have been deliberately inaccurate."

"But why should it be?"

"Because in the twenty-first century, army installations were always being attacked by political terrorists. That's why they made this place so impregnable."

"But in that case, surely they would have hidden the arsenal?"

Doggins snapped his fingers. "Of course—that's the answer. Below ground." He turned to Milo. "Is there a cellar in this place?"

"Yes, but it's locked."

"Show me where it is."

Milo led them along the corridor and down a flight of stairs. At the bottom, there was a steel-covered door. When its handle refused to turn, Doggins placed the blaster against it and fired.

The door swung open, drops of molten metal cascading to the floor.

But the rooms beyond proved to be storerooms. They contained filing cabinets, boxes of papers, and cassettes of microfilm. Doggins ordered everyone to examine the walls for signs of a secret door, but a long search revealed nothing.

"You've got to be right," Doggins said. "With a barracks in the middle of a city, they couldn't take the risk of making the armory accessible. One terrorist bomb could blow them all off the planet. The only sensible thing would be to construct it underground." He stared with sour frustration at the floor beneath his feet.

Again, Niall closed his eyes and tried to envisage the map. He said finally: "The word 'Arsenal' wasn't on the building itself. It was somewhere in front of it."

Only Doggins' eyes betrayed a glint of satisfaction. "Show me."

Outside, Niall pointed to the area adjacent to the building's northern wall. "About there."

Doggins turned to the others. "All right, we're looking for some kind of entrance, probably a concealed trapdoor. Spread out over there and stamp your feet. Keep on stamping until it sounds hollow."

Niall joined them as they stamped over an area of twenty square yards. The ground under their feet was smooth and black, and after ten minutes, both his feet felt sore. Doggins was crawling on his hands and knees, looking for a hairline crack; Niall could sense his increasing disappointment. The others gradually ceased their efforts.

Mostig's assistant said wearily: "Now if it was water, my old grandad could have found it in two minutes. He was the best dowser for miles."

It reminded Niall that he himself had often located underground springs; such an ability was part of the survival equipment of every desert dweller. Jomar had even claimed to be able to sense the burrows of rodents. He took the telescopic rod from his pocket and made it expand.

Doggins asked curiously: "What's that?"

He smiled. "A magic wand."

He observed with satisfaction that the metal seemed to tingle against his fingertips. Holding the two ends firmly in clenched fists, he turned his hands outward so the springy metal curved like a powerful bow. Then, forcing both hands down, so the curve was parallel to the ground, he walked forward slowly, closing his eyes to increase his concentration. When he reached the wall of the building, he turned and traced a diagonal path towards the perimeter wall. Within ten feet, the rod twisted upward with an irresistible force. Niall stopped and pointed to his feet.

"There's something down there."

Doggins said: "Bring the lights."

He and Niall both crouched on all fours and examined the hard asphalt. But the closest examination revealed no evidence of a trap-door. Doggins asked: "Are you sure there's something there?"

"Yes." The rod had spoken more clearly than words.

"All right." Doggins stood up. "Stand back." He pointed the blaster at the ground and pulled the trigger. The blue thread crackled like a miniature bolt of forked lightning, and the air filled with the ozone smell and with the pungent odor of burning asphalt. As they watched, the ground sagged, then dissolved. The edges of a two-foot hole bubbled and hissed, sending up plumes of white smoke. Niall joined Doggins at its rim; the ground felt hot through his sandals.

"Look at that!" Doggins gave a chuckle of delight and slapped Niall on the shoulder. "No wonder it didn't sound hollow."

From their position directly above the hole, they could see that the asphalt at this point was more than two feet thick. A lowered oil lamp showed a flight of steep concrete stairs descending into the darkness.

Doggins ordered them to fetch curtains; they returned with arms full of the moldy and disintegrating cloth, and these were packed over the molten edges. Then Doggins was lowered into the hole, a rope tied under his armpits. Niall and Milo followed.

From below, Niall could see that the asphalt had covered a wide trapdoor whose edges were supported by curved steel buttresses, each six inches wide. He asked: "How could anyone lift that from above? It must weigh half a ton."

"It wasn't intended to be lifted from above. The doors are controlled from below—the switch is probably in the office building." Doggins stepped carefully around the pool of tar that was slowly solidifying on the steps. "Follow me and watch out. This place may be booby trapped."

Niall said: "In that case, you'd better let me go first. I'll use this." He extended the telescopic rod in front of him.

"All right, but for God's sake be . . ."

The sentence was never finished. As Niall took his first step from the bottom of the stairway, there was a click, followed by a thud. Something flashed before his eyes and he found himself looking at a solid metal barrier which had slid across the corridor in the blink of an eyelid. It had snatched the telescopic rod from his hand and trapped it against the opposite wall. There could be no possible doubt that if it had been Niall's body that had intercepted the door, it would now be crushed flat, or perhaps divided in two as if by the stroke of some enormous axe.

Yet the sense of control engendered by the thought mirror was so powerful that Niall experienced only a mild sense of shock; his brain had already countermanded the flow of adrenaline before it had time to reach his bloodstream. As he reached out to try and pull the rod free, his hand was perfectly steady. But the rod was trapped as if in a vice.

Doggins said drily: "You see what I mean." But his face revealed how deeply shaken he felt. "Stand back."

He pointed the blaster at the edge of the door, a foot below the rod. In the blackness, the blue light made the enclosed space look like a wizard's cave, Niall observed that it caused faint sparks to crackle in Doggins' hair. As the door became red hot, then white hot, they had to move back up the stairs. A few drops of molten metal ran like drops of water, then a hole the size of a fist appeared. There was a click, then the door was no longer there. It had moved so fast that it was no more than a blur, and had vanished into the wall before the telescopic rod had reached the ground.

Niall bent to pick it up, and swore as the metal burnt his fingers. He knelt down and examined it by the light of the lamp. Incredibly, the metal was not even dented.

Once again, he extended the rod at arm's length. This time, nothing happened; whatever mechanism had triggered the release of the door had been destroyed by the heat.

Another twenty yards brought them to a heavy metal grid like a prison gate; it looked formidable, but its lock melted immediately under the heat of the blaster. Ten feet beyond this was another solid steel door with a combination lock. Doggins raised the blaster, then changed his mind. "No, let's play it safe." Niall watched with fascination as he placed his ear against the dial, then moved the knob gently back and forth with his fingertips. After ten minutes, there was a series of clicks and Doggins was able to pull the door open. It was then that they realized the wisdom of his decision not to use the blaster; stacked immediately behind the door were piles of red explosives cases, each decorated with a skull and crossbones.

These cases proved to be the final barrier. When they had been removed and restacked in the corridor, their lamps showed them a long, low-ceilinged chamber that was full of wooden cases and metal boxes. As they stood in the entrance, their lamps raised above their heads, Niall caught a glimpse of Doggins' face. His eyes were shining with the expression of a man who has achieved the goal of a lifetime.

Niall asked him curiously: "Did you know this place existed?"

Doggins started, like a man awakened from a dream. "I'd heard rumors. There were always lots of rumors. But I didn't really believe them." He drew in a deep breath. "My God, there's enough stuff here to start a war." He went forward and peered at the labels on the cases. "Rockets, firebombs, fission capsules, atom grenades . . ." He was like a man repeating some sacred litany.

Niall turned to Milo. "You'd better go and get the others." When Milo had gone, he went and joined Doggins, whose light glimmered at the far end of the storeroom. He found him sitting on an ammunition case, his hands drooping loosely between his knees.

"Are you all right?"

"Yes. Why?"

"You look ill."

Doggins shook his head slowly. "I'm not ill. Just . . . a little frightened."

"Of what?"

"Of all this power." He was staring straight in front of him. Niall sat beside him. "You realize what this represents? It's power to change the world. Power to do what you like."

"To get rid of the spiders?"

"Oh, yes, even that."

Niall was puzzled. "I don't understand. You've always had explosives."

"Not just explosives." He pointed. "Do you see that?"

He was pointing to a pile of black metal boxes, each about three inches thick and eighteen inches long. The label fixed to the wall above them said: "AFLs."

"What does AFL stand for?"

"Automatic fission laser." He went across to the pile and opened the topmost case. "Better known as Reapers."

"Yes. I've heard of those."

But Doggins was not listening. He was staring down into the case with a gentle, almost meditative expression. Then he reached down and brought out the weapon. To Niall, it looked disappointingly small, hardly more than a toy. It was black, little more than a foot long, with a short wooden butt and a short, heavily reinforced barrel. Below the barrel there was a curved hand grip.

Doggins brought it back to his seat and examined it slowly and carefully; he handled it as if it were a newborn baby.

Niall asked: "Haven't you ever seen one before?"

"Not in good working order."

The others were waiting inside the door. "Come here." Doggins beckoned. "I've something to show you." He allowed the weapon to swing upside down by its shoulder strap. "You wouldn't think this was the deadliest weapon ever invented, would you?"

It was obvious they had never seen a Reaper before. Milo asked: "Deadlier than the hydrogen bomb?"

"Far deadlier. Nobody dared to use the hydrogen bomb because it was too indiscriminate. This little thing could wipe out an individual or a whole army."

Niall asked: "Is it more powerful than your blaster?"

"Far more. And far more accurate. The trouble with the blaster is that the beam spreads out, so it's useless at a range of more than forty yards. This thing has a range of two miles."

Niall asked dubiously: "Isn't that too powerful?"

"No, because it's adjustable. This lever can increase or decrease its range. Set it on zero and it won't fire at all. Set it on one, and it has a range of fifty feet. And so on up to ten. If you set it on ten when you want to knock down a wall, you'll end up destroying half the city." He turned to Mostig's assistant. "Ulic, I want you to hand one out to everybody. Then I want you all to spend a few minutes familiarizing yourselves with the adjustable control. And don't forget—never—and I mean *never*—point it at another man unless you mean to kill him."

The word "kill" produced in Niall a curious inner contraction, as if some cold wind had caused his heart to shrink. It was not the word itself, but the way Doggins had said it—as if killing were some normal and perfectly legitimate activity.

Milo handed him a Reaper. It was surprisingly heavy for its size— at least fourteen pounds—and most of this weight seemed to be concentrated in the swollen cylindrical chamber immediately above the trigger guard. Its weight made it natural to hold it with the butt pressed into the muscles above the hip, the left hand clenched tightly around the projection below the barrel. As he held it in this position,

Niall experienced a sensation that puzzled and disturbed him. It was a sense of familiarity, as if he had been handling weapons all his life.

Doggins, meanwhile, had been exploring the other aisles of the storeroom. He had found a crowbar and was forcing open a long wooden packing case. This proved to contain an eight-foot metal tube and a number of bomb-like projectiles. Doggins chuckled with satisfaction as he tossed one of these up and down in his hand.

"Look at this little beauty."

"What is it?"

Doggins pointed at the tube. "That's a Brodsky Battering Ram, and it's the greatest anti-tank weapon ever made. It's deadly accurate up to a range of a mile." He looked fondly at the projectile. "This thing could knock a hole in a ten-foot wall."

Suddenly, Niall knew what had disturbed him a few minutes before. It was the fact that the Reaper gave him a sensation of control and power. It was a completely negative power—since the weapon had no purpose but destruction—yet it was strangely satisfying nevertheless. The Reaper concentrated his will in exactly the same manner as the thought mirror.

Milo approached them. "What are these?" He was holding out a handful of shining metal spheres, each one hardly more than an inch in diameter.

"Fire bombs. How many are there?"

"A dozen cases."

"Good. Make sure everybody fills his pockets with them. Then get ready to leave. It's time we got out of here." He replaced the lid on the packing case.

Niall said: "Do you mind if I ask you a question?"

"Go ahead."

"When we set out this evening, were you hoping to find Reapers?"

"Of course."

"Then what made you change your mind?"

"About what?"

"About fighting the spiders."

Doggins shook his head. "Let's get one thing clear. I don't intend to fight the spiders." He hefted the Reaper in his hand. "This isn't for fighting. It's for bargaining."

"About what?"

"Freedom."

"But I thought . . ."

Doggins interrupted him. "Freedom from interference. Why do you suppose we use oil lamps instead of electric torches? Why do you think I light the damn things with a tinder box instead of matches? Because of the spiders."

"I didn't think they had any control over the beetles."

"It's in the Peace Treaty: 'No servant of the beetles shall be allowed to use or construct a machine.' So, no dynamos, no engines, no computers—not even a clock. And it's been like that for more than two hundred years."

"And what would they do if you broke the agreement?"

"Go to war, I suppose. And this time they'd make sure they destroyed us."

"Could they destroy you?"

"Easily. When they made the treaty, there were about the same number of beetles as spiders. Now the spiders outnumber beetles by a thousand to one." He grinned and patted the Reaper. "But with this thing, we outnumber the spiders by a thousand to one."

Milo approached and saluted. "We're all ready, sir."

"Right. Take them up on to the barrack square and wait for me."

Niall asked: "What would happen if the spiders found this place?"

"It wouldn't matter. They wouldn't be able to get in."

"You shouldn't underestimate Kazak."

"I don't." They had reached the door. "Help me move these boxes."

Together, Niall and Doggins stacked the red explosives cases inside the door where they had found them. When the last one was in place, Doggins closed the massive door and twisted the dial of the combination lock. Then he struck the dial with the crowbar until it lay smashed on the floor.

"There. Even Kazak shouldn't be able to open that. And if he does, he may regret it."

As they mounted the concrete steps, Doggins stopped and placed his hand on Niall's arm.

"There's something I want to say to you."

"Yes?"

"Just—thanks for helping me to find this place. Perhaps I'll be able to do you a good turn one of these days."

Niall smiled. "You already have."

Outside it was unexpectedly dark. The wind had risen and a black raincloud obscured the moon. The tiny flames of the oil lamps only seemed to increase the surrounding blackness. Doggins cursed under his breath.

"I don't like this. It means the spiders can see us and we can't see them."

"Then let's wait until daylight."

Doggins shook his head; Niall could sense his indecision. "I don't want to stay here a minute longer than I have to."

Someone asked: "What are we going to do with poor Cyprian?"

"We'll have to leave him where he is."

"Couldn't we find somewhere to bury him?"

Doggins shrugged. "All right. Bring him with us."

Four of them picked up the body, two holding the arms and two the legs. Doggins led them to the rear gate. He took the blaster from his pocket.

"I want to show you something. Watch."

He pointed the blaster at the center of the metal door and pulled the trigger. As the thread of blue lightning flickered from the barrel, the air filled with the smell of heated metal; the gate turned red, then white hot. But, to Niall's surprise, it showed no sign of melting. Doggins lowered the blaster.

"It's a special blaster-proof metal called lattrix—designed to stop terrorists. The wall's made of a similar material. Now watch."

He adjusted the lever on the Reaper, then pointed it at the gate. The thin blue beam that emerged from the barrel was like an illuminated glass rod. Where it struck the gate, a small hole appeared in the metal. Casually, Doggins raised the Reaper; it made a tiny blue flame as it burnt and left a thin, straight line behind it. Within a few seconds, Doggins had sliced a large section out of the gate; it fell outward with a dull crash that emphasized its weight. Niall could see that the metal was six inches thick.

Doggins said: "Put the lamps out and follow me. Keep your guns at the ready, but don't fire unless I give the order."

He led the way. As Niall passed through the aperture in the gate, he ran his finger over the metal; it was cold to the touch.

The others had stopped. Niall assumed they were taking their bearings until he heard the soft thud; it was unmistakably the sound of a body being dropped. Then, as he stepped clear of the gate, the paralysis struck him and held him frozen in mid-stride. As the moon emerged from behind the cloud, he saw the spiders who were waiting for them. They were standing on the opposite side of the road, and they looked like black statues. The moonlight was reflected from their blank eyes.

This time Niall experienced no fear. He even observed that although the paralysis affected his muscles—so that his arms felt dead as though their circulation had been cut off by a tourniquet—his eyes were still able to move normally, and his brain was totally unaffected. Moreover, since the thought mirror was still turned inward, he was able to intensify his concentration, bringing the familiar sense of focused power. As he did this, the paralysis in his arms and shoulders began to melt away; if he relaxed the concentration, it returned. It was a curiously satisfying sensation, like pushing back a tide of impotence. A more powerful effort pushed back the tide towards his feet, so that his whole body was free. It was clear that the spiders were totally unaware of what was happening.

Then one of the spiders moved towards them and he decided it was time to act. He raised the Reaper and pulled the trigger. Nothing happened, and he realized that the lever was still in the safety position. He pushed it forward with his thumb and pulled the trigger.

The spider disappeared. So did the railings behind it, and a large section of the facade of the building. The blue pencil of light was dazzling in its intensity, and the weapon made a distinct recoil against the muscles of his stomach. When he released the trigger, his eyes were still dazzled by the flash. The momentary silence seemed frightening and unnatural.

The other spiders—there were perhaps six of them—were still immobile, but now it was the immobility of shock. And as Niall turned the Reaper on them, he was already aware that it was unnecessary. Their will force had snapped at the moment the first spider disappeared. It was as if they were connected and the destruction of one affected all. This is why, although he pointed the weapon towards them, he made no attempt to pull the trigger. Their help-lessness somehow disarmed him.

As he hesitated, another beam lanced through the darkness and struck the nearest spider, then traveled sideways, cutting them down before they could move. The effect was at once fascinating and sicken-ing. The beam sliced them in half, like some immense knife, at the same time cutting through the railings behind them. A moment later, the smell of burning flesh filled the air. The top half of a spider's body rolled into the gutter, while the legs and the lower part of its belly collapsed on to the pavement. There was no convulsive twitching, nothing to indicate death by violence. The bodies looked as though they had never been alive. All this had taken place so swiftly that it seemed instantaneous.

Doggins lowered the Reaper. He nodded at the weapon in Niall's hands. "You turned it up too high."

"I know." The lever was on five.

"But thanks all the same."

It was a signal for the others to surround him; some tried to hug him, some shook his hand, others patted him on the back until he winced. Their gratitude was overwhelming, both emotionally and physically—a measure of the terror it had replaced. None of them had ever experienced paralysis of the will, and the experience had shaken them more than the death of their comrades. Niall could understand this; it seemed a denial of the most basic human assumption: of con-trol over the body. The experience was like a premonition of death.

"All right," Doggins said, "that's enough. We've got to move." He was adjusting the lever on his gun. As he pressed the trigger, Niall closed his eyes involuntarily. When he opened them, the remains of the spiders had vanished; in their place, there was a shallow crater in the pavement. Niall asked: "Wouldn't it be better to take shelter in the Fortress until daylight?"

"Yes, but not in the Fortress. That's the first place they'll search. We'll find a basement somewhere." He turned to Milo. "Do you still want to bring Cyprian?"

Milo hesitated. "Whatever you say."

Doggins pointed his Reaper at the corpse, then seemed to change his mind.

"Bring him along. We'll try and hide him until we can get back."

As they lifted the body, a few drops of rain fell on the pavement. In the windy blackness they could not even see one another; so they stumbled on in a chaotic group, frequently colliding but deriving a certain comfort from the physical contact. When a blast of cold wind indicated that they had reached a street corner, Doggins asked Niall: "Any idea where we are?"

"The town hall is over there."

"All right. We'll make for that."

A glimmer of moonlight revealed a street running in a northerly direction. It was wide, and its buildings looked relatively undamaged. Because there were no cobwebs overhead, they marched in the middle of the road. But the weight of the corpse slowed their progress. After they had traveled only half a block, Doggins said: "Stop here. Put him down. I'm going to see if I can find a basement."

They waited in the darkness, shivering in the wind that flowed past them like an icy current. A few moments later, there was a yellow flicker of light from below the level of the pavement. This was followed by the blue flash of the blaster. Then Doggins' voice called: "All right. Bring him down here."

He was waiting at the bottom of a flight of steps that led into the basement area. Behind him, a door stood open. As they entered, the rain began to fall in torrents. A gust of wind caught the open door and slammed it behind them.

The lamp revealed that they were in a large furnished room. The floor was carpeted, and there were tables, armchairs, and a glass-fronted bookcase. Even Niall could tell that this had once been a comfortable flat. Now it smelt of dust, mold, and decaying plaster. Yet the sound of the rain on the pavement, and the wind that shook the windows, induced in them all a sense of relief and comfort.

The window curtains were of a heavy, stiff material, and unlike those in the barracks—untorn and undecayed. When these had been drawn, Doggins allowed them to light all the lamps. A heavy chair was lifted against the door to prevent it from blowing open—the Reaper had destroyed its lock. Then they attempted to make themselves comfortable and settled down to wait for the dawn.

All looked strained and exhausted, and Niall could see that some were close to breaking point. Only a few hours ago, they had been full of euphoria, amused and exhilarated at the thought of defying the authority of the spiders. Now three of their number were dead, and the rest were aware that they might never see their homes again. Yet none of them showed resentment; none seemed to blame Doggins for leading them into this grim situation. As he looked at their pale, tired faces, Niall felt admiration as well as pity.

It was when one of them took an apple from his pocket and began to eat that Niall remembered the food tablets; he produced the box from his pocket.

"Is anyone hungry?" They all looked up hopefully, but their faces fell as they saw the tiny brown capsules. Nevertheless, each took one; even Doggins, who at first waved them away impatiently, was induced to swallow one. Niall chewed his own, and within minutes experienced the wave of pleasure and relief as the warmth coursed down his throat, then slowly expanded until his stomach was filled with the comforting sensation of a hot meal. On the others, the effect was immediate. The air of listlessness vanished as the color returned to their cheeks; suddenly, they were talking as animatedly as if the past few hours had been a dream.

Doggins asked: "Where did you get these?"

"From a machine."

Doggins gave him an odd look, but said nothing.

The rest of the flat proved to consist of a kitchen and two bedrooms. The kitchen walls were covered with black mold, and the red floor tiles were half-buried in plaster that had fallen from the ceiling. But the bedrooms were surprisingly dry, and in these they found blankets, eiderdowns, and pillows. They were intrigued by the clothes they found in the wardrobes, and some of them proceeded to try them on. There seemed to be a general agreement that the male garments of these ancient times, particularly the trousers, were funny as well as ugly, while the female dresses were altogether more practical.

Ulic discovered a wall cabinet full of bottles and glasses. Doggins' eyes gleamed as he examined a bottle of amber liquid.

"Scotch whisky. It's an old drink like wine. I once found a bottle in a sunken wreck." He peeled off the leadfoil from the neck, removed the cork, and sniffed it. Then, to their alarm, he raised it to his lips. All watched with concern, expecting him to collapse or spit it out; instead, he grunted with approval, and took a longer drink. He handed the bottle to Niall. "Try it."

Niall found the taste startling and disagreeable, completely unlike the golden liquid he had shared with Odina on the ship. But a few minutes later he realized that the effect was much the same: the soothing, glowing sensation, and the expanding euphoria. As he watched the others pouring the fiery liquid into glasses, he experienced a flood of emotion that startled him. It was as if they were participating in some religious ceremony, or some ritual of blood-brotherhood. It lasted only for a few moments, but during that time achieved a remarkable intensity. For the first time in his life, Niall was overwhelmed by a feeling of love for his fellow men, and for the human race as a species. These young men whose names he scarcely knew—Ulic, Milo, Yorg, Crispin, Hastur, Renfred, Kosmin— had suddenly become as dear to him as his own mother or brother.

As the heat of the oil lamps and of their bodies gradually increased the temperature, the room became pleasantly warm. It was then that they all became aware of an unpleasant smell: that of decaying meat. Niall, who had smelt it before, realized after a moment that it came from the body that lay stretched out in the corner. The face had turned purple, and the ankles and wrists were beginning to swell. The scratch on the underside of the forearm had become a gaping black wound, and this seemed to be the source of most of the stench. Cyprian's body was dragged into the kitchen and left under a table. As an afterthought, Niall covered it over with the plastic tablecloth. As a mark of respect, Milo insisted on leaving one of the lamps burning on a chair beside the body. Cyprian had been his cousin.

Suddenly, they were all tired. Niall tried to look through the books in the bookcase but his eyes refused to focus. It had been twenty-four hours since he had last slept. He settled into an armchair, pulled a blanket around his shoulders, and surrendered to the fatigue. The voices around him seemed to be filtered through some dense, stifling medium, yet they still aroused a sense of warmth and kinship. This feeling of contentment carried him like a wave into a dreamless sleep.

He woke up with a curious sense of discomfort, as if something sticky was pressed against his face. As he raised his hands to try and push it away, it seemed to dissolve. The room was now illuminated by a single lamp, and everyone was asleep. For a moment the silence worried him; then he realized that the wind had dropped and the rain was no longer beating on the windows. In the next armchair, Doggins was snoring softly. At his feet, a black-haired youth named Kosmin was sleeping on his back, his mouth wide open. He seemed to be having some kind of nightmare and kept gasping uncomfortably.

Then Niall became aware of the sound. It was very soft and difficult to define: a bubbling, liquid noise, with an element like the rustling of dry leaves. For some reason, Niall associated it with the suffocating sensation that had awakened him. At first it seemed to be coming from the other side of the front door, and he imagined it to be connected with rainwater; then he became aware that it was coming from the kitchen. When he tried to move, a pain shot through his skull and he realized that he had fallen asleep with the thought mirror turned inward. He reached inside his shirt and turned it over; the sense of relief was instantaneous.

He stood up cautiously, allowing the blanket to drop to the floor, and took the lamp from the table; then, stepping over recumbent forms, he made his way to the kitchen.

What he saw made him gasp and take a step backward. The space underneath the table seemed to be a seething mass of grey slime, heaving like the scum on top of a bubbling cauldron. When he stooped and held the lamp closer, he realized what had happened. A squid fungus had made its way through a hole in the ceiling, and was now consuming the corpse. Niall picked up a broom that was lying on the floor, and poked the bubbling mass; it ignored him.

A voice whispered: "What is it?" Doggins had been awakened by his movements. When he saw the fungus, he recoiled with disgust. After watching it for a few moments, he shrugged. "Oh, well, perhaps it's the best thing that could happen."

"Is there any way of killing it?"

"Fire or the blaster. Otherwise it's almost impossible."

"What would happen if you cut it in half?"

"Nothing much." Doggins produced the broken knife, and slashed at a writhing grey tentacle. It fell to the floor, where it wriggled like a worm. Niall watched with horrified astonishment as the main body of the fungus seemed to spread sideways like a viscous liquid, while at the same time, the writhing fragment moved towards the fungus. They joined, and the fragment was absorbed by invisible mouths.

"Are they dangerous?"

"Only if you can't get away. Otherwise they move too slowly to do much harm."

"But what do they feed on most of the time?"

"No one's sure. They seem to be able to live for years without food." Doggins yawned and went back to his chair.

For another five minutes, Niall continued to watch the fungus with a mixture of fascination and disgust. It was diffusing a smell of rotting vegetation, and its thousand tiny mouths made a continuous liquid noise as it devoured the body. A trail of slime, running from the hole in the ceiling and down the kitchen wall, revealed that the creature had the ability to cling to smooth surfaces. It seemed to eat at an extraordinary speed; through the heaving slime, the outline of Cyprian's body had already ceased to be distinguishable.

As disgust gave way to curiosity, he deliberately focused the process of inner-contraction until his inner being was as still as water on a windless day. For a moment, he shared the predatory consciousness of the fungus, its total absorption in the process of digestion, and was interested to realize that the creature was aware of his presence. It could sense him as a diffused mass of life-force, a potential meal and a potential danger. But while it was eating, Niall was unimportant. Then his awareness slipped beyond the low-grade consciousness of the fungus, and once more became aware of the rippling, pulsating energy that seemed to spread through the earth like wavelets on a pond. Suddenly, he knew beyond all shadow of doubt that the life of the squid fungus was in some way dependent upon this energy source. It was difficult to grasp the precise nature of this dependence. At first he was tempted to believe that the fungus had no life of its own, but received life directly from the energy-pulse; but this was obviously absurd. A more accurate way of putting it might have been to say that the fungus was "subsidized" by the energy-pulse as a tree is subsidized by the living soil. This would explain how the fungus could live in empty buildings for years without dying of starvation. . . .

Niall's hair prickled, and a feeling of excitement drenched him as if someone had emptied a bucket of icy water over his head. The insight that surged through his mind was vague and half-formed, yet he felt it to be of tremendous significance. Not a tree, but a plant . . . This creature was a kind of mobile plant. It was now feeding on this corpse exactly as the roots of a plant feed on decaying organisms in the soil.

But the energy-pulse was trying to raise this mass of fungoid vegetation to a higher level; it was trying to turn it into a kind of animal. This was part of the insight that filled Niall with such excitement. It was the recognition that although this creature possessed no intelligence, it was nevertheless being driven and controlled by a force that possessed intelligence. This recognition filled him with a feeling of delight mixed with vague alarm, but also with a consuming curiosity to understand more about the mysterious pulse. Could it, for example, sense his own presence?

He went back into the other room, stepping carefully across recumbent bodies.

"Could I borrow your blaster?"

Doggins, who was still wide awake, asked: "What for?"

"I want to try something."

Doggins pulled it from his pocket. "Be careful. It's getting low, but it could still set the place on fire."

Niall returned to the kitchen. He knelt down, pointing the blaster at the edge of the slimy mass, and pulled the trigger. The blue lightning filled the air with the smell of ozone. A six-inch area of the fungus turned into black charcoal. The rest of the fungus shuddered and contracted with alarm. And as this happened, the pulse itself faltered. Then the grey protoplasm withdrew from the carbonized area, leaving it stuck to the floor. The creature went on feeding as if nothing had happened. It lacked the intelligence to flee.

Yet it had told Niall what he wanted to know. As the blast had struck it, Niall had been able to sense a momentary interruption of the pulse, revealing that it was aware of the attack. There was a two-way relation between the fungus and the energy-source.

Five minutes later, the fungus ceased to feed. Moving very slowly, it slid from under the table with a contractile motion, not unlike a slug, and reared up against the wall. Nothing remained of Cyprian's body; on the slime-covered tiles, there were only a few buttons and other indigestible objects. Niall pointed the blaster at the creature, tempted to destroy it; only the thought of the smell deterred him. It seemed to sense his intention and moved up the wall with surprising swiftness; a few moments later, it had disappeared through the hole in the ceiling.

Idly, merely in order to observe the effect, Niall concentrated his will and ordered the creature to stop moving. Although it was now invisible, he could sense its presence. He could also sense its reluctance to obey. Its one desire was to retreat to some dark, damp corner and digest the food it had absorbed so efficiently. Using the thought mirror to direct and concentrate his will, Niall ordered it to return. It started to do so, and a grey tentacle appeared around the edge of the hole. And at that point, the energy-pulse intervened, and countermanded Niall's order; the tentacle withdrew. Now thoroughly intrigued, Niall concentrated his inner-force and again ordered it to return. For a moment, a kind of tug of war ensued. Then the energy-source seemed to give way. The reason, Niall was convinced, was that it sensed that nothing important was at issue. The fungus wriggled through the hole, and started to cross the ceiling.

Niall had lost interest, and he relaxed his will. He expected the creature to stop, then to retreat. Instead, it continued to wriggle across the ceiling, then down the wall. Puzzled, he continued to watch its progress. It reached the floor, then flowed across the tiles, brushing aside chunks of fallen plaster, and reached his feet. He pointed the blaster, prepared to destroy it if it made any attempt to attack. But it merely waited there, an enormous, pulsating mass of semi-vegetable, semi-liquid greyness, waiting for further orders. With astonishment, Niall realized that it had come to accept him as the source of its instructions. Suddenly, the temptation to destroy it had disappeared. Instead, Niall ordered it to return. Once again, he relaxed his will as soon as he had given the order. But the fungus retreated obediently up the wall and vanished through its hole.

Now the kitchen was empty; it seemed pointless to leave the lamp burning. Niall leaned over, cupped one hand over the bulblike chimney and blew it out. A grey light filtered through the dusty window pane, and when he peered upward past the railings he could see the first rays of sunlight striking the clouds above the eastern rooftops. With a contraction of alarm, he realized that the lamp had been visible from the street. He stood there for perhaps five minutes, staring up into the greyness; then, seeing no sign of movement, went back into the other room. Doggins was the only one awake. He accepted the blaster without comment and pushed it back into his pocket.

Niall said: "It will soon be daylight."

"Thank God for that." Doggins stretched and yawned, then clapped his hands. "All right, boys, time to get up. With luck we'll be home for breakfast." He went to the nearest window and peered through the curtains. "We'll get started in ten minutes."

They woke with sighs and yawns, but all became instantly alert when they remembered where they were.

Milo went to the kitchen and a moment later called out: "Cyprian has gone!"

Doggins said irritably: "We already know that. We'll talk about it later. Get ready to leave."

But Milo's words had introduced a sense of foreboding, and it hung over them as they stood up and rubbed the sleep out of their eyes. They had lost their eagerness to venture out into the dawn.

Doggins said: "Now, before we set out, I want to say something, and I want you all to listen as if your lives depended on it. Now, listen." He held up the Reaper. "This weapon is more than a match for any spider. With this in your hands, you could defy an army of spiders. But remember that it's just as dangerous to human beings as to spiders. One false move, and you've killed the man standing in front of you—or, worse still, sliced off his arm or leg. So if we're attacked, don't panic. Keep your nerve, and don't pull the trigger until you can see your way clear. Don't take any risks.

"Now, there's one more thing I want to say. You may be afraid that a spider can paralyze your will before you can pull the trigger. So I want to tell you something that I've been keeping to myself. I realized a long time ago that this willpower of the spiders isn't as irresistible as we think. In fact it's a mistake to call it willpower. It's more like a force of *suggestion*." It was obvious that they were puzzled and doubtful. Doggins smiled reassuringly. "Look, why do you obey me when I give you an order? I don't force you to obey it, do I? You do it because you've come to accept the idea that I give the orders. Suppose somebody came up behind you and shouted in your ear 'Stand up straight!' You'd probably obey—but not because of his willpower. You'd obey because you've been taught to obey orders. Now I'll tell you what I believe. I believe that when a spider paralyzes your will, it sends out a kind of beam of suggestion, and the beam affects your subconscious mind. You could say it's a kind of hypnotism, if you know what that means. But you can refuse to be hypnotized. And with one of these things in your hands, you've got a damn good reason for refusing.

"So next time a spider tries to paralyze your will, don't let it get away with it. Fight back. Tell yourself there's nothing to be afraid of.

"All right, that's enough. When that door is open, I'll go first. Follow me one by one. Niall, you come last. Set your weapons to one, but don't fire unless I give the order. Crispin, move that chair out of the way. Then Milo open the door."

Niall said: "Wait. . . ."

Because his mind was still open to the vibrations of the energy-pulse, he sensed what was about to happen even as the fair-haired youth took a step towards the chair. It was like the breath of wind that signals the coming of a hurricane. Instinctively, he contracted his will as if tensing to receive a blow. So when the paralysis struck a moment later, like a chain of freezing metal, his own mind was already clenched like a fist. In that brief moment of preparation, he knew that Doggins was right. The will-force of the spiders was like an order suddenly bellowed into the depths of the mind. But although his muscles felt as though he had been plunged into freezing water, his will remained unaffected. When he reached up to push forward the safety catch of the Reaper, his fingers felt numb and frozen, yet they obeyed his will.

The door was being pushed open with such force that the heavy armchair began to move even though it was wedged under the handle. Niall waited calmly, his finger curled round the trigger. But a movement made him glance sideways. Doggins' face seemed to be distorted with agony, and his lips were drawn back from his clenched teeth. He looked like a man struggling to raise some enormous weight. Then his arm jerked, and blue flame leapt from the muzzle of his gun, sliced through the back of the armchair and penetrated the door. A moment later, Niall also fired into the widening gap.

Instantly, the will-force snapped, leaving them free. Niall darted forward and pushed the chair back against the door; it encountered no resistance. The others were staggering drunkenly and some stumbled or fell to the floor. Doggins turned and grinned at them.

"All rights, lads, round one to us." But his voice was strained and breathless. "Remember what I said: don't lose your nerve." His face suddenly became grey and he took a step backwards and sat down heavily.

Niall asked: "Are you all right?"

Doggins nodded. "I'm fine. Give me five minutes and I'll be ready to go."

Niall asked incredulously: "You're going out there?"

"Of course. We can't stay here all day." He closed his eyes and leaned his head back. The beaky nose gave the sallow face a corpse-like appearance.

For the next five minutes no one spoke. They were all watching the door, their weapons at the ready, and Niall was struck by the fact that no one looked tense or anxious. In this situation of extreme danger, there was no room for doubts or misgivings.

They were startled into alertness by a creaking sound; it was unmistakably the gate in the area railings. A moment later, they heard the noise of feet descending the steps. No one moved. There was a knock on the door, and a voice called:

"May I come in?"

Niall said: "It's Kazak."

Doggins called: "Are you alone?"

"Yes."

Doggins called to Ulic, who dragged aside the armchair and opened the door. Outside, it was daylight. Kazak bowed and smiled as he came into the room.

"I am King Kazak." He regarded Niall with a kind of ironical affection. "Yes, I thought I'd find you here." Doggins had risen to his feet. "And you must be Mr. Doggins. May I sit down?"

Someone hastened to push forward a chair. It was plain that Kazak's dignity, and his obvious lack of fear, had made an immediate impression on the young men. He sat down carefully and deliberately. Doggins also sat. Kazak said: "I am here as an emissary of the spiders. I've come to bring you their offer. They have asked me to say that you are all free to go."

His words caused astonishment. Doggins said incredulously: "You mean we can go back home?"

"That is correct, but on one condition—that you hand over all your weapons."

Doggins shook his head vigorously: "Never."

Kazak seemed mildly surprised. "May I ask why?"

Doggins grinned. "Because I don't trust them. We'd never get out of this place alive."

Kazak shook his head. "You are mistaken." He said it with total conviction, and Niall could see that he was sincere. "If you handed over your weapons, the spiders would come to an agreement with the bombardier beetles. Once that had happened, it would be a question of keeping their word. Your safety would be guaranteed. They have no wish to go to war."

Niall said: "If we handed over our weapons, they wouldn't need to go to war. They could destroy us whenever they liked."

Kazak nodded. "Possibly. But I am quite certain that they would keep their promise."

Doggins asked: "How can you be certain?"

"Because I am certain that the spiders want peace."

Doggins shook his head. "I'm afraid the answer has to be no."

It was obvious that Kazak was not surprised by this reply. He considered it carefully for a moment, frowning at the floor.

He asked finally. "So, you intend to destroy the spiders?"

"No. We want peace."

"They have offered you peace."

"But on their terms. They might change their minds when we've surrendered."

"I believe you are wrong." Again, Niall could see that he was sincere. "But in any case, let me try another suggestion. Suppose we could reach an agreement to destroy these weapons, so that neither side possessed them. Would you agree to that?"

Doggins thought about this for a long time, then shook his head, as Niall had known he would. "No."

"May I ask why not?"

"Because while we have these things we have bargaining power. They cost the lives of three of our men. Why should we throw that away?"

"They have also cost the lives of seven spiders." Niall was surprised that he knew the precise number. "Why not let one debt wipe out another?"

Doggins said patiently: "For a very simple reason. At the moment, you're a slave and I'm a slave. With these things, we needn't be slaves any more."

"I do not feel myself to be a slave." The contraction of Kazak's forehead showed that the notion offended him.

Doggins shook his head stubbornly: "Yet you are, just as I'm a slave of the beetles."

Kazak's neck flushed. "Are the spiders any worse than the beetles?"

"Much worse." It was Niall who answered. "When I first came to the spider city, I talked to your nephew Massig. He is quite convinced that he has nothing to fear from the spiders. He thinks he'll spend the next twenty years of his life working for them, then be allowed to retire to the great happy place. Even the slaves believe they're perfectly safe. When I first came to the slave quarter, I saw a child throw something at a spider in its web. I expected to see him killed instantly. Instead, the spider rolled him over on the ground and everybody thought it was a marvelous joke. It wasn't until last night that I realized what's really happening. The slaves are kept on the move all the time—they're not even allowed to sleep in the same place for two nights running. So when a slave gets eaten, nobody notices. Massig knew all about the slaves being eaten, but it didn't worry him because he was quite sure *he* was safe."

Kazak listened politely, but the tightness of his lips betrayed his impatience. "All that I know."

"Yet you still trust the spiders?"

Kazak shrugged. "For the moment, I have no alternative. They are the masters. What message do you wish me to take back to them—that you wish to be the masters?"

Doggins said: "Not masters. Just equals."

Kazak nodded thoughtfully: "Perhaps even that could be arranged."

Doggins smiled broadly. "If you can do that, you've got yourself a deal."

Kazak stood up. "Let me go and see what can be done." He moved towards the door, and Ulic and Milo pushed the chair aside. At the door, Kazak turned to face them again.

"Would you be willing to give up even one of your weapons? Merely as a token of good faith?"

Doggins patted the Reaper. "Not one of these, I'm afraid. They could blast us all out of this place before we could bat an eyelid."

"Have you nothing you could offer me as a bargaining counter? Something I could show them as a symbol of your good faith?"

Doggins took the blaster from his pocket. "How about this?"

"Very well." Kazak took it from him by the barrel and dropped it into the pocket of his toga. "I will return in a few minutes."

When the door had closed behind him, Niall asked: "Was that a good idea?"

Doggins shrugged, smiling. "I don't see why not. Those things are peashooters compared to these. Anyway, it's running out of power. I noticed that when I used it to blast the lock. It won't last much longer."

The youth called Kosmin asked: "May I ask a question?"

"Of course."

Kosmin said awkwardly: "I'm not questioning your judgment, but would it be such a bad idea to accept their offer?"

Milo said: "I was going to ask the same thing."

Kosmin said: "Suppose we agreed to destroy the Reapers, and they reached a diplomatic agreement with the beetles—wouldn't that be good for everyone?"

Another said: "While we've got these weapons, they won't stop trying to destroy us."

Doggins nodded. "That's true, Hastur. But while we have these weapons, we have the power to destroy them. As soon as we hand them over—or allowed them to be destroyed—we are at their mercy."

Milo said: "But do you think we can get out of here alive unless we make some concessions?"

Doggins said: "Yes, I do. For two reasons. The first is that we're stronger than they are. The second is that they know it. That's why they sent Kazak to bargain with us. We'd be stupid to throw away that advantage."

Niall said: "They could have had another reason."

Doggins looked at him curiously. "Such as?"

"To gain time."

Before Doggins could reply, there was a knock on the door and Kazak's voice called: "May I come in?"

Milo pushed the chair aside, and Kazak came past him. This time he stood near the door. Niall thought he showed signs of uneasiness. He cleared his throat and began: "First of all, the spiders have begged me to try again. They emphasize that they only wish for peace. They would even be willing for you to return to the city of the beetles with your weapons, providing you will promise to destroy them when you are there." He went on quickly as Doggins started to speak. "You see, they don't seem to trust human beings. I don't mean they doubt your word. But they don't believe there can be any permanent peace while you are armed with Reapers. They believe that men have a curiously criminal or destructive streak, and that sooner or later, the weapons would be turned against the spiders. As a human being, I must confess that I'm inclined to agree. Aren't you?" He looked around at all of them as he spoke, and Niall could see that most of the young men were nodding. Kazak undoubtedly had a way with words.

But Doggins shook his head decisively. "I'm sorry, Kazak. There's no way in which we're going to agree to part with the Reapers. If they won't allow us to leave freely, then we shall be forced to shoot our way out. And if necessary, we could annihilate ten thousand spiders—and I mean literally annihilate."

Kazak sighed. "In that case, you force me to deliver the second part of the message—and I can assure you that I hate it as much as you will. I am merely the messenger." He looked squarely at Doggins, and at Niall, who was standing beside him. "They have asked me to point out that they are holding Niall's mother and brother as hostages. . . ." He paused, and Niall could sense his nervousness. "They also ask me to tell you that they have now captured the city of the bombardier beetles, and that all your families are also hostages. If you hand over your weapons, or agree to their destruction, they will all be freed. Moreover, Niall's mother and brother, and anyone else he wants, will be allowed to move to the city of the beetles." He lowered his eyes. "That is my message."

Doggins had gone red, and veins stood out on his forehead. "If those bastards harm a single one of our people, I swear I'll destroy every spider in this city."

His eyes were so fierce that Kazak looked away. He cleared his throat. "I can only repeat what I say. They have no intention of harming anyone. They only wish for peace. They will exchange the lives of your families for the Reapers."

Niall glanced at Doggins. From his look of bafflement and helpless fury, he could see that Doggins felt he had no alternative.

Niall touched his arm. "This is something we need to discuss."

Kazak smiled with relief. "Please take all the time you like. Would you like me to withdraw?"

Niall said quickly: "Yes, perhaps that might be best."

Kazak bowed gravely, smiled his thanks at Milo for opening the door, and backed out. No one spoke until his footsteps reached street level. In the silence, Niall could sense their shock and dismay.

Doggins said in a flat voice: "Well, I'm afraid that's it."

But Niall had already turned the thought mirror so it faced inward, and the sudden concentration had dissipated his own sense of defeat.

"You intend to surrender?"

Doggins shrugged. "Can you see any alternative?"

"Yes. To refuse."

"How can we take that risk? They wouldn't hesitate to kill our families."

Niall looked round at the others; he could see they all shared this opinion. He said: "Listen to me. My own family is also being held hostage, so I understand your feelings. But what good would it do to surrender? You don't trust the spiders. Try to put yourself in the place of the Spider Lord. You have defied him once. You might do so again. The only way to prevent that from happening is to destroy you and your families. Do you think they would hesitate if you placed yourself in their power?"

He could see that his words had filled them with dejection and foreboding and went on quickly: "But suppose you refuse to surrender. It is true that they may carry out their threat against your families. But if they do, they know you would never rest until you have taken the life of a hundred spiders for every human being. While you have the weapons, you are in a position of power, and they can only take that away by destroying you. Why throw yourselves on their mercy? You are only inviting them to kill you as well." He turned to Doggins. "And how do you know they are telling the truth? Is the city of the beetles undefended?"

"Of course, not. But it could be captured—especially if they launched a surprise attack."

"And would that be easy?"

Doggins smiled grimly. "No. The beetles don't trust the spiders."

"So, the spiders may be trying to trick you into handing over your weapons?"

Doggins thought about this, frowning at the floor. He looked at the others. "What do you think?"

This appeal obviously embarrassed them; they were used to being given orders.

Milo said hesitantly: "I think Niall may be right."

Doggins came to a decision. "Open the door. Take the chair away."

Daylight streamed in. For a moment they were all dazzled. Doggins strode to the doorway. "Kazak, can you hear me?"

Kazak's voice shouted: "Yes."

"Tell them we're coming out." He turned to the others. "Keep your weapons ready, but don't fire unless I give the order. And keep a watch above your heads—don't forget they can drop out of the sky."

He advanced into the daylight and mounted the steps. The others followed in a single file, all held their weapons at the ready. As he mounted the steps, Niall glanced upward. There was now a cobweb that stretched across the street between the rooftops, but he could see no sign of an ambush.

As he stepped out of the gate, Niall was shocked to realize how many spiders were waiting for them. There must have been ten thousand, packed closely together in both directions, to the corners of the street and beyond. The only empty space in the road was immediately in front of the area gate. The spiders had withdrawn in a wide semicircle; the nearest were standing with Kazak on the far side of the road. Yet to Niall, even this distance brought an almost uncontrollable sense of being trapped. With a shock, he realized that spiders regard human beings with as much dislike as men regard spiders or poisonous snakes. They saw him as a disgusting, pale-skinned, venomous creature who threatened their lives, and every one of them would have been delighted to plunge its fangs into his throat. Once again, he experienced a sense of physical coldness as their blank eyes stared at him.

Niall could see that the others were badly unnerved. In an effort to prevent his hands from shaking, Milo was holding his weapon so tightly that his knuckles were white. Kosmin looked as if he was about to be sick. Doggins was very pale, his face beaded with sweat. The wall of sheer hostility seemed to drain their vitality. Even with the thought mirror turned inward, Niall felt that his own control was on the point of dissolution. Black patches were drifting across his vision.

Kazak called: "Well, have you decided to accept our terms?"

His voice restored Niall to a sense of normality; the feeling of suffocation suddenly vanished. He stepped forward in front of the others and answered firmly: "I'm afraid the answer is no."

Kazak was obviously surprised. He asked gravely: "Don't you think that is a rash decision?"

"No." Suddenly, Niall knew that the time for words had passed, that this deadlock could only be broken by some form of action. He pointed. "Do you see that building?" He turned his weapon on the ten-story building on the southeastern corner of the street and raised it so that it pointed above the heads of the spiders. Then he pulled the trigger.

What happened shocked him, even though he had been expecting it. The gun recoiled so it almost jerked itself out of his hands, and the blinding flash of blue energy struck the building and seemed to turn it into a dazzling blue haze. The recoil swung the barrel through an angle of a few degrees, and even this slight movement was enough to tear a fifty-foot hole in the wall. With incredulity, Niall realized that the blast had cut through the building as if it were made of paper; he could see the blue sky through its far wall. Then the whole building sagged and collapsed, showering slabs of masonry down on to the street.

Niall had released the trigger almost immediately, appalled at the magnitude of the catastrophe he had unleashed, but the collapse continued as if the building had been devastated by some tremendous explosion. A vast section of wall fell directly into the street below and onto the massed ranks of spiders. At the same moment, the spiders facing them surged forward, as the agony of dying spiders battered them like some tidal wave. Niall was aware that their minds had been momentarily destroyed by horror; but his companions, who had no way of realizing this, opened fire. Their Reapers, set at a lower level than Niall's, acted like flame throwers, cutting pathways through the massed bodies of the spiders and filling the air with a sickening stench of burnt spider flesh. Then, suddenly, they were surrounded by fleeing spiders, none of whom made any effort to attack them. All control had vanished. The agony, communicated from mind to mind, had destroyed the living as much as the dead.

Only Niall could understand what had happened. For the others, it was a baffling miracle. They had braced themselves for destruction, and now their enemies had vanished. But for Niall, the defeat of the spiders had left behind a nausea that was spiritual, not physical, in origin.

Something moved in the gutter on the far side of the road. It was Kazak. He stood up slowly, then came across the road towards them, his steps as unsteady as those of a drunken man. His toga was torn, and both knees were gashed and bleeding. So was his face; a flap of skin hung loosely under his left eye, which was already beginning to turn black. He stopped in front of Niall, and asked in a thick voice:

"Was that necessary?"

Niall tried to speak, but his voice seemed to be trapped in his throat. It was Doggins who answered.

"Well, it seems to have done the trick." He wiped his dripping forehead. "I didn't think we were going to get out of that alive."

Niall found his voice. "I'm sorry, I didn't intend that to happen. I only wanted to show them how powerful these things are." He was surprised by the waves of calm that were now flooding over him.

Doggins laughed. "You certainly succeeded." He turned to Kazak. "Well, are you going to stick with us?"

Kazak looked like a tired animal; the blood was now running down his cheek. He stared at Doggins for a long time, and it was difficult to guess what was going on in his mind. He said finally, "No," then turned and limped slowly away from them, moving in the direction of the river.

Doggins obviously found his decision incomprehensible.

"Is he cunning, or just stupid?" he asked Niall.

But Niall was also baffled. He stared after the limping figure with an odd feeling of concern.

"I don't know."

Doggins shrugged cheerfully. "Oh, well, it doesn't matter one way or the other." He turned to the others. "Are you lads ready to go?"

They marched in a northerly direction, advancing down the center of the wide street to avoid the risk of a surprise attack. All felt instinctively that this was unlikely; but it would have been foolish to relax their precautions. Doggins used his Reaper to slice through the webs that stretched overhead, and their strands hung like festive streamers down the walls of the buildings, fluttering in the stiff breeze from the south.

At the far end of the street, they found themselves at the edge of the town hall square. The City Hall was a massive pseudo-Greek building with fluted columns that had long ago turned black, but the surrounding lawns were smooth and well kept. Although the square was totally deserted, they paused to survey it, wondering if they were being observed from the buildings around or from the City Hall itself.

Doggins said: "I don't like this. Surely they can't be stupid enough to let us march straight out of their city without any attempt to stop us?"

The same thought had occurred to Niall. The spiders were badly demoralized. Yet the Spider Lord must know that if he allowed them to escape now, he would have lost a major opportunity—perhaps the only opportunity—to destroy them. Surrounded by buildings, Niall and his companions would be vulnerable to a sudden rush. And at close quarters, the spiders were almost irresistible. Once they had paralyzed their victim, even for a moment, by sheer willpower, they could dispatch him instantly with their poisoned fangs.

Niall was staring thoughtfully at the City Hall. "Do you know anything about spider balloons?"

"Of course. Our people manufacture them."

Niall pointed. "That place is a silk factory. Perhaps they also store balloons there."

Doggins frowned, shaking his head. "That's no good. We'd also need porifids."

"Porifids?"

"Short for Porifera Mephitis, the things that make them fly. Also known as the skunk sponge. It's a kind of sponge that produces a lighter-than-air gas."

"But if there are balloons, there may be porifids too."

Doggins glanced at the sun to calculate the time. "All right. I suppose it's worth a try."

They approached the City Hall cautiously, their weapons raised; but there seemed no sign of life. In the beds outside, banks of colored flowers filled the air with a spring-like fragrance. Birds sang in the surrounding trees, which rustled in the cool breeze. Niall was interested to observe how danger sharpened his appreciation of these things.

The carved oak doors were locked, but yielded immediately to the thin beam of the Reaper. Inside was a large hallway with marble columns and two wide flights of stairs sweeping in a curve to the upper story. It was not unlike Kazak's palace, but larger.

Facing them was another pair of imposing wooden doors, which also proved to be locked. Doggins sliced out the lock with his Reaper and kicked open the door. He gave a chortle of delight, and flung his arm round Niall's neck.

"You're a brilliant little lad! How did you know?"

The hall that faced them had evidently been used once for public ceremonies; the walls were covered with banners bearing municipal emblems; now it was a workshop and storeroom, full of ladders, wooden planks, handcarts, and building materials. And in the far corner were piles of neatly-folded silk which Niall recognized as spider balloons.

Niall shrugged modestly. "It was just a guess."

Doggins turned to the others. "You lads spread out all over the building and stand guard at the windows. We can't risk a surprise attack. Wedge the front doors closed. If you see any sign of movement, let me know immediately." He turned back to Niall. "Let's see if we can find a skunk sponge."

"Where are they usually kept?"

"In some kind of a tank."

In an alcove behind the balloons, they found a locked door; when this was kicked open, they were met by a stench of rotting vegetation that made them both recoil. Holding his nose, Doggins peeped into the room. He nodded with satisfaction.

"That's what we need."

There was a large glass tank, its sides almost as high as a man, containing slimy green water. Propped beside it were a number of nets with long handles. Niall peered into the scummy liquid but could see very little. Doggins climbed a flight of wooden steps beside the tank, took one of the nets and fished about in the water.

"There we are." He held out the net. Lying in the bottom, among slimy weed, was a green pulsating object shaped like a doughnut. The hole in its center was closed, but when Doggins prodded with his finger it opened for a moment, then closed on his finger. Inside this mouth Niall caught a glimpse of a pointed green tongue. Doggins pulled his finger away with a faint plop. The air was immediately filled with the disgusting smell of decay.

"But how does it make the balloons fly?"

"I'll show you."

Doggins crossed to a cylindrical metal container that stood on a table in a corner. When he removed the lid, a stench of rotting meat mingled with the vegetation smell. Doggins picked up a rusty saucepan from the table and dipped it into the cylinder. When it emerged, it was half-full of big grubs, some of them as much as two inches long and thick as a finger. Still holding his nose and retching with disgust, Doggins tilted the saucepan over the creature shaped like a doughnut. The mouth promptly opened, and closed again hungrily on the wriggling grubs. Once more the air filled with the smell of decay.

Doggins put the saucepan down. "Ugh! Let's get out of here." As they left the room, he carefully closed the door behind him. Niall observed that other porifids were now swimming at the edge of the tank, obviously hoping for grubs.

Back in the hall, they lifted down one of the folded balloons and laid it out on a clear floor-space. Unfolded, it was thirty feet across. This was the first time Niall had seen a spider balloon at close quarters, and he examined it with curiosity. He had often wondered how the spider was supported; now he could see there was a kind of flat, silken bag underneath the balloon. This had room for a large body and could easily hold two or three human beings.

The balloon itself was not spherical, but flattened like two dinner plates held face to face, and the finely woven silk was slightly sticky to the touch.

Spread out on the floor, the balloon formed a huge blue-white disc on the edge of which there was a six-inch loop of rope held in place by a powerful clip. When this was released and pulled, the side of the balloon opened like a gutted fish. Niall, who was barely familiar with the principal of the slide fastener, found this remarkable. Inside the balloon, at its central point, there was a reinforced cup about a foot in diameter, covered with two broad straps.

Doggins pointed. "That's where the porifid goes."

"But how do you make it produce the gas?"

"You don't have to. They hate the darkness, so as soon as they're sealed in, they begin to produce gas."

"And how do you release it?"

"Through a valve in the undercarriage. Help me get this thing outside."

Large windows behind a speaker's rostrum revealed a courtyard in the center of the building. They dragged the balloon outside and spread it on the flagstones. Doggins then fetched the fishing net and emptied the porifid into the cup-like container, enclosing it with the straps—since the creature seemed to have no power of locomotion, these were obviously intended to prevent it from falling out rather than from escaping. The balloon was then closed and sealed with the slide fastener. Even as this happened, it began to swell. Doggins found a coil of rope and secured the balloon to a metal ring in the flagstones. While he was doing so, it began to float clear of the ground. Half a minute later, it was fully distended and floating sideways at the end of a taut rope some twenty feet above their heads. Niall tried pulling on the rope, but the balloon seemed to actively resist any attempt to drag it towards the ground. He chuckled.

"How are we supposed to get inside it?"

"I'll show you."

Doggins placed his hands on his hips and stared up at the balloon, wearing a frown of intense concentration. His face became red, and a vein began to throb in the middle of his forehead. For about a minute, nothing happened; then the balloon began to deflate and drifted down towards them. Doggins expelled his breath in a long gasp and wiped the perspiration from his face.

"It's hard work. But I'm told it gets easier once you've got used to it. You can make them reabsorb their own gas. That's how the spiders control them." The balloon was already reinflating and rising again.

They heard running footsteps in the hall; a moment later, Milo came into the courtyard.

"There's something happening out there, sir."

In the entrance hall Ulic and Hastur were looking out of the windows, their weapons at the ready. The lawns surrounding the building were still deserted; so was the large paved area of terrace in front of them. But on the pavements on the edge of the square, there was a continual movement of spiders and human beings.

From the top of the staircase, Renfred called: "They're all around the edge of the square. You can get a better view from the roof."

They followed him up to the third story and out through a door onto the flat roof. From this vantage point there was an excellent view of the whole square. It revealed that all the surrounding streets were full of spiders and human beings. Yet there was no sign of any attempt to advance towards them; the square itself remained deserted.

Doggins frowned. "I wish I knew what they're up to. I daresay they mean to try and rush us."

Renfred was looking nervous. "I suppose we shall have to shoot our way out?"

Doggins shook his head. "We're leaving by balloon. Hastur, Milo, collect the others and bring them into the courtyard. Renfred, you wait there and keep watch—don't hesitate to open fire on full power if they attack."

Niall said: "I think I'd better stay and keep watch." Renfred would be an easy victim if the spiders launched a sudden attack.

"All right. We'll send for you as soon as we're ready to leave."

Alone on the roof, Niall used the thought mirror to concentrate his perceptions. The apparently aimless movement of spiders and human beings worried him. He tried to put himself into the place of the Spider Lord. If he wanted to prevent a group of dangerous enemies from escaping, how would he go about it? The simplest method would be a sudden rush. A spider could move at a terrifying speed; those who were now five hundred yards away could be swarming all over the City Hall within twenty seconds. But if they intended such an attack, why were they not massing in ranks on the pavements at the edge of the square?

He tried to relax and attune his mind to what was happening, but found it difficult. There were too many spiders, and all seemed preoccupied with their own affairs. He was expecting to sense an atmosphere of hostility, a determination to destroy their human enemies; instead, the spiders seemed to be waiting for something. But for what? An order to attack? That seemed unlikely; there was no sense of immediate expectation.

Niall strolled to the inner edge of the roof and looked down into the courtyard. They were bringing out balloons one by one and piling them on top of one another. Doggins was talking earnestly to a small group that included Milo and Kosmin, obviously explaining the steering mechanism of the balloons. The inflated balloon was floating within a few feet of Niall's face, its skin taut. The porifid inside was evidently producing large quantities of gas. It was leaking from some escape valve, and the stench of putrid vegetation drifted towards him; Niall moved hastily upwind.

As he watched, Ulic brought out another porifid in its net; this was sealed into the balloon at the top of the pile. A few moments later, the balloon began inflating. Milo, Kosmin, and Hastur clambered quickly into the undercarriage, and Doggins once more pointed out the position of the release valve. The undercarriage was made for the large, flat body of a spider, not for upright human beings, and its three occupants slid into uncomfortable positions in which their bodies reclined at an angle of forty-five degrees, while their feet met in the center. Horizontal slits served as windows, allowing them to look out. The balloon was already rising into the air, and those who were trying to hold it down had to let go. A moment later, it shot past Niall, pushing the other balloon aside. Niall caught Hastur's eye and thought he looked at once terrified and exalted. Then the balloon rose above the roof and was caught by the strong breeze. It continued to shoot upward with alarming speed, and within thirty seconds was a mere dot against the clear blue of the northern sky.

All movement at the edge of the square had ceased; spiders and human beings were all staring upward. Niall tightened his grip on the Reaper. If there was going to be a sudden attack, it should happen now, as the spiders realized their enemies were escaping. But as the balloon turned into a dot and then vanished, the movement of the spiders resumed. Again, Niall tried hard to attune himself to their minds, but found it impossible; there was too much confusion and activity. But again he received the impression that they were waiting for something.

Five minutes later, a second balloon went up. Once again, the movement among the spiders ceased. This time, Niall felt he could detect a certain tension; but it vanished as the balloon receded out of sight. But when a third, and then a fourth balloon rose up from the courtyard, he could sense a change. As they saw their enemies escaping, the spiders were becoming impatient. The aimless movement had ceased, and he once more experienced the curious sense of physical coldness that told him he was the object of scrutiny. In spite of the warmness of the morning, his arms were covered in goosepimples as if he were standing in a cold wind.

Doggins looked up at him; the fifth balloon was already inflating. "Come on down. We'll be ready to go in a moment."

But Niall experienced a curious reluctance to leave his post. He preferred to stay where he could see the spiders.

"I'd better wait until the other two have gone."

Doggins shrugged; he obviously felt Niall was being overcautious.

As the fifth balloon rose clear of the roof, the feeling of coldness seemed to increase. He began to experience the sense of nausea that he had felt half an hour before, when he was surrounded by spiders. It had the curious effect of blurring his vision and making the sweat stand out on his forehead, although it felt as cold as rain. He became aware that this was not due to a deliberately-directed hostility, but simply to the feeling of loathing of which he was the object. He had to take long, deep breaths to keep his senses clear.

The sixth balloon shot past him, making him start with alarm. Now there was only Doggins in the courtyard. "Come on down now," he called. "We're ready."

Niall cast a final glance round the square, then hurried through the door that led down off the roof. At that moment, the feeling of oppression vanished so abruptly that he felt as if some physical load had been lifted from his head. Then, as he passed a window on the stairs, he understood the reason. The square had turned into a black mass of spiders, all racing towards the building. The first of them were already crossing the surrounding lawns. He ran down the stairs three at a time, but as he reached the hallway, the double doors shuddered under the impact of a heavy body. He raised his weapon and started to press the trigger, then saw that the door had been wedged with a heavy balk of timber and that it would take a battering ram to burst through. He ran across the storeroom and out into the courtyard.

"Quick. We're being attacked."

As he spoke, there was a sound of shattering glass from the hallway. Doggins began to scramble into the undercarriage of the balloon which was hovering four feet above the ground. Niall slammed the courtyard door behind him and heaved a large stone flower vase against it, astonished by his own strength. Then, helped by Doggins, he climbed into the undercarriage, sliding head-downward. As he scrambled into an upright position, he felt the balloon beginning to rise. At the same moment, the first of the spiders arrived at the edge of the roof surrounding the courtyard. It leapt, and they heard its soft impact on the top of the balloon. Doggins was sawing at the rope that held them, but its slackness made it difficult to cut. Then Niall became aware that, instead of ascending, the balloon was returning towards the flagstones. Doggins cursed and struck with his clenched fist above his head, where a damp patch indicated the presence of the porifid. The effect was instantaneous; there was a violent upward surge and the frayed rope parted with a jerk. Another spider launched itself from the roof, struck the balloon and plunged onto the flagstones below. Then the roof was below them, and they could see the swarming black bodies of the spiders. A gust of wind tilted the balloon, and a spider hurtled past them, legs flailing, and plunged towards the roof. It struck the edge of the parapet, bounced off on to the lawn below and lay still. Both of them began to laugh uncontrollably; if the undercarriage had felt less unstable, they would have flung their arms round each other.

In less than a minute, the City Hall was only one building among many. They could see the barracks and the river, and beyond that, the main square with the white tower and the headquarters of the Spider Lord. And in the barrack yard, Niall saw something that made his heart contract: a crowd of men and of spiders gathered in the corner where the armory was situated.

The balloon could be controlled by two ropes that were attached to fin-like rudders on the underside. Now, as the red spires of the beetle city appeared in the distance, Doggins began to steer a course towards it. He also tugged on the cord of the release valve and for a moment they were sickened by the overpowering stench of decay. As the fabric of the balloon became less taut, it began to descend.

Niall was staring back towards the city, thrilled by this panoramic view which reminded him of his vision in the tower and filled him with an absurd sense of being lighter than air. In the distance, beyond the hills on the southern edge of the city, the sea was glittering in the sunlight like a clouded mirror. To the east, there was a wild countryside of dense woodland, with mountains on the horizon.

Then his attention was drawn back to the city they had just left. There was an orange flash, followed by the thunder of an explosion; he could see clearly that it came from the barracks. A black cloud of smoke began to rise into the air, carrying with it large fragments of solid material. As he shouted to Doggins and pointed there was a second and far greater explosion which was followed by a whole series of smaller explosions; these seemed to be spread over a far larger area than the barracks. As the noise roared in their ears, the wind struck them like a blow and sent them spinning through the sky. They were hurled up, and then down, and Niall caught a glimpse of the earth up above his head. With sudden terror he realized he was on the roof of the balloon, the naked sky above him and the undercarriage collapsed around him. Doggins was thrashing wildly in an attempt to escape the enveloping folds of silk, and Niall saw stars as he was kicked on the side of the head. Another blast of wind struck them and again the balloon was sent spinning, Niall clinging frantically to the loose silk. As his grip began to slacken and he felt himself slipping off the edge, the balloon performed a somersault and he found himself once more in the safety of the undercarriage. The Reaper was sticking into his back, and Doggins was lying across his chest and suffocating him with his weight. Niall twisted away from under him and managed to turn over on to his knees. The balloon was still tossing like a ship in a storm, and the sounds of explosions continued to roll past them like volleys of thunder. Finally, Niall succeeded in separating himself from Doggins and standing upright.

What he saw shocked him. It looked as if the whole city had disappeared. Instead, there was a billowing black cloud of dust and smoke that seemed to be moving upward and sideways in slow motion, like sand disturbed at the bottom of a river. Niall's first thought was of his family. Then, as some of the smoke drifted aside, he saw with relief that the explosion had been confined to the slave quarter; he could clearly see the white tower and the headquarters of the Spider Lord behind the expanding clouds.

Doggins pulled himself up beside him. "My God, that was a close one." He was obviously shaken; his knuckles were white as he clung to the fabric of the undercarriage. As he stared at the heaving smoke, his expression changed to one of awe. He drew a deep breath.

"Well, that's the last you'll see of your friend Kazak."

"Kazak?" For a moment Niall failed to understand, "What makes you think he was responsible?"

Doggins grinned with malicious amusement. "It was Kazak all right. He tried to get into the armory with my blaster."

Niall shuddered as he realized how close they had been to destruction. "So that's what they were waiting for!"

Doggins turned away. "The treacherous bastard got what he deserved." He shook his head. "But what a waste of explosive!"

They were both so fascinated by the spreading black cloud that neither had paid any attention to the land immediately below. Now, suddenly, Doggins gave a cry of alarm and pulled violently on the cord of the release valve; the stench hissed past them and was whipped away by the wind. The balloon gave a shudder and began to descend. They were almost directly over the twisted spires of the beetle city. And all round the city, staining the green landscape like a black mildew, was an army of spiders.

Doggins began to laugh. Niall stared at him in surprise, then realized that he was laughing with sheer relief, and was, in fact, close to tears. Doggins placed a hand on his shoulder.

"You were right. They *were* bluffing. They haven't captured the city."

"Can you be sure?" Niall was still suspicious of a trap.

"Look." Niall followed the direction of his pointing finger. At first he was not sure what Doggins was trying to indicate. He seemed to be pointing at the main square, with its expanse of green lawn. Then Niall observed a movement and realized that the lawn was covered with a densely-packed mass of green-backed beetles—so many that the paths were no longer visible.

"But why are they all there? Why aren't they defending the town?"

"They are."

"I don't understand."

But Doggins was no longer listening. He was staring below, and at the same time thumping the balloon above his head with his clenched fist. When Niall looked down he understood why. Instead of descending at an angle towards the city, they were plummeting almost directly downward, on a course that would take them into the midst of the spiders. At the same time, the sense of physical coldness told him what was happening. The combined will of the spiders was being directed at the porifid inside the balloon, causing it to reabsorb its gas so that the half-filled balloon was falling like a stone.

Doggins said between his teeth: "Right, if that's what you want." He unslung the Reaper from his back and pushed its lever forward. Then he braced himself against the side of the undercarriage and pointed the weapon downward.

In the bright sunlight, the beam of energy was almost invisible. But as it struck the ground, blue flame seethed in all directions like a sea of blue fire. Spiders shriveled and vanished and the earth became black. Then, suddenly, black bodies were fleeing, colliding and scrambling over one another in their terror. Niall was fascinated to observe that those who ran towards the beetle city were suddenly halted, as if they had crashed into an invisible wall. Then, almost immediately, they struggled to their feet and fled in another direction. He was witnessing the same mass panic he had seen earlier that morning—a panic in which the instant communication of physical agony produced a mindless terror and total loss of control.

Once again the balloon was struck by a force like a hurricane. This time it was the heat blast rising from the ground like the updraught of some immense bonfire. Niall was flung to his knees, and for a moment the heat was so intense that he was afraid the fabric would begin to burn. The undercarriage swung wildly from side to side as the balloon was hurled upwards. When he stood up and looked over the side, the ground was again receding fast.

Doggins shouted: "I'll steer, you release the gas." He handed Niall the cord of the release valve. For the next five minutes, Doggins performed a miracle of control, sometimes apparently steering the balloon directly into the wind. Niall held the cord but made no attempt to use it; it was simpler to control the porifid by willpower. The creature seemed to be remarkably sensitive to mental commands, releasing and re-absorbing gas with a precision that made it possible to achieve total control of the vertical component of their descent. At one point, when the wind almost carried them into one of the twisted spires, Niall caused the balloon to rise so that it missed the top by a few inches.

By now, people were running below them, trying to keep up with the balloon. In the forefront of the crowd, Niall recognized Doggins' wife Selima. The balloon caught momentarily in the branches of a tall tree, brushed the wall of a house and finally touched down beside an ornamental pool. Hands reached out to grasp theirs and to help them out of the collapsing undercarriage. Selima threw her arms round Doggins' neck and kissed him repeatedly. Niall found himself surrounded by people who were asking questions, while a young girl placed a colored paper chain round his neck. A small boy was clinging to his hand and asking if he could have a ride in the balloon. Further confusion ensued as the balloon started to rise again; but when Doggins pulled the slide fastener that released the pressure, there were cries of disgust and one child was violently sick. Niall held his breath until he had moved upwind from the stench.

He had been scanning the faces, hoping to see Odina, but there was no sign of her. For a moment, the sight of a blonde head made his heart pound; then he realized it was Doggins' wife Lucretia. He pushed his way towards her.

"Where is Odina?"

"Odina?" For a moment she did not seem to understand him. "Oh, she's with the beetles."

"Is there something the matter?" Her face looked drawn and tired.

She gave him a strange sidelong glance. "What do you think?" She pushed her way towards her husband, brushed Selima impatiently aside, and whispered something in his ear. Doggins' smile suddenly vanished and was replaced by a look of anxiety. With some difficulty, Niall reached his side.

"What is it?"

"Trouble."

"Spiders?"

Doggins gave a twisted smile. "Far worse than that. I've been summoned before the council."

"But why?"

Doggins shrugged. "Causing trouble, I suppose."

"Shall I come with you?"

Lucretia interposed sharply: "The Master sent for you alone."

Doggins grimaced. "Not allowed. You go back with Lucretia. I'll see you later." He turned and strode off in the direction of the town hall. Selima looked as if she were about to run after him, but a glance from Lucretia checked her.

Niall turned to Lucretia and was met by a hard stare. He asked: "Can you tell me what's wrong?"

"Wrong?" She raised her eyebrows with mild sarcasm. "Oh, nothing's wrong. You've just started a war, that's all."

Selima touched his arm gently. "Come back with us now. You must be tired."

Lucretia gave a snort of irritation and walked off.

Niall said: "I don't understand. He's saved your lives."

She gave him a sad smile. "That is for the Master to decide."

Her submission irritated him.

"But don't you feel proud of him? He's saved your city from the spiders."

"Perhaps that is true. But yesterday we had no quarrel with the spiders."

Neither of them spoke as they crossed the green lawns and turned down the smooth marble road that led to the town hall. Then the sight of a collapsed balloon by the side of the road reminded him of the others.

"How many more balloons have landed?"

"Two. But we saw another one pass overhead."

Now they had reached the town hall square. But its wide lawn was no longer crowded with beetles. As they were crossing it, a woman rushed up to Niall and seized his arm.

"Can you tell me what has happened to my son Yorg?"

"He escaped in a balloon. If he is not among those who landed, then he has been carried beyond the city. He should be quite safe."

Another woman approached him. "And my son Marcus?"

Niall lowered his eyes from her face. "I am sorry. He is dead."

The woman collapsed on the ground and began to moan and wail, beating her forehead on the hard turf. Niall felt convulsed by misery and guilt. The other woman asked: "How was he killed?"

"He was . . . he was killed by a spider." He was about to say "eaten," but stopped himself in time.

A small crowd had gathered round them. Selima said: "He cannot answer more questions now. We have to go back."

But at that moment a beetle came down the steps of the town hall and hurried across to them. It reached out with its long front leg and touched Niall on the shoulder, then made a series of gestures with its feelers. Selima said: "He is saying that you must go with him. They want to speak to you."

Niall stared at the blank face with its goggle eyes. It was not unlike the face of a spider, yet conveyed no feeling of menace. In spite of their enormous size, and the obvious strength in their armored legs, the beetles somehow communicated an atmosphere of gentleness and good nature. Without hesitation, Niall followed it back into the town hall.

It took several moments for his eyes to become accustomed to the dim light. Then he saw that the entrance hall was full of beetles and that they were communicating in their peculiar, sibilant voices, which sounded not unlike the chirping of a cicada. A moment later, to his joy, he saw Odina sitting on a bench in a corner. He rushed across to her and seized her hands.

"Are you all right?"

She raised her eyes to his face; to his astonishment, she seemed not to recognize him.

"Don't you know me?"

"Yes." Her lips scarcely moved.

"Then what is it?" The emptiness of her gaze chilled him.

The beetle touched him on the shoulder. Odina looked as if she were about to speak, then shook her head. Niall turned away and followed his escort feeling saddened and shaken. He cast a glance back towards her but she was no longer visible among the beetles.

He was led down a curved, sloping ramp that led into a basement; the light here was even dimmer than in the upper part of the building. The walls were of rough, unsmoothed stone, and as he followed his guide down a long, sloping corridor, he felt as though he were entering some kind of underworld. The floor under his feet was also rough, and he had to walk carefully to avoid stumbling. Yet he could understand intuitively why this lower part of the building had been left in an apparently unfinished state. For beetles the earth is a place of refuge and safety. So it would be natural to construct a council chamber—a place demanding deep thought and calm deliberation—under the ground.

The tunnel turned a right angle, and the slope became even steeper; now the walls were of hard-packed earth, supported by unplaned wooden beams. Like Kazak's underground city, this corridor was lighted by oil lamps set in alcoves. They came to a place where the walls opened out and where the corridor appeared to come to an end; in fact, the earth wall that faced them was a massive door made of some fibrous material like peat. As they waited, it swung slowly open. Niall expected to find himself confronted by some insect guardian of the threshold, and was surprised and amused to see that it was Doggins who was struggling to pull open the heavy door, which was more than a foot thick. Doggins gave him a brief nod of recognition; Niall thought he looked grim and rather harassed. When they were inside, Niall's beetle escort closed the door with a single powerful thrust of its front legs.

They were in a large, dimly-lighted room whose floor was a shallow oval bowl. The walls were of earth, supported by pillars of undressed stone; the light came from flickering oil lamps set close to the ceiling. The oval space contained a number of protuberances, like small hillocks, and on each of these sat a bombardier beetle. As his eyes became accustomed to the poor light, Niall could see that each of these hillocks had a steeply sloping upper surface, so the beetles were able to rest on them in an upright position, each folded leg resting in a groove; it was the beetle equivalent of an armchair, designed so its occupant could peer over the raised back.

There were, he counted, fifteen beetles facing him in a semi-oval. Their blank faces reminded him of toads. The beetle at the center of the arc was obviously older than the others, and its horny skin looked cracked and mottled. One of its goggling black eyes was flecked with white. Yet Niall sensed immediately that this was the Master.

Doggins took his arm and led him to the central point of the arc. They stood side by side. Niall was glad of Doggins' moral support. The gaze of the beetles produced in him a peculiar and uncomfortable sensation. It was completely unlike the physical coldness produced by the spiders, which seemed to be some physical expression of hostility. Yet he felt, nevertheless, as if their eyes were penetrating the surface of his skin and seeing into his body. They gave him the impression that they were ignoring his physical appearance and somehow looking directly into his feelings and emotions. It was an uncomfortable sensation, like being naked. He felt that it would be pointless to try to lie or deceive; they would sense the lie even before he spoke.

The beetle sitting to the right of the ruler raised its feelers and made rapid signs.

"Saarleb asks how old you are," Doggins interpreted.

Niall replied: "I am not sure. Perhaps some seventeen summers."

The beetle on the other side of the ruler asked a question, which Doggins translated as: "Saarleb asks why did you come to this country?" Saarleb was clearly a title, not a name.

Niall replied: "I was taken prisoner. My father was killed by the spiders."

When Doggins translated this reply, there was a long pause; then a beetle to his right asked: "Do you want revenge on the spider who killed your father?"

Niall answered truthfully: "No."

Another beetle asked: "Do you want revenge on all spiders?"

Niall thought about this before he answered: "I do not want revenge. But I want to be free."

There was another silence. Then, for the first time, the Master spoke: "If the spiders would allow you to leave in peace, would you be contented?"

"No."

"Why not?"

Niall was thinking of how to phrase his reply when, to his astonishment, he heard Doggins repeating the question and realized that the Master had addressed him directly. It was quite unlike the sensation he had experienced when the Spider Lord or the Steegmaster had addressed him telepathically; in that case he had experienced the voice inside his chest or his head. But the Master had seemed to address him as if speaking aloud.

Niall looked into the blank, worn face and answered: "Because even in my own country, we are not free. We have to spend our lives hiding from the spiders."

As Doggins started to translate this reply, the Master made a sign to him to be silent. Doggins looked surprised. Then, once again, Niall picked up the thought of the Master as naturally as if they were holding a normal conversation.

"If your people were permitted to live unhindered, would you be content?"

This time, the Master made no accompanying gestures, and it was obvious from Doggins' baffled expression that he could hear nothing. Niall thought for a long time before he answered: "No. I have seen the way the spiders treat their servants and their slaves, and I regard them as my enemies. I could not be happy in my own land."

These words caused a buzz of conversation to break out among the beetles; they began addressing one another in their strange sibilant language and waving their feelers. Only the Master continued to look at Niall with his mask-like face. Niall glanced sideways at Doggins and saw immediately that he was worried.

It was several minutes before silence was restored. Then the Master said: "What you have said places us in a difficult position. We have no quarrel with the spiders. Can you give us any reason why we should not hand you over to them?"

Niall made an intense effort of concentration, using the thought mirror to clarify his intuitions. He was aware that the Master was not asking him to excuse or justify himself; he was not asking for argument or persuasion. Behind his question lay his own objective assessment of the situation. They wanted peace with the spiders, and the key to peace was to hand Niall over to the Spider Lord. They were asking Niall, in an equally objective spirit, whether he did not agree that this was the most sensible thing to do. And suddenly, Niall understood what form his reply should take. He stared at the floor and placed his hands behind him in an attempt to clarify his thoughts. It was vital not to lose the thread.

"My people were once lords of the earth. Now we are either servants or fugitives. That is perhaps as it should be: we lost our position through weakness. Many of our people are content to be servants, and that is also as it should be; it is their own choice. But I was also offered a position as a servant of the spiders and I knew that it was impossible. And that is not simply because the spiders killed my father." He looked up, and stared directly at the Master. "It is because I have no wish to be a servant. My strongest desire is to be free."

The Master interrupted: "But you are free. To be alive is to be free."

Niall shook his head. "That may be true for beetles and spiders, but it is not true for human beings. We seem to have a kind of . . . of freedom function." He could sense the bewilderment of the Beetle Lord. "It is a feeling that our minds can be free as well as our bodies." He was feeling confused by their lack of understanding, and found it difficult to explain what he meant. He finished lamely: "For human beings, it is not true that to be alive is to be free."

There was a long silence. Finally, the Master said: "What you have just said is either very profound or very stupid. I do not profess to understand it. I am free. You are free. There is no other kind of freedom."

Niall asked: "Do you mean I am free to go now?"

"No. That is still for us to decide. We must consult with the Spider Lord." He beckoned to the beetle who was guarding the door. "Fetch the Spider Lord."

Niall was struck dumb with astonishment, and felt the muscles of his scalp contracting. Niall glanced at Doggins as the beetle went out and was puzzled that he showed no sign of surprise; Doggins was staring at the floor and looked only nervous and depressed.

With an immense effort, Niall controlled the pounding of his heart, but could still feel the blood throbbing in his toes and finger-ends. The minutes seemed to drag by. It seemed to him that his last hope had gone. If the beetles had permitted the Spider Lord to enter their city, then they were anxious for peace at any price, and it was merely a matter of time before they acceded to his demands.

The door opened. Niall experienced a wave of surprise and relief when the guard stood aside to permit Odina to enter the room. But as she came closer, he saw she was wearing the same stunned, blank expression that he had seen in the entrance hall. Her eyes met his without recognition; she looked as if she were in a trance. She came and stood beside him, standing to attention like a soldier. As Niall glanced sideways at her bare breasts and sunburnt arms, he experienced a flood of misery, the sense of having lost her.

The Master made a sign to the guard. "Bring the Death Lord a seat."

"I prefer to stand."

Niall stared at Odina with amazement. The voice had issued from her lips; yet it was the distinctive voice of the Spider Lord. At the same time, Odina's face changed. It had become older and stronger, the face of a stern old woman.

The Master spoke in the strange, hissing language of the beetles; yet Niall could understand the words as clearly as before.

"Greetings, again, to the Death Lord."

"Greetings." The voice was impatient.

"We have spoken to our servant Bildo, and he confirms what you have told us." It took Niall a moment to realize that Bildo referred to Doggins. "He agrees that he entered your city without permission. But he claims that his only purpose was to find explosives."

The Spider Lord said: "A servant has no business to do things without permission."

"He points out that he had been promoted to the rank of Saarleb only that afternoon, and that therefore he had the right to make that decision. But that, of course, is no excuse. He should have raised the matter in council first. And the council would have refused permission."

"Does it give him the right to kill spiders?"

"Of course not. That is the law. No human creature is permitted to raise his hand against a beetle or any of their allies."

The Death Lord said: "And the penalty for breaking that law?"

"Death."

"Do you propose to carry out that penalty?"

"If you insist, yes."

Niall glanced at Doggins; he was looking at the floor, his face emotionless.

"Will you carry it out yourself, or will you hand him over to us?"

The Master said: "We will hand him over to you."

"That is as it should be." The Death Lord was obviously mollified. "And what of the other prisoner?"

The Master hesitated. "That is a more difficult case. He is not a servant but a prisoner. Therefore he has every right to try to escape."

"Has he also the right to kill spiders?"

"He points out that the spiders killed his father, and that he regards them as his enemies. That seems to me a reasonable attitude."

"But he is an enemy of the spiders. And you are our ally. Therefore it is your duty to hand him over to us."

"I agree with you. But there seems to be some doubt among my council members. They point out that we only have a non-aggression treaty. That does not involve us in your quarrels."

"That is an unfriendly attitude."

"It is neither friendly nor unfriendly. We only wish to do what is right according to the law."

"So, you propose to let him go?" The Death Lord was beginning to lose his temper, and Niall was interested in this sign of weakness; it was evidence of vulnerability.

"We have not yet decided. The council has expressed a wish to hear what you have to say on the matter."

There was a long silence. Then the Death Lord said: "Very well. If what I have to say carries any weight, I advise you to listen to me very carefully."

"We shall always be willing to do that."

"Good." The Death Lord was obviously impatient of interruption. "Then listen. You know, as we do, that these human creatures were once the masters of the earth. That was because my ancestors and yours were small enough to be ignored. But we also know that they spent all their times quarreling and killing one another. They were incapable of living in peace. Finally, the gods grew tired of them, and made us the masters. And ever since then, the earth has been at peace.

"You beetles have treated your servants with indulgence, and this was the cause of the quarrel between us. That quarrel ended in the Great Treaty, under which you agreed that your servants should never be allowed to gain their independence. Ever since then, you and I have been allies. Is that not true?"

"It is true." The Master spoke as if making a ritual response.

"Good." The Death Lord was obviously pleased. "Bear that in mind, and we shall have no cause for quarrel. It is in your interest, as well as in ours, to keep these creatures in their place. You may feel that it would make no difference to let one of our enemies go free. But if human beings ever cease to be our servants you would soon learn the difference. These creatures are not capable of living in peace. They would not be content until they were the masters and you and I the servants. Is that what you want?"

"The answer to that question is obvious." Niall could detect a note of impatience in the Master's voice. "But I am unable to follow your reasoning. Why should the release of one young male creature bring about this catastrophe? He does not look particularly dangerous."

"I agree. But that is your mistake. It was he who persuaded your servant Bildo to enter the spider city without permission."

The Master turned his eyes on Doggins. "Is this true?"

Doggins cleared his throat and said uncertainly: "Not as far as I know."

The Master asked Niall: "Is it true?"

Niall shook his head in bewilderment. "No."

The Death Lord said: "Ask him to show you what he is wearing next to his heart."

The Master looked at Niall.

"What are you wearing next to your heart?"

Niall's hand crept inside his tunic and clutched the thought mirror. The idea of being parted from it filled him with alarm and dread.

But as he felt the eyes of the Master staring into his own, he took hold of the cord and allowed the thought mirror to hang outside his tunic.

"Give it to me," the Master said.

And although Niall wanted to keep the thought mirror more than anything in the world, he knew there was no question of refusal; the authority of the Master made him feel like a child. He took the cord from around his neck and handed it to the Master, who took it in his claw. Then he looked at the Death Lord.

"It is a simple thought amplifier. We have one in our history museum." To Niall's immense relief, he handed it back to him. "Did you use it to influence our servant Bildo?"

As Niall opened his mouth to reply, he suddenly knew that it would be impossible to answer with a simple "no." He recognized that the Death Lord could be correct. Doggins *had* changed his mind—just as Niall had wanted him to. His voice reflected his uncertainty as he answered: "I don't think so. But I'm not sure."

The Master turned his eyes on the Death Lord. "Are you saying that he did it deliberately?"

"I am saying that he did it. That is why he is dangerous."

As Niall moved back to take his place beside the Death Lord, he saw something that astonished him. For a brief moment his eyes met those of the Death Lord, and in that moment, he found himself looking at Odina. She was still there inside her body, listening to all that was going on. And as he again took his place beside her, it seemed to Niall that he had glimpsed a look of warning and of anguish. For a moment, he found this revelation so disturbing that he ceased to pay attention to what was being said. When he again became aware of their voices, the Death Lord was saying: "How long will it take your council to decide this matter?"

The Master replied: "I cannot tell you. But it will be soon."

"Good." The Spider Lord seemed about to take his leave. "But let me tell you once again what I have said before. If you decide to release our enemy, it will be a declaration of war."

The tone contained an unmistakable threat. As the Master and the Death Lord stared at each other, Niall became aware that two powerful wills were locked in conflict. He knew—as did everybody else in the room—that the Master was outraged by this attempt to intimidate his council. Yet when the Master spoke, his voice was calm and controlled.

"You are saying that the spiders will declare war on the beetles?"

"I am saying that it is time for the wise to take action."

There was something in the tone of this last word that stirred Niall to alertness, and he started to turn. As he did so, the hands of the Death Lord closed round his throat, and the fingers sank like steel into his flesh. But the moment of alertness had allowed him to move so the hands missed their intended grip; instead of crushing his windpipe, the thumbs were pressing into the flesh below the angle of the jaw. Yet the force was so immense that he felt himself being bent over backwards as if his muscles were paralyzed. At the same time, he found himself looking into the eyes of the Death Lord. Once again, he became aware of Odina's presence. And he realized with amazement that she was resisting the will of the Death Lord, and trying to prevent her muscles from obeying his orders to kill.

Then, over her shoulder, he saw the face of the beetle guard. There was a violent jerk, and he felt his feet leave the ground. The choking grip was suddenly relaxed and he was on his knees, trying to crawl and feeling as if he were swimming. His cheek was pressed to the floor. As his vision cleared, Doggins began helping him into a sitting position.

The first thing he saw was Odina, lying close to the door. She was obviously dead. The body was grotesquely curved, the knees spread out at an angle and one arm twisted underneath her. As Niall flung himself beside her, he saw that her neck was broken; when he took hold of the head and tried to hold it between his hands, it was as loose as if it was no longer attached to the body. The right side of her head had obviously struck the door with enormous force; the right cheek was cut open, and a trickle of blood ran from the corner of her mouth. The beetle guard, who had torn her free, was looking bewildered, as if astonished by his own strength.

Niall tried to stand, but his legs refused to support him. He sat on the floor, his head between his knees, feeling the pulse that beat behind his closed eyelids and hearing the sibilant chatter of the beetles as if it came from another room. When he tried to swallow, the pain made him gasp; it was as if someone had filled his gullet with fragments of broken glass.

The thought of Odina dissipated his self-pity. He used the thought mirror to concentrate his attention and immediately felt better. But he decided to make no further attempt to stand upright. Instead, he stared at the Beetle Lord from his position on the floor.

The Master made a gesture that brought silence. When he spoke, his voice betrayed his anger.

"What you have just witnessed was a deliberate act of treachery. It was also an act of calculated disrespect for our council. He intended to murder a prisoner who was still under our protection. This means that he has forfeited all right to our cooperation. He must realize that we have no alternative except to let the prisoner go free."

Niall tried to speak, but his voice was only a croak. Then he realized that speech was unnecessary; his thought had conveyed his question.

The Master said: "You may go wherever you please. We have decided that we have no right to restrict your freedom. But I would advise you to return to your own country and to remain there. The spiders will now make every attempt to destroy you. And I think it would be a pity if they were allowed to succeed. It would be more than their treachery deserves."

Niall forced himself to rise to his feet, and to make a bow as a gesture of thanks. But as soon as he stood upright, darkness washed over his senses. Doggins caught him as he fell.

Hampton Roads Publishing Company

. . . for the evolving human spirit

Hampton Roads Publishing Company
publishes books on a variety of subjects,
including metaphysics, health, integrative medicine,
visionary fiction, and other related topics.

For a copy of our latest catalog, call toll-free
(800) 766-8009, or send your name and address to:

Hampton Roads Publishing Company, Inc.
1125 Stoney Ridge Road
Charlottesville, VA 22902

e-mail: hrpc@hrpub.com
www.hrpub.com